Prize Stories 1998

THE O. HENRY AWARDS

Past Jurors
1997: Louise Erdrich, Thom Jones, David Foster Wallace

Past Magazine Award Winners
1997: *Epoch*

Prize Stories

1998

The O. Henry Awards

Edited and with an Introduction
by Larry Dark

ANCHOR BOOKS
DOUBLEDAY
New York London Toronto Sydney Auckland

An Anchor Book
PUBLISHED BY DOUBLEDAY
a division of Bantam Doubleday Dell Publishing Group, Inc.
1540 Broadway, New York, New York 10036

Anchor Books, Doubleday, and the portrayal of an anchor are trademarks
of Doubleday, a division of Bantam Doubleday Dell Publishing Group, Inc.

Permissions begin on page 444.

Library of Congress Cataloging-in-Publication Data

Prize stories, 1947–
New York, N.Y., Doubleday.
v. 22 cm.
Annual.
The O. Henry awards.
None published 1952–53.
Continues: O. Henry memorial award prize stories.
1. Short stories, American—Collected works.
PZ1.011   813′.01′08—dc19   21-9372
MARC-S

ISBN 0-385-48958-7
Printed in the United States of America
First Anchor Books Edition: September 1998

10   9   8   7   6   5   4   3   2   1

Dedicated to the memory of William Abrahams, series editor of *The O. Henry Awards* from 1967 to 1996.

Publisher's Note

WILLIAM SYDNEY PORTER, who wrote under the pen name O. Henry, was born in North Carolina in 1862. He started writing stories while in prison for embezzlement, a crime for which he was convicted in 1898 (it is uncertain if he actually committed the crime). His writing career was short and started late, but O. Henry proved himself a prolific and widely read short story writer in the twelve years he devoted to the craft, and his name has become synonymous with the American short story.

His years in Texas inspired many lively Westerns, but it was New York City that galvanized his creative powers, and his New York stories became his claim to fame. Loved for their ironic plot twists, which made for pleasing surprise endings, his highly entertaining tales appeared weekly in Joseph Pulitzer's *New York World*.

His best known story, "The Gift of the Magi," was written for the *World* in 1905 and has become an American treasure. Dashed off past deadline in a matter of hours, it is the story of a man who sells his watch to buy a set of hair combs as a Christmas present for his wife, who in the meantime has sold her luxurious locks to buy him a watch chain. "The Last Leaf" is another O. Henry favorite. It is the story of a woman who falls ill with pneumonia and pronounces that she will die when the last leaf of ivy she sees outside her Greenwich Village window falls away. She hangs on with the last stubborn leaf, which gives her the resolve to recover. She eventually learns that her inspirational leaf wasn't a real leaf at all, but rather a painting of a leaf. Her neighbor, who has always dreamed of painting a masterpiece, painted it on the wall and caught pneumonia in the process.

His work made him famous, but O. Henry was an extremely private man who, sadly, preferred to spend his time and money on drink, and ultimately it was the bottle that did him in. He died alone and penniless in 1910. O. Henry's legacy and his popularization of the short story was such that in 1918 Doubleday, in conjunction with the Society of Arts and Sciences, established the O. Henry Awards, an annual anthology of short stories, in his honor. At the end of the century the short story continues to flourish. Styles have radically changed and there can be no greater evidence of the evolution and high achievement today's short story writers enjoy than the contents of this 1998 edition of *Prize Stories: The O. Henry Awards* selected and compiled by the series editor, Larry Dark. Anchor Books and Doubleday are proud, with the seventy-eighth edition of the series, to continue the tradition of publishing this much beloved collection of outstanding short stories in O. Henry's name.

Acknowledgments

I would like to thank my editor at Anchor Books, Tina Pohlman, for her energy, intelligence, and patience, and my wife, Alice Elliott Dark, who read and discussed many of these stories with me.

Contents

Introduction

YOU ARE WHAT some would call a serious reader. The very
fact that you have picked up this book, that you are reading
this introduction, that you are interested in these twenty stories is
proof enough. By some dire accounts, you may also be a member of
an endangered species. In a given week, far fewer people buy the
top-selling work of fiction than tune in to the lowest-rated show on
television or buy tickets at the Cineplex 16 to see the latest box-
office flop. And short stories reach a smaller audience than bestsell-
ing novels do.

Why is this so? Because television and movies are generally
easy—what you see and hear is what you get—whereas literature
makes demands on the imagination. Because the short story, considered as a form of entertainment, must also these days vie against
the likes of professional ice hockey, America Online, pornographic
videos, quarter slot machines, the Home Shopping Network, and a
hundred other diversions aimed at capturing our attention primarily to capture our coin.

So why aren't you watching a "Seinfeld" rerun, surfing the Internet, flipping through *Vanity Fair,* or playing with a Game Boy
handheld video-cartridge unit? Why are you interested in the short
story, given the myriad other options available to you? Because you
know that a good short story is not intellectual medicine, it is an
immensely satisfying entertainment. It is not just a diversion of the
moment but something more profound and long-lasting. A good

story can change you, change the way you think and look at the world, because its meaning is not delivered predigested but must be uncovered with thought over time. The kind of pleasure that only a short story can provide is what makes you a reader, is why you are here.

In truth, there are enough serious readers to sustain the short story, and it continues to flourish. In 1997, I read about three thousand short stories in some two hundred and forty U.S. and Canadian magazines in order to choose the twenty in this collection. Commercial and small-press publishing houses produce a sizable number of short story collections and anthologies every year. And many of the most gifted and successful fiction writers work in the form.

Considering the short story as an entertainment is apt in the context of a series established as a memorial to the writer O. Henry, who wrote stories that were eagerly read by a mass audience in the early part of this waning century. In fact, several of the stories in this year's collection are of types favored by O. Henry—the Western, the love story, and the humorous story. Needless to say, however, O. Henry could never have written a Western story like Annie Proulx's "Brokeback Mountain," in which the two lonely ranch hands fall in love not with the same woman but with each other. Contemporary love stories aren't limited to focusing on romance as a prelude to intimacy, but can be about intimacy as a prelude to romance, as in Akhil Sharma's "Cosmopolitan." And humorous stories have become edgier and darker. "Winky" by George Saunders, for instance, takes aim at both the comforting platitudes of religion and the smug imperatives of the self-help movement, making the reader not only laugh but also squirm.

The incredible diversity and variety of the stories I read made it difficult to choose just twenty for this collection. It also makes it difficult to characterize them as a group. Overall, the stories I chose were those I found most interesting, compelling, and well-written; those that not only entertained me but also excited me, intrigued me, and challenged me. The truth, as always, is in the details. But rather than go story by story in an effort to convey what moved me about each, I think it's best to let the stories and authors speak for themselves.

The exception is that this year each of the top three prizewinners is introduced by one of the three jurors who selected them—Andrea Barrett, Mary Gaitskill, and Rick Moody. Each read blind copies of the twenty prizewinning stories (that is, not knowing the names of the authors or magazines in which they originally appeared), then voted for a first, second, and third-prize winner. I compiled the votes and broke ties to arrive at the final selections: Lorrie Moore's "People Like That Are the Only People Here" for First Prize, Steven Millhauser's "The Knife Thrower" for Second Prize, and Alice Munro's "The Children Stay" as the Third-Prize winner. The eloquent introductions written by Moody, Gaitskill, and Barrett are testament not only to the stories but also to the intelligence and enthusiasm each of the jurors brought to the task of choosing the top prizewinners.

The O. Henry Award for best U.S. or Canadian magazine publishing fiction this year goes to *The New Yorker* on the strength of four O. Henry Award-winning stories and four Honorable Mentions. You'll find a citation for this prize toward the end of the book, before the listings of magazines consulted.

Last year *Prize Stories: The O. Henry Awards* was the first annual anthology to add Web site and e-mail addresses to its magazine listings. And there are even more Web sites provided this year. With a few exceptions, I've found that magazine home pages, at this early stage, exist primarily as a means of promoting the established print versions and don't offer much in the way of original content. Though many Web 'zines do publish original short fiction, I have decided to limit eligibility for the O. Henry Awards to the two-hundred-and-forty-plus print magazines and consider the Internet a separate medium outside the purview of this series. The O. Henry Awards does, however, maintain its own Web presence, with updated magazine listings and other features, at www.boldtype.com/ohenry.

While I don't have any illusions about serious fiction someday reaching an audience of *Titanic* proportions (though good stories have provided some of Hollywood's best material), I also don't see myself as a museum curator for a dying form. The story lives, I tell you. And the twenty you will find here are the proof. They are full of life, death, love, humor, passion, hubris, blood, guts, dirt, God, war, mystery, fear, and longing. Other entertainments have their place, but there's still nothing to match the power of language in the hands of a gifted writer. For my money, a few thousand well-chosen words are worth a million pictures.

LARRY DARK, 1998

People Like That
Are the Only People Here

By Lorrie Moore

Introduced by Rick Moody

"People Like That Are the Only People Here" was, in my view, the most arresting piece of short fiction produced in 1997, not only because it's beautifully written or because it very cannily offloads most contemporary presuppositions about the well-made short story (like that they need to have openings and closings: "A beginning, an end: there seems to be neither"); or because it refuses to bother with questions of genre, refuses even to admit that genre is a question worthy of attention ("I write fiction. This isn't fiction"); mainly Lorrie Moore's story is perfect because it unflinchingly takes on the most difficult of all dramas, the sickness of a child, without indulging once in sentimentality. Moore sets the tone with an opening paragraph of such clinical brutality that only the intrepid will continue to read. Then things get far worse. Then most bravely of all, "People Like That" refuses to find any moral in the suffering of this particular child or even in the suffering of his parents. Illness and recovery are possibilities that exist. What else do you want the story to say? This for me is the value of all great literature, descriptive rather than salvific. Because accurate description *is* salvation. "People Like That" is written in the prose rhythms of the truth, is marked by the paralyzing emotional reversals of the truth, with the menace and terror that the truth bears with it. What closure can there be to a story that so confounds our longing for security and affirmation? Only the best ending I have read in an American magazine in a long time, one that reveals this harrowing, magnificent work for what it really is. A way to save lives.

—RICK MOODY

Lorrie Moore

People Like That Are the Only People Here

From *The New Yorker*

A BEGINNING, an end: there seems to be neither. The whole thing is like a cloud that just lands, and everywhere inside it is full of rain. A start: the Mother finds a blood clot in the Baby's diaper. What is the story? Who put this here? It is big and bright, with a broken, khaki-colored vein in it. Over the weekend, the Baby had looked listless and spacey, clayey and grim. But today he looks fine—so what is this thing, startling against the white diaper, like a tiny mouse heart packed in snow? Perhaps it belongs to someone else. Perhaps it is something menstrual, something belonging to the Mother or to the Babysitter, something the Baby has found in a wastebasket and for his own demented baby reasons stowed away here. (Babies—they're crazy! What can you do?) In her mind, the Mother takes this away from his body and attaches it to someone else's. There. Doesn't that make more sense?

Still, she phones the children's-hospital clinic. Blood in the diaper, she says, and, sounding alarmed and perplexed, the woman on the other end says, "Come in now."

Such pleasingly instant service! Just say "blood." Just say "diaper." Look what you get!

In the examination room, the pediatrician, the nurse, and the head resident all seem less alarmed and perplexed than simply perplexed. At first, stupidly, the Mother is calmed by this. But soon, besides peering and saying "Hmm," the doctor, the nurse, and the head resident are all drawing their mouths in, bluish and tight—morning glories sensing noon. They fold their arms across their white-coated chests, unfold them again, and jot things down. They order an ultrasound. Bladder and kidneys. Here's the card. Go downstairs, turn left.

In Radiology, the Baby stands anxiously on the table, naked against the Mother, as she holds him still against her legs and waist, the Radiologist's cold scanning disk moving about the Baby's back. The Baby whimpers, looks up at the Mother. *Let's get out of here,* his eyes beg. *Pick me up!* The Radiologist stops, freezes one of the many swirls of oceanic gray, and clicks repeatedly, a single moment within the long, cavernous weather map that is the Baby's insides.

"Are you finding something?" asks the Mother. Last year, her Uncle Larry had a kidney removed for something that turned out to be benign. These imaging machines! They are like dogs, or metal detectors: they find everything but don't know what they've found. That's where the surgeons come in. They're like the owners of the dogs. *Give me that,* they say to the dog. *What the heck is that?*

"The surgeon will speak to you," says the Radiologist.

"Are you finding something?"

"The surgeon will speak to you," the Radiologist says again. "There seems to be something there, but the surgeon will talk to you about it."

"My uncle once had something on his kidney," says the Mother. "So they removed the kidney and it turned out the something was benign."

The Radiologist smiles a broad, ominous smile. "That's always the way it is," he says. "You don't know exactly what it is until it's in the bucket."

"In the bucket," the Mother repeats.

"That's doctor talk," the Radiologist says.

"It's very appealing," says the Mother. "It's a very appealing way to talk." Swirls of bile and blood, mustard and maroon in a pail, the colors of an African flag or some exuberant salad bar: *in the bucket*—she imagines it all.

"The surgeon will see you soon," he says again. He tousles the Baby's ringlety hair. "Cute kid," he says.

"Let's see now," says the Surgeon, in one of his examining rooms. He has stepped in, then stepped out, then come back in again. He has crisp, frowning features, sharp bones, and a tennis-in-Bermuda tan. He crosses his blue-cottoned legs. He is wearing clogs.

The Mother knows her own face is a big white dumpling of worry. She is still wearing her long, dark parka, holding the Baby, who has pulled the hood up over her head because he always thinks it's funny to do that. Though on certain windy mornings she would like to think she could look vaguely romantic like this, like some French Lieutenant's Woman of the Prairie, in all her saner moments she knows she doesn't. She knows she looks ridiculous—like one of those animals made out of twisted party balloons. She lowers the hood and slips one arm out of the sleeve. The Baby wants to get up and play with the light switch. He fidgets, fusses, and points.

"He's big on lights these days," explains the Mother.

"That's O.K.," says the Surgeon, nodding toward the light switch. "Let him play with it." The Mother goes and stands by it, and the Baby begins turning the lights off and on, off and on.

"What we have here is a Wilms' tumor," says the Surgeon, suddenly plunged into darkness. He says "tumor" as if it were the most normal thing in the world.

"Wilms'?" repeats the Mother. The room is quickly on fire again with light, then wiped dark again. Among the three of them here there is a long silence, as if it were suddenly the middle of the night. "Is that apostrophe 's' or 's' apostrophe?" the Mother says finally. She is a writer and a teacher. Spelling can be important—perhaps even at a time like this, though she has never before been at a time like this, so there are barbarisms she could easily commit without knowing.

The lights come on; the world is doused and exposed.

" 'S' apostrophe," says the Surgeon. "I think." The lights go back out, but the Surgeon continues speaking in the dark. "A malignant tumor of the left kidney."

Wait a minute. Hold on here. The Baby is only a baby, fed on organic applesauce and soy milk—a little prince!—and he was standing so close to her during the ultrasound. How could he have this terrible thing? It must have been *her* kidney. A fifties kidney. A DDT kidney. The Mother clears her throat. "Is it possible it was my kidney on the scan? I mean, I've never heard of a baby with a tumor, and, frankly, I was standing very close." She would make the blood hers, the tumor hers; it would all be some treacherous, farcical mistake.

"No, that's not possible," says the Surgeon. The light goes back on.

"It's not?" says the Mother. Wait until it's *in the bucket,* she thinks. Don't be so sure. *Do we have to wait until it's in the bucket to find out a mistake has been made?*

"We will start with a radical nephrectomy," says the Surgeon, instantly thrown into darkness again. His voice comes from nowhere and everywhere at once. "And then we'll begin with chemotherapy after that. These tumors usually respond very well to chemo."

"I've never heard of a baby having chemo," the Mother says. Baby and Chemo, she thinks: they should never even appear in the same sentence together, let alone the same life. In her other life, her life before this day, she was a believer in alternative medicine. Chemotherapy? Unthinkable. Now, suddenly, alternative medicine seems the wacko maiden aunt to the Nice Big Daddy of Conventional Treatment. How quickly the old girl faints and gives way, leaves one just standing there. Chemo? Of course: chemo! Why, by all means: chemo. Absolutely! Chemo!

The Baby flicks the switch back on, and the walls reappear, big wedges of light checkered with small framed watercolors of the local lake. The Mother has begun to cry: all of life has led her here, to this moment. After this there is no more life. There is something else, something stumbling and unlivable, something mechanical, something for robots, but not life. Life has been taken and broken, quickly, like a stick. The room goes dark again, so that the Mother can cry more freely. How can a baby's body be stolen so fast? How much can one heaven-sent and unsuspecting child endure? Why has he not been spared this inconceivable fate?

Perhaps, she thinks, she is being punished: too many babysitters too early on. ("Come to Mommy! Come to Mommy-Babysitter!" she used to say. But it was a joke!) Her life, perhaps, bore too openly the marks and wigs of deepest drag. Her unmotherly thoughts had all been noted: the panicky hope that his nap would last just a little longer than it did; her occasional desire to kiss him passionately on the mouth (to make out with her baby!); her ongoing complaints about the very vocabulary of motherhood, how it degraded the speaker. ("Is this a poopie onesie? Yes, it's a very poopie onesie!") She had, moreover, on three occasions used the formula bottles as flower vases. She twice let the Baby's ears get fudgy with wax. A few afternoons last month, at snack time, she placed a bowl of Cheerios on the floor for him to eat, like a dog. She let him play with the Dustbuster. Just once, before he was born, she said, "Healthy? I just want the kid to be rich." A joke, for God's sake. After he was born, she announced that her life had become a daily sequence of mind-wrecking chores, the same ones over and over again, like a novel by Mrs. Camus. Another joke! These jokes will kill you. She had told too often, and with too much enjoyment, the story of how the Baby had said "Hi" to his high chair, waved at the lake waves, shouted "Goody-goody-goody" in what seemed to be a Russian accent, pointed at his eyes and said "Ice." And all that nonsensical baby talk: wasn't it a stitch? *Canonical babbling,* the language experts called it. He recounted whole stories in it, totally made up, she could tell; he embroidered, he fished, he exaggerated. What a card! To friends she spoke of his eating habits (carrots yes, tuna no). She mentioned, too much, his sidesplitting giggle. Did she have to be so boring? Did she have no consideration for others, for the intellectual demands and courtesies of human society? Would she not even attempt to be more interesting? It was a crime against the human mind not even to try.

Now her baby, for all these reasons—lack of motherly gratitude, motherly judgment, motherly proportion—will be taken away.

The room is fluorescently ablaze again. The Mother digs around in her parka pocket and comes up with a Kleenex. It is old and thin, like a mashed flower saved from a dance; she dabs it at her eyes and nose.

"The baby won't suffer as much as you," says the Surgeon.

And who can contradict? Not the Baby, who in his Slavic Betty Boop voice can say only *mama, dada, cheese, ice, bye-bye, outside, boogie-boogie, goody-goody, eddy-eddy,* and *car.* (Who is Eddy? They have no idea.) This will not suffice to express his mortal suffering. Who can say what babies do with their agony and shock? Not they themselves. (Baby talk: isn't it a stitch?) They put it all no place anyone can really see. They are like a different race, a different species: they seem not to experience pain the way we do. Yeah, that's it: their nervous systems are not as fully formed, and *they just don't experience pain the way we do.* A tune to keep one humming through the war. "You'll get through it," the Surgeon says.

"How?" asks the Mother. "How does one get through it?"

"You just put your head down and go," says the Surgeon. He picks up his file folder. He is a skilled manual laborer. The tricky emotional stuff is not to his liking. The babies. The babies! What can be said to console the parents about the babies? "I'll go phone the oncologist on duty to let him know," he says, and leaves the room.

"Come here, sweetie," the Mother says to the Baby, who has toddled off toward a gum wrapper on the floor. "We've got to put your jacket on." She picks him up and he reaches for the light switch again. Light, dark. Peekaboo: Where's baby? Where did baby go?

At home, she leaves a message—Urgent! Call me!—for the Husband on his voice mail. Then she takes the Baby upstairs for his nap, rocks him in the rocker. The Baby waves goodbye to his little bears, then looks toward the window and says, "Bye-bye, outside." He has, lately, the habit of waving goodbye to everything, and now it seems as if he sensed some imminent departure, and it breaks her heart to hear him. *Bye-bye!* She sings low and monotonously, like a small appliance, which is how he likes it. He is drowsy, dozy, drifting off. He has grown so much in the last year he hardly fits in her lap anymore; his limbs dangle off like a Pietà.

His head rolls slightly inside the crook of her arm. She can feel him falling backward into sleep, his mouth round and open like the sweetest of poppies. All the lullabies in the world, all the melodies threaded through with maternal melancholy now become for her—abandoned as mothers can be by working men and napping babies—the songs of hard, hard grief. Sitting there, bowed and bobbing, the Mother feels the entirety of her love as worry and heartbreak. A quick and irrevocable alchemy: there is no longer one unworried scrap left for happiness. "If you go," she keens low into his soapy neck, into the ranunculus coil of his ear, "we are going with you. We are nothing without you. Without you, we are a heap of rocks. Without you, we are two stumps, with nothing any longer in our hearts. Wherever this takes you, we are following; we will be there. Don't be scared. We are going, too, wherever you go. That is that. That is that."

"Take notes," says the Husband, after coming straight home from work, midafternoon, hearing the news, and saying all the words out loud—*surgery, metastasis, dialysis, transplant*—then collapsing in a chair in tears. "Take notes. We are going to need the money."

"Good God," cries the Mother. Everything inside her suddenly begins to cower and shrink, a thinning of bones. Perhaps this is a soldier's readiness, but it has the whiff of death and defeat. It feels like a heart attack, a failure of will and courage, a power failure: a failure of everything. Her face, when she glimpses it in a mirror, is cold and bloated with shock, her eyes scarlet and shrunk. She has already started to wear sunglasses indoors, like a celebrity widow. From where will her own strength come? From some philosophy? From some frigid little philosophy? She is neither stalwart nor realistic and has trouble with basic concepts, such as the one that says events move in one direction only and do not jump up, turn around, and take themselves back.

The Husband begins too many of his sentences with "What if." He is trying to piece everything together, like a train wreck. He is trying to get the train to town.

"We'll just take all the steps, move through all the stages. We'll go where we have to go, we'll hunt, we'll find, we'll pay what we have to pay. What if we can't pay?"

"Sounds like shopping."

"I cannot believe this is happening to our little boy," he says, and starts to sob again.

What is to be said? You turn just slightly and there it is: the death of your child. It is part symbol, part devil, and in your blind spot all along, until it is upon you. Then it is a fierce little country abducting you; it holds you squarely inside itself like a cellar room, the best boundaries of you are the boundaries of it. Are there windows? Sometimes aren't there windows?

The Mother is not a shopper. She hates to shop, is generally bad at it, though she does like a good sale. She cannot stroll meaningfully through anger, denial, grief, and acceptance. She goes straight to bargaining and stays there. How much? She calls out to the ceiling, to some makeshift construction of holiness she has desperately though not uncreatively assembled in her mind and prayed to; a doubter, never before given to prayer, she must now reap what she has not sown; she must reassemble an entire altar of worship and begging. She tries for noble abstractions, nothing too anthropomorphic, just some Higher Morality, though if this particular Highness looks something like the Manager at Marshall Field's, sucking a Frango mint, so be it. Amen. Just tell me what you want, requests the Mother. And how do you want it? More charitable acts? A billion, starting now. Charitable thoughts? Harder, but of course! Of course! I'll do the cooking, honey, I'll pay the rent. Just tell me. *Excuse me?* Well, if not to you, to whom do I speak? Hello? To whom do I have to speak around here? A higher-up? A superior? Wait? I can wait. I've got the whole damn day.

The Husband now lies next to her on their bed, sighing. "Poor little guy could survive all this only to be killed in a car crash at the age of sixteen," he says.

The Mother, bargaining, considers this. "We'll take the car crash," she says.

"What?"

"Let's Make a Deal! Sixteen is a full life! We'll take the car crash. We'll take the car crash in front of which Carol Merrill is now standing."

Now the Manager of Marshall Field's reappears. "To take the surprises out is to take the life out of life," he says.

The phone rings. The Husband leaves the room.

"But I don't want these surprises," says the Mother. "Here! You take these surprises!"

"To know the narrative in advance is to turn yourself into a machine," the Manager continues. "What makes humans human is precisely that they do not know the future. That is why they do the fateful and amusing things they do: who can say how anything will turn out? Therein lies the only hope for redemption, discovery, and—let's be frank—fun, fun, fun! There might be things people will get away with. And not just motel towels. There might be great illicit loves, enduring joy—or faith-shaking accidents with farm machinery. But you have to not know in order to see what stories your life's efforts bring you. The mystery is all."

The Mother, though shy, has grown confrontational. "Is this the kind of bogus, random crap they teach at merchandising school? We would like fewer surprises, fewer efforts and mysteries, thank you. K through 8; can we just get K through 8?" It now seems like the luckiest, most beautiful, most musical phrase she's ever heard: K through 8—the very lilt. The very thought.

The Manager continues, trying things out. "I mean, the whole conception of 'the story,' of cause and effect, the whole idea that people have a clue as to how the world works, is just a piece of laughable metaphysical colonialism perpetrated upon the wild country of time."

Did they own a gun? The Mother begins looking through drawers.

The Husband comes back in the room and observes her. "Ha! The Great Havoc That Is the Puzzle of All Life!" he says of the Marshall Field's management policy. He has just gotten off a conference call with the insurance company and the hospital. The surgery will be Friday. "It's all just some dirty capitalist's idea of a philosophy."

"Maybe it's just a fact of narrative, and you really can't politicize it," says the Mother. It is now only the two of them.

"Whose side are you on?"

"I'm on the Baby's side."

"Are you taking notes for this?"

"No."

"You're not?"

"No. I can't. Not this! I write fiction. This isn't fiction."

"Then write nonfiction. Do a piece of journalism. Get two dollars a word."

"Then it has to be true and full of information. I'm not trained. I'm not that skilled. Plus, I have a convenient personal principle about artists not abandoning art. One should never turn one's back on a vivid imagination. Even the whole memoir thing annoys me."

"Well, make things up but pretend they're real."

"I'm not that insured."

"You're making me nervous."

"Sweetie, darling, I'm not that good. I can't *do this*. I can do— what can I do? I can do quasi-amusing phone dialogue. I can do succinct descriptions of weather. I can do screwball outings with the family pet. Sometimes I can do those. Honey, I only do what I can. I do *the careful ironies of daydream*. I do *the marshy ideas upon which intimate life is built*. But this? Our baby with cancer? I'm sorry. My stop was two stations back. This is irony at its most gaudy and careless. This is a Hieronymus Bosch of facts and figures and blood and graphs. This is a nightmare of narrative slop. This cannot be designed. This cannot even be noted in preparation for a design—"

"We're going to need the money."

"To say nothing of the moral boundaries of pecuniary recompense in a situation such as this—"

"What if the other kidney goes? What if he needs a transplant? Where are the moral boundaries there? What are we going to do, have bake sales?"

"We can sell the house. I hate this house. It makes me crazy."

"And we'll live—where, again?"

"The Ronald McDonald place. I hear it's nice. It's the least McDonald's can do."

"You have a keen sense of justice."

"I try. What can I say?"

The Husband buries his face in his hands: "Our poor baby. How did this happen to him?" He looks over and stares at the bookcase that serves as their nightstand. "And is any one of these baby books a help?" He picks up the Leach, the Spock, the "What to Expect." "Where in the pages or index of any of these does it say 'chemotherapy' or 'Hickman catheter' or 'renal sarcoma'? Where does it say 'carcinogenesis' or 'metastasis'? You know what these books are obsessed with? *Holding a fucking spoon.*" He begins hurling the books off the nightstand and against the far wall.

"Hey," says the Mother, trying to soothe. "Hey, hey, hey." But, compared with his stormy roar, her words are those of a backup singer—a Shondell, a Pip—a doo-wop ditty. Books, and now more books, continue to fly.

Take notes.

Is "fainthearted" one word or two? Student prose has wrecked her spelling.

It's one word. Two words—faint hearted—what would that be? The name of a drag queen.

Take notes.

In the end you suffer alone. But at the beginning you suffer with a whole lot of others. When your child has cancer you are instantly whisked away to another planet: one of bald-headed little boys. Pediatric Oncology. Peed-Onk. You wash your hands for thirty seconds in antibacterial soap before you are allowed to enter through the swinging doors. You put paper slippers on your shoes. You keep your voice down. "Almost all the children are boys," one of the nurses says. "No one knows why. It's been documented, but a lot of people out there still don't realize it." The little boys are all from sweet-sounding places, Janesville and Appleton—little heartland towns with giant landfills, agricultural runoff, paper factories,

Joe McCarthy's grave. (Alone a site of great toxicity, thinks the Mother. The soil should be tested.)

All the bald little boys look like brothers. They wheel their I.V.s up and down the single corridor of Peed-Onk. Some of the lively ones, feeling good for a day, ride the lower bars of their I.V.s while their large, cheerful mothers whizz them along the halls. *Wheee!*

The Mother does not feel large and cheerful. In her mind she is scathing, acid-tongued, wraith-thin, and chain-smoking out on a fire escape somewhere. Below her lie the gentle undulations of the Midwest, with all its aspirations to be—to be what? To be Long Island. How it has succeeded! Strip mall upon strip mall. Lurid water, poisoned potatoes. The Mother drags deeply, blowing clouds of smoke out over the disfigured cornfields. When a baby gets cancer, it seems stupid ever to have given up smoking. When a baby gets cancer, you think, Whom are we kidding? Let's all light up. When a baby gets cancer, you think, Who came up with *this* idea? What celestial abandon gave rise to *this*? Pour me a drink, so I can refuse to toast.

The Mother does not know how to be one of these other mothers, with their blond hair and sweatpants and sneakers and determined pleasantness. She does not think that she can be anything similar. She does not feel remotely like them. She knows, for instance, too many people in Greenwich Village. She mail-orders oysters and tiramisù from a shop in SoHo. She is close friends with four actual homosexuals. Her husband is asking her to Take Notes.

Where do these women get their sweatpants? She will find out. She will start, perhaps, with the costume and work from there.

She will live according to the bromides: Take one day at a time. Take a positive attitude. *Take a hike!* She wishes that there were more interesting things that were useful and true, but it seems now that it's only the boring things that are useful and true. *One day at a time.* And *At least we have our health.* How ordinary. How obvious. One day at a time: you need a brain for that?

While the Surgeon is fine-boned, regal, and laconic—they have correctly guessed his game to be doubles—there is a bit of the mad, over-caffeinated scientist to the Oncologist. He speaks quickly. He knows a lot of studies and numbers. He can do the math. Good! Someone should be able to do the math! "It's a fast but wimpy tumor," he explains. "It typically metastasizes to the lung." He rattles off some numbers, time frames, risk statistics. Fast but wimpy: the Mother tries to imagine this combination of traits, tries to think and think, and can only come up with Claudia Osk from the fourth grade, who blushed and almost wept when called on in class but in gym could outrun everyone in the quarter-mile, fire-door-to-fence dash. The Mother thinks now of this tumor as Claudia Osk. They are going to get Claudia Osk, make her sorry. All right! Claudia Osk must die. Though it has never been mentioned before, it now seems clear that Claudia Osk should have died long ago. Who was she, anyway? So conceited, not letting anyone beat her in a race. Well, hey, hey, hey—don't look now, Claudia!

The Husband nudges her. "Are you listening?"

"The chances of this happening even just to one kidney are one in fifteen thousand. Now, given all these other factors, the chances on the second kidney are about one in eight."

"One in eight," says the Husband. "Not bad. As long as it's not one in fifteen thousand."

The Mother studies the trees and fish along the ceiling's edge in the Save the Planet wallpaper border. Save the Planet. Yes! But the windows in this very building don't open, and diesel fumes are leaking into the ventilating system, near which, outside, a delivery truck is parked. The air is nauseous and stale.

"Really," the Oncologist is saying, "of all the cancers he could get, this is probably one of the best."

"We win," says the Mother.

"'Best,' I know, hardly seems the right word. Look, you two probably need to get some rest. We'll see how the surgery and histology go. Then we'll start with chemo the week following. A little light chemo: vincristine and—"

"Vincristine?" interrupts the Mother. "Wine of Christ?"

"The names are strange, I know. The other one we use is actinomycin-D. Sometimes called dactinomycin. People move the 'D' around to the front."

"They move the 'D' around to the front," repeats the Mother.

"Yup," the Oncologist says. "I don't know why, they just do!"

"Christ didn't survive his wine," says the Husband.

"But of course he did," says the Oncologist and nods toward the Baby, who has now found a cupboard full of hospital linens and bandages and is yanking them all out onto the floor. "I'll see you guys tomorrow, after the surgery." And with that the Oncologist leaves.

"Or, rather, Christ was his wine," mumbles the Husband. Everything he knows about the New Testament he has gleaned from the soundtrack of "Godspell." "His blood was the wine. What a great beverage idea."

"A little light chemo. Don't you like that one?" says the Mother. *"Eine kleine* dactinomycin. I'd like to see Mozart write that one up for a big wad o' cash."

"Come here, honey," the Husband says to the Baby, who has now pulled off both his shoes.

"It's bad enough when they refer to medical science as an inexact science," says the Mother. "But when they start referring to it as an art I get extremely nervous."

"Yeah. If we wanted art, Doc, we'd go to an art museum." The Husband picks up the Baby. "You're an artist," he says to the Mother with the taint of accusation in his voice. "They probably think you find creativity reassuring."

The Mother sighs. "I just find it inevitable. Let's go get something to eat." And so they take the elevator to the cafeteria, where there is a high chair, and where, not noticing, they all eat a lot of apples with the price tags still on them.

Because his surgery is not until tomorrow, the Baby likes the hospital. He likes the long corridors, down which he can run. He likes everything on wheels. The flower carts in the lobby! ("Please keep your boy away from the flowers," says the vender. "We'll buy the whole display," snaps the Mother, adding, "Actual children in a children's hospital—unbelievable, isn't it?") The Baby likes the other little boys. Places to go! People to see! Rooms to wander into! There is Intensive Care. There is the Trauma Unit. The Baby smiles and waves. What a little Cancer Personality! Bandaged citizens smile and wave back. In Peed-Onk there are the bald little boys to play with. Joey, Eric, Tim, Mort, and Tod. (Mort! Tod!) There is the four-year-old, Ned, holding his little deflated rubber ball, the one with the intriguing curling hose. The Baby wants to play with it. "It's mine, leave it alone," says Ned. "Tell the baby to leave it alone."

"Baby, you've got to share," says the Mother from a chair some feet away.

Suddenly, from down near the Tiny Tim Lounge, comes Ned's mother, large and blond and sweatpanted. "Stop that! Stop it!" she cries out, dashing toward the Baby and Ned and pushing the Baby away. "Don't touch that!" she barks at the Baby, who is only a baby and bursts into tears because he has never been yelled at like this before.

Ned's mom glares at everyone. "This is drawing fluid from Neddy's liver!" She pats at the rubber thing and starts to cry a little.

"Oh, my God," says the Mother. She comforts the Baby, who is also crying. She and Ned, the only dry-eyed people, look at each other. "I'm so sorry," she says to Ned and then to his mother. "I'm so stupid. I thought they were squabbling over a toy."

"It does look like a toy," agrees Ned. He smiles. He is an angel. All the little boys are angels. Total, sweet, bald little angels, and now God is trying to get them back for himself. Who are they, mere mortal women, in the face of this, this powerful and overwhelming and inscrutable thing, God's will? They are the mothers, that's who. You can't have him! they shout every day. You dirty old man! *Get out of here! Hands off!*

"I'm so sorry," says the Mother again. "I didn't know."

Ned's mother smiles vaguely. "Of course you didn't know," she says, and walks back to the Tiny Tim Lounge.

The Tiny Tim Lounge is a little sitting area at the end of the Peed-Onk corridor. There are two small sofas, a table, a rocking chair, a television, and a VCR. There are various videos: "Speed," "Dune," "Star Wars." On one of the lounge walls there is a gold plaque with the musician Tiny Tim's name on it: years ago, his son was treated at this hospital, and so he donated money for this lounge. It is a cramped little lounge, which one suspects would be larger if Tiny Tim's son had actually lived. Instead, he died here, at this hospital, and now there is this tiny room which is part gratitude, part generosity, part *Fuck you*.

Sifting through the videocassettes, the Mother wonders what science fiction could begin to compete with the science fiction of cancer itself: a tumor, with its differentiated muscle and bone cells, a clump of wild nothing and its mad, ambitious desire to be something—something inside you, instead of you, another organism but with a monster's architecture, a demon's sabotage and chaos. Think of leukemia, a tumor diabolically taking liquid form, the better to swim about incognito in the blood. George Lucas, direct that!

Sitting with the other parents in the Tiny Tim Lounge, the night before the surgery, having put the Baby to bed in his high steel crib two rooms down, the Mother begins to hear the stories: leukemia in kindergarten, sarcomas in Little League, neuroblastomas discovered at summer camp. *Eric slid into third base, but then the scrape didn't heal.* The parents pat one another's forearms and speak of other children's hospitals as if they were resorts. "You were at St. Jude's last winter? So were we. What did you think of it? We loved the staff." Jobs have been quit, marriages hacked up, bank accounts ravaged; the parents have seemingly endured the unendurable. They speak not of the *possibility* of comas brought on by the chemo but of the *number* of them. "He was in his first coma last July," says Ned's mother. "It was a scary time, but we pulled through."

Pulling through is what people do around here. There is a kind of bravery in their lives that isn't bravery at all. It is automatic, unflinching, a mix of man and machine, consuming and unquestionable obligation meeting illness move for move in a giant, even-Steven game of chess: an unending round of something that looks like shadowboxing—though between love and death, which is the shadow? "Everyone admires us for our courage," says one man. "They have no idea what they're talking about."

I could get out of here, thinks the Mother. I could just get on a bus and go, never come back. Change my name. A kind of witness-relocation thing.

"Courage requires options," the man adds.

The Baby might be better off.

"There are options," says a woman with a thick suède headband. "You could give up. You could fall apart."

"No, you can't. Nobody does. I've never seen it," says the man. "Well, not *really* fall apart." Then the lounge is quiet. Over the VCR someone has taped the fortune from a fortune cookie. *Optimism,* it says, *is what allows a teakettle to sing though up to its neck in hot water.* Underneath, someone else has taped a clipping from a summer horoscope. *Cancer rules!* it says. Who would tape this up? Somebody's twelve-year-old brother. One of the fathers—Joey's father—gets up and tears them both off, makes a small wad in his fist.

There is some rustling of magazine pages.

The Mother clears her throat. "Tiny Tim forgot the wet bar," she says.

Ned, who is still up, comes out of his room and down the corridor, whose lights dim at nine. Standing next to the Mother's chair, he says to her, "Where are you from? What is wrong with your baby?"

In the little room that is theirs, she sleeps fitfully in her sweatpants, occasionally leaping up to check on the Baby. This is what the sweatpants are for: leaping. In case of fire. In case of anything. In case the difference between day and night starts to dissolve and there is no difference at all so why pretend. In the cot beside her the Husband, who has taken a sleeping pill, is snoring loudly, his arms folded about his head in a kind of origami. How could either of them have stayed back at the house, with its empty high chair and empty crib? Occasionally the Baby wakes and cries out, and she bolts up, goes to him, rubs his back, rearranges the linens. The clock on the metal dresser shows that it is five after three. Then twenty to five. And then it is really morning, the beginning of this day, Nephrectomy Day. Will she be glad when it's over, or barely alive, or both? Each day of this week has arrived huge, empty, and unknown, like a spaceship, and this one especially is lit an incandescent gray.

"He'll need to put this on," says John, one of the nurses, bright and early, handing the Mother a thin greenish garment with roses and Teddy bears printed on it. A wave of nausea hits her: this smock, she thinks, will soon be splattered with—with what?

The Baby is awake but drowsy. She lifts off his pajamas. "Don't forget, *bubeleh*," she whispers, undressing and dressing him. "We will be with you every moment, every step. When you think you are asleep and floating off far away from everybody, Mommy will still be there." If she hasn't fled on a bus. "Mommy will take care of you. And Daddy, too." She hopes the Baby does not detect her own fear and uncertainty, which she must hide from him, like a limp. He is hungry, not having been allowed to eat, and he is no longer amused by this new place but worried about its hardships. Oh, my baby, she thinks. And the room starts to swim a little. The Husband comes in to take over. "Take a break," he says to her. "I'll walk him around for five minutes."

She leaves but doesn't know where to go. In the hallway she is approached by a kind of social worker, a customer-relations person, who had given them a video to watch about the anesthesia: how the parent accompanies the child into the operating room, and how gently, nicely the drugs are administered.

"Did you watch the video?"

"Yes," says the Mother.

"Wasn't it helpful?"

"I don't know," says the Mother.

"Do you have any questions?" asks the video woman. *Do you have any questions?* asked of someone who has recently landed in this fearful, alien place seems to the Mother an absurd and amazing little courtesy. The very specificity of a question would give the lie to the overwhelming strangeness of everything around her.

"Not right now," says the Mother. "Right now I think I'm just going to go to the bathroom."

When she comes back to the Baby's room, everyone is there: the Surgeon, the Anesthesiologist, all the nurses, the social worker. In their blue caps and scrubs they look like a clutch of forget-me-nots, and forget them who could? The Baby, in his little Teddy-bear smock, seems cold and scared. He reaches out and the Mother lifts him from the Husband's arms, rubs his back to warm him.

"Well, it's time!" says the Surgeon, forcing a smile.

"Shall we go?" says the Anesthesiologist.

What follows is a blur of obedience and bright lights. They take an elevator down to a big concrete room, the anteroom, the green-room, the backstage of the operating room. Lining the walls are long shelves full of blue surgical outfits. "Children often become afraid of the color blue," one of the nurses says. But of course. Of course! "Now, which one of you would like to come into the operating room for the anesthesia?"

"I will," says the Mother.

"Are you sure?" says the Husband.

"Yup." She kisses the Baby's hair. Mr. Curlyhead people keep calling him here, and it seems both rude and nice. Women look admiringly at his long lashes and exclaim, "Always the boys! Always the boys!"

Two surgical nurses put a blue smock and a blue cotton cap on the Mother. The Baby finds this funny and keeps pulling at the cap. "This way," says another nurse, and the Mother follows. "Just put the Baby down on the table."

In the video, the mother holds the baby and fumes from the mask are gently waved under the baby's nose until he falls asleep. Now, out of view of camera or social worker, the Anesthesiologist is anxious to get this under way and not let too much gas leak out into the room generally. The occupational hazard of this, his cho-sen profession, is gas exposure and nerve damage, and it has started to worry him. No doubt he frets about it to his wife every night. Now he turns the gas on and quickly clamps the plastic mouth-piece over the Baby's cheeks and lips.

The Baby is startled. The Mother is startled. The Baby starts to scream and redden behind the plastic, but he cannot be heard. He thrashes. "Tell him it's O.K.," says the nurse to the Mother.

O.K.? "It's O.K.," repeats the Mother, holding his hand, but she knows he can tell it's not O.K., because he can see that not only is she still wearing that stupid paper cap but her words are mechanical and swallowed, and she is biting her lips to keep them from trembling. Panicked, he attempts to sit, he cannot breathe, his arms reach up. *Bye-bye, outside.* And then, quite quickly, his eyes shut, he untenses and has fallen not into sleep but aside to sleep, an odd, kidnapping kind of sleep, his terror now hidden someplace deep inside him.

"How did it go?" asks the social worker, waiting in the concrete outer room. The Mother is hysterical. A nurse has ushered her out.

"It wasn't at all like the film strip!" she cries. "It wasn't like the film strip at all!"

"The film strip? You mean the video?" asks the social worker.

"It wasn't like that at all! It was brutal and unforgivable."

"Why, that's terrible," she says, her role now no longer misinformational but janitorial, and she touches the Mother's arm. The Mother shakes her off and goes to find the Husband.

She finds him in the large mulberry Surgery Lounge, where he has been taken and where there is free hot chocolate in small plastic-foam cups. Red cellophane garlands festoon the doorways. She has totally forgotten it is as close to Christmas as this. A pianist in the corner is playing "Carol of the Bells," and it sounds not only unfestive but scary, like the theme from "The Exorcist."

There is a giant clock on the far wall. It is a kind of porthole into the operating room, a way of assessing the Baby's ordeal: forty-five minutes for the Hickman implant; two and a half hours for the nephrectomy. And then, after that, three months of chemotherapy. The magazine on her lap stays open at a ruby-hued perfume ad.

"Still not taking notes," says the Husband.

"Nope."

"You know, in a way, this is the kind of thing you've *always* written about."

"You are really something, you know that? This is life. This isn't a 'kind of thing.'"

"But this is the kind of thing that fiction is: it's the unlivable life, the strange room tacked on to the house, the extra moon that is circling the earth unbeknownst to science."

"I told you that."

"I'm quoting you."

She looks at her watch, thinking of the Baby. "How long has it been?"

"Not long. Too long. In the end, those're the same things."

"What do you suppose is happening to him right this second?"

Infection? Slipping knives? "I don't know. But you know what? I've gotta go. I've gotta just walk a bit." The Husband gets up, walks around the lounge, then comes back and sits down.

The synapses between the minutes are unswimmable. An hour is thick as fudge. The Mother feels depleted; she is a string of empty tin cans attached by wire, something a goat would sniff and chew, something now and then enlivened by a jolt of electricity.

She hears their names being called over the intercom. "Yes? Yes?" She stands up quickly. Her voice has flown out before her, an exhalation of birds. The piano music has stopped. The pianist is gone. She and the Husband approach the main desk, where a man looks up at them and smiles. Before him is a Xeroxed list of patients' names. "That's our little boy right there," says the Mother, seeing the Baby's name on the list and pointing at it. "Is there some word? Is everything O.K.?"

"Yes," says the man. "Your boy is doing fine. They've just finished with the catheter and they are moving on to the kidney."

"But it's been two hours already! Oh, my God, did something go wrong, what happened, what went wrong?"

"Did something go wrong?" The Husband tugs at his collar.

"Not really. It just took longer than they expected. I'm told everything is fine. They wanted you to know."

"Thank you," says the Husband. They turn and walk back toward where they were sitting.

"I'm not going to make it," sighs the Mother, sinking into a fake-leather chair shaped somewhat like a baseball mitt. "But before I go I'm taking half this hospital out with me."

"Do you want some coffee?" asks the Husband.

"I don't know," says the Mother. "No, I guess not. No. Do you?"

"Nah, I don't, either, I guess," he says.

"Would you like part of an orange?"

"Oh, maybe, I guess, if you're having one." She takes a temple orange from her purse and just sits there peeling its difficult skin, the flesh rupturing beneath her fingers, the juice trickling down her hands, stinging the hangnails. She and the Husband chew and swallow, discreetly spit the seeds into Kleenex, and read from photocopies of the latest medical research which they begged from the interne. They read, and underline, and sigh and close their eyes, and after some time the surgery is over. A nurse from Peed-Onk comes down to tell them.

"Your little boy's in recovery right now. He's doing well. You can see him in about fifteen minutes."

How can it be described? How can any of it be described? The trip and the story of the trip are always two different things. The narrator is the one who has stayed home but then, afterward, presses her mouth upon the traveller's mouth, in order to make the mouth work, to make the mouth say, say, say. One cannot go to a place and speak of it, one cannot both see and say, not really. One can go, and upon returning make a lot of hand motions and indications with the arms. The mouth itself, working at the speed of light, at the eye's instructions, is necessarily struck still; so fast, so much to report, it hangs open and dumb as a gutted bell. All that unsayable life! That's where the narrator comes in. The narrator comes with her kisses and mimicry and tidying up. The narrator comes and makes a slow, fake song of the mouth's eager devastation.

It is a horror and a miracle to see him. He is lying in his crib in his room, tubed up, splayed like a boy on a cross, his arms stiffened into cardboard "no-no"s so that he cannot yank out the tubes. There is the bladder catheter, the nasal-gastric tube, and the Hickman, which, beneath the skin, is plugged into his jugular, then popped out his chest wall and capped with a long plastic cap. There is a large bandage taped over his abdomen. Groggy, on a morphine drip, still he is able to look at her when, maneuvering through all the vinyl wiring, she leans to hold him, and when she does he begins to cry, but cry silently, without motion or noise. She has never seen a baby cry without motion or noise. It is the crying of an old person: silent, beyond opinion, shattered. In someone so tiny, it is frightening and unnatural. She wants to pick up the Baby and run—out of there, out of there. She wants to whip out a gun: *No-nos, eh? This whole thing is what I call a no-no.* "Don't you touch him!" she wants to shout at the surgeons and the needle nurses. "Not anymore! No more! No more!" She would crawl up and lie beside him in the crib if she could. But instead, because of all his intricate wiring, she must lean and cuddle, sing to him, songs of peril and flight: "We gotta get out of this place, if it's the last thing we ever do. We gotta get out of this place. Baby, there's a better life for me and for you."

Very 1967. She was eleven then, and impressionable.

The Baby looks at her, pleadingly, his arms outstretched in surrender. To where? Where is there to go? Take me! Take me!

That night, post-op night, the Mother and the Husband lie afloat in their cots. A fluorescent lamp near the crib is kept on in the dark. The Baby breathes evenly but thinly in his drugged sleep. The morphine in its first flooding doses apparently makes him feel as if he were falling backward—or so the Mother has been told— and it causes the Baby to jerk, to catch himself over and over, as if he were being dropped from a tree. "Is this right? Isn't there something that should be done?" The nurses come in hourly, different ones—the night shifts seem strangely short and frequent. If the Baby stirs or frets, the nurses give him more morphine through the Hickman catheter, then leave to tend to other patients. The Mother rises to check on him herself in the low light. There is gurgling from the clear plastic suction tube coming out of his mouth. Brownish clumps have collected in the tube. What is going on? The Mother rings for the nurse. Is it Renee or Sarah or Darcy? She's forgotten.

"What, what is it?" murmurs the Husband, waking up.

"Something is wrong," says the Mother. "It looks like blood in his N-G tube."

"What?" The Husband gets out of bed. He, too, is wearing sweatpants.

The nurse—Valerie—pushes open the heavy door to the room and enters quietly. "Everything O.K.?"

"There's something wrong here. The tube is sucking blood out of his stomach. It looks like it may have perforated his stomach and now he's bleeding internally. Look!"

Valerie is a saint, but her voice is the standard hospital saint voice: an infuriating, pharmaceutical calm. It says, *Everything is normal here. Death is normal. Pain is normal. Nothing is abnormal. So there is nothing to get excited about.* "Well, now, let's see." She holds up the plastic tube and tries to see inside it. "Hmm," she says. "I'll call the attending physician."

Because this is a research and teaching hospital, all the regular doctors are at home sleeping in their Mission-style beds. Tonight, as is apparently the case every weekend night, the attending physician is a medical student. He looks fifteen. The authority he attempts to convey he cannot remotely inhabit. He is not even in the same building with it. He shakes everyone's hand, then strokes his chin, a gesture no doubt gleaned from some piece of dinner theatre his parents took him to once. As if there were an actual beard on that chin! As if beard growth on that chin were even possible! "Our Town"! "Kiss Me Kate"! "Barefoot in the Park"! He is attempting to convince if not to impress.

"We're in trouble," the Mother whispers to the Husband. She is tired, tired of young people grubbing for grades. "We've got Dr. 'Kiss Me Kate' here."

The Husband looks at her blankly, a mixture of disorientation and divorce.

The medical student holds the tubing in his hands. "I don't really see anything," he says.

He flunks! "You don't?" The Mother shoves her way in, holds the clear tubing in both hands. "That," she says. "Right here and here." Just this past semester she said to one of her own students, "If you don't see how this essay is better than that one, then I want you to just go out into the hallway and stand there until you do." Is it important to keep one's voice down? The Baby stays asleep. He is drugged and dreaming, far away.

"Hmm," says the medical student. "Perhaps there's a little irritation in the stomach."

"A little irritation?" The Mother grows furious. "This is blood. These are clumps and clots. This stupid thing is sucking the life right out of him!" Life! She is starting to cry.

They turn off the suction and bring in antacids, which they feed into the Baby through the tube. Then they turn the suction on again. This time on "low."

"What was it on before?" asks the Husband.

"High," says Valerie. "Doctor's orders, though I don't know why. I don't know why these doctors do a lot of the things they do."

"Maybe they're—not all that bright?" suggests the Mother. She is feeling relief and rage simultaneously: there is a feeling of prayer and litigation in the air. Yet essentially she is grateful. Isn't she? She thinks she is. And still, and still: look at all the things you have to do to protect a child, a hospital merely an intensification of life's cruel obstacle course.

The Surgeon comes to visit on Saturday morning. He steps in and nods at the Baby, who is awake but glazed from the morphine, his eyes two dark, unseeing grapes. "The boy looks fine," he announces. He peeks under the Baby's bandage. "The stitches look good," he says. The Baby's abdomen is stitched all the way across, like a baseball. "And the other kidney, when we looked at it yesterday face to face, looked fine. We'll try to wean him off the morphine a little, and see how he's doing on Monday."

"Is he going to be O.K.?"

"The boy? The boy is going to be fine," he says, then taps her stiffly on the shoulder. "Now, you take care. It's Saturday. Drink a little wine."

Over the weekend, while the Baby sleeps, the Mother and the Husband sit together in the Tiny Tim Lounge. The Husband is restless and makes cafeteria and sundry runs, running errands for everyone. In his absence, the other parents regale her further with their sagas. Pediatric cancer and chemo stories: the children's amputations, blood poisoning, teeth flaking like shale, the learning delays and disabilities caused by chemo frying the young, budding brain. But strangely optimistic codas are tacked on: endings as stiff and loopy as carpenter's lace, crisp and empty as lettuce, reticulate as a net—ah, words. "After all that business with the tutor, he's better now, and fitted with new incisors by my wife's cousin's husband, who did dental school in two and a half years, if you can believe that. We hope for the best. We take things as they come. Life is hard."

"Life's a big problem," agrees the Mother. Part of her welcomes and invites all their tales. In the few long days since this nightmare began, part of her has become addicted to disaster and war stories. She only wants to hear about the sadness and emergencies of others. They are the only situations that can join hands with her own; everything else bounces off her shiny shield of resentment and unsympathy. Nothing else can even stay in her brain. From this, no doubt, the philistine world is made, or should one say recruited? Together the parents huddle all day in the Tiny Tim Lounge—no need to watch "Oprah." They leave "Oprah" in the dust. "Oprah" has nothing on them. They chat matter-of-factly, then fall silent and watch "Dune" or "Star Wars," in which there are bright and shiny robots, whom the Mother now sees not as robots at all but as human beings who have had terrible things happen to them.

Some of their friends visit with stuffed animals and soft "Looking good"s for the dozing baby, though the room is way past the stuffed-animal limit. The Mother arranges, once more, a plateful of Mint Milano cookies and cups of takeout coffee for guests. All her nutso pals stop by—the two on Prozac, the one obsessed with the word "penis" in the word "happiness," the one who recently had her hair foiled green. "Your friends put the *de* in *fin de siècle*," says the Husband. Overheard, or recorded, all marital conversation sounds as if someone must be joking, though usually no one is.

She loves her friends, especially loves them for coming, since there are times they all fight and don't speak for weeks. Is this friendship? For now and here, it must do and is, and is, she swears it is. For one, they never offer impromptu spiritual lectures about death, how it is part of life, its natural ebb and flow, how we all must accept that, or other such utterances that make her want to scratch out somebody's eyes. Like true friends, they take no hardy or elegant stance loosely choreographed from some broad perspective. They get right in there and mutter "Jesus Christ!" and shake their heads. Plus, they are the only people who will not only laugh at her stupid jokes but offer up stupid ones of their own. *What do you get when you cross Tiny Tim with a pit bull?* A child's illness is a strain on the mind. They know how to laugh in a flutey, desperate way—unlike the people who are more her husband's friends and who seem just to deepen their sorrowful gazes, nodding their heads in Sympathy. How Exiling and Estranging are everybody's Sympathetic Expressions! When anyone laughs, she thinks, O.K. Horray! A buddy. In disaster as in show business.

Nurses come and go; their chirpy voices both startle and soothe. Some of the other Peed-Onk parents stick their heads in to see how the Baby is and offer encouragement.

Green Hair scratches her head: "Everyone's so friendly here. Is there someone in this place who isn't doing all this airy, scripted optimism—or are people like that the only people here?"

"It's Modern Middle Medicine meets the Modern Middle Family," says the Husband. "In the Modern Middle West."

Someone has brought in takeout lo mein, and they all eat it out in the hall by the elevators.

Parents are allowed use of the Courtesy Line.

"You've got to have a second child," says a friend on the phone, a friend from out of town. "An heir and a spare. That's what we did. We had another child to insure we wouldn't off ourselves if we lost our first."

"Really?"

"I'm serious."

"A formal suicide? Wouldn't you just drink yourself into a lifelong stupor and let it go at that?"

"Nope. I knew how I would do it even. For a while, until our second came along, I had it all planned."

"You did? What did you plan?"

"I can't go into too much detail, because—hi, honey!—the kids are here now in the room. But I'll spell out the general idea: R-O-P-E."

Sunday evening she goes and sinks down on the sofa in the Tiny Tim Lounge next to Frank, Joey's father. He is a short, stocky man with the currentless, flat-lined look behind the eyes that all the parents eventually get here. He has shaved his head bald in solidarity with his son. His little boy has been battling cancer for five years. It is now in the liver, and the rumor around the corridor is that Joey has three weeks to live. She knows that Joey's mother, Roseanne, left Frank years ago, two years into the cancer, and has remarried and had another child, a girl named Brittany. The Mother sees Roseanne here sometimes with her new life—the cute little girl and the new full-haired husband, who will never be so maniacally and debilitatingly obsessed with Joey's illness the way Frank, her first husband, is. Roseanne comes to visit Joey, to say hello and now goodbye, but she is not Joey's main man. Frank is.

Frank is full of stories—about the doctors, about the food, about the nurses, about Joey. Joey, affectless from his meds, sometimes leaves his room and comes out to watch TV in his bathrobe. He is jaundiced and bald, and though he is nine he looks no older than six. Frank has devoted the last four and a half years to saving Joey's life. When the cancer was first diagnosed, the doctors gave Joey a twenty-per-cent chance of living six more months. Now here it is almost five years later, and Joey's still here. It is all due to Frank, who, early on, quit his job as vice-president of a consulting firm in order to commit himself totally to his son. He is proud of everything he's given up and done, but he is tired. Part of him now really believes that things are coming to a close, that this is the end. He says this without tears. There are no more tears.

"You have probably been through more than anyone else on this corridor," says the Mother.

"I could tell you stories," he says. There is a sour odor between them, and she realizes that neither of them has bathed for days.

"Tell me one. Tell me the worst one." She knows he hates his ex-wife and hates her new husband even more.

"The worst? They're all the worst. Here's one: one morning I went out for breakfast with my buddy—it was the only time I'd left Joey alone ever, left him for two hours is all—and when I came back his N-G tube was full of blood. They had the suction on too high, and it was sucking the guts right out of him."

"Oh, my God. That just happened to us," said the Mother.

"It did?"

"Friday night."

"You're kidding. They let that happen again? I gave them such a chewing out about that!"

"I guess our luck is not so good. We get your very worst story on the second night we're here."

"It's not a bad place, though."

"It's not?"

"Naw. I've seen worse: I've taken Joey everywhere."

"He seems very strong." Truth is, at this point Joey seems like a zombie and frightens her.

"Joey's a fucking genius. A biological genius. They'd given him six months, remember."

The Mother nods.

"Six months is not very long," says Frank. "Six months is nothing. He was four and a half years old."

All the words are like blows. She feels flooded with affection and mourning for this man. She looks away, out the window, out past the hospital parking lot, up toward the black marbled sky and the electric eyelash of the moon. "And now he's nine," she says. "You're his hero."

"And he's mine," says Frank, though the fatigue in his voice seems to overwhelm him. "He'll be that forever. Excuse me," he says. "I've got to go check. His breathing hasn't been good. Excuse me."

"Good news and bad," says the Oncologist on Monday. He has knocked, entered the room, and now stands there. Their cots are unmade. One wastebasket is overflowing with coffee cups. "We've got the pathologist's report. The bad news is that the kidney they removed had certain lesions, called 'rests,' which are associated with a higher risk for disease in the other kidney. The good news is that the tumor is Stage I, regular cell structure, and under five hundred grams, which qualifies you for a national experiment in which chemotherapy isn't done but your boy is simply monitored with ultrasound. It's not all that risky, given that the patient's watched closely, but here is the literature on it. There are forms to sign, if you decide to do that. Read all this and we can discuss it further. You have to decide within four days."

Lesions? Rests? They dry up and scatter like M&M's on the floor. All she hears is the part about no chemo. Another sigh of relief rises up in her and spills out. In a life where there is only the bearable and the unbearable, a sigh of relief is an ecstasy.

"No chemo?" says the husband. "Do you recommend that?"

The Oncologist shrugs. What casual gestures these doctors are permitted! "I know chemo. I like chemo," says the Oncologist. "But this is for you to decide. It depends how you feel."

The Husband leans forward. "But don't you think that now that we have the upper hand with this thing we should keep going? Shouldn't we stomp on it, beat it, smash it to death with the chemo?"

The Mother swats him angrily and hard. "Honey, you're delirious!" She whispers, but it comes out as a hiss. "This is our lucky break." Then she adds gently, "We don't want the Baby to have chemo."

The Husband turns back to the Oncologist. "What do you think?"

"It could be," he says, shrugging. "It could be that this is your lucky break. But you won't know for sure for five years."

The Husband turns back to the Mother. "O.K.," he says. "O.K."

The Baby grows happier and strong. He begins to move and sit and eat. Wednesday morning they are allowed to leave, and to leave without chemo. The Oncologist looks a little nervous. "Are you nervous about this?" asks the Mother.

"Of course I'm nervous." But he shrugs and doesn't look that nervous. "See you in six weeks for the ultrasound," he says, then he waves and leaves, looking at his big black shoes.

The Baby smiles, even toddles around a little, the sun bursting through the clouds, an angel chorus crescendoing. Nurses arrive. The Hickman is taken out of the Baby's neck and chest, antibiotic lotion is dispensed. The Mother packs up their bags. The baby sucks on a bottle of juice and does not cry.

"No chemo?" says one of the nurses. "Not even a little chemo?"

"We're doing watch-and-wait," says the Mother.

The other parents look envious but concerned. They have never seen any child get out of there with his hair and white blood cells intact.

"Will you be O.K.?" says Ned's mother.

"The worry's going to kill us," says the Husband.

"But if all we have to do is worry," chides the Mother, "every day for a hundred years, it'll be easy. It'll be nothing. I'll take all the worry in the world if it wards off the thing itself."

"That's right," says Ned's mother. "Compared to everything else, compared to all the actual events, the worry is nothing."

The Husband shakes his head. "I'm such an amateur," he moans.

"You're both doing admirably," says the other mother. "Your baby's lucky, and I wish you all the best."

The Husband shakes her hand warmly. "Thank you," he says. "You've been wonderful."

Another mother, the mother of Eric, comes up to them. "It's all very hard," she says, her head cocked to one side. "But there's a lot of collateral beauty along the way."

Collateral beauty? Who is entitled to such a thing? A child is ill. No one is entitled to any collateral beauty.

"Thank you," says the Husband.

Joey's father, Frank, comes up and embraces them both. "It's a journey," he says. He chucks the Baby on the chin. "Good luck, little man."

"Yes, thank you so much," says the Mother. "We hope things go well with Joey." She knows that Joey had a hard, terrible night.

Frank shrugs and steps back. "Gotta go," he says. "Goodbye!"

"Bye," she says, and then he is gone. She bites the inside of her lip, a bit tearily, then bends down to pick up the diaper bag, which is now stuffed with little animals; helium balloons are tied to its zipper. Shouldering the thing, the Mother feels she has just won a prize. All the parents have now vanished down the hall in the opposite direction. The Husband moves close. With one arm he takes the Baby from her; with the other he rubs her back. He can see she is starting to get weepy.

"Aren't these people nice? Don't you feel better hearing about their lives?" he asks.

Why does he do this, form clubs all the time—why does even this society of suffering soothe him? When it comes to death and dying, perhaps someone in this family ought to be more of a snob.

"All these nice people with their brave stories," he continues as they make their way toward the elevator bank, waving goodbye to the nursing staff as they go, even the Baby waving shyly. *Bye-bye! Bye-bye!* "Don't you feel consoled, knowing we're all in the same boat, that we're all in this together?"

But who on earth would want to be in this boat? the Mother thinks. This boat is a nightmare boat. Look where it goes: to a silver-and-white room, where, just before your eyesight and hearing and your ability to touch or be touched disappear entirely, you must watch your child die.

Rope! Bring on the rope.

"Let's make our own way," says the Mother, "and not in this boat."

Woman Overboard! She takes the Baby back from the Husband, cups the Baby's cheek in her hand, kisses his brow and then, quickly, his flowery mouth. The Baby's heart—she can hear it—drums with life. "For as long as I live," says the Mother, pressing the elevator button—up or down, everyone in the end has to leave this way—"I never want to see any of these people again."

There are the notes.

Now, where is the money?

The Knife Thrower

By Steven Millhauser

Introduced by Mary Gaitskill

I like "The Knife Thrower" because it is elegant and has lyric beauty which Millhauser, like Poe and Angela Carter, uses to evoke nightmarish unease. There is an almost old-fashioned purity in the simplicity of its structure and characterizations—the characters, except for the narrator, are realized entirely through exquisite descriptions of their physical actions and qualities. They have the odd, arresting power of the images on playing cards; they are static, but their very stasis suggests a bottomless pit of slithering motion.

I was surprised by some of Millhauser's language because it seemed slightly archaic, a bit like the language of Victorian pornography: ". . . there were many, young women especially, who longed to be wounded by the master and to bear his mark proudly." Good grief—who else would write that way? There would be something silly about it, except that the fastidious theatricality suits the story perfectly. "At that moment, we felt in our arms and along our backs a first faint flutter of anxious excitement, for there they stood before us, the dark master and the pale maiden, like figures in a dream from which we were trying to awake." It's just so . . . corny. And yet, somehow, we are not yet awake.

The knife thrower's show has the innocuous grotesquery of a cheap carnival, it has a kind of brutish innocence (". . . the smell of sawdust and cotton candy, the glittering woman on the turning wheel"), it has the ancient allure of cruelty. The story is like an especially good "Twilight Zone" episode, or a young child's dream of something terrible—except that it is told by an adult.

—MARY GAITSKILL

Steven Millhauser

The Knife Thrower

From *Harper's Magazine*

WHEN WE LEARNED that Hensch, the knife thrower, was stopping at our town for a single performance at eight o'clock on Saturday night, we hesitated, wondering what we felt. Hensch, the knife thrower! Did we feel like clapping our hands for joy, like leaping to our feet and bursting into smiles of anticipation? Or did we, after all, want to tighten our lips and look away in stern disapproval? That was Hensch for you. For if Hensch was an acknowledged master of his art, that difficult and faintly unsavory art about which we knew very little, it was also true that he bore with him certain disturbing rumors, which we reproached ourselves for having failed to heed sufficiently when they appeared from time to time in the arts section of the Sunday paper.

Hensch, the knife thrower! Of course we knew his name. Everyone knew his name, as one knows the name of a famous chess player or magician. What we couldn't be sure of was what he actually did. Dimly we recalled that the skill of his throwing had brought him early attention, but that it wasn't until he had changed the rules entirely that he was taken up in a serious way. He had stepped boldly, some said recklessly, over the line never before crossed by knife throwers, and had managed to make a reputation out of a disreputable thing. Some of us seemed to recall reading that in his early carnival days he had wounded an assistant badly; after a six-month retirement he had returned with his new act. It was here that he had introduced into the chaste discipline of knife throwing the idea of the artful wound, the mark of blood that was the mark of the master. We had even heard that among his followers there were many, young women especially, who longed to be wounded by the master and to bear his scar proudly. If rumors of this kind were disturbing to us, if they prevented us from celebrating Hensch's arrival with innocent delight, we nevertheless acknowledged that without such dubious enticements we'd have been unlikely to attend the performance at all, since the art of knife throwing, for all its apparent danger, is really a tame art, an outmoded art—little more than a quaint old-fashioned amusement in these times of ours. The only knife throwers any of us had ever seen were in the circus sideshow or the carnival ten-in-one, along with the fat lady and the human skeleton. It must, we imagined, have galled Hensch to feel himself a freak among freaks; he must have needed a way out. For wasn't he an artist, in his fashion? And so we admired his daring, even as we deplored his method and despised him as a vulgar showman; we questioned the rumors, tried to recall what we knew of him, interrogated ourselves relentlessly. Some of us dreamed of him: a monkey of a man in checked pants and a red hat, a stern officer in glistening boots. The promotional mailings showed only a knife held by a gloved hand. Is it surprising we didn't know what to feel?

At eight o'clock precisely, Hensch walked onto the stage: a brisk unsmiling man in black tails. His entrance surprised us. For although most of us had been seated since half-past seven, others were still arriving, moving down the aisles, pushing past half-turned knees into squeaking seats. In fact we were so accustomed to delays for latecomers that an 8:00 performance was understood to mean one that began at 8:10 or even 8:15. As Hensch strode across the stage, a busy no-nonsense man, black-haired and top-bald, we didn't know whether we admired him for his supreme indifference to our noises of settling in, or disliked him for his refusal to countenance the slightest delay. He walked quickly across the stage to a waist-high table on which rested a mahogany box. He wore no gloves. At the opposite corner of the stage, in the rear, a black wooden partition bisected the stage walls. Hensch stepped behind his box and opened it to reveal a glitter of knives. At this moment a woman in a loose-flowing white gown stepped in front of the dark partition. Her pale hair was pulled tightly back and she carried a silver bowl.

While the latecomers among us whispered their way past knees and coats, and slipped guiltily into their seats, the woman faced us and reached into her bowl. From it she removed a white hoop about the size of a dinner plate. She held it up and turned it from side to side, as if for our inspection, while Hensch lifted from his box half a dozen knives. Then he stepped to the side of the table. He held the six knives fanwise in his left hand, with the blades pointing up. The knives were about a foot long, the blades shaped like elongated diamonds, and as he stood there at the side of the stage, a man with no expression on his face, a man with nothing to do, Hensch had the vacant and slightly bored look of an overgrown boy holding in one hand an awkward present, waiting patiently for someone to open a door.

With a gentle motion the woman in the white gown tossed the hoop lightly in the air in front of the black wooden partition. Suddenly a knife sank deep into the soft wood, catching the hoop, which hung swinging on the handle. Before we could decide whether or not to applaud, the woman tossed another white hoop. Hensch lifted and threw in a single swift smooth motion, and the second hoop hung swinging from the second knife. After the third hoop rose in the air and hung suddenly on a knife handle, the woman reached into her bowl and held up for our inspection a smaller hoop, the size of a saucer. Hensch raised a knife and caught the flying hoop cleanly against the wood. She next tossed two small hoops one after the other, which Hensch caught in two swift motions: the first at the top of its trajectory, the second near the middle of the partition.

We watched Hensch as he picked up three more knives and spread them fanwise in his left hand. He stood staring at his assistant with fierce attention, his back straight, his thick hand resting by his side. When she tossed three small hoops, one after the other, we saw his body tighten, we waited for the thunk-thunk-thunk of knives in wood, but he stood immobile, sternly gazing. The hoops struck the floor, bounced slightly, and began rolling like big dropped coins across the stage. Hadn't he liked the throw? We felt like looking away, like pretending we hadn't noticed. Nimbly the assistant gathered the rolling hoops, then assumed her position by the black wall. She seemed to take a deep breath before she tossed again. This time Hensch flung his three knives with extraordinary speed, and suddenly we saw all three hoops swinging on the partition, the last mere inches from the floor. She motioned grandly toward Hensch, who did not bow; we burst into vigorous applause.

Again the woman in the white gown reached into her bowl, and this time she held up something between her thumb and forefinger that even those of us in the first rows could not immediately make out. She stepped forward, and many of us recognized, between her fingers, an orange and black butterfly. She returned to the partition and looked at Hensch, who had already chosen his knife. With a gentle tossing gesture she released the butterfly. We burst into applause as the knife drove the butterfly against the wood, where those in the front rows could see the wings helplessly beating.

That was something we hadn't seen before, or even imagined we might see, something worth remembering; and as we applauded we tried to recall the knife throwers of our childhood, the smell of sawdust and cotton candy, the glittering woman on the turning wheel.

Now the woman in white removed the knives from the black partition and carried them across the stage to Hensch, who examined each one closely and wiped it with a cloth before returning it to his box.

Abruptly, Hensch strode to the center of the stage and turned to face us. His assistant pushed the table with its box of knives to his side. She left the stage and returned pushing a second table, which she placed at his other side. She stepped away, into half-darkness, while the lights shone directly on Hensch and his tables. We saw him place his left hand palm up on the empty tabletop. With his right hand he removed a knife from the box on the first table. Suddenly, without looking, he tossed the knife straight up into the air. We saw it rise to its rest and come hurtling down. Someone cried out as it struck his palm, but Hensch raised his hand from the table and held it up for us to see, turning it first one way and then the other: the knife had struck between the fingers. Hensch lowered his hand over the knife so that the blade stuck up between his second and third fingers. He tossed three more knives into the air, one after the other: rat-tat-tat they struck the table. From the shadows the woman in white stepped forward and tipped the table toward us, so that we could see the four knives sticking between his fingers.

Oh, we admired Hensch, we were taken with the man's fine daring; and yet, as we pounded out our applause, we felt a little restless, a little dissatisfied, as if some unspoken promise had failed to be kept. For hadn't we been a trifle ashamed of ourselves for attending the performance, hadn't we deplored in advance his unsavory antics, his questionable crossing of the line?

As if in answer to our secret impatience, Hensch strode decisively to his corner of the stage. Quickly the pale-haired assistant followed, pushing the table after him. She next shifted the second table to the back of the stage and returned to the black partition. She stood with her back against it, gazing across the stage at Hensch, her loose white gown hanging from thin shoulder straps that had slipped down to her upper arms. At that moment we felt in our arms and along our backs a first faint flutter of anxious excitement, for there they stood before us, the dark master and the pale maiden, like figures in a dream from which we were trying to awake.

Hensch chose a knife and raised it beside his head with deliberation; we realized that he had worked very quickly before. With a swift sharp drop of his forearm, as if he were chopping a piece of wood, he released the knife. At first we thought he had struck her upper arm, but we saw that the blade had sunk into the wood and lay touching her skin. A second knife struck beside her other upper arm. She began to wriggle both shoulders, as if to free herself from the tickling knives, and only as her loose gown came rippling down did we realize that the knives had cut the shoulder straps. Hensch had us now, he had us. Long-legged and smiling, she stepped from the fallen gown and stood before the black partition in a spangled silver leotard. We thought of tightrope walkers, bare-back riders, hot circus tents on blue summer days. The pale yellow hair, the spangled cloth, the pale skin touched here and there with shadow, all this gave her the remote, enclosed look of a work of art, while at the same time it lent her a kind of cool voluptuous-ness, for the metallic glitter of her costume seemed to draw attention to the bareness of her skin, disturbingly unhidden, dan-gerously white and cool and soft.

Quickly the glittering assistant stepped to the second table at the back of the stage and removed something from the drawer. She returned to the center of the wooden partition and placed on her head a red apple. The apple was so red and shiny that it looked as if it had been painted with nail polish. We looked at Hensch, who stared at her and held himself very still. In a single motion Hensch lifted and threw. She stepped out from under the red apple stuck in the wood.

From the table she removed a second apple and clenched the stem with her teeth. At the black partition she bent slowly back-ward until the bright red apple was above her upturned lips. We could see the column of her trachea pressing against the skin of her throat and the knobs of her hips pushing up against the silver spangles. Hensch took careful aim and flung the knife through the heart of the apple.

Next from the table she removed a pair of long white gloves, which she pulled on slowly, turning her wrists, tugging. She held up each tight-gloved hand in turn and wriggled the fingers. At the partition she stood with her arms out and her fingers spread. Hensch looked at her, then raised a knife and threw; it stuck into her fingertip, the middle fingertip of her right hand, pinning her to the black wall. The woman stared straight ahead. Hensch picked up a clutch of knives and held them fanwise in his left hand. Swiftly he flung nine knives, one after the other, and as they struck her fingertips, one after the other, bottom to top, right-left right-left, we stirred uncomfortably in our seats. In the sudden silence she stood there with her arms outspread and her fingers full of knives, her silver spangles flashing, her white gloves whiter than her pale arms, looking as if at any moment her head would drop forward—looking for all the world like a martyr on a cross. Then slowly, gently, she pulled each hand from its glove, leaving the gloves hanging on the wall.

Now Hensch gave a sharp wave of his fingers, as if to dismiss everything that had gone before, and to our surprise the woman stepped forward to the edge of the stage, and addressed us for the first time.

"I must ask you," she said gently, "to be very quiet, because this next act is very dangerous. The master will mark me. Please do not make a sound. We thank you."

She returned to the black partition and simply stood there, her shoulders back, her arms down but pressed against the wood. She gazed steadily at Hensch, who seemed to be studying her; some of us said later that at this moment she gave the impression of a child who was about to be struck in the face, though others felt she looked calm, quite calm.

Hensch chose a knife from his box, held it for a moment, then raised his arm and threw. The knife struck beside her neck. He had missed—had he missed?—and we felt a sharp tug of disappointment, which changed at once to shame, deep shame, for we hadn't come out for blood, only for—well, something else; and as we asked ourselves what we had come for, we were surprised to see her reach up with one hand and pull out the knife. Then we saw, on her neck, the thin red trickle, which ran down to her shoulder; and we understood that her whiteness had been arranged for this moment. Long and loud we applauded, as she bowed and held aloft the glittering knife, assuring us, in that way, that she was wounded but well, or well-wounded; and we didn't know whether we were applauding her wellness or her wound, or the touch of the master, who had crossed the line, who had carried us, safely, it appeared, into the realm of forbidden things.

Even as we applauded she turned and left the stage, returning a few moments later in a long black dress with long sleeves and a high collar, which concealed her wound. We imagined the white bandage under the black collar; we imagined other bandages, other wounds, on her hips, her waist, the edges of her breasts. Black against black they stood there, she and he, bound now it seemed in a dark pact, as if she were his twin sister, or as if both were on the same side in a game we were all playing, a game we no longer understood; and indeed she looked older in her black dress, sterner, a schoolmarm or maiden aunt. We were not surprised when she stepped forward to address us again.

"If any of you, in the audience, wish to be marked by the master, to receive the mark of the master, now is the time. Is there anyone?"

We all looked around. A single hand rose hesitantly and was instantly lowered. Another hand went up; then there were other hands, young bodies straining forward, eager; and from the stage the woman in black descended and walked slowly along an aisle, looking closely, considering, until she stopped and pointed: "You." And we knew her, Susan Parker, a high school girl, who might have been our daughter, sitting there with her face turned questioningly toward the woman, her eyebrows slightly raised, as she pointed to herself; then the faint flush of realization; and as she climbed the steps of the stage we watched her closely, wondering what the dark woman had seen in her, to make her be the one, wondering too what she was thinking, Susan Parker, as she followed the dark woman to the wooden partition. She was wearing loose jeans and a tight black short-sleeved sweater; her reddish-brown and faintly shiny hair was cut short. Was it for her white skin she had been chosen? or some air of self-possession? We wanted to cry out: sit down! you don't have to do this! but we remained silent, respectful. Hensch stood at his table, watching without expression. It occurred to us that we trusted him at this moment; we clung to him; he was all we had; for if we weren't absolutely sure of him, then who were we, what on earth were we, who had allowed things to come to such a pass?

The woman in black led Susan Parker to the wooden partition and arranged her there: back to the wood, shoulders straight. We saw her run her hand gently, as if tenderly, over the girl's short hair, which lifted and fell back in place. Then taking Susan Parker's right hand in hers, she stepped to the girl's right, so that the entire arm was extended against the black partition. She stood holding Susan Parker's raised hand, gazing at the girl's face—

comforting her, it seemed; and we observed that Susan Parker's arm looked very white between the black sweater and the black dress, against the black wood of the partition. As the women gazed at each other, Hensch lifted a knife and threw. We heard the muffled bang of the blade, heard Susan Parker's sharp little gasp, saw her other hand clench into a fist. Quickly the dark woman stepped in front of her and pulled out the knife; and turning to us she lifted Susan Parker's arm, and displayed for us a streak of red on the pale forearm. Then she reached into a pocket of her black dress and removed a small tin box. From the box came a ball of cotton, a patch of gauze, and a roll of white surgical tape, with which she swiftly bound the wound. "There, dear," we heard her say. "You were very brave." We watched Susan Parker walk with lowered eyes across the stage, holding her bandaged arm a little away from her body; and as we began to clap, because she was still there, because she had come through, we saw her raise her eyes and give a quick shy smile, before lowering her lashes and descending the steps.

Now arms rose, seats creaked, there was a great rustling and whispering among us, for others were eager to be chosen, to be marked by the master, and once again the woman in black stepped forward to speak.

"Thank you, dear. You were very brave, and now you will bear the mark of the master. You will treasure it all your days. But it is a light mark, do you know, a very light mark. The master can mark more deeply, far more deeply. But for that you must show yourself worthy. Some of you may already be worthy, but I will ask you now to lower your hands, please, for I have with me someone who is ready to be marked. And please, all of you, I ask for your silence."

From the right of the stage stepped forth a young man who might have been fifteen or sixteen. He was dressed in black pants and a black shirt and wore rimless glasses that caught the light. He carried himself with ease, and we saw that he had a kind of lanky and slightly awkward beauty, the beauty, we thought, of a water bird, a heron. The woman led him to the wooden partition and indicated that he should stand with his back against it. She walked to the table at the rear of the stage and removed an object, which she carried back to the partition. Raising the boy's left arm, so that it was extended straight out against the wall at the level of his shoulder, she lifted the object to his wrist and began fastening it into the wood. It appeared to be a clamp, which held his arm in place at the wrist. She then arranged his hand: palm facing us, fingers together. Stepping away, she looked at him thoughtfully. Then she stepped over to his free side, took his other hand, and held it gently.

The stage lights went dark, then a reddish spotlight shone on Hensch at his box of knives. A second light, white as moonlight, shone on the boy and his extended arm. The other side of the boy remained in darkness.

Even as the performance seemed to taunt us with the promise of danger, of a disturbing turn that should not be permitted, or even imagined, we reminded ourselves that the master had so far done nothing but scratch a bit of skin, that his act was after all public and well traveled, that the boy appeared calm; and though we disapproved of the exaggerated effect of the lighting, the crude melodrama of it all, we secretly admired the skill with which the performance played on our fears. What it was we feared, exactly, we didn't know, couldn't say. But there was the knife thrower bathed in blood-light, there was the pale victim manacled to a wall; in the shadows the dark woman; and in the glare of the lighting, in the silence, in the very rhythm of the evening, the promise of entering a dark dream.

And Hensch took up a knife and threw; some heard the sharp gasp of the boy, others a thin cry. In the whiteness of the light we saw the knife handle at the center of his bloody palm. Some said that at the moment the knife struck, the boy's shocked face shone with an intense, almost painful joy. The white light suddenly illuminated the woman in black, who raised his free arm high, as if in triumph; then she quickly set to work pulling out the blade, wrapping the palm in strips of gauze, wiping the boy's drained and sweating face with a cloth, and leading him off the stage with an arm firmly around his waist. No one made a sound. We looked at Hensch, who was gazing after his assistant.

When she came back, alone, she stepped forward to address us, while the stage lights returned to normal.

"You are a brave boy, Thomas. You will not soon forget this day. And now I must say that we have time for only one more event, this evening. Many of you here, I know, would like to receive the palm mark, as Thomas did. But I am asking something different now. Is there anyone in this audience tonight who would like to make"—and here she paused, not hesitantly, but as if in emphasis—"the ultimate sacrifice? This is the final mark, the mark that can be received only once. Please think it over carefully, before raising your hand."

We wanted her to say more, to explain clearly what it was she meant by those riddling words, which came to us as though whispered in our ears, in the dark, words that seemed to mock us even as they eluded us—and we looked about tensely, almost eagerly, as if by the sheer effort of our looking we were asserting our vigilance. We saw no hands, and maybe it was true that at the very center of our relief there was a touch of disappointment, but it was relief nonetheless; and if the entire performance had seemed to be leading toward some overwhelming moment that was no longer to take place, still we had been entertained by our knife thrower, had we not, we had been carried a long way, so that even as we questioned his cruel art we were ready to offer our applause.

"If there are no hands," she said, looking at us sharply, as if to see what it was we were secretly thinking, while we, as if to avoid her gaze, looked rapidly all about. "Oh: yes?" We saw it too, the partly raised hand, which perhaps had always been there, unseen in the half-darkened seats, and we saw the stranger rise, and begin to make her way slowly past drawn-in knees and pulled-back coats and half-risen forms. We watched her climb the steps of the stage, a tall mournful-looking girl in jeans and a dark blouse, with lank long hair and slouched shoulders. "And what is your name?" the woman in black said gently, and we could not hear the answer. "Well then, Laura. And so you are prepared to receive the final mark? Then you must be very brave." And turning to us she said, "I must ask you, please, to remain absolutely silent."

She led the girl to the black wooden partition and arranged her there, unconfined: chin up, hands hanging awkwardly at her sides. The dark woman stepped back and appeared to assess her arrangement, after which she crossed to the back of the stage. At this point some of us had confused thoughts of calling out, of demanding an explanation, but we didn't know what it was we might be protesting, and in any case the thought of distracting Hensch's throw, of perhaps causing an injury, was repellent to us, for we saw that already he had selected a knife. It was a new kind of knife, or so we thought, a longer and thinner knife. And it seemed to us that things were happening too quickly, up there on the stage, for where was the spotlight, where was the drama of a sudden darkening, but Hensch, even as we wondered, did what he always did— he threw his knife. Some of us heard the girl cry out, others were struck by her silence, but what stayed with all of us was the absence of the sound of the knife striking wood. Instead there was a softer sound, a more disturbing sound, a sound almost like silence, and some said the girl looked down, as if in surprise. Others claimed to see in her face, in the expression of her eyes, a look of rapture. As she fell to the floor the dark woman stepped forward and swept her arm toward the knife thrower, who for the first time turned to acknowledge us. And now he bowed: a deep, slow, graceful bow, the bow of a master, down to his knees. Slowly the dark red curtain began to fall. Overhead the lights came on.

As we left the theater we agreed that it had been a skillful performance, though we couldn't help feeling that the knife thrower had gone too far. He had justified his reputation, of that there could be no question; without ever trying to ingratiate himself with us, he had continually seized our deepest attention. But for all that, we couldn't help feeling that he ought to have found some other way. Of course the final act had probably been a setup, the girl had probably leaped smiling to her feet as soon as the curtain closed, though some of us recalled unpleasant rumors of one kind or another, run-ins with the police, charges and countercharges, a murky business. In any case we reminded ourselves that she hadn't been coerced in any way, none of them had been coerced in any way. And it was certainly true that a man in Hensch's position had every right to improve his art, to dream up new acts with which to pique curiosity, indeed such advances were absolutely necessary, for without them a knife thrower could never hope to keep himself in the public eye. Like the rest of us, he had to earn his living, which admittedly wasn't easy in times like these. But when all was said and done, when the pros and cons were weighed, and every issue carefully considered, we couldn't help feeling that the knife thrower had really gone too far. After all, if such performances were encouraged, if they were even tolerated, what might we expect in the future? Would any of us be safe? The more we thought about it, the more uneasy we became, and in the nights that followed, when we woke from troubling dreams, we remembered the traveling knife thrower with agitation and dismay.

The Children Stay

By Alice Munro

Introduced by Andrea Barrett

This capacious and lovely story explicitly suggests parallels with the myth of Orpheus and Eurydice but then resists being read on those terms; as it also invokes but then turns away from *Anna Karenina* and *Madame Bovary*. Pauline, the story's heroine, wants "a love that is outside of ordinary life." She thinks "it's intolerable, at last, to stay in two skins, two envelopes with their own blood and oxygen sealed in their solitude"; she believes "that there is this major difference in lives or in marriages or unions between people. That some of them have a necessity, a fatefulness about them, which others do not have." Perched on the coast of Vancouver Island, in a fever of love and longing, she seeks "the feelings she doesn't have to strive for but only to give in to like breathing or dying."

Wonderfully romantic notions, all—but Munro is after something deeper and darker than mere romance. "The Children Stay" is anti-mythic, anti-romantic, profoundly unsettling in its denial of the central American myth: that we can always start over, that a life can be abandoned, a new life begun, without lasting damage. Like many of Chekhov's greatest stories, it's about being driven to a place where no good choices exist, and from which there is no return. Pauline believes she will not be left behind, or turned to stone, or turned into a version of her parents; she will not be ordinary; she will not be fenced in. But the gesture she makes—that gesture toward the self, toward making the self—backs her into the "radiant explosion" of her ordinary, heartbreaking life.

—ANDREA BARRETT

Alice Munro

The Children Stay

From *The New Yorker*

THIRTY YEARS AGO, a family was spending a holiday together on the east coast of Vancouver Island. A young father and mother, their two small daughters, and an older couple, the husband's parents.

What perfect weather. Every morning, every morning it's like this, the first pure sunlight falling through the high branches, burning away the mist over the still water of Georgia Strait.

If it weren't for the tide, it would be hard to remember that this is the sea. You look across the water to the mountains on the mainland, the ranges that are the western wall of the continent of North America. These humps and peaks coming clear now through the mist are of interest to the grandfather and to his son, Brian. The two men are continually trying to decide which of these shapes are actual continental mountains and which are improbable heights of the islands that ride in front of the shore.

There is a map, set up under glass, between the cottages and the beach. You can stand there looking at the map, then looking at what's in front of you and back at the map again, until you get things sorted out. The grandfather and Brian usually get into an argument—though you'd think there would not be much room for disagreement with the map right there.

Brian's mother won't look at the map. She says it boggles her mind. Her concern is always about whether anybody is hungry yet, or thirsty, whether the children have their sun hats on and have been rubbed with protective lotion. She makes her husband wear a floppy cotton hat and thinks that Brian should wear one, too—she reminds him of how sick he got from the sun that summer they went to the Okanagan, when he was a child. Sometimes Brian says to her, "Oh, dry up, Mother." His tone is mostly affectionate, but his father may ask him if that's the way he thinks he can talk to his mother nowadays.

"She doesn't mind," says Brian.

"How do you know?" says his father.

"Oh, for Pete's sake," says his mother.

Pauline, the young mother, slides out of bed as soon as she's awake every morning, slides out of reach of Brian's long, sleepily searching arms and legs. What wakes her is the first squeaks and mutters of the baby, Mara, in the children's room, then the creak of the crib as Mara—sixteen months old now, getting to the end of baby-hood—pulls herself up to stand hanging on to the railing. She continues her soft amiable talk as Pauline lifts her out—Caitlin, nearly five, shifting about but not waking, in her nearby bed—and as she is carried into the kitchen to be changed, on the floor. Then she is settled into her stroller, with a biscuit and a bottle of apple juice, while Pauline gets into her sundress and sandals, goes to the bathroom, combs out her hair—all as quickly and quietly as possible. They leave the cottage and head for the bumpy unpaved road that runs behind the cottages, a mile or so north till it stops at the bank of the little river that runs into the sea. The road is still mostly in deep morning shadow, the floor of a tunnel under fir and cedar trees.

The grandfather, also an early riser, sees them from the porch of his cottage, and Pauline sees him. But all that is necessary is a wave. He and Pauline never have much to say to each other (though sometimes there's an affinity they feel, in the midst of some long-drawn-out antics of Brian's or some apologetic but insistent fuss made by the grandmother, there's an awareness of not looking at each other, lest their look reveal a bleakness that would discredit others).

On this holiday Pauline steals time to be by herself—being with Mara is still almost the same thing as being by herself. Early morning walks, the late morning hour when she washes and hangs out the diapers. She could have had another hour or so in the afternoons, while Mara is napping. But Brian has fixed up a shelter on the beach, and he carries the playpen down every day, so that Mara can nap there and Pauline won't have to absent herself. He says his parents might be offended if she's always sneaking off. He agrees, though, that she does need some time to go over her lines for the play she's going to be in, back in Victoria, this September.

Pauline is not an actress. This is an amateur production, and she didn't even try out for the role. She was asked if she would like to be in this play by a man she met at a barbecue, in June. The people there were mostly teachers, and their wives or husbands—it was held at the house of the principal of the high school where Brian taught. The woman who taught French was a widow—she had brought her grown son, who was staying for the summer with her and working as a night clerk in a downtown hotel. She told everybody that he had got a job teaching at a college in western Washington State and would be going there in the fall.

Jeffrey Toom was his name. "Without the 'b,' " he said, as if the staleness of the joke wounded him.

What was he going to teach?

"Dram-ah," he said, drawing the word out in a mocking way.

He spoke of his present job disparagingly as well.

"It's a pretty sordid place," he said. "Maybe you heard—a hooker was killed there last February. And then we get the usual losers checking in to O.D. or bump themselves off."

People did not quite know what to make of this way of talking and drifted away from him. Except for Pauline.

"I'm thinking about putting on a play," he said. He asked her if she had ever heard of "Eurydice."

Pauline said, "You mean Anouilh's?" and he was unflatteringly surprised. He immediately said he didn't know if it would ever work out. "I just thought it might be interesting to see if you could do something different here in the land of Noël Coward."

Pauline did not remember when there had been a play by Noël Coward put on in Victoria, though she supposed there had been several. She said, "We saw 'The Duchess of Malfi' last winter at the college."

"Yeah. Well," he said, flushing. She had thought he was older than she was, at least as old as Brian—who was thirty, though people were apt to say he didn't act it—but as soon as he started talking to her, in this offhand, dismissive way, never quite meeting her eyes, she suspected that he was younger than he'd like to appear. Now, with that flush, she was sure of it.

As it turned out, he was a year younger than she was. Twenty-five.

She said that she couldn't be Eurydice—she couldn't act. But Brian came over to see what the conversation was about and said at once that she must try it.

"She just needs a kick in the behind," Brian said to Jeffrey. "She's like a little mule—it's hard to get her started. No, seriously, she's too self-effacing. I tell her that all the time. She's very smart. She's actually a lot smarter than I am."

At that Jeffrey did look directly into Pauline's eyes—impertinently and searchingly—and she was the one who was flushing.

He had chosen her immediately as his Eurydice because of the way she looked. But it was not because she was beautiful. "I'd never put a beautiful girl in that part," he said. "I don't know if I'd ever put a beautiful girl onstage in anything. It's distracting."

So what did he mean about the way she looked? He said it was her hair, which was long and dark and rather bushy (not in style at that time), and her pale skin ("Stay out of the sun this summer") and, most of all, her eyebrows.

"I never liked them," said Pauline, not quite sincerely. Her eyebrows were level, dark, luxuriant. They dominated her face. Like her hair, they were not in style. But if she had really disliked them, wouldn't she have plucked them?

Jeffrey seemed not to have heard her. "They give you a sulky look and that's disturbing," he said. "Also your jaw's a little heavy and that's sort of Greek. It would be better in a movie, where I could get you close up. The routine thing for Eurydice would be a girl who looked ethereal. I don't want ethereal."

As she walked Mara along the road, Pauline did work at the lines. There was a long speech at the end that was giving her trouble. She bumped the stroller along and repeated to herself, "You are terrible, you know, you are terrible like the angels. You think everybody's going forward, as brave and bright as you are— oh, don't look at me, please, darling, don't look at me— Perhaps I'm not what you wish I was, but I'm here, and I'm warm, I'm kind, and I love you. I'll give you all the happiness I can. Don't look at me. Don't look. Let me live."

She had left something out. "Perhaps I'm not what you wish I was, but you feel me here, don't you? I'm warm and I'm kind—"

She had told Jeffrey that she thought the play was beautiful.

He said, "Really?" What she'd said didn't please or surprise him—he seemed to feel it was predictable, superfluous. He would never describe a play in that way. He spoke of it more as a hurdle to be got over. Also a challenge to be flung at various enemies. At the academic snots, as he called them, who had done "The Duchess of Malfi." And at the social twits, as he called them, in the little theatre. He saw himself as an outsider heaving his weight against these people, putting on his play—he called it his—in the teeth of their contempt and opposition. In the beginning Pauline thought that this must be all in his imagination. Then something would happen that could be, but might not be, a coincidence—repairs to be done on the church hall where the play was to be performed, making it unobtainable, an unexpected increase in the cost of printing advertising posters—and she found herself seeing it his way. If you were going to be around him much, you almost had to see it his way—arguing was dangerous and exhausting.

"Sons of bitches," said Jeffrey between his teeth, but with some satisfaction. "I'm not surprised. I'm going to get to the bottom of this."

The rehearsals were held upstairs in an old building on Fisgard Street. Sunday afternoon was the only time that everybody could get there, though there were fragmentary rehearsals during the week. Pauline had to depend on sometimes undependable high-school babysitters—for the first six weeks of the summer Brian was busy teaching summer school. And Jeffrey himself had to be at his hotel job by eight o'clock in the evening. But on Sunday afternoons they were all there, laboring in the dusty high-ceilinged room on Fisgard Street. The windows were rounded at the top as in some plain and dignified church, and propped open in the heat with whatever objects could be found—ledger books from the nineteen-twenties, belonging to the hat shop that had once operated down-stairs, pieces of wood left over from the picture frames made by the artist whose canvases were now stacked against one wall and ap-parently abandoned. The glass was grimy, but outside the sunlight bounced off the sidewalks, the empty gravelled parking lots, the low stuccoed buildings, with what seemed a special Sunday bright-ness. Hardly anybody moved through these downtown streets. Nothing was open except the occasional hole-in-the-wall coffee shop or lackadaisical, flyspecked convenience store.

Pauline was the one who went out at the break to get soft drinks and coffee. She was the one who had the least to say about the play and the way it was going—even though she was the only one who had read it before—because she alone had never done any acting. So it seemed proper for her to volunteer. She enjoyed her short walk in the empty streets—she felt as if she had become an urban person, someone detached and solitary, who lived in the glare of an important dream. Sometimes she thought of Brian at home, work-ing in the garden and keeping an eye on the children. Or perhaps he had taken them to Dallas Road—she recalled a promise—to sail boats on the pond. That life seemed ragged and tedious compared to what went on in the rehearsal room—the hours of effort, the concentration, the sharp exchanges, the sweating and tension. Even the taste of the coffee, its scalding bitterness, and the fact that it was chosen by nearly everybody in preference to a fresher-tasting and maybe more healthful drink out of the cooler, seemed satisfy-ing to her.

❏ ❏ ❏ ❏

When she said that she had to go away for the two-week holiday, Jeffrey looked thunderstruck, as if he had never imagined that things like holidays could come into her life. Then he turned grim and slightly satirical, as if this were just another blow that he might have expected. Pauline explained that she would miss only the one Sunday—the one in the middle of the two weeks—because she and Brian were driving up the Island on a Monday and coming back on a Sunday morning. She promised to get back in time for rehearsal. Privately she wondered how she would do this—it always took so much longer than you expected to pack up and get away. She wondered if she could possibly come back by herself, on the morning bus. That would probably be too much to ask for. She didn't mention it.

She couldn't ask him if it was only the play he was thinking about, only her absence from a rehearsal that caused the thundercloud. At the moment, it very likely was. When he spoke to her at rehearsals there was never any suggestion that he ever spoke to her in any other way. The only difference in his treatment of her was that perhaps he expected less of her, of her acting, than he did of the others. And that would be understandable to anybody. She was the only one chosen out of the blue, for the way she looked—the others had all shown up at the audition he had advertised on signs put up in cafés and bookstores around town.

Yet she thought they all knew what was going on, in spite of Jeffrey's offhand and abrupt and none too civil ways. They knew that after every one of them had straggled off home he would walk across the room and bolt the staircase door. (At first Pauline had pretended to leave with the rest and had even got into her car and circled the block, but later such a trick had come to seem insulting, not just to herself and Jeffrey but to the others, whom she was sure would never betray her, bound as they all were under the temporary but potent spell of the play.)

Jeffrey crossed the room and bolted the door. Every time, this was like a new decision that he had to make. Until it was done, she wouldn't look at him. The sound of the bolt being pushed into place, the ominous or fatalistic sound of metal hitting metal, gave her a localized shock of capitulation. But she didn't make a move, she waited for him to come back to her with the whole story of the afternoon's labor draining out of his face, the expression of matter-of-fact and customary disappointment cleared away, replaced by the live energy she always found surprising.

"So. Tell us what this play of yours is about," Brian's father said. "Is it one of those ones where they take their clothes off on the stage?"

"Now, don't tease her," said Brian's mother.

Brian and Pauline had put the children to bed and walked over to his parents' cottage for an evening drink. The sunset was behind them, behind the forests of Vancouver Island, but the mountains in front of them, all clear now and hard cut against the sky, shone in its pink light. Some high inland mountains were capped with pink summer snow.

"The story of Orpheus and Eurydice is that Eurydice died," Pauline said. "And Orpheus goes down to the underworld to try to get her back. And his wish is granted, but only if he promises not to look at her. Not to look back at her. She's walking behind him—"

"Twelve paces," said Brian. "As is only right."

"It's a Greek story, but it's set in modern times," said Pauline. "At least this version is. More or less modern. Orpheus is a musician travelling around with his father—they're both musicians—and Eurydice is an actress. This is in France."

"Translated?" Brian's father said.

"No," said Brian. "But don't worry, it's not in French. It was written in Transylvanian."

"It's so hard to make sense of anything," Brian's mother said with a worried laugh. "It's so hard, with Brian around."

"It's in English," Pauline said.

"And you're what's-her-name?"

She said, "I'm Eurydice."

"He get you back O.K.?"

"No," she said. "He looks back at me and then I have to stay dead."

"Oh, an unhappy ending," Brian's mother said.

"You're so gorgeous?" said Brian's father skeptically. "He can't stop himself from looking back?"

"It's not that," said Pauline. But at this point she felt that something had been achieved by her father-in-law, he had done what he meant to do, which was the same thing that he nearly always meant to do, in any conversation she had with him. And that was to break through the careful structure of some explanation he had asked her for, and she had unwillingly but patiently given, and with a seemingly negligent kick knock it into rubble. He had been dangerous to her for a long time in this way, though he wasn't particularly so tonight.

But Brian did not know that. Brian was still figuring out how to come to her rescue.

"Pauline is gorgeous," Brian said.

"Yes indeed," said his mother.

"Maybe if she'd go to the hairdresser," his father said. But Pauline's long hair was such an old objection of his that it had become a family joke. Even Pauline laughed. She said, "I can't afford to till we get the veranda roof fixed." And Brian laughed boisterously, full of relief that she was able to take all this as a joke. It was what he had always told her to do.

"Just kid him back. It's the only way to handle him."

"Yeah, well, if you'd got yourselves a decent house," said his father. But this, like Pauline's hair, was such a familiar sore point that it couldn't rouse anybody. Brian and Pauline had bought a handsome house in bad repair on a street in Victoria where old mansions were being turned into ill-used apartment buildings. The house, the street, the messy old Garry oaks, the fact that no basement had been blasted out under the house, was all a horror to Brian's father. So what he said now about a decent house might be some kind of peace signal. Or could be taken so.

Brian was an only son. He was a math teacher. His father was a civil engineer, and part owner of a contracting company. If he had hoped that he would have a son who was an engineer and might come into the company, there was never any mention of it. Pauline had asked Brian whether he thought the carping about their house, and her hair, and the books she read, might be a cover for this larger disappointment, but Brian had said, "Nope. In our family we complain about just whatever we want to complain about. We ain't subtle, Ma'am."

Pauline still wondered, when she heard his mother talking about how teachers ought to be the most honored people in the world and they did not get half the credit they deserved and that she didn't know how Brian managed it, day after day. Then his father might say, "That's right," or "I sure wouldn't want to do it, I can tell you that. They couldn't pay me to do it."

And Brian would turn that into a joke, as he turned nearly everything into a joke.

"Don't worry, Dad. They don't pay you much."

Brian in his everyday life was a much more dramatic person than Jeffrey. He dominated his classes by keeping up a parade of jokes and antics, extending the role that he had always played, Pauline believed, with his mother and father. He acted dumb, he bounced back from pretended humiliations, he traded insults. He was a bully in a good cause—a chivying, cheerful, indestructible bully.

"Your boy has certainly made his mark with us," the principal said to Pauline. "He has not just survived, which is something in itself. He has made his mark."

Your boy.

He called his students boneheads. His tone was affectionate, fatalistic. He said that his father was the King of the Philistines, a pure and natural barbarian. And that his mother was a dishrag, good-natured and worn out. But however he dismissed such people, he could not be long without them. He took his students on camping trips. And he could not imagine a summer without this shared holiday. He was mortally afraid, every year, that Pauline would refuse to go along. Or that, having agreed to go, she was going to be miserable, take offense at something his father said, complain about how much time she had to spend with his mother, sulk because there was no way they could do anything by themselves. She might decide to spend all day in their own cottage, reading, and pretending to have a sunburn.

All those things had happened, on previous holidays. But this year she was easing up. He told her he could see that, and he was grateful to her.

"I know it's an effort," he said. "It's different for me. They're my parents and I'm used to not taking them seriously."

Pauline came from a family that took things so seriously that her parents had got a divorce. Her mother was now dead. She had a distant, though cordial, relationship with her father and her two much older sisters. She said that they had nothing in common. She knew Brian could not understand how that could be a reason. She saw what comfort it gave him, this year, to see things going so well. She had thought it was laziness or cowardice that kept him from breaking the arrangement, but now she saw that it was something far more positive. He needed to have his wife and his parents and his children bound together like this, he needed to involve Pauline in his life with his parents and to bring his parents to some recognition of her—though the recognition, from his father, would always be muffled and contrary, and from his mother too profuse, too easily come by, to mean much. Also he wanted Pauline to be connected—and the children, too—to his own childhood. He wanted these holidays to be linked to the holidays of his youth with their lucky or unlucky weather, car troubles, boating scares, bee stings, marathon Monopoly games, to all the things that he told his mother he was bored to death hearing about. He wanted pictures from this summer to be taken, and fitted into his mother's album, a continuation of all the other pictures that he groaned at the mention of.

The only time they could talk to each other was in bed, late at night. But they did talk then, more than was usual with them at home, where Brian was so tired that often he fell immediately asleep. And in ordinary daylight it was hard to talk to him because of his jokes. She could see the joke brightening his eyes. (His coloring was very like hers—dark hair and pale skin and gray eyes—but her eyes were cloudy and his were light, like clear water over stones.) She could see it pulling at the corners of his mouth as he foraged among your words to catch a pun or the start of a rhyme—anything that could take the conversation away, into absurdity. His whole body, tall and loosely joined together and still almost as skinny as a teenager's, twitched with comic propensity. Before she married him, Pauline had a friend named Gracie, a rather grumpy-looking girl, subversive about men. Brian had thought her a girl whose spirits needed a boost, and so he made even more than the usual effort. And Gracie said to Pauline, "How can you stand the non-stop show?"

"That's not the real Brian," Pauline had said. "He's different when we're alone." But, looking back, she wondered how true that had ever been. Had she said it simply to defend her choice, as you did when you had made up your mind to get married?

Even in the cottage, with the window open on the unfamiliar darkness and stillness of the night, he teased a little. He had to speak of Jeffrey as Monsieur le Directeur, which made the play, or the fact that it was a French play, slightly ridiculous. Or perhaps it was Jeffrey himself, Jeffrey's seriousness about the play, that had to be called into question.

Pauline didn't care. It was such a pleasure and a relief to her to mention Jeffrey's name.

Though most of the time she didn't mention him, she circled around that pleasure. She described all the others instead. The hairdresser and the harbor pilot and the busboy and the old man who claimed to have once acted on the radio. He played Orphée's father, and gave Jeffrey the most trouble, because he had the stubbornest notions of his own about acting.

The middle-aged impresario, M. Dulac, was played by a twenty-four-year-old travel agent. And Mathias, who was Eurydice's former boyfriend, presumably around her own age, was played by the manager of a shoe store, who was married and a father.

"Why didn't Monsieur le Directeur cast those two the other way round?" said Brian.

"That's the way he does things," Pauline said. "What he sees in us is something different from the obvious."

For instance, she said, the busboy was a difficult Orphée.

"He's only nineteen, he's terribly shy, but he's determined to be an actor. Even if it's like making love to his grandmother. Jeffrey has to keep at him. 'Keep your arms around her a little longer, stroke her a little—' "

"He might get to like it," Brian said. "Maybe I should come around and keep an eye on him."

At this Pauline snorted. When she had started to quote Jeffrey she had felt a giving-way in her womb or the bottom of her stomach, a shock that had travelled oddly upward and hit her vocal cords. She had to cover up this quaking by growling in a way that was supposed to be an imitation (though Jeffrey never growled or ranted or carried on in any theatrical way at all).

Stroke her a little.

"But there's a point about him being so innocent," she said hurriedly. "Being not so physical. Being awkward." She began to talk about Orphée in the play, not the busboy—Orphée's problems with love and reality. Orphée will not put up with anything less than perfection. He wants a love that is outside of ordinary life. He wants a perfect Eurydice.

"Eurydice is more realistic. She's carried on with Mathias and with M. Dulac. She's been around her mother and her mother's lover. She knows what people are like. But she loves Orphée. She loves him better, in a way, than he loves her. She loves him better because she's not such a fool. She loves him like a human person."

"She's slept with those other guys?"

"Well, with M. Dulac she had to, she couldn't get out of it. She didn't want to, but probably after a while she enjoyed it, because after a certain point she couldn't help enjoying it. Just because she's slept with those men doesn't mean she's corrupt," Pauline said. "She wasn't in love then. She hadn't met Orphée. There's one speech where he tells her that everything she's done is sticking to her, and it's disgusting. Lies she's told him. The other men. It's all sticking to her forever. And then of course M. Henri plays up to that. He tells Orphée that he'll be just as bad and that one day he'll walk down the street with Eurydice and he'll look like a man with a dog he's trying to lose."

Brian laughed. He said, "That could be true."

"But not inevitably," said Pauline. "That's what's silly. It's not inevitable at all."

So Orphée is at fault, Pauline said decidedly. He looks back at Eurydice on purpose to kill her and get rid of her because she isn't perfect. Because of him she has to die a second time.

Brian, on his back and with his eyes wide open (she knew that because of the tone of his voice), said, "But doesn't he die, too?"

"Yes. He chooses to."

"So then they're together?"

"Yes. Like Romeo and Juliet. Orphée is with Eurydice at last. That's what M. Henri says. That's the last line of the play. That's the end." Pauline rolled over onto her side and touched her cheek to Brian's shoulder—not to start anything but to emphasize what she said next. "It's a beautiful play in one way but in another it's so silly. And it isn't really like 'Romeo and Juliet,' because it isn't bad luck or circumstances. It's on purpose. So they don't have to go on with life and get married and have kids and buy an old house and fix it up and—"

"And have affairs," said Brian. "After all, they're French."

Then he said, "And be like my parents."

Pauline laughed. "Do they have affairs? I can't imagine."

"Oh, sure," said Brian. "I meant their life."

"Oh."

"Logically I can see killing yourself so you won't turn into your parents. I just don't believe anybody would do it."

They went on speculating, and comfortably arguing, in a way that was not usual, but not altogether unfamiliar to them. They had done this before, at long intervals in their married life—talked half the night about God or fear of death or how children should be educated or whether money was important. At last they admitted to being too tired to make sense any longer, and arranged themselves in a comradely cuddle and went to sleep.

Finally a rainy day. Brian and his parents were driving into Campbell River to get groceries, and gin, and to take Brian's father's car to a garage. Brian had to go along, with his car, just in case the other car had to be left in the garage overnight. Pauline said that she had to stay home because of Mara's nap.

She persuaded Caitlin to lie down, too—allowing her to take her music box to bed with her if she played it under the covers. Then Pauline spread the script on the kitchen table, and drank coffee and went over the scene in which Orphée says that it's intolerable, at last, to stay in two skins, two envelopes with their own blood and oxygen sealed up in their solitude, and Eurydice tells him to be quiet.

"Don't talk. Don't think. Just let your hand wander, let it be happy on its own."

Your hand is my happiness, says Eurydice. Accept that. Accept your happiness.

Of course he says he cannot.

Caitlin called out frequently to ask what time it was, and Pauline could hear the music box. She hurried to the bedroom door and hissed at her to turn it off, not to wake Mara.

"If you play it like that again I'll take it away from you. O.K.?"

But Mara was already rustling around in her crib and in the next few minutes there were sounds of soft, encouraging conversation from Caitlin, designed to get her sister wide awake. Then of Mara rattling the crib railing, pulling herself up, throwing her bottle out onto the floor, and starting the bird cries that would grow more and more desolate until they brought her mother.

"I didn't wake her," Caitlin said. "She was awake all by herself. It's not raining anymore. Can we go down to the beach?"

She was right. It wasn't raining. Pauline changed Mara, told Caitlin to get her bathing suit on and find her sand pail. She got into her own bathing suit and put on her shorts on top of it, in case the rest of the family arrived home while she was down there. ("Dad doesn't like the way some women just go right out of their cottages in their bathing suits," Brian's mother had said to her. "I guess he and I just grew up in other times.") She picked up the script to take it along, then laid it down. She was afraid that she would get too absorbed in it and take her eye off the children for a moment too long.

The thoughts that came to her, of Jeffrey, were not really thoughts at all—they were more like alterations in her body. This could happen when she was sitting on the beach (trying to stay in the half shade of a bush and so preserve her pallor, as Jeffrey had ordered). Or when she was wringing out diapers, or when she and Brian were visiting his parents. In the middle of Monopoly games, Scrabble games, card games. She went right on talking, listening, working, keeping track of the children, while some memory of her secret life disturbed her like a radiant explosion. Then a warm weight settled, reassurance filling up all her hollows. But it didn't last, this comfort leaked away, and she was like a miser whose windfall has vanished and who is convinced such luck can never strike again. Longing buckled her up and drove her to the discipline of counting days. Sometimes she even cut the days into fractions to figure out more exactly how much time had gone.

She thought of going in to Campbell River, making some excuse, so that she could get to a phone booth and call him. The cottages had no phones—the only public phone was in the hall of the Lodge, across from the entrance to the dining room. But she did not have the number of the hotel where Jeffrey worked. And, besides that, she could never get away to Campbell River in the evening. She was afraid that if she called him at home in the daytime his mother the French teacher might answer. He said she hardly ever left the house in the summer. Just once, she had taken the ferry to Vancouver for the day. Jeffrey had phoned Pauline to ask her to come over. Brian was teaching and Caitlin was at her play group.

Pauline said, "I can't. I have Mara."

"Couldn't you bring her along?" he asked.

She said no.

"Why not? Couldn't you bring some things for her to play with?"

No, said Pauline. "I couldn't," she said. "I just couldn't." It seemed too dangerous to her, to trundle her baby along on such a guilty expedition. To a house where cleaning fluids would not be bestowed on high shelves and all pills and cough syrups and cigarettes and buttons put safely out of reach. And even if she escaped poisoning or choking, Mara might be storing up time bombs—memories of a strange house where she was strangely disregarded, of a closed door, noises on the other side of it.

"I just wanted you," Jeffrey said. "I just wanted you in my bed."

She said again, weakly, "No."

Those words of his kept coming back to her. I wanted you in my bed. A half-joking urgency in his voice but also a determination, a practicality, as if "in my bed" meant something more, the bed he spoke of taking on larger, less material dimensions.

Had she made a great mistake, with that refusal? With that reminder of how fenced in she was, in what anybody would call her real life?

The beach was nearly empty—people had got used to its being a rainy day. The sand was too heavy for Caitlin to make a castle or dig an irrigation system—projects she would undertake only with her father, anyway, because she sensed that his interest in them was wholehearted, and Pauline's was not. She wandered a bit forlornly at the edge of the water, missing the presence of other children, the nameless instant friends and occasional stone-throwing, water-kicking enemies, the shrieking and splashing and falling about. A boy a little bigger than she was and apparently all by himself stood knee deep in the water farther down the beach. If these two could get together it might be all right, the whole beach experience might be retrieved. Pauline couldn't tell if Caitlin was now making those little splashy runs into the water for his benefit, or whether he was watching her with interest or scorn.

Mara didn't need company, at least for now. She stumbled toward the water, felt it touch her feet and changed her mind, stopped, looked around, and spotted Pauline. "Paw. Paw," she said, in happy recognition. "Paw" was what she said for "Pauline," instead of "Mother" or "Mommy." Looking around overbalanced her; she sat down half on the sand and half in the water, made a squawk of surprise which turned into an announcement, and then, by some determined ungraceful maneuvers that involved putting her weight on her hands, rose to her feet, wavering and triumphant. She had been walking for half a year, but getting around on the sand was still a challenge. Now she came back toward Pauline, making some reasonable casual remarks in her own language.

"Sand," said Pauline, holding up a clot of it. "Look. Mara. Sand."

Mara corrected her, calling it something else—it sounded like "whap." Her thick diaper under her plastic pants and her terry-cloth playsuit gave her a fat bottom, and that, along with her plump cheeks and shoulders and her sidelong important expression, made her look like a roguish matron.

Pauline became aware of someone calling her name. It had been called two or three times, but because the voice was unfamiliar she had not recognized it. She stood up and waved. It was the woman who worked in the store at the Lodge. She was leaning over the porch rail and calling, "Mrs. Keating. Mrs. Keating? Telephone, Mrs. Keating."

Pauline hoisted Mara onto her hip and summoned Caitlin. She and the little boy were aware of each other now: they were both picking up stones from the bottom and flinging them out into the water. At first she didn't hear Pauline, or pretended not to hear.

"Store," called Pauline. "Caitlin. Store." When she was sure Caitlin would follow—it was the word "store" that had done it, the reminder of the tiny store in the Lodge where you could buy ice cream and candy—she began the trek across the sand and up the flight of wooden steps. Halfway up she stopped, said, "Mara, you weigh a ton," and shifted the baby to her other hip. Caitlin followed, banging a stick against the railing.

"Can I have a Fudgsicle? Mother? Can I?"

"We'll see."

The public phone was beside a bulletin board on the other side of the main hall and across from the door to the dining room. A bingo game had been set up in there, because of the rain.

"Hope he's still hanging on," the woman who worked in the store called out. She was unseen now behind her counter.

Pauline, still holding Mara, picked up the dangling receiver and said breathlessly, "Hello?" She was expecting to hear Brian telling her about some delay in Campbell River or asking her what it was she had wanted him to get at the drugstore. It was just the one thing—calamine lotion—so he had not written it down.

"Pauline," said Jeffrey. "It's me."

Mara was bumping and scrambling along Pauline's side, eager to get down. Caitlin came along the hall and went into the store, leaving wet sandy footprints. Pauline said, "Just a minute, just a minute." She let Mara slide down and hurried to close the door that led to the steps. She did not remember telling Jeffrey the name of this place, though she had told him roughly where it was. She heard the woman in the store speaking to Caitlin in a sharper voice than she would use to children whose parents were beside them.

"Did you forget to put your feet under the tap?"

"I'm here," said Jeffrey. "I didn't get along so well without you. I didn't get along at all."

Mara made for the dining room, as if the male voice calling out "Under the N" were a direct invitation to her.

"Here. Where?" said Pauline.

She read the signs that were tacked up on the bulletin board beside the phone:

No Person Under Fourteen Years of Age Not Accompanied
by Adult Allowed in Boats or Canoes.

Fishing Derby.

Bake and Craft Sale, St. Bartholomew's Church.

Your life is in your hands. Palms and Cards read.
Reasonable and Accurate. Call Claire.

"In a motel. In Campbell River."

Pauline knows where she is before she opens her eyes. Nothing surprises her. She has slept, but not deeply enough to let go of anything.

She had waited for Brian in the parking area of the Lodge, with the children in tow, and then she had asked for the keys. She told him in front of his parents that there was something else she needed, from Campbell River. He asked what was it? And did she have any money?

"Just something," she said, so he would think that it was tampons or birth-control supplies, something that she didn't want to mention.

"Sure. O.K., but you'll have to put some gas in," he said.

Later she had to speak to him on the phone. Jeffrey said she had to do it.

"Because he won't take it from me. He'll think I kidnapped you or something. He won't believe it."

But the strangest thing of all the things that day was that Brian did seem, immediately, to believe it. Standing where she had stood not so long before, in the public hallway of the Lodge—the bingo game over now, but people going past, she could hear them, people on their way out of the dining room after dinner—Brian had said, "Oh. Oh. Oh. O.K.," in a voice that would have to be quickly controlled but that seemed to draw on a supply of fatalism or foreknowledge that went far beyond that necessity.

"O.K.," he said. "What about the car?"

He said something else, something impossible, and then hung up, and she came out of the phone booth beside a row of gas pumps in Campbell River.

"That was quick," Jeffrey said. "Easier than you expected?"

Pauline said, "I don't know."

"He may have known it subconsciously. People do know."

She shook her head, to tell him not to say any more, and he said, "Sorry." They walked along the street not touching or talking.

Now, looking around at leisure—the first real leisure or freedom she's had since she came into that room—Pauline sees that there isn't much of anything in it. Just a junky dresser, the bed without a headboard, an armless upholstered chair. On the window a Venetian blind with a broken slat. Also a noisy air-conditioner—Jeffrey turned it off in the night and left the door open on the chain, since the window was sealed. The door is shut now. He must have got up in the night and shut it.

This is all she has. Her connection with the cottage where Brian lies now asleep or not asleep is broken. Also her connection with the house that has been an expression of her life with Brian, of the way they wanted to live. She has cut herself off from all the large solid acquisitions, like the washer and dryer and the oak table and the refinished wardrobe and the chandelier that is a copy of the one in a painting by Vermeer. And just as much from those things that were particularly hers—the pressed-glass tumblers that she had been collecting and the prayer rug that was probably not authentic, but beautiful. Especially from those things. The skirt and blouse and sandals she put on for the trip to Campbell River might as well be all she has now to her name. She would never go back to lay claim to anything. If Brian got in touch with her to ask what was to be done with things, she would tell him to do what he liked—throw everything into garbage bags and take it to the dump, if that was what he liked. (In fact she knows that he will probably pack up a trunk, which he does, sending on, scrupulously, not only her winter coat and boots but things like the waist cincher she wore at her wedding and never since, with the prayer rug draped on top of everything like a final statement of his generosity, either natural or calculated.)

She believes that she will never again care about what sort of rooms she lives in or what sort of clothes she puts on. She will not be looking for that sort of help to give anybody an idea of who she is, what she is like. Not even to give herself an idea. What she has done will be enough, it will be the whole thing.

What she has done will be what she has heard about and read about. It will be what Anna Karenina did and what Mme. Bovary wanted to do. And what a teacher at Brian's school did, with the school secretary. He ran off with her. That was what it was called. Running off with. Taking off with. It was spoken of disparagingly, humorously, enviously. It was adultery taken one step further. The people who did it had almost certainly been having an affair already, committing adultery for quite some time before they became desperate or courageous enough to take this step. Once in a long while a couple might claim their love was unconsummated and technically pure, but these people would be thought of—if anybody believed them—as being not only very serious and high-minded but almost devastatingly foolish, almost in a class with those who gave up everything to go and work in some poor and dangerous country.

The others, the adulterers, were seen as irresponsible, immature, selfish, or even cruel. Also lucky. They were lucky because the sex they had been having in parked cars or the long grass or in each other's sullied marriage beds or most likely in motels like this one must surely have been splendid. Otherwise they would never have got such a yearning for each other's company at all costs or such a faith that their shared future would be altogether better and different in kind from what they had in the past.

Different in kind. That is what Pauline must believe now—that there is this major difference in lives or in marriages or unions between people. That some of them have a necessity, a fatefulness about them, which others do not have. Of course she would have said the same thing a year ago. People did say that, they seemed to believe that, and to believe that their own cases were all of the first, the special kind, even when anybody could see that they were not.

It is too warm in the room. Jeffrey's body is too warm. Conviction and contentiousness seem to radiate from it, even in sleep. His torso is thicker than Brian's, he is pudgier around the waist. More flesh on the bones, yet not so slack to the touch. Not so good-looking in general—she is sure most people would say that. And not so fastidious. Brian in bed smells of nothing. Jeffrey's skin, every time she's been with him, has had a baked-in, slightly oily or nutty smell. He didn't wash last night—but, then, neither did she. There wasn't time. Did he even have a toothbrush with him? She didn't, but she had not known she was staying.

When she met Jeffrey here it was still in the back of her mind that she had to concoct some colossal lie to serve her when she got home. And she—they—had to hurry. When Jeffrey said to her that he had decided that they must stay together, that she would come with him to Washington State, that they would have to drop the play because things would be too difficult for them in Victoria, she had looked at him just in the blank way you'd look at somebody the moment that an earthquake started. She was ready to tell him all the reasons why this was not possible, she still thought she was going to tell him that, but her life was coming adrift in that moment. To go back would be like tying a sack over her head.

All she said was "Are you sure?"

He said, "Sure." He said sincerely, "I'll never leave you."

That did not seem the sort of thing that he would say. Then she realized he was quoting—maybe ironically—from the play. It was what Orphée says to Eurydice within a few moments of their first meeting in the station buffet.

So her life was falling forward, she was becoming one of those people who ran away. A woman who shockingly and incomprehensibly gave everything up. For love, observers would say wryly. Meaning, for sex. None of this would happen if it weren't for sex.

And yet what's the great difference there? It's not such a variable procedure, in spite of what you're told. Skins, motions, contact, results. Pauline isn't a woman from whom it's difficult to get results. Brian got them. Probably anybody would, who wasn't wildly inept or morally disgusting.

But nothing's the same, really. With Brian—especially with Brian, to whom she had dedicated a selfish sort of good will, with whom she's lived in married complicity—there can never be this stripping away, the inevitable flight, the feelings she doesn't have to strive for but only to give in to like breathing or dying. That she believes can only come when the skin is on Jeffrey, the motions made by Jeffrey, and the weight that bears down on her has Jeffrey's heart in it, also his habits, thoughts, peculiarities, his ambition and loneliness (that for all she knows may have mostly to do with his youth).

For all she knows. There's a lot she doesn't know. She hardly knows anything about what he likes to eat or what music he likes to listen to or what role his mother plays in his life (no doubt a mysterious but important one, like the role of Brian's parents). One thing she's pretty sure of: whatever preferences or prohibitions he has will be definite. Plates in his armor.

She slides out from under Jeffrey's hand and from under the top sheet, which has a harsh smell of bleach, slips down to the floor where the bedspread is lying and wraps herself quickly in that rag of greenish-yellow chenille. She doesn't want him to open his eyes and see her from behind and note the droop of her buttocks. He's seen her naked before, but generally in a more forgiving moment.

She rinses her mouth and washes herself, using the bar of soap that is about the size of two thin squares of chocolate and firm as stone. She's hard used between the legs, swollen and stinking. Urinating takes an effort and it seems she's constipated. Last night when they went out and got hamburgers she found she could not eat. Presumably she'll learn to do all these things again, they'll resume their natural importance in her life. At the moment it's as if she can't quite spare the attention.

She has some money in her purse. She has to go out and buy a toothbrush, toothpaste, deodorant, shampoo. Also vaginal jelly. Last night they used condoms the first two times but nothing the third time.

She didn't bring her watch and Jeffrey doesn't wear one. There's no clock in the room, of course. She thinks it's early—there's still an early look to the light in spite of the heat. The stores probably won't be open, but there'll be someplace where she can get coffee.

Jeffrey has turned onto his other side. She must have wakened him, just for a moment.

They'll have a bedroom. A kitchen, an address. He'll go to work. She'll go to the laundromat. Maybe she'll go to work, too. Selling things, waiting on tables, tutoring students. She knows French and Latin—do they teach French and Latin in American high schools? Can you get a job if you're not an American? Jeffrey isn't.

She leaves him the key. She'll have to wake him to get back in. There's nothing to write a note with, or on.

It is early. The motel is on the highway at the north end of town, beside the bridge. There's no traffic yet. She scuffs back and forth under the cottonwood trees at the edge of the lot for quite a while before a vehicle of any kind rumbles over the bridge—though the traffic on it shook their bed regularly late into the night.

Something is coming now. A truck. But not just a truck—there's a large bleak fact coming at her. And it has not arrived out of nowhere—it's been waiting, cruelly nudging at her ever since she woke up or even all night.

Caitlin and Mara.

Last night on the phone, after speaking in such a flat and controlled and almost agreeable voice—as if he prided himself on not being shocked, not objecting or pleading—Brian cracked open. He said with contempt and fury and no concern for whoever might hear him, "Well, then—what about the kids?"

The receiver began to shake against Pauline's ear.

She said, "We'll talk—" but he did not seem to hear her.

"The children," he said, in this same shivering and vindictive voice. Changing the word "kids" to "children" was like slamming a board down on her—a heavy, formal, righteous threat.

"The children stay," Brian said. "Pauline. Did you hear me?"

"No," said Pauline. "Yes. I heard you, but—"

"All right. You heard me. Remember. The children stay."

It was all he could do. To make her see what she was doing, what she was ending, and to punish her if she did so. Nobody would blame him. There might be finagling, there might be bargaining, there would certainly be humbling of herself, but there it was, like a round cold stone in her gullet, like a cannonball. And it would remain there unless she changed her mind entirely. The children stay.

Their car—hers and Brian's—is still sitting in the motel parking lot. Brian will have to ask his father or his mother to drive him up here today to get it. She has the keys in her purse. There are spare keys—he will surely bring them. She unlocks the car door and throws her keys on the seat, then locks the door from the inside and shuts it.

Now she can't go back. She can't get into the car and drive back and say that she'd been insane. If she did that he would forgive her but he'd never get over it and neither would she. They'd go on, though, as people did.

She walks out of the parking lot, she walks along the sidewalk, into town.

The weight of Mara on her hip yesterday. The sight of Caitlin's footprints on the floor.

Paw. Paw.

She doesn't need the keys to get back to them, she doesn't need the car. She could beg a ride on the highway. Give in, give in, get back to them any way at all—how can she not do that?

A sack over her head.

This is acute pain. It will become chronic. Chronic means that it will be permanent but perhaps not constant. It may also mean that you won't die of it. You won't get free of it but you won't die of it. You won't feel it every minute but you won't spend many days without it, either. And you'll learn some tricks to dull it or banish it or else you'll end up destroying what you've got. What you incurred this pain to get. It isn't his fault. He's still an innocent or a savage, who doesn't know there's a pain so durable in the world. Say to yourself, You lose them anyway. They grow up. For a mother there's always waiting this private, slightly ridiculous desolation. They'll forget this time, in one way or another they'll disown you. Or hang around till you don't know what to do about them, the way Brian has.

And, still, what pain. To carry along and get used to until it's only the past you're grieving for and no longer any possible present.

Her children have grown up. They don't hate her. For going away or staying away. They don't forgive her, either. Perhaps they wouldn't have forgiven her anyway, but it would have been about something different.

Caitlin remembers a little about the summer at the Lodge, Mara nothing. Caitlin calls it "that place Grandma and Grandpa stayed at."

"The place we were at when you went away," she says. "Only we didn't know you went away with the man who was Orphée."

Pauline has told them about the play.

Pauline says, "It wasn't Orphée."

"It wasn't Orphée? Oh, well. I thought it was."

"No."

"Who was it, then?"

"Just a man connected," says Pauline. "It wasn't him."

Maxine Swann

Flower Children

From *Ploughshares*

THEY'RE FREE to run anywhere they like whenever they like, so they do. The land falls away from their small house on the hill along a prickly path; there's a dirt road, a pasture where the steer are kept, swamps, a gully, groves of fruit trees, and then the creek from whose far bank a wooded mountain surges—they climb it. At the top, they step out to catch their breaths in the light. The mountain gives way into fields as far as their eyes can see— alfalfa, soybean, corn, wheat. They aren't sure where their own land stops and someone else's begins, but it doesn't matter, they're told. It doesn't matter! Go where you please!

They spend their whole lives in trees, young apple trees and old tired ones, red oaks, walnuts, the dogwood when it flowers in May. They hold leaves up to the light and peer through them. They close their eyes and press their faces into showers of leaves and wait for that feeling of darkness to come and make their whole bodies stir. They discover locust shells, tree frogs, a gypsy moth's cocoon. Now they know what that sound is in the night when the tree frogs sing out at the tops of their lungs. In the fields, they collect groundhog bones. They make desert piles and bless them with flowers and leaves. They wish they could be plants and lie very still near the ground all night and in the morning be covered with tears of dew. They wish they could be Robin Hood, Indians. In the summer, they rub mud all over their bodies and sit out in the sun to let it dry. When it dries, they stand up slowly like old men and women with wrinkled skin and walk stiff-limbed through the trees towards the creek.

Their parents don't care what they do. They're the luckiest children alive! They run out naked in storms. They go riding on ponies with the boys up the road who're on perpetual suspension from school. They take baths with their father, five bodies in one tub. In the pasture, they stretch out flat on their backs and wait for the buzzards to come. When the buzzards start circling, they lie very still, breathless with fear, and imagine what it would be like to be eaten alive. That one's diving! they say, and they leap to their feet. No, we're alive! We're alive!

The children all sleep in one room. Their parents built the house themselves, four rooms and four stories high, one small room on top of the next. With their first child, a girl, they lived out in a tent in the yard beneath the apple trees. In the children's room, there are three beds. The girls sleep together and the youngest boy in a wooden crib which their mother made. A toilet stands out in the open near the stairwell. Their parents sleep on the highest floor underneath the eaves in a room with skylights and silver-papered walls. In the living room, a swing hangs in the center from the ceiling. There's a woodstove to one side with a bathtub beside it; both the bathtub and the stove stand on lion's feet. There are bookshelves all along the walls and an atlas, too, which the children pore through, and a set of encyclopedias from which they copy fish. The kitchen, the lowest room, is built into a hill. The floor is made of dirt and gravel, and the stone walls are damp. Blacksnakes come in sometimes to shed their skins. When the children aren't outside, they spend most of their time here; they play with the stones on the floor, making pyramids or round piles and then knocking them down. There's a showerhouse outside down a steep, narrow path and a round stone well in the woods behind.

There's nowhere to hide in the house, no cellars or closets, so the children go outside to do that, too. They spend hours standing waist-high in the creek. They watch the crayfish have battles and tear off each other's claws. They catch the weak ones later, off-guard and from behind, as they crouch in the dark under shelves of stone. And they catch minnows, too, and salamanders with the soft skin of frogs, and they try to catch snakes, although they're never quite sure that they really want to. It maddens them how the water changes things before their eyes, turning the minnows into darting chips of green light and making the dirty stones on the bottom shine. Once they found a snapping turtle frozen in the ice, and their father cut it out with an axe to make soup. The children dunk their heads under and breathe out bubbles. They keep their heads down as long as they can. They like how their hair looks underneath the water, the way it spreads out around their faces in wavering fans. And their voices sound different, too, like the voices of strange people from a foreign place. They put their heads down and carry on conversations, they scream and laugh, testing out these strange voices that bloom from their mouths and then swell outwards, endlessly, like no other sound they have ever heard.

The children get stung by nettles, ants, poison ivy, poison oak, and bees. They go out into the swamp and come back, their whole heads crawling with ticks and burrs. They pick each other's scalps outside the house, then lay the ticks on a ledge and grind their bodies to dust with a pointed stone.

They watch the pigs get butchered and the chickens killed. They learn that people have teeth inside their heads. One evening, their father takes his shirt off and lies out on the kitchen table to show them where their organs are. He moves his hand over the freckled skin, cupping different places—heart, stomach, lung, lung, kidneys, gall bladder, liver here. And suddenly they want to know what's inside everything, so they tear apart everything they find, flowers, pods, bugs, shells, seeds, they shred up the whole yard in search of something; and they want to know about every-thing they see or can't see, frost and earthworms, and who will decide when it rains, and are there ghosts and are there fairies, and how many drops and how many stars, and although they kill things themselves, they want to know why anything dies and where the dead go and where they were waiting before they were born. In the hazelnut grove? Behind the goathouse? And how did they know when it was time to come?

Their parents are delighted by the snowlady they build with huge breasts and a penis and rock-necklace hair. Their parents are delighted by these children in every way, these children who will be like no children ever were. In this house with their children, they'll create a new world—that has no relation to the world they have known—in which nothing is lied about, whispered about, and nothing is ever concealed. There will be no petty lessons for these children about how a fork is held or a hand shaken or what is best to be said and what shouldn't be spoken of or seen. Nor will these children's minds be restricted to sets and subsets of rules, rules for children, about when to be quiet or go to bed, the causes and effects of various punishments which increase in gravity on a gradated scale. No, not these children! These children will be different. They'll learn only the large things. Here in this house, the world will be revealed in a fresh, new light, and this light will fall over everything. Even those shady forbidden zones through which they themselves wandered as children, panicked and alone, these, too, will be illuminated—their children will walk through with torches held high! Yes, everything should be spoken of in this house, everything, and everything seen.

Their father holds them on his lap when he's going to the bathroom, he lights his farts with matches on the stairs, he likes to talk about shit and examine each shit he takes, its texture and smell, and the children's shits, too, he has theories about shit that unwind for hours—he has theories about everything. He has a study in the toolshed near the house where he sits for hours and is visited regularly by ideas, which he comes in to explain to their mother and the children. When their mother's busy or not listening, he explains them to the children or to only one child in a language that they don't understand, but certain words or combinations of words bore themselves into their brains, where they will remain, but the children don't know this yet, ringing in their ears for the rest of their lives—repression, Nixon, wind power, nuclear power, Vietnam, fecal patterns, sea thermal energy, civil rights. And one day these words will bear all sorts of meaning, but now they mean nothing to the children—they live the lives of ghosts, outlines with no form, wandering inside their minds. The children listen attentively. They nod, nod, nod.

Their parents grow pot in the garden, which they keep under the kitchen sink in a large tin. When the baby-sitter comes, their mother shows her where it is. The baby-sitter plays with the children, a game where you turn the music up very loud, Waylon Jennings, "The Outlaws," and run around the living room leaping from the couch to the chairs to the swing, trying never to touch the floor. She shows them the tattoo between her legs, a bright rose with thorns, and then she calls up all her friends. When the children come down later to get juice in the kitchen, they see ten naked bodies through a cloud of smoke sitting around the table, playing cards. The children are invited, but they'd rather not play.

Their parents take them to protests in different cities and to concerts sometimes. The children wear T-shirts and hold posters and then the whole crowd lets off balloons. Their parents have peach parties and invite all their friends. There's music, dancing, skinny-dipping in the creek. Everyone takes off their clothes and rubs peach flesh all over each other's skin. The children are free to join in, but they don't feel like it. They sit in a row on the hill in all their clothes. But they memorize the sizes of the breasts and the shapes of the penises of all their parents' friends and discuss this later amongst themselves.

One day, at the end of winter, a woman begins to come to their house. She has gray eyes and a huge mound of wheat-colored hair. She laughs quickly, showing small white teeth. From certain angles, she looks ugly, but from others she seems very nice. She comes in the mornings and picks things in the garden. She's there again at dinner, at birthdays. She brings presents. She arrives dressed as a rabbit for Easter in a bright yellow pajama suit. She's very kind to their mother and chatters to her for hours in the kitchen as they cook. Their father goes away on weekends with her; he spends the night at her house. Sometimes he takes the children with him to see her. She lives in a gray house by the river that's much larger than the children's house. She has six Siamese cats. She has a piano and many records and piles of soft clay for the children to play with, but they don't want to. They go outside and stand by the concrete frog pond near the road. Algae covers it like a hairy, green blanket. They stare down, trying to spot frogs. They chuck rocks in, candy, pennies, or whatever else they can find.

In the gray spring mornings, there's a man either coming or going from their mother's room. He leaves the door open. Did you hear them? I heard them. Did you see them? Yes. But they don't talk about it. They no longer talk about things amongst themselves. But they answer their father's questions when he asks.

And here again they nod. When their father has gone away for good and then comes back to visit or takes them out on trips in his car and tells them about the women he's been with, how they make love, what he prefers or doesn't like, gestures or movements of the arms, neck, or legs described in the most detailed terms— And what do they think? And what would they suggest? When a woman stands with a cigarette between her breasts at the end of the bed and you suddenly lose all hope— And he talks about their mother, too, the way she makes love. He'd much rather talk to them than to anyone else. These children, they're amazing! They rise to all occasions, stoop carefully to any sorrow—and their minds! Their minds are wide open and flow with no stops, like damless streams. And the children nod also when one of their mother's boyfriends comes by to see her—she's not there—they're often heartbroken, occasionally drunk, they want to talk about her. The children stand with them underneath the trees. They can't see for the sun in their eyes, but they look up, anyway, and nod, smile politely, nod.

The children play with their mother's boyfriends out in the snow. They go to school. They're sure they'll never learn to read. They stare at the letters. They lose all hope. They worry that they don't know the Lord's Prayer. They realize that they don't know God or anything about him, so they ask the other children shy questions in the schoolyard and receive answers that baffle them, and then God fills their minds like a guest who's moved in, but keeps his distance, and worries them to distraction at night when they're alone. They imagine they hear his movements through the house, his footsteps and the rustling of his clothes. They grow frightened for their parents, who seem to have learned nothing about God's laws. They feel that they should warn them, but they don't know how. They become convinced one night that their mother is a robber. They hear her creeping through the house alone, lifting and rattling things.

At school, they learn to read and spell. They learn penmanship and multiplication. They're surprised at first by all the rules, but then they learn them too quickly and observe them all carefully. They learn not to swear. They get prizes for obedience, for following the rules down to the last detail. They're delighted by these rules, these arbitrary lines that regulate behavior and mark off forbidden things, and they examine them closely and exhaust their teachers with questions about the mechanical functioning and the hidden intricacies of these beings, the rules: If at naptime, you're very quiet with your eyes shut tight and your arms and legs so still you barely breathe, but really you're not sleeping, underneath your arms and beneath your eyelids you're wide awake and thinking very hard about how to be still, but you get the prize anyway for sleeping because you were the stillest child in the room, but actually that's wrong, you shouldn't get the prize or should you, because the prize is really for sleeping and not being still, or is it also for being still . . . ?

When the other children in the schoolyard are whispering themselves into wild confusion about their bodies and sex and babies being born, these children stay quiet and stand to one side. They're mortified by what they know and have seen. They're sure that if they mention one word, the other children will go home and tell their parents who will tell their teachers who will be horrified and disgusted and push them away. But they also think they should be punished. They should be shaken, beaten, for what they've seen. These children don't touch themselves. They grow hesitant with worry. At home, they wander out into the yard alone and stand there at a terrible loss. One day, when the teacher calls on them, they're no longer able to speak. But then they speak again a few days later, although now and then they'll have periods in their lives when their voices disappear utterly or else become very thin and quavering like ghosts or old people lost in their throats.

But the children love to read. They suddenly discover the use of all these books in the house and turn the living room into a lending library. Each book has a card and a due date and is stamped when it's borrowed or returned. They play card games and backgammon. They go over to friends' houses and learn about junk food and how to watch TV. But mostly they read. The read about anything, love stories, the lives of inventors and famous Indians, blights that affect hybrid plants. They try to read books they can't read at all and skip words and whole paragraphs and sit like this for hours lost in a stunning blur.

They take violin lessons at school and piano lessons and then stop one day when their hands begin to shake so badly they can no longer hold to the keys. What is wrong? Nothing! They get dressed up in costumes and put on plays. They're kings and queens. They're witches. They put on a whole production of *The Wizard of Oz*. They play detectives with identity cards and go searching for the kittens who have just been born in some dark, hidden place on their land. They store away money to give to their father when he comes. They spend whole afternoons at the edge of the yard waiting for him to come. They don't understand why their father behaves so strangely now, why he sleeps in their mother's bed when she's gone in the afternoon and then gets up and slinks around the house, like a criminal, chuckling, especially when she's angry and has told him to leave. They don't know why their father seems laughed at now and unloved, why he needs money from them to drive home in his car, why he seems to need something from them that they cannot give him—everything—but they'll try to give him—everything—whatever it is he needs, they'll try to do this as hard as they can.

Their father comes and waits for their mother in the house. He comes and takes them away on trips in his car. They go to quarries, where they line up and leap off cliffs. They go looking for caves up in the hills in Virginia. There are bears here, he tells them, but if you ever come face to face with one, just swear your heart out and he'll run. He takes them to dances in the city where only old people go. Don't they know how to fox-trot? Don't they know how to waltz? They sit at tables and order sodas, waiting for their turn to be picked up and whirled around by him. Or they watch him going around to other tables, greeting husbands and inviting their wives, women much older than his mother, to dance. These women have blue or white hair. They either get up laughing or refuse. He comes back to the children to report how they were— like dancing with milk, he says, or water, or molasses. He takes them to see the pro-wrestling championship match. He takes them up north for a week to meditate inside a hotel with a guru from Bombay. He takes them running down the up-escalators in stores and up Totem Mountain at night in a storm. He talks his head off. He gets speeding tickets left and right. He holds them on his lap when he's driving and between his legs when they ski. When he begins to fall asleep at the wheel, they rack their brains, trying to think of ways to keep him awake. They rub his shoulders and pull his hair. They sing rounds. They ask him questions to try to make him talk. They do interviews in the back seat, saying things they know will amuse him. And when their efforts are exhausted, he tells them that the only way he'll ever stay awake is if they insult him in the cruelest way they can. He says their mother is the only person who can do this really well. He tells them that they have to say mean things about her, about her boyfriends and lovers and what they do, or about how much she hates him, thinks he's stupid, an asshole, a failure, how much she doesn't want him around. And so they do. They force themselves to invent insults or say things that are terrible but true. And as they speak, they feel their mouths turn chalky and their stomachs begin to harden as if with each word they had swallowed a stone. But he seems delighted. He laughs and encourages them, turning around in his seat to look at their faces, his eyes now completely off the road.

He wants them to meet everyone he knows. They show up on people's doorsteps with him in the middle of the day or late at night. He can hardly contain himself. These are my kids! he says. They're smarter than anyone I know, and ten times smarter than me! Do you have any idea what it's like when your kids turn out smarter than you?! He teaches them how to play bridge and to ski backwards. At dinner with him, you have to eat with your eyes closed. When you go through a stoplight, you have to hold on to your balls. But the girls? Oh yes, the girls—well, just improvise! He's experiencing flatulence, withdrawal from wheat. He's on a new diet that will ruthlessly clean out his bowels. There are turkeys and assholes everywhere in the world. Do they know this? Do they know? But he himself is probably the biggest asshole here. Still, women find him handsome—they do! They actually do! And funny. But he *is* funny, he actually is, not witty but funny, they don't realize this because they see him all the time, they're used to it, but other people—like that waitress! Did they see that waitress? She was laughing so hard she could barely see straight! Do they know how you get to be a waitress? Big breasts. But he himself is not a breast man. Think of Mom—he calls their mother Mom— she has no breasts at all! But her taste in men is mind-boggling. Don't they think? Mind-boggling! Think about it too long, and you'll lose your mind. Why do they think she picks these guys? What is it? And why are women almost always so much smarter than men? And more dignified? Dignity for men is a completely lost cause! And why does anyone have kids, anyway? Come on, why?! Because they like you? Because they laugh at you? No! Because they're fun! Exactly! They're fun!

Around the house there are briar patches with berries and thorns. There are gnarled apple trees with puckered gray skins. The windows are all open—the wasps are flying in. The clothes on the line are jumping like children with no heads but hysterical limbs. Who will drown the fresh new kitties? Who will chain-saw the trees and cut the firewood in winter and haul that firewood in? Who will do away with all these animals, or tend them, or sell them, kill them one by one? Who will say to her in the evening that it all means nothing, that tomorrow will be different, that the heart gets tired after all? And where are the children? When will they come home? She has burnt all her diaries. She has told the man in the barn to go away. Who will remind her again that the heart has its own misunderstandings? And the heart often loses its way and can be found hours later wandering down passageways with unexplained bruises on its skin. On the roof, there was a child standing one day years ago, his arms waving free, but one foot turned inward, weakly— When will it be evening? When will it be night? The tree frogs are beginning to sing. She has seen the way their toes clutch at the bark. Some of them are spotted, and their hearts beat madly against the skin of their throats. There may be a storm. It may rain. That cloud there looks dark—but no, it's a wisp of burnt paper, too thin. In the woods above, there's a house that burnt down to the ground, but then a grove of lilac bushes burst up from the char. A wind is coming up. There are dark purple clouds now. There are red-coned sumacs hovering along the edge of the drive. Poisonous raw, but fine for tea. The leaves on the apple trees are all turning blue. The sunflowers in the garden are quivering, heads bowed—empty of seed now. And the heart gets watered and recovers itself. There is hope, everywhere there's hope. Light approaches from the back. Between the dry, gnarled branches, it's impossible to see. There are the first few drops. There are the oak trees shuddering. There's a flicker of bright gray, the underside of one leaf. There was once a child standing at the edge of the yard at a terrible loss. Did she know this? Yes. The children! (They have her arms, his ears, his voice, his smell, her soft features, her movements of the hand and head, her stiffness, his confusion, his humor, her ambition, his daring, his eyelids, their failure, their hope, their freckled skin—)

Brian Evenson

Two Brothers

From *Dominion Review*

I. Daddy Norton

DADDY NORTON had fallen and broken his leg. He lay on the floor of the entry hall, the rug bunched under his back, a crubbed jag of bone tearing his trousers at the knee.

"I have seen all in vision," he said, grunting against the pain. "God has foreseen how we must proceed."

He forbade Aurel and Theron to depart the house, for God had called them to witness and testify the miracles He would render in that place. Mama he forbade to summon an ambulance on threat of everlasting fire, for his life was God's affair alone.

He remained untouched on the floor into the evening and well through the night, allowing Mama near dawn to touch his face with a damp cloth and to slit back his trouser leg with a butcher knife. Aurel and Theron slept fitfully, leaned against the front door, touching shoulders. The leg swelled and grew thick with what to Aurel's imperfect vision appeared flies but which were, before Daddy Norton's pure spiritual eye, celestial messengers cleansing the wound with God's holy love. Dawn broke and the sun reared suddenly up the side of the house and flooded the marbled glass at the peak of the door, creeping across the floor until it mottled the broken leg. Daddy Norton beheld unfurled in the light the face of God, and spoke with God of his plight, and felt himself assured.

When the light fell beyond the leg and Daddy Norton lay silent and panting, Theron called for his breakfast. Mama had risen for it when Daddy Norton raised his hand and denied him, for *He that trusteth in the Lord is nourished by his word alone.*

"Bring us rather the Holy Word, Mama," Daddy Norton said. "Bring us the true book of God's awful comfort. We shall feast therein."

Theron declared loudly that he loved God's Holy Word as well as any of God's anointed, but he wanted some breakfast. Daddy Norton feigned not to hear, neglecting Theron until Mama returned armed with the Holy Word. She spread it before him, beside his face, tilting the book so her husband could read from it prone.

Daddy Norton tightened his eyes.

"Jesus have mercy," he said. "I can't find the pages."

Mama brought the book closer, kept bringing it forward until the pages were pressed against Daddy Norton's face. "Closer!" he called, "Closer!" Until his head rolled to one side and he stopped altogether.

"Make me some breakfast, Mama," said Theron.

"You heard what Daddy Norton said," said Mama.

"I'm starved, Mama," said Theron.

She took up the Holy Word and began to read, though without the lilt and fall of voice which Daddy Norton had learned to afflict on the words. Aurel could not feel the nourishment in Mama's voice, sounding as it did as mere words rattling forth without the spirit spurring them. He made at first to listen but in a few words paid heed only to Daddy Norton's leg. Crawling closer, he looked at it, watched God's love seethe.

"Goddamn if I don't make my own breakfast," Theron said, standing.

"Theron," said Mama, marking the verse with her thumb. "Be Mama's good boy and sit."

Theron ventured a step. Mama heaved her bulk up and stood filling the hallway, the Holy Word lifted over her head.

"Damned if I won't brain you," she said.

"Now, Mama," said Theron. "It's your Theron you're talking to. You don't want to hurt your own sweet child."

In his dreams Daddy Norton gave utterance to some language devoid of distinction, spilling out a continual and incomprehensible word. He lifted his head, his eyes furzing about the sockets, his tongue thrust hard between his teeth. He tried to pull himself up, the bone thrusting up through the flesh and the blood welling forth anew.

"Listen to what he's saying, Theron," said Mama. "He's talking to you."

Theron listened, carefully sat down.

Daddy Norton continued to speak liquids, his mouth flecking with blood. Aurel and Theron stayed against the outer door, silent, watching the light slide across the floor and vanish up over the house. Aurel's mouth was so dry he couldn't swallow. He kept clearing his throat and trying to swallow for hours, until the sun streamed in the window at the other end of the hall and began its descent.

"Tell Daddy to ask God what time lunch is served, Mama," said Theron.

Mama glared at him. She opened the *Holy Word of God as revealed to Daddy Norton, Beloved* and read aloud from the revelations of the suffering of the wicked. As she read, Daddy Norton's voice grew softer then seemed to stop altogether, though the lips never stopped moving. The light made its way toward them until they could see, through the glass at the end of the hall, the sun flatten into the sill and collapse.

Mama clutched the Holy Word to her chest and rocked back and forth, her eyes shut. Theron nudged Aurel, then arose and edged past Daddy Norton. He skirted Mama, his boots creaking, without her eyes opening. He strode down the hall and into the kitchen, the door banging shut behind him.

Mama started, opening her eyes.

"Where's Theron?" she asked.

Aurel pointed to the kitchen door.

"That boy is godless," she said. "And you, Aurel, hardly better. A pair of sorry sinners, the goddamn both of you."

She closed her eyes and rocked. In the dim, Aurel examined Daddy Norton. The man's face had gone pale and floated in the coming darkness like a buoy. Theron returned, toting half a loaf of bread and a bell jar of whiskey. He edged around Mama and straddle-stepped over Daddy Norton, seating himself against the door. He ripped the loaf apart, gave a morsel to Aurel. Aurel took it, tore off a mouthful. Mama watched them dully. They did not stop chewing. She closed her eyes, clung tighter to the Holy Word.

"Holy Word won't save you now, Mama," said Theron. "You need bread."

"Shut up," said Aurel. "Leave her alone."

"Won't save Daddy either," said Theron. "Nor angels neither."

"Shut up!" shouted Aurel, hiding his ears in his hands.

Unscrewing the lid of the whiskey, Theron took a swallow. "Drink, Mama?" he asked, holding the jar out.

She would not so much as look at him. He offered the jar to Aurel, who removed his hands from his ears long enough to take and drink.

"Aurel knows, Mama," said Theron. "He don't like it, but he knows."

Turning away from them, she lay down on the floor. Aurel swallowed his bread and lay down as well. Theron took the remainder of the whiskey. He leaned back against the door, whispering softly to himself, and watched the others sleep.

In the early light, Aurel awoke. Daddy Norton, he saw, had risen and was leaning against the wall on his whole leg. In one hand he held a butcher knife awkwardly, trying to hack off his other leg just above the broken joint, crying out with each blow.

He stopped long enough to regard Aurel with burning, red-rimmed eyes, the knife poised, his gaze drifting slowly upward. Shaking his head, he continued to gash the leg, the dull knife making poor progress, at last turning skew against the bone and clattering from his fingers.

Bending his good leg, he tried to take the blood-smeared knife off the floor. He could not reach it. He cast his gaze about until it stuck onto Aurel.

"Aurel," he said, his voice greding with pain. "Be a good boy and give Daddy the knife."

Aurel did not move. They looked at one another, Aurel unable to break Daddy Norton's gaze. He began to move slowly backward across the floor, pulling himself until he struck against the door.

"Aurel," Daddy Norton said. "God tells you to pick up the knife."

Aurel swallowed, stayed pressed to the door.

"You're a sorry sinner," said Daddy Norton.

Daddy Norton extended an arm, pointing one finger at Aurel, his other hand raised open-palmed to support the heavens. Stepping onto the injured leg, he listed toward the boy and fell. His leg folded, turning under him so as to look like he was attempting to couple with it. He lay on the floor slick-faced with sweat, his eyes misfocussed.

"Give me the knife, Aurel," he said.

He began to pull himself around by his fingers, twisting his body around until it became wedged between the hall walls. Grunting, he rolled over, twisting the broken leg, and fainted.

Aurel shook Theron. Theron blinked his eyes and mumbled, his voice still thick with liquor. Aurel motioned to Daddy Norton, who came conscious again and stared them through with God's awful hate.

"Stop staring at me," said Theron.

Daddy Norton neither stopped nor moved. There was a smell coming up from him, from his leg too. Theron stood, holding his nose, and stepped over him, taking up the butcher knife, Daddy Norton's eyes following him almost in reflex. "Stop staring," Theron said again, and pushed the blade in.

Aurel closed his eyes. For a long time he could hear the damp sound of Theron working the knife in and out, and then the noise finally stopped.

He opened his eyes to see Theron leaning over Daddy Norton, holding the remains of the man's eyelids closed with his fingertips, though when he released them they crept up to reveal the emptied sockets. Theron twisted the man's neck and rolled the head, directing the eyeholes toward the floor. He wiped the knife on Daddy Norton's shirt. Putting the knife into Daddy Norton's hand, he stood back. The fingers straightened and the knife slipped out. He folded the fingers around the haft, watched them straighten again.

"Theron?" said Aurel.

"Not now, Aurel."

"What about Mama?" asked Aurel.

Theron seemed to consider it, then stood and took the knife in his own hands and approached Mama.

"Don't kill her, Theron," said Aurel. "Not Mama."

"Be quiet about it," said Theron. He prodded her head with his boot. "Wake up, Mama," he said.

She did not move. Theron pushed her head again.

"Daddy needs you, Mama," he said.

"I can't bear to have you do it," said Aurel.

"You don't know at all what you can bear," said Theron.

Kneeling down beside her, he took the Holy Word out of her hands and dropped it aside. He placed the knife into her hand, carefully, so as not to awaken her. The knife fit, held.

"You can have only one of us, Aurel," said Theron. "Me or Mama?"

"Mama," said Aurel.

"It's me you want," said Theron. "You aren't thinking straight. I got to think for you."

He picked up Mama under the shoulders and dragged her closer to Daddy Norton. He took her wrists and pushed her hands into Daddy Norton's body until they came away stained, the knife gory too.

"Besides," said Theron. "You don't have a choice. Mama gone and died while we were jawing. You got only me."

II. The Funeral

For the funeral Preacher Thrane collected from his congregation enough for a shirt and a pair of presentable trousers for both boys—though, he said, they would have to secure collar and cravat of their own initiative, did they care for them. This he suggested they find the means to do by taking up the cup and pleading door for door to members of Daddy Norton's former congregation.

"But," said Thrane, "I want you to give by any plans you have of being prophets after the manner of Daddy Norton. You aren't Daddy Nortons. You come worship with me from now on."

"We're Daddy Norton's boys," said Aurel.

"What?" said Thrane.

"We got to carry on Daddy Norton's work," said Aurel.

"Don't listen to Aurel," said Theron. "We had enough of Daddy to last a lifetime."

Thrane hesitated then patted them both on the shoulders, passed to Theron a brown paper package wrapped in twine.

"There are good boys hidden in you somewhere," Thrane said, touching their hair. "All you got to do is let them out."

They took a tin cup from beneath the sink and left it on the porch of the house beneath a hand-lettered placard reading "Comfort for the Bereav'd" with a crude arrow pointing down. They wore their new clothes to loosen them a little before the funeral. They wore the clothes in the hall, sitting on the floor, admiring what they could see. Each time the clock chimed they stood on their toes and looked out the panes along the top of the door, but never saw that anyone approached the cup to give into it.

"Thrane should damn well have the decency to buy us some collars and cravats too, all that Daddy did for him," said Theron. "I have a mind not to attend their funeral at all."

Aurel said nothing. Theron strode up and down the entry hall. Snatching his hat and coat from their pegs, he went out.

Aurel stood tiptoe at the door and watched his brother pick up the tin cup, stare into it, put it back down. Theron put his hat on, then his coat, then stood on the porch looking out over the fields. He stood like that for a long while, then came back inside.

"Hell if I'll beg," said Theron. "You?"

"I don't want to go to any funeral," said Aurel.

"What?" asked Theron.

"I don't want to go," Aurel said.

Theron stripped off his hat, his coat, hanging them from their pegs. He sat down on the floor, began to work off his boots.

"I am not going," said Aurel. "Theron, you heard me?"

"I heard you, Aurel," said Theron.

"We could stay here," said Aurel. "Nobody would know the difference."

"Preacher Thrane would," said his brother.

"What do we care about Preacher Thrane?" asked Aurel.

"He gave us these clothes, didn't he?"

"He only wants us coming to his church," said Aurel. "He wants us to be his boys."

"We aren't nobody's boys," said Theron.

"We are Daddy Norton's boys," said Aurel.

"No," said Theron. "Don't say that, Aurel."

Theron looked briefly into his boots, then set them to one side. Sliding back, he leaned against the door.

"I am not going," said Aurel, "I mean it."

"Nobody said you were," said Theron. "We'll stay," he said. He stretched his hands toward his brother. "Come sit with me," he said.

Aurel looked at him carefully, but came and sat down next to him.

Theron made a point of looking up and down his brother's body.

"Fine clothing," said Theron. "But if we aren't attending the funeral, take them off. They reek of Thrane's God."

Aurel began to unbutton the shirt, stopped.

"You aren't taking yours off," he said.

"All in time, brother," said Theron. "You lead the way."

Aurel stood and turned into the corner. He unbuttoned the shirt, stripped it off his shoulders, let it fall. Unbuttoning the trousers, he stepped out of them.

"Briefs, too," said Theron.

"The briefs are mine," said Aurel. "No preacher gave me them."

"You got them from Daddy Norton, didn't you?" said Theron. "You better do all I say."

"I don't want it," said Aurel.

"Doesn't matter," said Theron. He stood and shook loose his own belt. "This is all my church now. I take what I want."

They sat against the door, touching each other, staring down the hall. Preacher Thrane came and pounded on the door and cursed them, but they did not open for him, and once they dropped the clothes he had given them out the window he took leave. Others came by, and knocked, and called out, but the two brothers remained silent and holding onto each other with a certain desperation and did not respond.

Near evening someone knocked, and, when they did not answer, tried to turn the knob, then began to strike a shoulder against the door, weakly.

Theron stood and looked out to see a woman there, rubbing her shoulder. She stood rubbing it for some time then turned the other shoulder to the door and started again.

"By God," whispered Theron, crouching. "She thinks she can break down the door."

"Can she?" asked Aurel.

Theron snorted. "Not the likes of her," he said.

"I heard that!" the woman yelled from the outside. "Open the door!"

"Theron, she knows we're here," whispered Aurel.

"Let's see her do anything about it," Theron said.

"You got to let her in," said Aurel.

"Let her in?" said Theron. "And then what are we going to do with her?"

Aurel looked. Theron, he saw, was bare of body, his sides scarred where Daddy Norton had beat the devil out of him and made paths for the penetration of God. He looked down at himself, saw his red hands fidget and swim on his pale thighs, his belly slack, the dull tip of his sex prodding the floorboards between his body.

"I am naked," said Aurel.

"I want to know what you think you are going to do to her once we get her in."

"Don't let her in," pleaded Aurel, covering his sex with both hands.

Theron stood and turned to the door. "Just a minute," he called. "A moment please."

"No," said Aurel. "Please, Theron."

"Who do you love, Aurel?"

"What?"

"Do you love her?"

"I don't love her," said Aurel.

"Nobody said you did, Aurel," said Theron. "But who?"

Aurel brought his head down against his knees, tipped over onto his side. "Don't ask me that, Theron," he said.

"Think about it," said Theron. "Think it through."

The thumping at the door resumed.

"Who do you love? Who is all you have in this world, Aurel?" asked Theron. "With Mama and Daddy Norton dead and gone?"

"God?" said Aurel.

"In *this* world," said Theron, kicking Aurel in the side. "God isn't in this world. Think, goddamn it."

Aurel remained silent a long time, his side darkening where Theron had kicked him. He kept touching his ribs and pulling his fingers away and staring at them. Theron took Aurel's hands, held them away from his body, stilled them.

"You?" asked Aurel. "Is it you?"

Letting go of Aurel's hands, Theron cupped his own hands around Aurel's face. He drew the face forward, kissed it on the mouth.

"Yes," said Theron. "Me."

He let Aurel's head go and watched Aurel collapse, his eyes rolling back into his head. He went and unlocked the door. He tugged it open.

"God almighty," said the woman outside.

Aurel came conscious and tried to crawl out of line of the woman's voice, but Theron kept opening the door wider until the door was pressed against the wall and there was nowhere left to crawl. Aurel got up and stumbled down to the far end of the hall, covering his sex, then came stumbling back, moaning.

"You come on in," said Theron.

The woman seemed to be trying to keep her eyes on his face. "Will you put on some clothing?" she asked.

"Not me," he said.

"We are clothed in God's spirit," said Aurel.

"Shut up, Aurel," said Theron. He rendered his best smile. "What can we do for you?" he asked the woman.

She looked at Aurel, then back to Theron, then at Aurel again, her eyes drawn down then quickly up. "I am here about the property," she said.

"Won't you come in?" Theron asked.

He stretched his hand toward her, his palm opening and closing. Aurel came up behind Theron and hid behind his body, his sex beginning to exert itself more severely. He peered over Theron's shoulder at her. He tried to push the door shut, but Theron kept it blocked open with his foot.

"No," she said, stepping backward, "I don't think I can."

"What's thinking got to do with it?" asked Theron. "Just come on."

She took a few more steps backward until she stepped off the edge of the porch and fell hard.

"The property," said Theron. "We'll pay you whatever you want. We have it inside."

"We don't have any money, Theron," said Aurel.

"Shut up, Aurel," said Theron. "Soon," he said to the woman. "We'll pay you soon. Is it money you want?"

She sat in the weeds holding her ankle, rocking back and forth, her face grimacing.

"I think she likes you, Aurel," said Theron.

Aurel just watched until Theron nudged him. "What's her name?" Aurel asked.

"What's your name?" asked Theron of the woman.

She had taken her shoe off and was rotating the foot manually and with care, wincing. She did not choose to answer.

"My name is Theron," said Theron. "This is my brother Aurel. Our Daddy and Mama are dead."

"Pleased to meet you," Aurel said, trying to shut the door.

"Maybe you have a name too?" asked Theron. He stared at her, watched her stand and put her weight tenuously on the foot. "Looks like she's hurt, Aurel," he said. "She won't get far."

"I bet her name is Arabella," said Aurel. "That's a pretty name, all right."

"Is that your name?" asked Theron.

She looked at them. Slowly, as if to avoid startling them, she began to limp away, flimmering her hands for balance.

"Go fetch her, Aurel," said Theron. "Bring her back here."

Aurel did not move.

"I mean it, Aurel," said Theron.

Aurel went to the far end of the hall and crouched there, shaking and hugging himself around the knees. Theron watched the woman stumble away for a while and then came back into the house, closing and locking the door.

He came down the hall toward his brother.

"You'll have to do," said Theron.

He sat on the floor beside him, leaning in, putting his hand inside his brother's thigh. He kissed Aurel on the shoulder, the neck, the cheek.

"See now," he said throatily, "we only got each other. Nobody in the world but you and me."

III. The Dog

Aurel would hardly leave the hall, at most taking a step out onto the front porch or going through the extreme door into the bathroom. He would not enter the kitchen and Theron had to bring food to him, though he swore each time that he would not bring it the next.

Theron left him so as to rummage through the rest of the rooms—excepting Daddy Norton's private room, the door to that room being locked and he (though he dared not admit so before Aurel) not having quite the nerve to kick it down. Had it been open, he told himself, he would have entered. But he could not bring himself to break in.

The sprawling house was even larger than he had imagined,

running into a half-dozen levels and half-levels, and strung into labyrinths of makeshift rooms, especially on the upper floors, that Theron could not make sense of nor later recover. He at first made some effort to restrict himself to the two lower floors, as he had done when Daddy Norton was alive, but as the days passed he went farther up. To make sense of the upper levels, he tried to trace his way in and then out of a floor along the same path, but always seemed to lose his way. Often he found himself in trying to leave passing through chambers that did not seem to have existed before.

He searched through the rooms and found clothing which seemed to belong neither to him nor his brother, nor Mama, nor Daddy Norton. He could make no sense of it nor piece it together in complete outfits, for no matter how many times he coupled articles, they seemed mismatched in color, style, size. He abandoned the clothing and took to gathering objects that interested him, carrying them with him for fear of never finding them again. He gathered them and then, when sufficiently burdened, tried to find his way back, in the process discovering more than he could ever hope to carry. He heaped what he could in kitchen and hall, dividing objects into piles according to an interior logic he could not fathom but felt compelled to obey.

Aurel sat almost entirely still, seemed hardly to breathe. He could still arise and walk up and down the length of the hall when he chose, though he moved now with an excess of precision, as if even his most subtle motions were the result of a tremendous and impeccable focussing of the will. He spoke in a similar way, his voice measured and taut, his inflection oddly spaced but so well controlled as to impact the words much harder.

"You have begun to talk like Daddy Norton," said Theron. "Are you thinking of reopening the ministry?"

"No," said Aurel, "Daddy Norton has begun to talk like me."

Unable to puzzle through what Aurel meant, Theron came to watch his brother more closely. He noticed that when his brother moved it was as if he were hardly resident within his own body, or was resident only in a strictly mechanic sense. When Aurel was motionless, he did not seem present at all.

Watching him like that made Theron conscious of a strange kinship between himself and Aurel, and between the two of them and the dead, a kinship that made it difficult for him to keep always in mind who he was. He took to nudging Aurel when he came into the hall, prodding him gently until the eyes focussed in, so as not to have to watch. He kept this current for a few days, until Aurel learned to ignore it.

In one of the upper rooms, under a blanket, Theron found an air rifle and a box of hard plastic pellets. He pumped the gun and shot it into a rat-eaten mattress, raising puffs of dust. Taking the rifle downstairs, he brandished it before Aurel.

"Where was it?" asked Aurel.

"Upstairs," said Theron. "One of the rooms."

"Daddy Norton's room?" asked Aurel.

"No."

"What is in Daddy Norton's room?" asked Aurel.

Theron claimed that he had entered Daddy Norton's room but could not remember precisely what was within. Nothing important, he told Aurel. The next time, he thought, I will go in.

The next time, however, he did not go in. He stood for some time beside the door and even twisted the knob again, but it would not turn. Bending down, he applied his eye to the keyhole but found the aperture blocked. He shot the doorknob with the air rifle, listening to the pellets ping off and roll about the floor.

He began, to please Aurel, to imagine Daddy Norton's room, to flesh it forth out of nothing in his head and then recount it as real before his brother. He claimed it a simple room, spare in decor, austere, little substance to it, a few books, a few ordinary objects. When Theron described Daddy Norton's room, Aurel seemed almost attentive and might even ask a few questions. It became so that Theron had to keep a series of notes in the kitchen and review them frequently, for Aurel noticed any inconsistency. He seemed to remember every detail, even to the point of requesting certain items from the room itself, asking for the private trinity of holy books Theron claimed Daddy Norton had written: *Father of Light: The Autobiography of God, Unaccustomed Sinners,* and a refutation, *Body of Lies.*

"I won't bring his rubbish to you," said Theron. "Get it yourself."

Aurel came to his feet, his knees crackling, and swayed down the hall. Before he reached the door of the stairs, he slowed, sat deliberately down.

"What's the matter?" asked Theron.

"I am not ready," said Aurel. "Not yet."

Sometimes Theron left the hall not to wander the upper rooms, but to remain behind one of the five doors leading off the main hall, his ear pressed to the door or the door cracked open slightly and he peering through the site of the air rifle, observing Aurel. Aurel did not appear to notice him, nor in fact to notice anything at all. Each time Theron returned to the hall and shook him conscious, Aurel would say, "You've been to Daddy Norton's room?" and, when Theron shook his head, "I'll have to go myself."

"Why don't you go?" Theron asked.

"I am going," said Aurel. "Here I go," he said, but could not rise.

The pantry, which at first had seemed to Theron to always replenish itself, was nearly empty. Creditors and bastards of the slickest varieties took to coming to the door and posting legal notices and other formal threats. The brothers did not answer. A wet-haired man in a tightbuttoned shirt tried to crack open the door with a crowbar until Theron opened it himself and threatened him with the air rifle.

"You can't shoot me," said the man. "You are naked."

Theron jabbed the man in the belly and pulled the trigger, the pellet burying itself in the fat. Wheezing, pressing his hands to his belly, the man backed away.

The food in the kitchen ran out. Theron grew hungry. He searched the upper rooms for food, found nothing.

Returning to the entrance hall, he grabbed the air rifle, pulling Aurel to his feet and toward the front door. Aurel leaned against him, moving languidly, as if drugged. He allowed himself to be propelled through the door, onto the porch, before beginning weakly to resist.

"Where are we going?" he managed.

"To get something to eat," said Theron.

"This is the outside," said Aurel. "We need clothes."

Theron bent his brother over the porch rail, went back into the house. Kicking through the piles in the hall and kitchen, he uncovered a pair of bathing trunks and a pair of briefs. He slipped into the former, carried the briefs outside.

Aurel had fallen off the porch, was lying curled up and hardly moving in the dirt.

"What's wrong with you, brother?" asked Theron.

"What do you mean?" asked Aurel.

Theron stepped off the porch and slipped the briefs over Aurel's feet, working them up to rim about his brother's knees. He lifted his brother off the ground, pulled the briefs up until they caught on his sex, lifted the elastic out and over.

"I have to go back inside," said Aurel.

"We need something to eat," said Theron.

He dragged Aurel forward until he began to move his legs of his own accord. Theron slowly slacked his support, Aurel tottering forward on his own.

"I want to go home," begged Aurel.

They travelled alongside the town road for a time then slipped away into the fields. They waded through a vacant plot, the ground dawked and uneven. Theron stuffed Aurel through a barbed wire fence, the wires combing his body with lines of blood, then crawled through himself.

Passing through wheat fields, they fell onto a dirt track and were led to a house. They went around to the back. In the shade of one of the trees was a dog on a chain. He got to his feet when he saw them and stretched. Theron started pumping the air rifle. The dog came forward, wagging its tail, its chain paying out.

Theron pushed Aurel against the side of the house and levelled the air rifle at the dog's head. The dog sniffed at the muzzle, the tip of it, and tried to pass underneath. Theron pushed the barrel flush against the dog's forehead. Closing his eyes, he shot.

He heard the dog yelp. Opening his eyes, he found the dog's eye burst and bubbling, the dog staggering to revolve a mutilated and partial circle, its paws tangling in the chain. He began to pump the rifle. The dog started to moan, wavering its way back toward the tree.

Theron followed it, pumping the rifle. He slipped the barrel's end between the shoulder blades. As the dog turned and snapped, he jerked the trigger.

The dog stumbled to its belly and lay spread a moment, then heaved back up. Theron could see a small burr of blood rising where the pellet had gone in, the lump resting just under the skin.

"Aurel, this dog don't want to die," Theron called.

"Leave it alone," said Aurel.

Theron pumped the rifle and got around by the dog where it was spread under the tree and on its side, palsied. He reached his bare foot out and put it against the dog's jaw, pushing the head down, exposing the throat.

"I want to go home," said Aurel.

Theron pointed the gun and fired, shooting the dog through the throat, the pellet lodging somewhere within the breathpipe. The dog whimpered, the fur of its throat slowly leaking full of blood. Theron pushed his foot down harder and lined the gun again, pumping. Wriggling beneath him, the dog shook its jaw free and bit him.

He cried out and began to jab at the dog's snout with the barrel, the dog chacking its jaws tighter. Reversing the rifle, he brought the gunstock down hard across the dog's skull, feeling in the blow the dog's teeth to shear deep through his flesh. The dog shuddered, let go.

Theron limped back a little distance and dropped to examine the wound, blood pushing up in the teethmarks and running in streaks down the side of the foot. The dog tried to get to its feet but could not and just stayed pawing the ground in front of it until it could not do that either, and curled its legs underneath itself and died.

He looked up for Aurel and found Aurel gone. Leaving the dog and the gun beside it, he hobbled around to the front of the house. Aurel he found on the front porch clawing at a window.

"What is it?" asked Theron.

"I need air," said Aurel. "Let me out."

"Come off of there," said Theron, taking him by the hair and dragging him down. "This is not even our house."

Limping, he pulled Aurel back to the dog and let go. He unchained the dog and took it by the hind legs and began to drag it away.

"Come on, Aurel," said Theron. "Time to go home."

Aurel stayed put, watching him. "I don't want to go," he said.

"Jesus Christ," said Theron. "First you don't want to leave, then you don't want to go home. What's the matter with you?"

"Don't say that name, Theron," said Aurel. "You want to go to hell?"

"Are you walking or do I have to drag you?" asked Theron.

Aurel remained a moment standing and then sat down. Theron let go of the dog's legs and came over to hit Aurel in the face. He picked his brother up under the arms and found him light and cold to the touch. When Theron lifted and carried him, Aurel did not seem to notice, but lay in his arms without regard for anything.

Theron stumbled past the dead dog and a few meters later set Aurel down on the ground. He went down stiffly. Theron went back for the dog, dragged it alongside his brother. Crouching down, he stared at first one then the other until Aurel's eyes opened.

"Can you walk?" he asked Aurel.

"I won't," said Aurel.

He alternated between lugging Aurel and the dog's carcass until he reached the main road, and then gave it up to carry the one while dragging the other. He tried to drag the dog and carry Aurel, but kept dropping his brother. He found it easier to drag Aurel by the feet, the boy's head jouncing across the asphalt while he slung the dog over his shoulders.

He could hardly walk for the pain in his foot. People slowed as they passed in cars, at times even pointed, shouted. He cursed them thoroughly and kept on.

The dog grew heavy around his neck, his chest and shoulders spattering with blood and foam. Behind, Aurel seemed to have fallen asleep though his eyes were still open. Theron kept turning around and asking, *Hey, you dead? Hey, you dead?* After a while, Theron stopped asking.

IV. The Holy Word

The foot festered, and soon he could not walk on it. He left the carcass in the hall, slitting the skin and fur off of it with an old kitchen knife cutting raw hunks for himself and Aurel until it was too difficult to pick out the maggots. He pulled himself back a few yards, watching the flesh vanish and the bones push through, the structure collapsing into a mere arthritic pile, flies turning circles on the walls and cling to his face. Maggots struck across the floor out from the carcass and only Aurel had stomach enough to believe they were creatures of God and to eat them.

Soon both dog and maggots seemed to have vanished, though Theron discovered no inclination to leave the hall or stand. Aurel, on the contrary, seemed to have regained his strength. He had risen suddenly to his feet, and was now rarely found in the hall. He seemed to have acquired color in his cheeks, and his eyes were less inclined to delirium. He roamed the upper rooms of the house, though unlike Theron he never returned with anything. He would vanish for days, and then Theron would awaken to find him crouched and peering over him. And then Aurel would vanish again.

The maggots returned, this time pushing their way out of Theron's injured foot. Aurel scraped them from the wound and swallowed them, but they originated deeper within the foot than Theron would permit him to scrape, and kept returning. The smaller, individual wounds became a single wound, the wound growing purple and deep, the flesh sloughing away almost painlessly at a touch.

Theron faded in and out of consciousness, Aurel seeming to grow immense. Theron could hear his brother's feet creak upon the ceiling above, the structure of the house swaying beneath his weight. He took to not seeing things, then to not hearing them. He kept his eyes closed and pulled himself, over the days, to a damp corner and leaned into it. His nerves dried out and his skin ceased to feel. His thoughts ran on for a while in all directions and then seemed to establish an equilibrium of sorts, and then fell silent.

He felt himself shaken. After some time, he brought himself to open his eyes. Before him was Aurel.

He tried to turn his head. He swallowed, coughed forth a web of phlegm, spread it along the wall.

"What did you do with Daddy Norton's eyes?" asked Aurel.

"His eyes?"

"You removed them," said Aurel. "Where are they?"

Theron fumbled his hand into the corner behind him and seemed to fall asleep. Aurel nudged him and he brought his hand forth and opened his palm out, an irregular mass within.

Aurel took the eye from Theron's hand and examined it, the surface withered and collapsed, the lens sunken in and grown opaque.

"It might be Daddy's," said Theron. "It might be the dog's."

"Where's the other eye?" Aurel asked.

Theron swallowed, looked into his wound. "This is the one that has been watching me," he said. "You must cut my leg off, before it is too late."

Aurel sniffed the eye. He lifted it, held it against first one of his eyes then the other, then stretched it toward Theron. Theron let it come close then closed his eyes.

"Please," said Theron.

"Look," said Aurel. "Please look."

He brought the eye toward Theron slowly and Theron let him do it. He brought the eye near to Theron's living eye.

"What do you see?" he asked.

"Nothing," said Theron. "Not a goddamn thing."

Upstairs, Aurel broke down Daddy Norton's door by simply leaning into it, the cheap hinges bursting apart. The room inside was dark and damp, reeking of Daddy Norton's pomade. He left the door open and felt around beside the door for a light mechanism, but did not find one. He took a few steps inside and waited there, waiting for the dark to acquire depth and texture. He took a few more steps, then a few more, standing still until he started to see.

One side of the room was lined with religious tokens of all sects and creeds, strung along the wall. There were, as well, holy books, many of them still in wrapping and apparently never opened, scattered over the floor.

The other side of the room was nearly empty—a stiff austere bed, a low basin, a lectern which supported Daddy Norton's Holy Word.

Aurel went to the Holy Word and opened it up. He began to read.

Those who strike against God's True and Everlasting Covenant as revealed by Him to Daddy Norton shall be numbered among the damned and cast into the outer dark.

Those who have known God's Own Truth, as revealed to Daddy Norton and written by his hand, guided by God's hand, in this holy book, and who turn against it, shall be numbered most visibly among the damned and cast into the outer dark.

To afflict Daddy Norton is to afflict God himself. Those who, knowingly or unknowingly, within faith or outside of it, challenge Daddy Norton or his path toward Truth, will be damned with the damnation that sticks and cast well beyond the outer dark.

He took the book downstairs and shook Theron alive and read the verses to him.

"It's a good thing the bastard's dead," said Theron.

"Be quiet," said Aurel. "Do you want to be cast into the outer dark?"

"As long as Daddy Norton isn't there to wait for me."

Aurel shook his head. In closing the book, his eye passed across a line, and he opened the book again and read the verse in its full body.

He who converses with my enemies, though he claim loyalty to me and every whit of doctrine, is my enemy, for the law must be fulfilled. Brother shall turn against brother for my sake, and father against child.

He studied the words out and pondered them in his mind and wondered upon its application until the hall had fallen dark.

"Theron," he said. "Let me read this to you."

Theron did not answer yea or nay. Aurel read the passage slowly, haltingly, in his own voice, then looked up to see what his brother would say. Theron did not say anything, just stayed pressed up into the corner, pale, silent.

"I'm sorry, brother," said Aurel.

He closed the book. He stood and looked down at Theron. He prodded the festered leg with his own foot, his toes sinking into the flesh. He stood and left the hall.

He travelled through the upper rooms, the air hardly breathable, at one time stumbling into an attic filled with dead swallows, their heads screwed off and heaped in a corner. He lived for some time on the armload of swallows he carried out, stripping them free of their larger feathers and choking them down whole as he wandered on.

He could feel the house creak and sway beneath him, the wood groaning as if the rooms he now travelled were never meant to be walked in. Many of the rooms were dark, and he found in these his eyes could not gather sufficient light to glean wisdom from the Holy Word, so he avoided them. Others rippled with heat, and these he came to avoid as well. He kept instead to the most narrow and rickety rooms nearest the top, chinks in their walls and ceilings, their floors as well, which howled with wind and in which he had to hold the pages of the Holy Word pressed flat so they could not go adrift.

He read the book from cover to cover, a little in each room, and by the end came again to believe in the divinity of the book and in the divine election of Daddy Norton, alive or dead, and in his own divine election as Daddy Norton's disciple, called of God in this, God's only true church. And then he read the book a second time and found himself no longer certain. It did not seem to him the same book the second time, for it began to reveal to him faces that he had not wanted to see before. He saw that his faith would fall in jeopardy were he to continue reading, and so, to preserve his faith, he abandoned the book in one of the upper rooms and never saw it again.

He lived on what scraps he could find, when these were gone

peeling off the wallpaper and eating the paste underneath. He began to find other books in the rooms. These at first he left where they were, passing them clinging close to the wall and moving into the rooms beyond. But when he began to find them more often, he took to picking them up and hiding them beneath beds and tables, so as not to see them again. Still, the books appeared everywhere, in each new room he entered as well as in rooms he thought he had entered before, as if someone were moving them.

He stopped trying to hide the books and left them where they were. He tried to find his way downstairs but had no inkling of the way. He came into a room with a split-board floor where he thought the stairs should be. Light shone up hard through the floorcracks, the walls musted and blotched with mold. Kicking a hole through a wall, he crawled out into a narrow room, a globed glass fixture hanging from the ceiling and aglow. Lying on the floor, he watched the light and listened to fleas ping inside the globe, and fell asleep.

He awoke to find fleas strung up and down his veins and grown fat upon him. He began to crush them with stiff thumbs, leaving smears of blood. Getting to his feet he saw a book on a table, and this he took up and opened and read from silently without avail or feeling though like every other book it was most likely some god or other's sacred word. He read on blankly for many pages, until was given to him:

He that loveth his brother abideth in light, and there is none occasion of stumbling in him.

He put the book down as if struck and then as quickly scooped it up again. He took Daddy Norton's dessicated eye out of his underwear and held it toward the words, then put the eye away. Putting the book under his arm, he went out of the room through a door and from there through chambers with irregular floors and from there fell down a ramshackle staircase face first. He found himself in a room that seemed familiar to him, though he could place nothing about it. Making his way out through a door broken from its hinges, he passed along a hall and down a staircase missing its treads. He entered what seemed at one time to have been a kitchen but which now seemed a repository for refuse of all kinds.

Wading across the room, he opened a door and came out into a long hall, a door at one end of it, a window at the other. In the corner, beneath the window, was a figure, vaguely human. The smell of it was hard to breathe at first, and then became sweet and made his head dance with light.

He could feel God watching. He approached the figure and sat beside it, pulling it over to lean against him. What he touched was soggy in his hands, as if impregnated with water, and it left portions of itself adhered to the wall even as it came away.

He read the verse aloud, but his brother did not respond. He pulled him closer and felt him come apart in his hands.

He gathered what he could and pushed it back into the corner. He took off the briefs he wore, the eye falling out and dropping away. He shaped the pile in the corner like a pillow and lay his head onto it.

"Brothers always," he claimed. And closed his eyes.

George Saunders

Winky

From *The New Yorker*

EIGHTY people waited in a darkened meeting room at the Hyatt wearing mass-produced paper hats. The White Hats were Beginning to Begin. The Pink Hats were Moving Ahead in Beginning. The Green Hats were Very Firmly Beginning, all the way up to the Gold Hats, who had Mastered Living and were standing in a group around the snack table, whispering and conferring and elbowing one another whenever someone in a lesser hat walked by.

Trumpets sounded from a concealed tape deck. An actor in a ripped flannel shirt stumbled across the stage with a sign around his neck that said "You."

"I'm lost!" You cried. "I'm wandering in a sort of wilderness!"

"Hey, You, come on over!" shouted a girl across the stage, labelled "Inner Peace." "I bet you've been looking for me your whole life!"

"Boy, have I!" said You. "I'll be right over!"

But then out from the wings sprinted a number of other actors, labelled "Whiny" and "Self-Absorbed" and "Blames Her Fat on Others," and so on, who draped themselves across You and began poking him in the ribs and giving him noogies.

"Oh, I can't believe you love Inner Peace more than you love me, You!" said Insecure. "That really hurts."

"Frankly, I've never been so disappointed in my life," said Disappointed.

"Oh, God, all this arguing is giving me a panic attack," said Too High-Strung to Function.

"I'm waiting, You," said Inner Peace. "Do you want me or not?"

"I do, but I seem to be trapped!" You shouted. "I can't seem to get what I want!"

"You and about a billion other people in this world," said Inner Peace sadly.

"Is there no hope for me?" asked You. "If only someone had made a lifelong study of the roadblocks people encounter on their way to Inner Peace!"

"And yet someone has," said Inner Peace.

Another fanfare sounded from the tape deck, and a masked Gold Hat, whose hat appeared to be made of actual gold, bounded onto the stage, flexed his muscles, and dragged Insecure to a paper jail, on which was written "Pokey for Those Who Would Keep Us from Inner Peace." Then the Gold Hat dragged Chronically Depressed and Clingy and Helpless and the rest across the stage and shoved them into the Pokey.

"See what I just did?" said the Gold Hat. "I just liberated You from those who would keep him from Inner Peace. So good for You! Question is, is You going to be able to stay liberated? Maybe what You needs is a repeated internal reminder. A mantra. A mantra can be thought of as a repeated internal reminder, can't it? Does anyone out there have a good snappy mantra they could perhaps share with You?"

The crowd was delighted, because they knew the mantra. Even the lowly White Hats knew the mantra—even Neil Yaniky, who sat spellbound and insecure in the first row, sucking his mustache, knew the mantra, because it was on all the TV commercials and also on the front cover of the Orientation Text in big bold letters.

"Give it to me, folks!" shouted the Gold Hat. "What time is it?"

"Now Is the Time for Me to Win!" the crowd shouted.

"You got that right, baby!" said the Gold Hat exultantly, ripping off his mask to reveal what many already suspected: this was not some mere Gold Hat but Tom Rodgers himself, founder of the Seminars.

"What fun!" he shouted. "To have something to give, and people who so badly need what I have to offer. Here's what I have to offer, folks, although it's not much, really, just two simple concepts, and the first one is: oatmeal."

From out of his suit he pulled a bowl and a box of oatmeal, and filled the bowl with the oatmeal and held the bowl up.

"Simple, nourishing, inexpensive," he said. "This represents your soul in its pure state. Your soul on the day you were born. You were perfect. You were happy. You were good.

"Now, enter Concept No. 2: crap. Don't worry, folks, I don't use actual crap up here. Only imaginary crap. You'll have to supply the crap, using your mind. Now, if someone came up and crapped in your nice warm oatmeal, what would you say? Would you say, 'Wow, super, thanks, please continue crapping in my oatmeal'? Am I being silly? I'm being a little silly. But, guess what, in real life people come up and crap in your oatmeal all the time—friends, co-workers, loved ones, even your kids, especially your kids!—and that's exactly what you do. You say, 'Thanks so much!' You say, 'Crap away!' You say, and here my metaphor breaks down a bit, 'Is there some way I can help you crap in my oatmeal?'

"Let me tell you something amazing: I was once exactly like you people. A certain someone, a certain guy who shall remain nameless, was doing quite a bit of crapping in my oatmeal, and simply because he'd had some bad luck, simply because he was in some pain, simply because, actually, he was in a wheelchair, this certain someone expected me to put my life on hold while he crapped in my oatmeal by demanding round-the-clock attention, this brother of mine, this Gene, and, whoops, there goes that cat out of the bag, but does this maybe sound paradoxical? Wasn't he the one with the crap in his oatmeal, being in a wheelchair? Well, yes and no. Sure, he was hurting. No surprise there. Guy drops a motorcycle on a gravel road and bounces two hundred yards without a helmet, yes, he's going to be somewhat hurting. But how was that my fault? Was I the guy riding the motorcycle too fast, drunk, with no helmet? No, I was home, studying my Tacitus, which is what I was into at that stage of my life, so why did Gene expect me to consign my dreams and plans to the dustbin? I had dreams! I had plans! Finally, and this is all in my book, 'People of Power,' I found the inner strength to say to Gene, 'Stop crapping in my oatmeal, Gene, I'm simply not going to participate.' And I found the strength to say to our sister Ellen, 'Ellen, take the ball that is Gene and run with it, because if I sell myself short by catering to Gene I'm going to be one very angry puppy, and anger does the mean-and-nasty on a person, and I for one love myself and want the best for me, because, I am, after all, a child of God.' And I said to myself, as I describe in the book, 'Tom, now is the time for you to win!' That was the first time I thought that up. And do you know what? I won. I'm winning. Today we're friends, Gene and I, and he acknowledges that I was right all along. And as for Ellen, Ellen still has some issues. She'd take a big old dump in my oatmeal right now if I gave her half a chance, but, guess what, folks, I'm not giving her that half a chance, because I've installed a protective screen over my oatmeal—not a literal screen, but a metaphorical protective screen. Ellen knows it, Gene knows it, and now they pretty much stay out of my hair and away from my oatmeal, and they've made a nice life together, and who do you think paid for Gene's wheelchair ramp with the money he made from a certain series of seminars?"

The crowd burst into applause. Tom Rodgers held up his hand.

"Now, what about you folks?" he said softly. "Is now the time for you to win? Are you ready to screen off your metaphorical oatmeal and identify your own personal Gene? Who is it that's screwing you up? Who's keeping you from getting what you want? Somebody is! God doesn't make junk. If you're losing, somebody's doing it to you. Today I'll be guiding you through my Three Essential Steps: Identification, Screening, Confrontation. First, we'll identify your personal Gene. Second, we'll help you mentally install a metaphorical Screen over your symbolic oatmeal. Finally, we'll show you how to Confront your personal Gene and make it clear to him or her that your oatmeal is heretofore off limits."

Tom Rodgers looked intensely out into the crowd.

"So what do you think, guys?" he asked, very softly. "Are you up for it?"

From the crowd came a nervous murmur of assent.

"All right, then," he said. "Let's line up. Let's line up for a change. A *dramatic* change."

Then he crisply left the stage, and a spotlight panned across nine Personal Change Centers, small white tents set up in a row near the fire door.

Neil Yaniky rose with the rest and checked his Line Assignment and joined his Assigned Line. He was a tiny man, nearly thirty, balding on top and balding on the sides, and was still chewing on his mustache and wondering if anyone or everyone else at the seminar could tell that he was a big stupid faker, because he had no career, really, and no business but only soldered little triangular things in his basement, for forty-seven cents a little triangular thing, for CompuParts, although he had high hopes for something better, which was why he was here.

The flap of Personal Change Center 4 flew open and in he went, bending low.

Inside were Tom Rodgers and several assistants, and a dummy in a smock sitting in a chair.

"Welcome, Neil," said Tom Rodgers, glancing at Yaniky's name tag. "I'm honored to have you in my Seminar, Neil. Now. The way we'll start, Neil, is for you to please write across the chest of this dummy the name of your real-life, personal Gene. That is, the name of the person you perceive to be crapping in your oatmeal. Do you understand what I'm saying?"

"Yes," said Yaniky.

Tom Rodgers was talking very fast, as if he had hundreds of people to change in a single day, which of course he did. Yaniky had no problem with that. He was just happy to be one of them.

"Do you need help determining who that person is?" said Tom Rodgers. "Your oatmeal-crapper?"

"No," said Yaniky.

"Excellent," said Tom Rodgers. "Now write the name and under it write the major way in which you perceive this person to be crapping in your oatmeal. Be frank. This is just between you and me."

On an erasable marker board permanently mounted in the dummy's chest Yaniky wrote, "Winky: Crazy-looking and too religious and needs her own place."

"Super!" said Tom Rodgers. "A great start. Now watch what I do. Let's fine-tune. Can we cut 'crazy-looking'? If this person, this Winky, were to get her own place, would the fact that she looks crazy still be an issue? As much of an issue? Less of an issue?"

Yaniky pictured his sister looking crazy but in her own apartment.

"Less of an issue," he said.

"All right!" said Tom Rodgers, erasing "crazy-looking." "It's important to simplify so that we can hone in on exactly what we're trying to change. O.K. At this point, we've determined that if we can get her out of your house the crazy-looking can be lived with. A big step forward. But why stop there? Let me propose something: if she's out of your hair, what the heck do you care if she's religious?"

Yaniky pictured Winky looking crazy and talking crazy about God but in her own apartment.

"It would definitely be better," he said.

"Yes, it would," said Tom Rodgers, and erased until the dummy was labelled "Winky: needs her own place."

"See?" said Tom Rodgers. "See how we've simplified? We've got it down to one issue. Can you live with this simple, direct statement of the problem?"

"Yes," Yaniky said. "Yes, I can."

Yaniky saw now what it was about Winky that got on his nerves. It wasn't her formerly red curls, which had now gone white, so it looked like she had soaked the top of her head in glue and dipped it in a vat of cotton balls; it wasn't the bald spot that every morning she painted with some kind of white substance; it wasn't her shiny-pink face that was always getting weird joyful looks on it at bad times, like during his dinner date with Beverly Amstel, when he'd made his special meatballs but to no avail, because Bev kept glancing over at Winky in panic; it wasn't the way she came click-click-clicking in from teaching church school and hugged him for too long a time while smelling like flower water, all pumped up from spreading the word of damn Christ; it was simply that they were too old to be living together and he had things he wanted to accomplish and she was too needy and blurred his focus.

"Have you told this person, this Winky, that her living with you is a stumbling block for your personal development?" said Tom Rodgers.

"No, I haven't," Yaniky said.

"I thought not," said Tom Rodgers. "You're kindhearted. You don't want to hurt her. That's nice, but guess what? You are hurting her. You're hurting her by not telling her the truth. Am I saying that you, by your silence, are crapping in her oatmeal? Yes, I am. I'm saying that there's a sort of reciprocal crapping going on here. How can Winky grow on a diet of lies? Isn't it true that the truth will set you free? Didn't someone once say that? Wasn't it God or Christ, which would be ironic, because of her being so religious?"

Tom Rodgers gestured to an assistant, who took a wig out of a box and put it on the dummy's head.

"What we're going to do now is act this out symbolically," Tom Rodgers said. "Primitive cultures do this all the time. They might throw Fertility a big party, say, or paint their kids white and let them whack Sickness with palm fronds and so forth. Are we somehow smarter than primitive cultures? I doubt it. I think maybe we're dumber. Do we have fewer hemorrhoids? Were Incas killed on freeways? Here, take this."

He handed Yaniky a baseball bat.

"What time is it, Neil?" said Tom Rodgers.

"Time to win?" said Yaniky. "Time for me to win?"

"Now is the time for you to win," said Tom Rodgers, clarifying, and pointed to the dummy.

Yaniky swung the bat and the dummy toppled over and the wig flew off and the assistant retrieved the wig and tossed it back into the box of wigs, and Tom Rodgers gave Yaniky a big hug.

"What you have just symbolically said," Tom Rodgers said, "is

'No more, Winky. Grow wings, Winky. I love you, but you're killing me, and I am a good person, a child of God, and don't deserve to die. I deserve to live, I demand to live, and, therefore, get your own place, girl! Fly, and someday thank me!' This is to be your sub-mantra, Neil, O.K.? *Out you go!* On your way home today, I want you to be muttering, not angrily muttering but sort of joyfully muttering, to center yourself, the following words: 'Now is the time for me to win! *Out you go! Out you go!*' Will you do that for me?"

"Yes," said Yaniky, very much moved.

"And now here is Vicki," said Tom Rodgers. "One of my very top Gold Hats, who will walk you through the Confrontation step. Neil! I wish you luck, and peace, and all the success in the world."

Vicki had a face that looked as if it had been smashed against a steering wheel in a crash and then carefully reworked until it somewhat resembled her previous face. Several parallel curved indentions ran from temple to chin. She led Yaniky to a folding table labelled "Confrontation Center" and gave him a sheet of paper on which was written, "Gentle, Firm, Loving."

"These are the characteristics of a good Confrontation," she said, somewhat mechanically. "Now flip it over."

On the other side was written, "Angry, Wimpy, Accusatory."

"These are the characteristics of a bad Confrontation," said Vicki. "A destructive Confrontation. O.K. So let's say I'm this person, this Winky person, and you're going to tell me to hit the road. Gentle, Firm, Loving. Now begin."

And he began telling Vicki to her damaged face that she was ruining his life and sucking him dry and that she had to go live somewhere else, and Vicki nodded and patted his hand, and now and then stopped him to tell him he was being too severe.

Neil-Neil was coming home soon and she was way way behind.

Some days she took her time while cleaning, smiling at happy thoughts, frowning when she imagined someone being taken advantage of, and sometimes the person being taken advantage of was a frail little boy with a scar on his head and the person taking advantage was a big fat man with a cane, and other times the person being taken advantage of was a kindly, friendly British girl with a speech impediment and the person taking advantage was her rich, pushy sister who spoke in perfect diction and always got everything she wanted and went around whining while sucking little pink candies. Sometimes Winky asked the rich sister in her mind how she'd like to have the little pink candies slapped right out of her mouth. But that wasn't right. That wasn't Christ's way. You didn't slap the little pink candies out of her mouth, you let her slap your mouth, seventy times seven times, which was like four hundred times, and after she'd slapped you the last time she suddenly understood it all and begged your forgiveness and gave you some candy, because that was the healing power of love.

For crying out loud! What was she doing? Was she crazy? It was time to get going! Why was she standing in the kitchen thinking?

She dashed up the stairs with a strip of broken molding under her arm and a dirty sock over her shoulder.

Halfway up she paused at a little octagonal window and looked dreamily out, thinking, In a way, we own those trees. Beyond the Thieus' was the same old gap in the leaning elms showing the same old meadow that would soon be ToyTowne. But for now it still reminded her of the kind of field where Christ with his lap full of flowers had suffered with the little children, which was a scene she wanted to put on the cover of the singing album she was going to make, the singing album about God, which would have a watercolor cover like "Shoulder My Burden," which was a book but anyways it had this patient donkey piled high with crates and behind it this mountain, and the point of that book was that if you take on the worries and cares of others God or Jesus will take on your cares and worries, so that was why the patient donkey and why the crates, and why she prided herself on keeping house for Neil-Neil and never asked him for help.

Holy cow, what was she doing standing on the landing! Was she crazy? Today she was rushing! She was giving Neil-Neil a tea! She burst off the landing, taking two stairs at once. The molding had to go to the attic and the dirty sock to the hamper. While she was up, she could change her top. Because on it was some crusty soup.

The wallpaper at the top of the stairs had metal flocking and showed about a million of the same girl whacking a smiling goose with a riding crop. Hello, girls! Hello, girls! Ha ha! Hello, geese! Not to leave you out!

From a drawer in her room she took the green top, which Neil-Neil liked. Once when she was wearing it he had asked if it was new. When had that been? At the lunch at the Beef Barn, when he paid, when he asked would she like to leave Rustic Village Apartments and come live with him. Oh, that sweetie. She still had the matchbook. Those had been sad days at Rustic Village, with every friend engaged but Doris, who had a fake arm, and, boy, those girls could sometimes say mean things, but now it was all behind her, and she needed to send poor Doris a card.

But not today! Today she was rushing!

Down the stairs she pounded, still holding the molding, sock still over her shoulder.

In the kitchen she ripped open the cookie bag but there were no clean plates, so she rinsed a plate but there was no towel, so she dried the plate with her top. Hey, she still had on the yellow top. What the heck! Where was the green top? Hadn't she just gotten it out of her drawer? Ha ha! That was funny. She should send that in to *ChristLife*. They liked cute funny things that happened, even if they had nothing to do with Jesus.

The kitchen was a disaster! But first things first. Her top sucked. Not sucked, sucked was a bad word, her top was yugly. Dad used to say that, yugly. Not about her. He always said she was purty. Sometimes he said things were purty yugly. But not her. He always said she was purty purty, and then lifted her up. Oh Dad, Daddy, Poppy-Popp! Was Poppy-Popp one with the Saviour? She hoped so. Sometimes he used to swear and sometimes he used to drink, and once he swore when he fell down the stairs when he was drunk, but when she ran to him he hopped up laughing, and, oh, when he sang "Peace in the Valley" you could tell he felt things would be better beyond, which had been a super example for a young Christian kid to witness.

She flew back up the stairs to change her top. Here was the green top, on the top step! Bad top! I should spank! She gave the green top a snap to undust it and discipline it and, putting the strip of molding and the dirty sock on the bed, changed tops right then and there, picked up the molding, threw the dirty sock over her shoulder, and pounded back down the stairs.

There were so many many things to do! Not only now, for the tea, but in the future! It was time to get going! Now that she was out of that lonely apartment she could finally learn to play the piano, and, once she learned to play and write songs, she could write her songs about God, and then find out about making a record, her record about God, about how God had been good to her in this life, because look at her! A plain girl in a nice home! Oh, she knew she was plain, her legs were thick and her waist was thick and her hair, oh, my God—oh, my gosh, rather—her hair, what kind of hair was that to have, yugly white hair, and many was the time she had thought, This is not hair, this is a test. The test of white sparse hair, when so many had gorgeous manes, and that was why, when she looked in a mirror by accident and saw her white horrible hair, she always tried to think to herself, Praise God!

Neil-Neil was the all-time sweetie pie. Those girls were crazy! Did they think because a man was small and bald he had no love? Did they think bad things came in small packages? Neil-Neil was like the good brother in the Bible, the one who stayed home with his dad on the farm and never even got a small party. Except there was no bad brother, it was just the two of them, so still no party, although she'd get her party, a big party, in Heaven, and was sort of even having her party now, on earth, and when she saw that little man all pee-stained at Rexall Drug, not begging but just saying to every person who went in that he or she was looking dapper, she knew that he was truly the least of her brothers. The world was a story Christ was telling her. And when she told the pee-man at the Rexall that he was looking dapper himself and he said loudly that she was too ugly to f—, she had only thought to herself, O.K., praise God, he's only saying that because he's in pain, and she had smiled with the lightest light in her eyes that she could get by wishing it there, because even if she was a little yugly she was still beautiful in Christ's sight, and for her it was all a party, a little party before a bigger party, the biggest, but what about Neil-Neil, where was his party?

She would do what she could! This would be his party, one tiny installment on the huge huge party he deserved, her brother, her pal to the end, the only loving soul she had yet found in this world.

The bell rang and she threw open the door, and there was Neil-Neil.

"Welcome home!" she said grandly, and bowed at the waist, and the sock fell off her shoulder.

Yaniky had walked home in a frenzy, gazing into shopwindows, knowing that someday soon, when he came into these shops with his sexy wife, he'd simply point out items with his riding crop and they would be loaded into his waiting Benz, although come to think of it why a riding crop? Who used a riding crop? Did you use a riding crop on the Benz? Ho, man, he was stoked! He wanted a Jag, not a Benz! Golden statues of geese, classy vases, big porcelain frogs, whatever, when his ship came in he'd have it all, because when he was stoked nothing could stop him.

If Dad could see him now! Walking home in a suit from a seminar at the freaking Hyatt! Poor Dad, not that he was bashing Dad, but had Dad been a seeker? Well, no, Dad had been no seeker, life had beaten Dad. Dad had spent every evening with a beer on the divan, under a comforter, and he remembered poor Ma in her Sunday dress, which had a rip, which she'd taped because she couldn't sew, and Dad in his too big hat, recently fired again, and all of them on the way to church, dragging past a crowd of spick hoods on the corner, and one spick said something about Ma's boobs, which were big, but all of Ma was big, so why did the hood have to say something about her big boobs, as if they were nice? When they all knew they weren't nice, they were just a big woman's boobs in a too tight dress on a rainy Sunday morning, and on her head was a slit-open bread bag to keep her gray hair dry. The hood said what he said because one look at Dad told him he could. Dad, with his hunched shoulders and his constant blinking, just smirked and took Ma's arm and told the hood that a comment like that did more damage to the insulter than to the insulted, etc. etc. blah blah blah. Then the hood made a sound like a cow, at Ma, and Neil, who was nine, tried to break away and take a swing at the hood but Ma had his hand and wouldn't turn him loose and secretly he was glad, because he was scared, and then was ashamed at the relief he felt on entering the dark church, where the thin panicked preacher, who was losing his congregation, exchanged sly Biblical quotes with Dad as Winky stood beaming as if none of it outside had happened, the lower half of her body gone psychedelic in the stained-glass light.

Oh, man, the world had shit on Dad, but it wasn't going to shit on him. No way. If the world thought he was going to live in a neighborhood where spicks insulted his wife's boobs, if the world thought he was going to make his family eat bread dragged through bacon grease while calling it hobo's delight, the world was just wrong, he was going to succeed, like the men described in "People of Power," who had gardens bigger than entire towns and owned whole ships and believed in power and power only. Were thirty horse-drawn carts needed to save the roses? The call went out to the surrounding towns and at dusk lanterns from the carts could be seen approaching on the rocky bumpy roads. Was a serving girl found attractive? Her husband was sent away to war. Those guys knew how to find and occupy their Power Places, and he did, too, like when he sometimes had to solder a thousand triangular things in a night to make the rent, and drink coffee till dawn and crank WMDX full blast to stay psyched. On those nights, when Winky came up making small talk, he boldly waved her away, and when he waved her away, away she went, because she sensed in his body language that he was king, that what he was doing was essential, and when she went away he felt good, he felt strong, and he soldered faster, which was the phenomenon the book called the Power Boost, and the book said that Major Successes tended to be people who could string together Power Boost after Power Boost, which was accomplished by doing exactly what you felt like at any given time, with certainty and joy, which was what, he realized, he was about to do, by kicking out Winky!

Now was the time for him to win! Why the heck couldn't he cook his special meatballs for Beverly and afterward make love to her on the couch and tell her his dreams and plans and see if she was the one meant to be his life's helpmate, like Mrs. Thomas Alva Edison, who had once stayed up all night applying labels to a shipment of chemicals essential for the next day's work? But no. Bev was dating someone else now, some kind of guard at the mall, and he remembered the meatball dinner, Winky's pink face periodically thrusting into the steam from the broccoli as she trotted out her usual B.S. on stigmata and the amount of time necessary for an actual physical body to rot. No wonder her roommates had kicked her out, calling him in secret, no wonder her preacher had demanded she stop volunteering so much—another secret call, people had apparently been quitting the church because of her. She was a nut, a real energy sink, it had been a huge mistake inviting her to live with him and now she simply had to go.

It was sad, yes, a little sad, but if greatness were easy everyone would be doing it.

Yes, she'd been a cute kid and, yes, they'd shared some nice moments, yes yes yes, yes, she'd brought him crackers and his little radio that time he'd hid under the steps for nine straight hours after Dad started weeping during dinner, and, yes, he remembered the scared look in her eyes when she'd come running up to him after taking a fishhook in the temple while fishing with the big boys, and, yes, he'd carried her home as the big boys cackled, yes, it was sad that she sang so bad and thought it was good and sad that her panties were huge now when he found them in the wash but like it said in the book a person couldn't throw himself across someone else's funeral pyre without getting pretty God-damned hot.

She had his key so he rang the bell.

She appeared at the door, looking crazy as ever.

"Welcome home!" she said, and bowed at the waist, and a sock fell off her shoulder, and as she bent to pick it up she banged her head against the storm window, the poor dorky thing.

Oh shit, oh shit, he was weakening, he could feel it, the speech he'd practiced on the way home seemed now to have nothing to do with the girl who stood wet-eyed in the doorway, rubbing her bald spot. He wasn't powerful, he wasn't great, he was just the same as everybody else, less than everybody else, other people got married and had real jobs, other people didn't live with their fat clinging sisters, he was a loser who would keep losing for the rest of his life, because he'd never gotten a break, he'd been cursed with a bad Dad and a bad Ma and a bad sister, and was too weak to change, too weak to make a new start, and as he pushed by her into the tea-smelling house the years ahead stretched out bleak and joyless in his imagination and his chest went suddenly dense with rage.

"Neil-Neil," she said. "Is something wrong?"

And he wanted to smack her, insult her, say something to wake her up, but only kept moving toward his room, calling her terrible names under his breath.

Karen Heuler

Me and My Enemy

From *The Virginia Quarterly Review*

ALL MY LIFE perfect strangers have come up and confessed to me. They say I remind them of their sisters, their daughters, their first sweethearts, and it's perfectly true that most of these people have been men and they always confused me by their honesty so that I listened, like a girl who believes, to every one of them. I never knew what was expected of me. Maybe nothing was—but really, something is always expected, and by the very nature of their giving me something so freely and anonymously, they must have desired something back.

I hope that, even if by accident, they got it from me. Some of them at least. I know it couldn't be possible for all.

When I say that people confess to me, I mean they tell me things like an unburdening. An example? I went to the laundry the other day and while I stood there, loading wash, a man asked, "Did you do your taxes yet?"

He was an older man, tired and heavy with all those years of gravity. His eyes locked on me immediately. I pushed the coin slot into the washer.

"I haven't, no."

He shook his head wearily. "Sarah does it for me, over on Washington St. A lovely person." He blinked. "She's been doing it for us for 20 years." His eyes floated away. "I still say 'us.' My wife died two years ago."

His head bowed down even lower, and I sat next to him on the laundry bench as the windows spun their clothes around us, tumbling like his words, getting drier and older by the minute, and he told me all he could about Laura.

That's what it's like so often. Someone—gently, conversationally, as if there were no start to it—talks. Just like rain, it starts, and their sorrows mist down: I am poor, I am sick, I am lonely, I am sore.

At the grocer's, just the other night, as I lined up with my purchases, the cashier said, "That milk's no good for you." She held it up in front of her, cradling it. "It's irradiated. They say it can cause cancer." Her lip trembled. "I have cancer. I found out today."

"Today! You shouldn't be working!"

"No, it's all right, really. What else would I do? Go home? I live with my mom, she's a nervous woman. She'll be watching me constantly. I hate that. Last year I lost a baby—I wasn't very far along—but I think it nearly killed her."

"Lost a baby! And now cancer! It's too much, too much!"

That lifted her head a little bit. "It is, isn't it? I tell myself things like this happen all the time, but I don't know anyone else so many things have happened to. My girlfriend says it's enough to crush a person."

"It would bring most people to their knees."

And it would. It's amazing how misfortune sometimes chooses one special person, so the burdens pile on top of burdens, until a last small scrap brings it all crashing to a halt. I met one woman who lost an eye to a rare tropical disease, though she'd been out of the country only once. She married twice, both husbands died (one to suicide) and was about to retire on a company pension when the company went bankrupt and disappeared. It was this that broke her.

It's certainly true that money and emotions are intertwined. I guess it does make sense, because money in its own way creates relationships. My boss, for instance, has had more influence on my life than anyone I've known.

My boss is in love with me.

He tells me this constantly.

His story is a familiar one, and he repeats it often. "My wife?" he says dismissively. "She'll burn in hell. Why not? It'll be her turn—she's made my life hell."

He hangs his head in a caricature of despondence. His emotions are hard to ignore, they're blatant. They're too big for him to carry well, he uses them as weapons.

He looks at me from under the lids, as if he's hiding behind his eyes and occasionally needs to check on me.

He's a tall, stocky man with big ears whose body is constantly moving. He bobs his head, shrugs his shoulders, flings his arms out.

About a month after I started working in the traffic department of an import company (I fill out the invoices and transport assignments from the port to the store), I noticed my boss was gloomy. His head sunk low, he was silent, his shoulders were frozen. Because he looked unhappy, I did small things for him—got him coffee, picked up his mail. Nothing big, but he noticed it.

There's one other person in the department, an older woman named Doris, who works surrounded by ringing phones and retirement plans. I took the job only because they said I could start immediately. I figured I would do it until something better showed up, but it turned out they expect me to replace Doris. They did me a favor, really, by hiring me. And if Doris retires and then I quit— well, that wouldn't be fair. Of course I never promised them anything. But then, taking the job was a sort of promise, wasn't it?

That night, as I left, Eddie caught up with me at the elevator. He just appeared there, all of a sudden. As we waited, he hung his head and asked, "Did you ever have a day where you felt like giving up?"

I protested. "Oh no! Don't ever give up!"

"And why not? Go home to a house where they hate me? What's the point of that?"

I hesitated. I try to be quiet and unobtrusive at work. Sometimes, when people confide too much, they regret it. They don't want to be reminded of their weaknesses afterward; I understand that. So I blinked and tried to look comforting yet not inviting, but there are people whose sorrows spill out and spill over; they force you to step in.

"You wouldn't have time for a drink," he said as we got in the elevator. "For a quick drink? Just one I swear and you can be off." He gave me a humble smile and I said, Just one, because I thought we could be friends. You should never refuse to be a friend, never. It's my belief that people are cruel because they're unhappy, and they're unhappy because they've been treated unkindly and that's where the cycle must be broken: by those who can be kind. That's all I intended—to be kind.

We went to a bar right around the block, and he got us a table in a corner, ordered drinks and said, "All these years and I never knew what that woman was." His eyes almost rolled back in his head. "She's been having an affair with my neighbor. All these years. Twenty years. She threw it in my face. She laughed at me."

"Oh my God."

He shook his head. "Two children. Ha. Are they mine? Whose are they? How can I look them in the eye? All these years I loved them like they were my own." He gulped his whiskey and soda.

"I'm sure you love them," I said hastily. "And I'm sure they love you. And they could be your own, couldn't they?"

"Working all my life for them. Just like that, what a waste. Do you know what that's like? Your whole life wasted? No, you don't, you're too young, you're still a kid, you can't know what it's like. It's all ahead of you."

He lifted his glass, nodded, and drank. He had an oddly delicate habit of sticking his pinkie out. Someone, his mother perhaps, had told him it was the right thing to do, and he was still doing it so many years later. He had thick hands.

He ordered a second round, saying, "I've missed my bus. The next one's not for an hour. Keep me company, will you? No one should drink alone, the way I feel."

He swore it would be the last, and when he tried to order a

third drink, I said I had to go. I put money out for my share; he said that insulted him, so I took it back.

I live 20 minutes from work, and he insisted on walking me home. I thought the air might do him some good. He had missed the second bus and I thought the walk would keep him occupied until the third bus. On the way he told me that his neighbor Walter always had a smirk on his face and now he knew why. "I named my youngest after him," he said in anguish. "I loved him like a brother!"

I did my best to soothe him, I said anything that popped into my head. They loved him, I said—certainly his children did—and they were waiting for him and needed him.

At my building he thanked me almost formally: "You've saved my life. Nobody else has ever listened to me like this. *She* never did. Not like this. Now I have to get on that bus and go home—to what?" He shook his head, peering at me from his heavy lids. He left, still shaking his head.

I felt sympathy for him, but I'm not a fool, I know whoever tells a story has a way of selecting details. We had other drinks, other days, days when he looked glum or when he stood in the doorway, rattling his fat fingers on his heart to indicate misery. He quickly developed a kind of shorthand for his demands: a flick of the hand with pinkie extended meant a drink, rubbing his belly meant a meal, tapping his heart meant hours of talk. I grew to dread it. Within two weeks of our first conversation he had taken over my life.

I knew by then that he had a history, too: an affair with a secretary in another office. She had walked out on him—tortured him, he claimed; she had left town without a word. His head pumped up and down in misery.

"You've screwed around," I said one night, tired of listening to the same accusations, the same complaints. "You're not lily-white. Why can't you forgive her? Work it out?"

"Forget her," he said. "You know how I feel about you."

I was torn between my wish to be sympathetic and my growing unease. The more he told me he loved me, the more I wanted to get away from him. Sometimes that took 15 minutes of refusals and pleadings. I tried to sneak out of work without his seeing me, but he watched me. And as soon as I got home, the phone calls began. Just as I turned the stove on, put water on to boil, sliced onions or tomatoes, the phone would ring.

"I need to talk to you."

"No."

"Why not?"

"No."

"I won't take long."

"No."

"What are you doing that we can't have dinner? What's so important that you hurt me like this? You're killing me. What'll it cost you—an hour? Two hours?"

"I just need some time alone."

"I'll kill myself."

"Don't say that. It's not fair."

"You're my life."

"I don't love you. I told you that."

"You will, you will. I'll go to my grave thinking that."

"That's right, you will."

These conversations, these phone calls, became routine. From once a week to five times a week; from once a night to 10, 20 times.

I dreaded those calls. I didn't go home right away. I went for long walks. I went to movies.

One night, a man in line behind me said, "Excuse me, do you know what this film is about?" He had nervous eyes, nervous gestures.

"It's an adventure movie. Lots of action. I don't think it's violent."

"Thanks. I couldn't take violence." He jiggled his hands in his pockets and gave a snort of a laugh. "Not now. My wife has a complaint against me. Says I hit her." His face went dark and sour.

"And did you?"

"Self-defense. She pushed me to the limit, to the very limits of my soul." His eyes pooled up. "I'd give anything to change it. I don't see myself as a hitter. Not me. That's my dad. I'll never be my dad."

The line moved forward. "That's so hard," I said. "I think they call it learned behavior. You learned it even when you hated it."

"Yeah," he said, jiggling some more. "The worst thing is, I hit my kid."

I was silent.

"I know what you're thinking," he whispered. "I didn't hit him hard. Not one of those freaks you see on TV. I didn't hit him hard."

"Don't ever do it again," I said, and I think my voice shook. It was just at that moment that I saw Eddie walk down the street, coming towards me. I cut and run.

I know my neighborhood; I knew where to duck and how to make the shortcuts. But I got farther from home, choosing the worst path, always, just to get rid of Eddie. I stopped, finally, panting, in a part of town I'd never seen before. I looked around— overturned garbage cans, broken lights, no one in sight.

I walked in the street, which is what you're supposed to do in a bad neighborhood. Because it's harder to be dragged away without being seen, because someone in a car might come by and actually help.

This time, however, a car came slowly down the street, passed by me gently, and stopped. A man got out—young, grinning, call-ing, "Honey, sweetie-pie, you all alone here? You lost, honey?" He was big but he moved with a spring in his step, a jauntiness like good humor. He left his car running and came towards me. "You okay, there?" he sang out, coming towards me, and I had two impulses—one to run and one to stay. I didn't want to misjudge him, he might help me out.

But when he got to me his hand waved in front of my face—a little dancing prancing wave to show me the knife.

"Now sweetie, honey, just give me everything you've got. Money—no jewelry, huh? Cards, then. This it?" He frowned then, and I got a sick feeling in my legs as if they were about to buckle.

"What can I do with this kind of money?" he muttered, holding my wallet in his hands. He had already gone through my purse, dropping it in disgust in the street.

"Now don't start crying on me—I ain't done a thing to hurt

you. It's just money I need, just like everybody else. You think I like to do this, huh? I don't. I got pressures. I've got a life that ain't going right. I could tell you right now how many people are robbing me—doctors, landlords, tax people, you name it—but it's not gonna make me richer to tell you, is it?" He looked at me a moment, thoughtfully. "Your pockets. Empty out your pockets." His eyes got faraway and frightening and his knife jiggered fretfully. His voice dropped to a whisper. "No, forget the pockets. We're going for a ride. In my car, girlie, come on with me."

Every instinct in me said the safest thing to do was please him, but my knees bent and I fell down to the pavement. He dropped beside me. "Here? You wanna do it here?" His knife wavered over me—my neck, my breasts, my thighs, as if he were looking for the right place to start.

Just then a car turned the corner and we both looked up, blinded and frozen, as it slowed down and stopped. I no longer had any thoughts. The headlights made everything around us enormous.

A car door opened and a man asked, "What's going on out there?"

At once my attacker turned and ran. I sat up as I heard the squeal of his tires.

"Are you all right?" Footsteps tapped slowly down the pavement.

I knew I should run but I couldn't stop shaking. I thought this one, too, would have a knife, but he didn't. He was a kid who'd just gotten off from work. He drove me home, all the time twisting his head to look at me, and opening his mouth to say something, but he never actually did. He was a nice boy, a little young and skinny to be a hero, or maybe all heroes are young and skinny, and it's just the stories that supply the flesh. I had the feeling I was going to be his story.

I could hear my phone ringing while I was still in the hallway. It stopped by the time I made it in and stayed silent for 15 minutes but then it rang again, at least a dozen times. It stopped; it rang again. That went on until I took the phone off the hook.

The next day at work Eddie wouldn't even look up when I

came in. His anger rose off him like steam. I had a bruise on my face; I couldn't even remember how I'd gotten it. The night before seemed unreal; it couldn't possibly have happened. I couldn't bear to think of it, that was all. Fear was like a blanket—it smothered everything else, smoothing out the things I thought about. I didn't really directly think about that man and his knife, but he was there, in the background, everywhere. He was twisting that knife and whispering to me, whispering.

Eddie's silence—he managed to keep his back to me the whole day—was a relief. I felt myself drifting off occasionally—sinking down in the glare of the lights—and I had to snap back again; bite my finger, pinch my nose, anything like that.

But as it got time to leave I felt Eddie's eyes on me. He glared relentlessly; I sat with my head down, aware of it but holding out. It seemed a test of some kind, trying to keep away from his eyes.

"Where'd you get that bruise?" he asked finally when I looked at him. His voice was a mixture of outrage and self-pity.

"I don't know, I didn't even notice. I must have bumped into something."

His whole upper body moved with the emphasis of his nod. His voice twanged with injury. "Who is he? Who'd you meet?"

"I didn't meet anyone."

"I saw you. The guy you talked to in the line." He knew I was holding out on him; he had gained a moral ground. He was almost gloating.

"You saw me at the movies?"

"I saw you."

There was something about the triumphant way he said this that pulled me up short. "You just happened to go to the movies?"

"I followed you."

At once it seemed obvious—how the phone started ringing just minutes after I got home, how lately he had suddenly stopped making scenes when I insisted on going home. He was following me. He was watching me.

And what a simple life he had watched, too. Out the door, five blocks and turn right, two blocks and stop at the store owned by the man whose mother had gone to the laundromat one day and simply not come back. Two corners and a magazine, perhaps, or a newspaper. A chat with the newspaperman, whose son had dropped out of school and was possibly on drugs.

Eddie was watching me. His face was ugly; I had always thought before how sad it was to be so unattractive, but now it occurred to me that his face might, indeed, reflect his soul. It was a mean thought. For a moment I hated him.

"You ran off to meet someone," he said.

"No. I didn't." I almost said, I ran because I saw *you,* but I was ashamed. He was unhappy, horribly unhappy. That's why he behaved so badly. I knew that he brought it all on himself, but the pain was still real. How would it help if I insulted him? Still, I couldn't give in. "I don't want you following me," I said finally. But then I wavered. I thought how much I hated going home, the night ahead of me shaped only by memories of a man with a knife.

He saw me; he was alert to me. "Let's talk about it over dinner," he said.

And because I was a coward, I said, "Yes, but this time will be the last time. You have to understand that."

Of course, he agreed. And, in the course of his whiskey-and-sodas, he grew more expansive, more confident, more insistent. "Drop the jerk," he said, pointing at my bruise. "Or tell me who he is. I'll take care of it."

"I told you, it was an accident. And it's not important. What is important is to remember I'm your friend. I'll never be your lover. The phone calls have to stop, and following me home has to stop. You make people hate you when you do that."

He was crestfallen. "I won't do it," he promised. "But you drive me crazy. I sit next to you all day long, don't I? And I behave like a gentleman. And you have no idea how I feel."

"No I don't." I seized the opportunity. "Because I don't feel the way you do."

He glowered. "You want to hurt me? Go ahead then, hit me right here." He pounded his heart. "It would be easier to take."

But I got him to stop at two drinks and he let me end it without too much trouble after the bill was paid. I walked him to the bus station; I waited for the bus; I watched him get on it.

When I got home, the phone wasn't ringing, it didn't ring all night. I thought, it isn't so very hard to set things right.

But I was wrong. The next night he wanted dinner again and I said no. I took a different way home; I stopped in different stores, but I knew he was there even when I didn't see him. The hairs at the back of my neck were prickling.

The phone rang the moment I opened my door.

"I said don't call me," I hissed.

"Please," he said, "I'm going to leave my wife for you."

"Don't do it," I cried. "I'll quit my job, I'll leave town."

"No, no. I'm sorry. Don't quit. Just talk to me, meet me for a drink."

"I'm unplugging the phone," I said. And I did.

Ten minutes later the bell started ringing. I thought it would drive me mad, the way he wouldn't stop. I could picture him, down there, jabbing at the button, outraged, jabbing again.

No matter what, I wasn't going to give in. Why couldn't he take no for an answer? Why couldn't he behave reasonably? Why did he push so hard—forcing me to hate him—me, who hated no one, on principle?

The bell stopped finally. I heard shouting in the hallway. I covered my ears again; I wanted peace, peace, peace.

I crept out later to the store for bread and eggs—and I looked back over my shoulder the whole time, I checked the streets constantly.

The super was putting out the garbage when I got back. He beckoned to me. "You've got a problem," he said. "About 45 or so, pudgy, funny looking, ugly son of a bitch."

"My boss."

"Kept ringing and ringing your bell. You know how it is. The first floor hears the bells. The apartments around you hear the bells. We *all* hear the bells. I had to tell him I called the cops. He doesn't give up easily."

"No. He doesn't."

"The thing is," he said, looking at me closely, "there's three complaints against you now."

"Against me? Why me? I didn't ring the bell."

"You're the attraction." He looked uncomfortable. "I don't want to see you get thrown out."

I panicked. "No, no. I'll take care of it. I promise."

He sighed in relief. "That's good. I can't take any more problems, not now. My son's wife ran off with their money, just went to the bank and took it all out. The kid is crushed, he's like a baby, he doesn't know what to do. Trouble like this, I have to be careful, I have to keep this job. I'm not alone." His face got deeper lines on it just standing there thinking of his troubles.

"It's all right," I said, trying to stop the flow of worries. "None of this is your problem. I'm sorry if you were bothered. I'll take care of it."

My stomach was in a knot. I fried some eggs, buttered some toast, and threw it all away.

I got a screwdriver and disconnected my bell. I put the phone in the closet. I went to bed and stared at the ceiling. Where had I gone wrong? I believed, I truly believed, that I had a gift for listening—and yet it had gone wrong, terribly wrong. I had encouraged Eddie's obsessions, I might even be evicted because of it. How had such good intentions gone so far astray?

The next day I found copies of my work on my desk with angry red circles around typos and mistakes of all kinds. I leafed through them slowly, my neck getting hot, my heart speeding. We did so much work that perfection wasn't the rule, efficiency was. I wasn't a schoolchild; this wasn't homework. I looked again: the orders had all been filled already. I threw them out.

While Eddie was out of the room I told Doris I didn't feel well and was going home.

I had no plan, that was the problem. I needed to think of a plan. I didn't want to hurt Eddie, I just wanted him to leave me alone. But what if he wasn't capable of that?

I was so lost in thought that I took my usual route home, meeting the mailman whose house had burned down and a neighbor whose cat had died.

I opened the front door and turned to close it just as Eddie's fat fingers wrapped themselves around the edge. I jumped back and he grinned. "I have to talk to you," he said.

I started backing up the stairs. "No. I don't want to talk to you right now."

"Just talking. What's the problem?" He came up the stairs slowly, grinning in a foolishly triumphant way.

"I want you to go away. Now." I hated the way he kept walking up the stairs, each step a little mountain he crested. When I got to the top of the flight I knew I couldn't stand it anymore, I had lost the use of all reasonable words, and I pushed him away—not even forcefully, it was an indecisive push. But it was enough, it took him by surprise, and those fat hands of his flew up, looking for support, and found nothing. His eyes, still on me, registered irritation, only, at another interruption in his plans, and then he tipped over backwards, like a jar off a shelf.

All my life I've tried to do the right thing and only the right thing. It isn't just that I was willing to listen to them all; I wanted to. I wanted them to throw a little of their sorrowing away, that's all, these people staggering under their worries and guilts. I wanted to be the little blessed secret in their life, touching them, leaving them better off.

I ran down the stairs and checked him; his eyes were closed and his chest was still. I called for help from the phone around the corner, but I doubted it would still matter.

It's so simple, how the world changes irrevocably. There was no way I could go back—five minutes ago, an hour ago—to the time when I was innocent and free. People are most obsessed when they surprise themselves. Unexpected heroism, unexpected cowardice— these things that seem to leap out from someone else's history and land in yours—well, you're never released from it.

Because what could be so remarkable as this—with the best of intentions, without thinking at all about it—change from what I was to what I am, a murderer?

I walked to the police station, waited for the desk sergeant to notice me and said, "I killed someone." He lost his bored expression for only a moment, then sent me upstairs to a large room with cracked gay linoleum on the floor and four old metal desks. A man waved me over to his desk and I sat down on a folding chair.

"I murdered someone."

Det. Clark gave me a tired smile.

"He was my boss. He followed me constantly, tracking me down. I told him to stop, but he was an unhappy man."

"A stalker," Det. Clark murmured.

"I disconnected my bell and the phone. To stop him from bothering me."

"You must have been frightened."

"I wasn't frightened until I saw the knife."

"He had a knife? It was self-defense?"

I had to concentrate harder. "I didn't mean that, no." I was ruining my case. "He didn't have a knife, that was someone else."

"Take it easy," Det. Clark said. "Take your time. No one's gonna hurt you. Now, how'd he die? He *is* dead, right?"

It was impossible, but the detective had a sympathetic glint in his eye. He looked at me kindly, he was steering me gently away from my own statements. "He might have stepped back on his own, you know. Like he forgot where he was."

"I know I pushed him."

"Don't worry, we'll straighten this out."

He made a call, his head turned from me, then turned back and smiled. "You've never been in trouble before, have you? No, I didn't think so. The man stalked you. Probably wanted to get you into bed. That's right, isn't it?" He shook his head sadly. "When I was growing up, I had a friend who was stalked. Like you, a nice girl, easy to talk to. A daddy fell in love with her." He snorted. "That's how young we were, that's how she said it. She disappeared, 14 years old. You look like her, the same kind of eyes, the way you listen. You're just like Annie. She always looked like she was taking in every word. You have that look. Sympathetic. You have a gift for making a person feel listened to. I think I would have married her, you know. I have a wife and kids, but just sometimes you think of different things and I always think of her."

His voice was drifting over me. I would have told him, Stop, please stop and listen to me, but he already had the gaze they get when they confess to me—densely abstracted, cushioned in memories. I heard all about Annie as he filled out the forms, interrupting himself every once in a while to check a fact.

"You said he threatened to kill himself?"

"I don't think he meant it."

"Annie always thought the best of people, too. There was a woman next door that everyone hated, I hated too, I did a terrible thing to her once and only Annie knew. . . ." And his voice went off, recollecting Annie and his own lost days.

I didn't want to listen to him. I hated listening to him. But my lips must have smiled and maybe my eyes softened automatically, the way he said Annie's had. Because he kept on talking.

In fact they all keep talking, even now, when I have my own story, a story just as sad as theirs. But still they keep on talking, as if I couldn't possibly have sorrows of my own.

As if it isn't, somehow, unbearable to be told it was all an accident when I know it wasn't, to be told I'm innocent when the guilt rises up in my throat, to be treated as if I were exactly the same as before. As soon as they see me, they throw their words at me like hail, and it doesn't matter how I feel. It doesn't matter that I need forgiveness too, I need relief, because all they care about, beating their breasts and wiping their eyes, is the personal, quite comfortable, recital of their sins.

Well, damn their sins.

And damn their sorrows.

Damn them all.

Thom Jones

Tarantula

From *Zoetrope: All-Story*

JOHN HAROLD HAMMERMEISTER arrived at W. E. B. Du Bois High School with grand ambitions. Harold loved to work, thrived on challenge, and could scarcely contain his excitement at the prospect of a new and difficult assignment.

Postings such as these were like the great wars, they provided one with opportunities for distinguishment. There was another thing, too—hard work took Harold's mind off the inner turmoil resulting from so many recent life changes. He had been wracking up big numbers on the Hans Seyle Stress Scale. In less than two years he had weathered a divorce, suffered the death of both parents, and then, with the last of his inheritance, had come down from Canada—come down to Detroit to polish off the course work on a Ph.D. Now everything was done except for the thesis. It was just one last detail. A little trifling. Why, he would have it out of the way faster than you could say John Harold Hammermeister.

The principal who hired Hammermeister was scheduled to retire in a year, and Hammermeister, with his doctorate all but finished, had a "feeling" that the principal's job was his. All he needed was to whirl like a dervish for one year, a mere two hundred and twenty-six school days—dazzle them senseless—and the kingdom from on high would be his. And Harold was most definitely in contact with the kingdom. Before falling asleep each night

Hammermeister tuned into the Universal Cosmic Broadcast. He was a psychic radioman who not only transmitted but received. He was connected, on the inside. It was beautiful, wonderful, mar-ve-lous!

Yeah, eyes closed at night, in red flannel pajamas, Hammermeister lay in the ancient Murphy bed of his studio apartment and *created* the future—and in that future he saw himself in the principal's office, in full command, in one year's time, a mere two hundred and twenty-six school days. The principal's office was just a little pit stop on the way over to district office proper, and he would most certainly ascend the ladder there. From the Murphy bed he created the glorious visions of supreme success. He watched himself climb from the modest position of junior vice-principal all the way up to the summit of State Superintendent of Public Instruction! Why not try *that one* on for size? Heh heh.

The old Murphy bed was Harold's magic Persian carpet from which he could encompass the "entire situation." From there he plotted his moves and savored future pleasures. Harold saw, smelled, felt, and practically *tasted* the smooth, dove-gray leather seats of the burnished black Lincoln Town Car that would replace his ancient Ford. A car so quiet, the only thing he could ever hear was the ticking of his handcrafted Swiss watch. In their gold-plated frames, the Lincoln's vanity plates would read: HAMMER!

In the mind-movie there was also a second wife, a newer and better model than the first. Beauty, brainpower, and refinement ("behind every great man. . . ."). When she wasn't supporting him in his Machiavellian schemes, number two would be a well-rounded person in her own right. *Yeah, she gon' be so fine!* And the school district administration center would be Harold's seventh heaven of joy—secretaries in short skirts with a little piquant bantering among them by day. A little bit of hanky-panky, while nights and weekends involved a walled country estate with polo, fox hunting, and high society available at his pleasure. Yes, a *walled* estate! Wasn't that how the rich did the world over? They put up buffers and walls against the detritus of the everyday life. It was every man for himself in the swinish cesspool of the twentieth century. And why not be absolutely selfish? Was not beauty more pleasing to the eye than ugliness and squalor? To think of this new beginning, to think that it would all take off from a place like Du Bois High School—a veritable war zone, a sinkhole of black despair, a continued scene of barbarous violence! Well, no problem, Harold would soon have it all squared away. They would have to do a double segment on *60 Minutes* to showcase Harold and the new reformation revolution in American schools. Du Bois would become the exemplar ghetto success story. Hope would replace despair. Yes, fairy tales could come true. Harold was going to turn things around on a dime. Only fair that he should reap the rewards.

The bestseller that his thesis would become would provide the means. Written in the snappy, popular vernacular, it was a multifaceted jewel. Americans would read Harold's terse, spellbinding prose with a curious admixture of horror and astonishment. The *All-New Blackboard Jungle: An American High School in 1997.* Probably make a movie, and playing the role of the visionary reformer—the only actor capable of playing real-life John Harold Hammermeister—may I have the envelope, please?—*ta da!* Ladies and gentlemen, the only actor with sufficient authority and range to catch the infinite subtleties—with the scope, the voice, intelligence, maturity, the physical presence—ladies and gentlemen, I present to you . . . yet another gifted Canadian, Mr. Donald Sutherland. Was it Sir Donald? Well, it would be. The Queen Mother could hop off her ass and beknight the man. The dear fellow. It was high time. Just 'bout time, all right.

Boy oh boy, what the mind could behold, the mind could make real. Hammermeister gave the kids a watered-down version of his visualization techniques whenever it was time to light a fire under somebody's dead ass. Take pride! Pull yourself up by your bootstraps. It was always in one ear and out the other; they didn't have a snowball's chance, but you had to try. Professional ethics required one to take the idle stab.

Nobody but nobody knew anything about elbow grease anymore. People were so friggin' lazy. Work like a German! It was the golden key to riches and prosperity beyond imagining. Most American educators were shell-shocked, blown. In the trench warfare of public schooling, one needed to concentrate, work hard, confront problems and wrestle them down. Engage the mind. Work! In the trenches, friends, family, and personal recreation were inexcusable diversions. Insipid fuck-fiddle. You could pick up on that action later. Climb the ladder and then harvest the bounty . . . in the meantime, later, alligator.

In Hammermeister's office, on the left side of his desk in a small glass cage—the bottom covered with pea gravel, the top fixed with a warming lamp—Hammermeister kept a tarantula named Lulu. Hammermeister waited a few days before he brought the spider in. He wanted to get the lay of the land first. Lulu was a statement, and he wasn't totally sure how to "play" these Americans. A big-ass hairy spider could get to be *too much,* but then, with his pleasant, affable good looks, his Mr. Nice Guy demeanor, Hammermeister wanted to establish a darker aspect of himself—a presentation of danger. If it gets down to it, boys and girls, *if it comes down to it,* I'll fuck you up in a second! I'll mess up yo' face!

Did he really say that?

No, but he *conveyed* it just the same. He put out the vibe. When a recalcitrant student was sent to his office, Hammermeister liked to rock back in his executive's chair, tapping the edge of his desk with a number one Dixon Executive pencil, affecting a debonair Donald Sutherland style and say, "You aren't getting through to me, my friend." Tap, tap, tap. "You aren't getting through." It got to even the baddest of the bad—the sneaky quiet malefactors, the toughest thugs, the sulkers, wrong-doers of various shapes and descriptions. Hang a leading question on the guilty soul and they spilled their guts. It never failed.

Hammermeister was the first administrator to show up in the morning and the last to leave at night. He attended the football games, the band, orchestra, and choir recitals—plays. He even showed up at girls' B-squad volleyball games. He wanted everyone to know that he was at the school and of it, and that because of him and through the sheer force of his personality, the school was going to get better, improve, blaze into the heavens—and the plan was working. A man has to have a plan, and Harold had a righteous plan. Beautiful, wonderful, *mar-ve-lous!*

The students and discipline were his forte. He soon had them all under control—the wild-ass freshman girls, the dopers, the gang bangers; the whole spectrum of adolescent vermin. It didn't have to be: "I'll fuck you up!" It hardly ever was . . . really. With Lulu on the desk he could focus totally.

The principal complimented him often about how well he handled the whole arena of discipline, but when Hammermeister asked for more responsibilities, Dr. White put him off.

"Not just yet. Why don't you settle in for a while, huh-huh-huh-Harold? Don't want to burn out, do you? Meltdown by May. That happens to the best of us, you know, even when things are guh-guh-guh-going well."

Christ, you could stand there for an hour to hear the motherfucker deliver one complete sentence.

"Seriously, Dr. White, I want to learn everything I can. I want to know this school inside and out. I'm part of the team, and I don't like sitting on the bench."

"Okay then. There is one little trouble spot that seems to duh-duh-duh-defy our coping skills: the cuh-cuh-cuh-custodians. They're yuh-yuh-yuh-yours."

Hammermeister quickly scheduled a meeting with all thirteen of the men. He had pizza brought in to foster conviviality, but instead of the friendly get-together he envisioned, all thirteen janitors started in on him at once: the year had never been off to a worse start! It was terrible! There was a group of squirrely freshmen, and they were carrying food to all ends of the building—spilling pop on the rugs, spitting chew, sunflower seeds, and peanut shells. A particular bone of contention was a type of hot pink, new wave chewing gum. This stuff didn't freeze when you applied aerosol propelled gum hardener to it—freeze it so you could smack it to pieces with a putty knife, pick up the cold little broken shards, and throw them in the trash.

A red-faced custodian named Duffy harped on and on about the gum hardener. "For one thing, it erodes the ozone layer, and for another, it makes this fuckin' gum melt and soak *deeper* into the fiber of the carpet. Opposite of the very role for which it was intended, man. One piece of gum, fuck! One kid, thirty-two teeth, give or take, and one wad of gum equals twenty-five minutes of *my time* which translates into almost nine dollars of the district's money. One piece of gum! I could *ignore* it, let the rug go to shit, but I take pride. *I take pride!* For Christsakes, why doesn't somebody tell that jerkoff that fills up the vending machines to quit putting chewing gum in—huh? Or at least use a normal kind. I tried to talk to the man. I don't know what you have to do with that guy. I can't get through to him. Mastication of the South American chicle plant is against the law in Singapore, Harold, did you know that? I tell this guy that selling gum is against the law in Singapore! They got their shit squared away over there. I tell this to Vend-o-face, an' he ain't hearin' it. He's one of them passive-aggressive sons of bitches who likes to drive fifty in the passing lane or who will *hang up* an express line at the supermarket jacking around with a checkbook, buying lottery tickets, and asking questions when others are in a fuckin' life-and-death hurry. Forgive my digression, but are you getting the picture? I never met anyone like him before; he's just an absolute asshole. You know the character, John Waite from *The Nigger of the Narcissus?* That's this guy. There's just no other way to describe this human piece of shit."

Hammermeister was so shocked by Duffy's stream of invective that his face went pale. In Canada, a man such as Duffy would be fired on the spot. What gross insolence! That Duffy had the nerve to speak to him in this fashion—obviously, there were different rules of engagement going on. Detroit, shit, what a very strange energy inhabited the city where such scenes were commonplace. Harold was almost certain he could smell alcohol on this man's breath. "John Waite?"

"Waite from *The Nigger of the Narcissus.* For God's sake, you're a college man, aren't you? Read the book. Don't teachers have to read in college?"

Another of the custodians chimed in. "Hey, the man is right. He knows what he's talking about. This vending guy is Johnny Waite! He should be banned from the fuckin' building."

Throughout this all, an enormous black man with a shaved head and silver nose- and earrings fixed a hard stare on Hammermeister, like a heat-seeking missile. At last he said, "Hey! I'd like to get something off my chest. You called us all in here for a meeting, and nothing will change or get done as we all know. You have the secretary call me up to come to a fucking meeting at two-thirty in the afternoon when I work graveyard. Doesn't anybody have any consideration? I need to come in and hear all of this Mickey Mouse piss and moan. *The Nigger of the Narcissus!* Watch your mouth, Duffy! I don't even want to hear you *thinkin'* 'nigger.' You don't have the right, motherfucker! I'm the one's paid dues." Roused to a fury, the large custodian wheeled on Hammermeister and stuck a finger in his face. "How would you like it if I called you up and told you you had to come to work at three in the morning? *Three in the morning,* because that's what this is for me, goddamn it! Plus, I'm sick tonight. Call me a sub. You done fucked up my biological clock! I don't know when it will come back to normal, I'm still fucked over from fucking daylight savings back in May or whenever the fuck! Foolin' with Mother fucking Nature. God! Great God! Goddamn it, son of a bitch!" With that, Centrick Cline kicked a metal folding chair out of his way and stormed out of the room.

Mike, the head custodian, got up, ostentatiously glanced at his watch, and said, "There's a volleyball set up in the gym. Let's go. We're already two hours behind. Lord, we got to boogie, folks, or we're going to be here *awl* night long."

Hammermeister watched the custodians file out of the conference room. He looked down at the untouched pizzas, sixty dollars worth leaking warm grease onto the limp cardboard containers. He picked up a piece smothered with sausage, pineapple, olives, and onions and ate it in four bites. It was his first meal of the day.

All the screaming had caused Rider, the senior vice-principal, to pop his head in the door and catch Hammermeister in a state of panic—catch him in a situation over which he had no control. An abominable scene. Janitors . . . Dr. White had been right. They defied the usual . . . well, hell, they were out of control. He would call them in one by one. Isolate them. Break them down. Turn them into lap dogs.

They did have a point, however, the school did look like hell. The next afternoon Hammermeister got on the p.a. and told the students of W. E. B. Du Bois High School that while the year was off to a great start, food, candy, and pop were not permitted in the halls and classrooms. The following afternoon he repeated the message, shifting from the insouciant Donald Sutherland to the rather arch Donald. When Hammermeister continued to notice litter in the halls and classrooms, he ordered the pop and candy machines shut down for an unspecified period.

Hammermeister called the head custodian into his office and told him of this decision. "I want to help you guys out. We couldn't run this school without the custodians," he said with an ingratiating smile. "Anything you need in the way of supplies, or whatever, just let me know. And one other thing, the district has asked me to address the problem of sick-leave abuse. Du Bois is the worst school in the district in this regard."

No sooner were the words out of Hammermeister's mouth when Mike, the head custodian, proceeded to tell Hammermeister that his daughter had chicken pox and that he needed a sub for the rest of the week—moreover, Ralph, the day man, needed a sub for Monday because he was going in for some blood tests. And, oh, somebody else, too—he wasn't sure, well, yes, it was Ray. Ray had tickets for a rap concert and wanted to take a vacation day.

"So . . . Mike . . . at least talk to the guys. Can you do that much?"

"Yo," the head custodian piped as he turned and walked away. For a head custodian, Hammermeister felt the man had a very bad attitude in regard to chain of command. *Well wait a minute, Mike. Come on back here, my friend. Perhaps that's too much to lay on you all at once. Maybe you ought to go home and rest. Take a year off for mental health. I'll catch your area for you and make sure all your checks are mailed . . . r'hat on time, bro. Izzat cool or what? I mean, I'm hip to all the problems you guys go through. I know your job . . . ain't no day at th' beach. I'm in full sympathy. Really. You don't think I got a heart? I gotta heart. I got a heart.*

A week after the pop and candy machines were shut off, the associated student body complained that they were losing the revenue from these machines and made it plain to Hammermeister that this revenue was the lifeblood that bought band uniforms, sports equipment, and other essentials. Hammermeister was shocked when he learned the figures. The students at Du Bois drank enough fluid ounces of Coke, assorted beverages, and refreshments to half fill the swimming pool in a week. The Hammer didn't allow anything sweeter than fresh fruit back at the juvenile facility in Canada, and what a difference. There weren't any sugared-out junior gangsters like here, and the behavioral considerations, repercussions, etc. were extremely . . . interesting. Well, it would all be in the thesis. Soon the wide world would know.

In less than a week there was heavy pressure to turn the candy machines back on. Hammermeister lost his cool and exchanged heated words over the matter with senior vice-principal Rider. He came back later and made a cringing apology explaining that he wasn't used to making so many compromises. having come from a detentional facility where his word had been "law"; that he was grinding out his thesis and so on and when he reflected over the apology, it occurred to him how weak and desperate he had sounded—effete and obsequious. A wipe-out migraine could do that to him, turn him white. The pop machines went back on, and the school instantly became a pit.

Waiting for a pair of codeine #4s to kick in, Hammermeister dropped a succulent white grub into Lulu's cage and watched the spider attack it with such speed and ferocity that Hammermeister jerked back in his leatherette executive chair. He thought, "What if I were that worm? Lulu would show no mercy. And I wouldn't expect any."

The pace of the activities at Du Bois began to pick up. Hammermeister was getting hit with building requests from the science people—brainy types in KMart jogging shoes, who wore pen packs and watches with calculators on them and who, generally speaking, displayed the whole range of absentminded professor types of behavior. They were exasperating when you were trying to get from line "a" to line "b" within a certain time frame and didn't want to screw around with their spacey weirdness. It could mean a migraine that radiated down the back of Hammermeister's neck, accompanied by a Zulu spear chucked four inches deep in the region of vertebra C-6.

Worse than science were the special-education people, they were the most eccentric bunch of the entire faculty. Do-good, granola freaks in Birkenstock sandals, who came in with problems of every description. Stories from left field. All Harold could do was sympathize. He knew their burn-out rate was high, and he wasn't good when they came in weeping, half crazy . . . they would shed hot, salty tears over virtually anything! But there was no one to foist these people off on, and he sat with a number one Dixon tap-tapping. *I have never heard of a student openly masturbating in a classroom. This is a mental health issue. Let me make some phone calls.* When they left his office, he would mechanically open his top drawer and pop two Extra-Strength Excedrins, a couple of Advils, and a deuce of Canadian 222s.

The people who taught social studies and history were coaches, mostly, and their minds were seldom on innovating the curriculum. They wanted to do everything by the numbers. One thing they could do—they could read the sports page.

The teachers in language-arts complained that they had too many papers to grade. Harold hired part-time college English majors as assistants and fed as many student teachers into the language-arts program as he could. The math and business people, Hammermeister found dull. But dull could be good; it had its advantages. These people were undemanding and caused few problems. They were pure gravy in terms of his own job description. Ditto with the vocational-education types.

The group he cultivated most, although he had little interest in high-school sports, was the coaches. The coaches who were P.E. teachers didn't count so much as those who taught academic subjects. P.E. teachers tended to be happy with the status quo. It was the latter bunch, the so-called academic teachers, who were ambitious, who would eventually give up the classroom and move into administration where there was more money.

Coaches had popularity not only with the students and the general public but with the administration. Winning teams meant high student morale and coaches were very important. With these imbeciles Harold laughed, drank, farted, and clowned. Whenever the conversation turned to the gridiron, all Hammermeister had to do was listen intently, carefully orchestrating his body language and throwing in a line like, "Geez, you really know your football, coach. I'm impressed. I never *saw* it that way before. That's absolutely brilliant. No wonder the students love you." He despised coaches, but collectively they had more juice than any other group in the building.

It was only with the women in the administrative office that Harold could let his hair down and be himself. He could tell they found him attractive, and before long, as a joke, he had everyone in the office saying "a-boot" in the Canadian style rather than "about." He wondered if they had Peter Jennings fantasies about him.

Sex was something for the next lifetime. It was tough learning the new job, but since he lived alone in a tiny apartment and required little sleep, Hammermeister was able to throw himself into his work, body and soul. He longed to get out of this rough-and-tumble high school and into the cozy air-conditioned district office building with the two-hour lunches, plush carpets, and countless refinements and amenities as soon as possible. He saw himself there. And sex was for then. He was a dervish, and he was whirling this year. Things were poppin'. There was suddenly so much to do. He had forgotten almost entirely about the janitors.

Then one day the activity director received a shipment of folding chairs for a district-wide choir recital slated for the gymnasium, and of the thirteen custodians in the school, only four were on hand after school to unload the chairs and get the gym whipped into shape. The activity director was highly agitated, and not realizing how little real clout the man had, Hammermeister became hysterical as well. When Harold saw the head custodian, he demanded to know where all of the other janitors were.

Mike was either in his fool-in-paradise mood—or "high." He stood before Harold and scratched his head for a moment. Well, three custodians were out sick and no subs were available. There were the two who worked graveyard: somebody or other had driven off to pick up a prescription, yet another had not acknowledged the "all call," and finally, still another, the very one who worked the gym area, did not report to work until five. Hammermeister listened to this, all the while his headache picking up steam and mutating into a kind of epileptoid craziness. Still, he managed to maintain his composure, and said, "I want that man in at two like all the swing-shift people, have you got that?"

Later that afternoon this very janitor, Duffy, walked into Hammermeister's office and caught him writing notes on his thesis. "Can't you knock?" Hammermeister asked. Duffy, who was red with anger, made a perfunctory apology. Hammermeister saw Lulu stir in her glass box. Duffy's eyes followed her movement.

"Shit, man, a bug! Weird! *Goddamn it!*"

"It's a spider, Mr. Duffy. Tarantula. Now what can I do for you?" Tap, tap, tap.

Duffy nervously stroked his moustache and short beard. He looked at the spider and then back at Hammermeister. "Mike told me you changed my hours."

"That's right, Duffy. Did he tell you why?" Tap, tap.

"He said something about unloading chairs for the concert. Only four guys were here or something."

"Yes, exactly. The next time this kind of thing happens there will be five, minimum." Tap.

Duffy took a deep breath and shook his neck to loosen up a bit. "Can I say something, Harold? I want to say this: I've been here for ten years and this is the first time that anything like this has come up. It almost never happens. If I have to come in at two, there's nothing I can clean. The gym and the upper gym are in use, the locker rooms are in use—there's nothing I can do."

"I'm sure you'll think of something." Tap, tap, tap.

"Plus—after the game, like tonight. Tonight there's football. The team won't be out of the locker rooms until a quarter to eleven—everything will be muddy, a total mess, and I'm supposed to have gone home fifteen minutes previous—"

"On game nights come in at four. How's that?"

"Look . . . Harold. The reason I took that gym job was so I

could baby-sit until my wife gets home from the auto plant. She gets home at four-thirty. If you change my hours, I'm going to have to hire a baby-sitter—"

Hammermeister rocked back in his chair, steepling his fingers. "I am familiar with your union contract, and I can change your hours to suit the needs of the school. Is that clear?"

"All right, we can play it that way. I tried nice, but we can take this motherfucker to the union, and we can sit in hearing rooms . . . *by the hour!* I know you got lots of homework. It's going to be fun. You can really make progress on that thesis of yours. Or maybe you can read a little Joseph Conrad. It would do you good, Harold. Give you a little insight, Harold, into the ways of the world. I'm *filing.*"

"You pay union dues, and I encourage you to use the union," Hammermeister said evenly. He swiveled his chair away in a little half twist and busied himself with a file folder, dismissing the custodian with a wave of the hand. He wasn't going to let the man scream or give him the satisfaction of making eye contact. Anger— for a lot of people, it was a hobby. They liked it. Why play their silly-ass game?

Duffy slammed the door so hard a draft of air lifted Hammermeister's thin, fluffy, light brown hair, which was combed forward to cover a receding hairline. He zipped open his drawer, popped two Excedrin, two Advil, swallowed a double glug of Pepto Bismol, and then hunched over his desk and restyled his hair using a comb and hand mirror.

A few days later Hammermeister got a note from the district custodial coordinator stating that because of activities scheduling, Duffy's shift would revert back to the original five p.m. to one-thirty a.m., semi-graveyard shift. Hammermeister got on the phone and talked to the man, one Bob Graham, who told him Sean Duffy was one of the better custodians in the district and that he was not going to stand still for any aggravation. Furthermore, Graham characterized Duffy as one of the nicest, most easygoing people he knew. *Right! White was black, and black was white!* What *perfect* logic!

Whenever Harold needed time to "think," or to let his various headache medicines kick in, he would take a stroll over in the area of the gym and look at Duffy's work. It was hard to fault, but Hammermeister was quick to jot down "dings" with a retractable ballpoint—especially if he found them two or three days in a row. He would leave notes to Duffy. Pin them on the custodians' bulletin board for all of the classified staff to see. "To S. Duffy from H. Hammermeister: Black mark on benches, boys locker room. Why?"

When basketball season started, Hammermeister grabbed Duffy by the arm and pointed out a spilled Pepsi under the bleachers. It was the first thing you saw when you walked into the gym, and he told Duffy to go get a mop and clean it up. It was an eyesore. "Hurry up, there, chop-chop!" Hammermeister said, with heat in his voice.

Later that night, at halftime, when Duffy was giving the basketball court a quick sweep, the drill team came out, and Hammermeister made a theatrical throat-slashing gesture for Duffy to get off the court. Duffy waited at the opposite end of the gym, his face blazing scarlet with bilious fury, and after the drill team finished its routine, Hammermeister noted with satisfaction Duffy's embarrassment as he finished the job. Duffy was an aneurysm waiting to blow.

Well, there were the teachers, too, who were slackers—a good number of them. Hammermeister made note. They were easy to spot. They liked to show films or assign book reports and theme papers blocking out days at a time in the library. They followed the same curriculum year in and year out. Playing one clique off the other, Hammermeister ascertained who the lazy ones were and, if they were not coaches, he gave them heat, too.

Woodland, down in the portables, for instance. He dressed like some kind of Salvation Army bum. Beard right off a pack of Smith Brothers' Cough Drops. When Hammermeister caught Woodland smoking one day after school, he reminded the man that he was a master teacher and wondered out loud what his future goals were.

"I used to be gung ho and *all thangs,* but now I'm getting short. Have you got a problem with that, Hammermeister?"

"I'm not saying you need to wear a suit and tie. But you have to remember you are still on the job and you are a role model, Woodland. You are a senior teacher. Where's your self-respect, man? You want to be a good teacher, then work at it. You're *getting paid,* aren't you?"

As he walked down the ramp from Woodland's portable, he turned back and saw Woodland flip him the "bird." Jesus, look at them wrong and an American could get a hair up his ass and lose it. This Woodland had murder in his heart. There was less free-floating hostility at the prison back in Canada, which was tame by comparison. Hammermeister locked eyes with Woodland, but before violence was done, he abruptly turned and stalked back to the main building with his pulse pounding. He could feel the surge of it in his neck and temples. He already had a Tylenol #4 headache over that one, but you had to give them a little jab, to let them know who was running the show. He had given Woodland a jab, and the man had showed him as much disrespect as that custodian, Duffy—well, these people would be excised. Duffy sooner and Woodland later, when the time was right . . . in a bloodless Machiavellian style. For some short-term revenge, Harold managed to "lose" a work order Woodland had recently put in to have his air conditioner fixed. He balled it up and slam dunked it into his wastebasket. The next thing he did was write a note reminding himself to call Woodland into his office, on Harold's turf, where he could reverse any notions the teacher had about blowing him off. He would feign consideration, all the better to ultimately crush Woodland to dust. Hah!

W. E. B. Du Bois was far from an ideal school, and the more he got to know it and was dragged down by the inertia of it, the more Hammermeister was inclined to jab these slackers or to outright get in their faces. But he had to watch himself and keep it under control, at least for this first crucial year. He really belonged in the district office, and he would be there when he whipped this place into shape. He had done well at the detention facility in Canada; he would do well here. Working in a low-morale school where so many of his colleagues were just going through the motions made Hammermeister shine like a red, white, and blue comet streaking through a night sky of blackest India ink—so, in a way, it was all to the good. *Blackboard Jungle 1997* was coming along, and in the meantime, the dervish continued to whirl.

Once the buses arrived and students started filing in, there was heavy action. Metal detectors going off. Fights picked up where they had left off the previous afternoon. Open drug transactions. Before you knew it, they were calling Hammermeister to put out one brushfire after another and another and another—all day long. Although he thrived on adrenaline, the pace of events at Du Bois was getting to be relentless. Harold was racking up some more big numbers on the Hans Seyle Stress Scale. Points that took you beyond the limits of human endurance! His stomach had become a volcano from all of the aspirin he was swallowing, and his tongue was black with bismuth from the cherry-flavored Pepto Bismol tablets that he constantly chewed.

The high school was overcrowded, and after the first few weeks of timidity, the students mostly threw their good intentions *("I be goin' to Princ'sun!")* out the window. The joint became as bad as it had been advertised: *The Lord of the Flies.* The chaos at Du Bois made it seem far more dangerous to Harold than his well-regulated penal institution back in Canada, where Hammermeister had fond memories of courteous and compliant murderers, rapists, and stickup artists. These American kids were savages. And those candy machines—all of that refined sugar was just adding fuel to the fire. It was in Harold's thesis, the magnum opus; you could read all about it there, or you could wait for the movie. Heh heh heh. Harold didn't know if he would have all that much say-so in the casting, but he needed to throw a glamorous woman into the picture—a kind of gal Friday. Something along the lines of a . . . Whitney Houston, say. Janet Jackson would be a stretch but . . . maybe Gloria Estefan. Or you could get a tough bird. Oprah Winfrey? He wondered if Whoopi was lined up with commitments.

Sean Duffy was giving the head custodian a hard time about Hammermeister, the custodians' new boss. Who *was* this asshole? Who did the motherfucker think he was? "Just because he's a vice-principal, does he think he's running the place? And Dr. White is letting him get away with it. That's what really riles me!" Duffy said. "White's going to retire, and he just doesn't give a shit anymore."

Mike knew that Duffy was hitting the juice pretty hard, but he could never quite catch him with liquor on his breath. Not that he really cared to—not as long as the man did his work. Was Duffy drinking vodka or something odorless? He always looked fairly fresh on Mondays, but as the week wore on, Duffy would get red-faced with bloodshot eyes. Increasingly, he would launch long tirades against Hammermeister—tirades that went beyond normal fury. Tirades inspired by alcohol.

One night after the swing-shift custodians left and the school was all but vacant, Centrick Cline started complaining to Duffy about Hammermeister. Hammermeister didn't like his nose- and earrings, was a racist motherfucker—"Hey, man, why didn't they hire Alec Baldwin for the job? This geek motherfucker said he comes by at three a.m. and he better not catch me in the weight room. I *clean* the weight room," Centrick Cline said, "an' I ain't 'posed to be in the weight room?"

Duffy's own latent anger flared. They stood together and pissed about Hammermeister for forty-five minutes. Then Duffy took a customary inspection of his area, making sure he had not left a beer can on a desk somewhere before turning out the lights. When this was done, it was close to one a.m. and Duffy slugged down two quick cans of Hamms, lit a Gitanes cigarette, and furtively entered Hammermeister's office. He stood before the tarantula cage a moment and then lifted the lid. He took another puff on the Gitanes and blew it on the spider.

The hairy spider shocked Duffy somewhat by setting itself down. But rather than confirming his worst fear by jumping, it froze. Duffy removed a long pencil from Hammermeister's desk and nervously positioned it over the spider's thorax. Closer and closer until suddenly Duffy thrust down at it, and the large body of the spider exploded like an egg, spurting yellow matter all over the room. When Duffy let go of the pencil the spider sprung straight up in the air and landed on his shoulder. He batted the spider down and scrambled out into the commons area, grabbed his coat, and fled the building.

Hammermeister came in Friday morning, and the first thing he noticed when he stepped into his office was that the lid of the tarantula cage was ajar. He hastily closed the door thinking that the spider had escaped, and he didn't want it to bolt out into the main office. Somehow he knew something like this was going to happen. He had a funny premonition.

Lulu lay dead on the seat of his executive chair, impaled with a number one Dixon. The Gitanes butt was there, but Hammermeister was struck dumb with grief and all he noticed as he looked about the room was the gruesome egg-yolk splattered essence of Lulu on his seat, the walls, and the ceiling. When he finally composed himself, he stepped out of his office and told the secretaries that the spider had been stabbed (already he had a pretty good idea which students did it), and that it had crawled up to his chair to die. This peculiar detail had Hammermeister on the verge of tears. He wrung his hands to no purpose. His face fell as if he were the comic Stan Laurel confronted with some absurd calamity. Hammermeister's favorite secretary, Cynthia—the nicest-looking woman in the building—put both of her hands on his shoulders and said, "Are you okay friend?" Hammermeister said that he was and woodenly made his way back into the office. Not fast enough for Rider to miss the tail end of the scene, however. Harold had a four-star migraine, but his gut lining was shredded from too much aspirin. He slammed down three Tylenol #4s and chased them with a Diet Coke. As he wiped the spider splatter from his chair with paper towels, the enormity of this personal loss caused his thighs to wobble. Harold gently lifted Lulu's corpse from the chair, neatly wrapped it in his handkerchief, and deposited the body in his top desk drawer. He sat at his desk with his head in his hands, wincing, waiting for the codeine to kick in, waiting possibly to just *blow,* perish, succumb to . . . internal spontaneous combustion! None of these things happened, and Hammermeister didn't get any worse. But he didn't get any better. He was alarmed to find that he stayed just the same for some time. At the foot of his chair he noticed a peculiar butt. It was a manufactured cigarette but the tobacco in it appeared to be almost black. He picked it up and examined it. No doubt it belonged to the assassin. He shoved it into an envelope for evidence and placed it in his top desk drawer, locking it.

The secretaries were so moved by Hammermeister's "nervous breakdown" that on the weekend they went to a pet shop and bought a replacement spider for fifty-five dollars. They pasted a little note on the cage that said, "Hey there, big boy, Lulu's back in town!"

On the following Friday Lulu number two was found murdered in the same fashion as number one had been: impaled with a number one Dixon. In evidence was another cigarette butt. A vile-smelling thing filled with blackish tobacco. This one was not a Gitanes, but it was unfiltered and it was foreign. Harold noticed such butts in an ashtray in Centrick Cline's janitor's closet. And what a place that was. There were militant anti-white slogans pasted on the wall, posters of Malcolm X and Huey Newton, and an accumulation of what seemed to be voodoo paraphernalia. Cline was not known to be a smoker. Yet most of the staff who smoked had keys to this closet and would sneak cigarettes there. Through-out the remainder of the day, Harold made hourly checks to see if any of the teachers had smoked such a cigarette during their prep periods. There were none to be found. But then there were none in the morning after the janitors' shift either.

Because of the pace and the pressing events of the school, Hammermeister found himself playing catch-up. This alarmed him since he was no procrastinator and was devoting his entire life to his job. How could life be so hard? On a number of occasions the senior vice-principal came down hard on him, implying that his Ph.D would have to wait until summer; there was a school to run. Hammermeister's objective "breath of fresh air"—the Canadian jet stream—was getting stale. Harold heard the talk and could only hope another burst of energy was available, and with it some new inspiration. When he was state superintendant of education, when the book was made into the movie and he was pulling in fifty-thousand-dollar speaking-engagement fees, Rider would still be on his fat, *Ahm a soul man, sweet potato pie* ass, forever mired deep in the middle of Detroit's blackboard jungle. In the meantime, not only was the staff all over him, but the students were becoming impossible to control. Harold was now somehow frightened by them—frightened terribly, and they could tell. Without Lulu next to him exuding encouragement, Harold was scared and overreacting. When he started nailing students with suspensions over petty grievances, Dr. White hit the ceiling.

White scheduled a personal one-on-one conference with Harold after school. He was far from courteous when he told Harold of the conference, and he did not stutter. The motherfucker was on the rag! Hammermeister staggered through the day, certain that he was about to be fired. But it wasn't that at all. White dumped a book challenge on Harold. At issue was John Steinbeck's *Cannery Row*—it had been called "filth" by an irate parent. White told Harold to handle it without saying exactly how. White just didn't want to get his hands dirty, that was all. There was a levy vote coming up and "how" had to mean: get the library to pull the book. Probably. Or did it?

After thinking the matter over, Harold went upstairs and spoke with the head librarian, who was horrified at the suggestion that the book be pulled. She vowed to "go to the wall." Hammermeister thoughtlessly warned her that librarians were a dime a dozen. It was the codeine talking. At least there were no witnesses.

That night Hammermeister left the building well after dark, and when he got to his car he discovered that all four tires were flat. Later, after a tow truck had hauled the car in, Hammermeister was informed that the tires were okay. The party that flattened them had simply removed the valve-core stems, then after the tires were deflated, poured Krazy Glue into the valves. They didn't pull the valves and run, they were brazen enough to wait until the tires went flat and then carefully squirted glue into the valves. They even took the trouble to screw the valve caps back on. Professionals! The valves were of a type that wasn't available at that hour of the night. The car would be ready tomorrow afternoon.

Head down, hands in pocket, Hammermeister furiously strode the three miles to his apartment through a biting *Nanook of the North* sleet storm. Just as he cut through the back entrance, where the covered parking stalls were located, he heard the abrupt rustling of leather jackets. He barely turned his head when a large tawny palm engulfed his face like an eclipse of the sun. The mighty hand snapped Harold's head back and firmly cradled it between the abductor's solid chest and a rock-hard bicep muscle. As his face was getting squashed Hammermeister suddenly felt his shins getting pounded with fierce woodpecker rapidity. The *tonk tonk tonk* sounds were those of an aluminum baseball bat. Hammermeister sagged halfway to the ground, but the large hand held him firmly like he was some kind of rag doll, and Hammermeister was not a small man. He stood over 6′2″, but with all the recent stress, he was down twenty pounds from his normal weight of two hundred and twelve.

The powerful hand that encased his face forced Harold's mouth to open in an "O" as a thick, wet, balled-up sock was rammed inside, a smelly cloth was placed over his eyes, and then, as Hammermeister heard the quick rip of duct ape, the stinking rag was adhered to his face like a layer of fast-drying cement.

There were two of them. The woodpecker with the bat continued to expertly peck at his legs, knees, and elbows, while the powerful strong-armed man spun him around, cranked a solid punch into Hammermeister's solar plexus, and then let him free fall to the ground. For the next moment Hammermeister was kicked and pounded mercilessly. He wondered if it was murder. The woodpecker was batting him in the head now but not with massive, clobbering blows. It felt like he was being poked with the knob end of the bat. Hammermeister felt himself sinking into the black vortex of hell, but then the shower of stars abruptly stopped, and in the frigid night air he heard his assailants' cold, rasping breaths tear through his brain like the sandpaper tongue of a lion. It occurred to Hammermeister that the dictum "when you lose your sight you become all eardrums" was profoundly true. Hammermeister could distinctly hear the different ways the two men breathed. If he lived to be a thousand, he would never forget the way these men breathed.

The stronger man grabbed his wrists and pulled them behind his back. As a knee came down on his spine, Hammermeister heard the sound of duct tape being unreeled and torn again, and soon his hands were bound as tightly as if he were displayed in a pillory. Then, with a suddenness that was frightening, he felt himself being lifted like a suitcase and lugged away from the lighted parking stalls to a very dark place. Even though his eyes were masked, he had been able to see shadows—now nothing. All the while the hollow bat rapped away at him. Neither of the abductors said a word. Hammermeister attempted to scream through the sock, but it was a scream that just couldn't get off the ground.

The pain in his shoulders felt like a crucifixion. Harold emitted a high-pitched scream through his nose as he was hauled off into yet a deeper forest of blackness. After what seemed like an interminable voyage, he was dropped roughly to the pavement, where he wet his pants in abject terror, waiting for the mechanical action of some sort of firearm—the rotation of a revolver cylinder, perhaps.

Both of the unseen men were panting heavily. Before they shot him, they were waiting to catch their breath. After a moment he felt their rough hands pulling at his pants, ripping them down to his knees as they turned him over on his stomach. Harold let his legs kick out wildly, and this only made the men laugh.

Suddenly there was a jolting, searing-hot pain in his right ass cheek. Hammermeister could smell his own smoldering flesh. The whole focus of his being gravitated to the burn.

The other pains were gone, he was nothing but a single right ass cheek. He writhed with the vigor of a freshly landed marlin. Then he felt himself lifted like a suitcase again. The two men heaved him up, and by the smell of things, Hammermeister realized he had been cast into the garbage dumpster before he even landed. His body was greeted by cardboard boxes, nail-embedded two-by-fours, metal cans, offal—the slime, grit, and stink of coffee grinds and cat litter, rib and chicken bones, and cigarette butts.

There was a loud clang as the two men dropped down the metal door. There was the sound of the metal lid reverberating, followed by the squeak of sneakers peeling across the snowy pavement of the back drive, as the thugs made a New Balance getaway.

The pain of the burn was incredible. It gave Hammermeister superhuman strength. In just seconds he was able to wrest his hands free from the tape. In another few seconds he pulled the tape from his face and spit out the sock that was choking him. By the time he slipped out of his bindings and pushed up the lid of the dumpster, the men were gone; the sleet had turned to snow, and a soft white blanket was laid about him like a kind of Currier and Ives/Edward Hopper Detroit. The Motor City.

Harold hastened to his room. After four tumblers of straight bourbon and a handful of Tylenol #4s, Hammermeister, still trembling, stood before his phone imagining what he would say to the police. When he finally called 911, a dispatcher answered with a disaffected tone and Hammermeister quickly replaced the phone in its cradle, afraid that his call would be traced and an aid car would be sent to his building.

He staggered into the bathroom and looked at the burn. It was hideous, his buttock exuded a watery yellow fluid, yet the letters KKK were crudely apparent. They had somehow taken him to a pre-arranged spot where the hot iron was cooking. This sort of vicious calculation made him think of gangs. Of gang planning. Somebody really was playing hardball. Not kids. Not janitors. But who else except fucking kids and fucking janitors? Funny that they didn't steal his wallet or shoot him. Rip-off artists shaking down a random victim in a parking lot would go for the money. Kids and janitors had access to a high-school metal shop where branding irons could be made.

Hammermeister went back to the phone to call an ambulance and was once again struck by indecision. It had been a warning. Maybe it would be best not to get the police involved. After all, how would he explain it to Dr. White?

One of the legs of his pants had been torn off completely. His legs were swollen with red and purple abrasions yet no bones were broken. He hurt all over, yet he really wasn't that hurt except for the searing pain on his buttock, which was an agony unlike anything he had ever known. Twenty minutes later, the burn seemed a thousand times more painful. Hammermeister took a warm shower and carefully soaped his wounds. It helped to take action. After he dried himself, he applied some antibiotic cream to his right butt cheek and placed a nonstick dressing on it. There was only one such dressing in his medicine cabinet that would fit it, a super jumbo—hell, in Detroit you would think that gun-trauma kits would be fast-moving items at every drugstore. After Hammermeister put on a pair of clean Jockey shorts, he went back to the phone where he found himself again paralyzed with indecision. As the booze and dope kicked in, Hammermeister felt a magical sense of relief. Suddenly he was packing his suitcase. He would drive back to Sondra in the morning. He missed her and the kids more than anything. God, he had been a dick. Sometimes it took a real shocker to bring you back to your senses. Well, this night had been an epiphany. The booze and the codeine were so good, so nice, he was thinking straight for the first time in years. He had a proper sense of perspective again.

In the morning Hammermeister abruptly came to in a world of pain. The burn felt more like a chemical burn, like a deep burn—like a *real deep* burn. He couldn't look at it. Instead he immediately dosed himself with vodka and codeine, and then, when he realized that his car was in the shop, he wondered about his plan for claiming the vehicle and driving back home after all. You could not drive when you could not sit down. Canada—shit, the bridge had been burned. He really hated his wife, and while he loved his kids in a way, it was one of those deals like "out of sight, out of mind." There was no going back.

Nipping from the pint of vodka, Hammermeister laced up a pair of heavy weatherproof brogues and walked to work, stopping at McDonalds for the two Egg McMuffins and a large coffee to go. He was going to the school where he would confront Duffy and Cline. He wouldn't even have to ask a question, all he would have to do is listen to them breathe.

It was a zoo day. The place was a zoo. First period the head of the English department—tough, smart, and formidable—came into his office and told him there was no way in hell her department was going to see John Steinbeck banished from the school. Hammermeister told her it was a matter between himself and the librarians, and she closed the door, took three powerful strides over to his desk where he stood looking through his memos. "Now you just wait here, buster!" In casting this role, Harold was suddenly thinking in terms of Bette Midler or Cher on a tirade.

Boy! Twenty-five Hans Seyle stress points for that one. Hammermeister had tried to appeal to her sense of reason. "We've got a levy coming up, we don't need this right now. What will you say if I tell you we can't buy new language-arts books this fall?" His voice was hollow. His legs, the shins especially, began to hurt more than the burn on his ass. He gulped down more codeine with the last of his cold coffee. Why in the hell had he come back to this zoo? To nail Centrick Cline and Sean Duffy, that's why—and from the stack of morning memos he could see that both of them had already called in sick. His secretary gave him their numbers, and he called them both at home. Neither of the malefactors answered their phones. Off somewhere together, drunk, sniggering in iniquitous delight.

Later that morning he was forced to phone the parent who had raised the hullabaloo about *Cannery Row*. She was a real kook. What the fuck! Yet Hammermeister deferred to her, sympathized and told her off the record that he was in full agreement with her. It was necessary to placate this woman. Dr. White had insisted upon it. Hadn't he?

Events quickly came to a head when the issue was thrown in at the tail end of the monthly board of directors meeting the next evening. The librarians throughout the district were on hand, as were librarians from nearby school districts. The word spread fast. "Oh God," Hammermeister thought, "a cause célèbre." He had to go home and crash before the meeting, and then, heavily medicated, he overslept and showed up looking like Howard Beals coming in to deliver that news in that old movie *Network*. Harold's buzzcut was sticky with tape, he needed a shave—he looked like a madman. But he was high and didn't care. He had not prepared for the debate; he had decided to just "wing it." Sometimes it paid to be spontaneous and genuine. You were walking on thin ice, but sometimes it did work.

The W. E. B. Du Bois High School librarian was dressed like a model of propriety. Armed with a thick packet of note cards, which she hardly ever seemed to look at, she gave a convincing

pro-First Amendment presentation. This was followed by an eloquent statement by the head of the English department. Then
Hammermeister suddenly found himself on his feet making
counterarguments, all weak and vapid. The beneficial effects of the
nap were short-lived. He was strung out from too much booze and
Tylenol #4, and as he scanned the room looking for a sympathetic
face, the fact that there seemed to be none inflamed him with
hollow fury. This was a setup. The board members, the superintendent, and his own principal looked at him hard. The formality
of the room was hard, as were the faces of the people sitting in the
gallery. A press photographer snapped photos of Hammermeister,
and as he did so, a feeling of depersonalization overcame the Canadian. Exhausted by the previous evening, the present onslaught
was too much for him. He found himself saying, over and over
again, that he was about to receive a doctorate in education, as if
that were germane to the situation at hand. He said something
about how a society that was too liberal became soft and festered
with decay. Harold said something about the rightness of trying to
change society for the better turning to "wrongness" when everyone focused on gender, sexual entitlement, and the color of skin.
Whatever happened to genuine achievement leading to entitlement? You couldn't play center for the Tigers just because you
were white. No! You had to be the best center fielder in Detroit. So
what was the problem? What did sex or color have to do with
genuine achievement? Why did society have to allocate prizes and
create heroes out of sex perverts and deluded, talentless know-
nothings, be they black, white, or brown? Why did they have to
hand the keys to power over to fools? The right-minded liberal
inclination to make the "all men are created equal" utopia had led
to ruin. Utopia-building, good in theory, simply did not work anymore. It only led to ruin, decay, and dispersion. It was time to
resort back to the police state. Like Duffy had said—Singapore!

Somewhere in the back of his brain he realized it was the codeine talking—a medicinal "misadventure," yet Hammermeister
could not stop himself. He told the audience that America was
going down the sewer as it coddled weaklings and slackers. He
began to talk of racial polarization and the subway shooters, until

finally the superintendent, aghast at Hammermeister's presentation from the first, shot him a withering look and cut him off. "That will do, Mr. Hammermeister. Thank you for your views."

In the morning, Dr. White was sitting in Hammermeister's chair reading through Hammermeister's thesis when Harold came in. He looked up at the Canadian and said, "We'll pay your salary through the year, but don't ask for any job recommendations. You aren't gonna want my recommendation. I'm sorry for you, huh-huh-huh-Harold. There are people of cuh-cuh-cuh-color out there who can dance circles around your qualifications. It's my fault for letting you buh-buh-buh-bullshit me during the interview. I wanted to hire a white man. I wanted some diversity. I wanted you to succeed, but you're a buh-buh-buh-bad person!"

"I didn't bullshit you. I can do this job. I can do this job!" Hammermeister began to spill his guts about the janitors, his beating and abduction. Dr. White drew his head back in alarm.

"You don't believe me, do you?" Hammermeister shouted. He pulled down his pants and showed the man the burn on his ass and the bruises on his legs. "It looks like Kaposki's or whatever they call it." Hammermeister began to spin his theory that the custodians—Duffy and Cline, the weight lifter—had beaten him, gang-bangers had stabbed his spiders . . . and so on.

"That's the most preposterous thing I've ever heard. For one thing, those spiders were ridiculous, and for another, Duffy has been with us for ten years and I've never heard a single buh-buh-buh-bad word—"

"Bullshit! He's an alcoholic! He's a drunk! Everybody knows it. Where have you been?"

"He hasn't taken a sick day in the whole ten years," the principal said incredulously. "The buh-buh-buh-best attendance record in the district, sh-sh-sh-short of my own."

"Alcoholics are *like* that. With their low self-esteem, they over-compensate at work. Have you ever read *The Nigger of the Narcissus*, Sidney? Do you know the character, Waite? That piss-and-moan, do-nothing crybaby! Well, *that's* who Duffy is. *Duffy is Johnny Waite!* And if you haven't read the book—judging by that vacant look on your face, I dare say you haven't—then by God you should!"

"Harold. I don't know what happened to your legs or how you got that burn, but the alcohol fumes in here are bad enough to knock a person down. I think you should check yourself into . . . a facility! The district has a progressive policy—"

"Duffy and that burrhead in the gym, Cline—that's what you call a bad nigger."

"That's it! I've heard enough—you've got fifteen minutes before I call the police!" Dr. White said, standing up. "Puh-puh-puh-pack your stuff and get out."

"Fine," Hammermeister said. "Fifteen minutes. That's just fine. 'The custodians are a little trouble spot,' remember? 'They seem to defy our coping skills,' remember? Shit, why did I have to be born white! It's a curse!"

The principal walked out of the room, shutting the door behind him.

Hammermeister began slamming his personal supplies into a box. There wasn't much. He picked up *Blackboard Jungle 1997* and began to read. There was the truth. The American public would be shocked if they came to these schools and observed. Something very dangerous was going on inside. Well, the public did come. They were invited to come with open arms, but only to well-orchestrated events with canned speeches, lies, bullshit inspiration. If America really knew what was going on, it would be shocked. If they could see the school, day in and day out. The quality of education was an abomination!

Harold began to dictate into his personal recorder. "The school-board system: you've got a superintendent. What is his job? Why, he goes to a meeting now and then. He gets a haircut. Plays golf. Around levy time he sweet-talks some newspaper people. The tax-payers would be better off if they let the district secretary run things! When I came into this field I thought that by hard work and determination I could make a difference, but I have been swallowed up in chaos and futility. The American public has been greatly deceived! It is not only your hard-earned tax dollars that I am concerned about, it is our youth and the future of this once great nation! We need parental involvement. You can't send them to us for seven hours and expect us to undo. They're going loco. We need more metal detectors in the school. We need drug testing. We need a crime-prevention program. There should even be AIDS testing and quarantine like they've got over in Cuba. Are we going to let the rotten apples spoil the whole barrel? Goddamn it, democracy just isn't cutting it anymore. Someone has to step in and get the fucking trains running on time again or it's closing time in the gardens of the West!"

Two uniformed police officers in squeaky leather jackets stepped warily into Hammermeister's office. Harold looked at his watch. Fifteen minutes? "It hasn't been fifteen minutes."

"It's time to go," one of the police officers said.

Hammermeister looked at the box. He threw his thesis in it. He attempted to place Lulu's glass cage in the box but it was too large. He set it back on the desk. He would have to carry the cage under one arm, and the box with the thesis, the Dixon pencils, coffee mug, Pepto Bismol, aspirin, Tylenol #4s, Advil, his spare sports coat and neckties, etc., under the other arm. Except that now he was so spaced from the codeine and round-the-clock vodka drinking that he knew he would never manage it.

"Let's go," the officer said.

Hammermeister stuffed his pockets with the codeine #4s, then on impulse flipped the thesis into the wastebasket, dumping the remainder of the box in after it—the pencils, coffee cup, neckties, spare sports jacket, everything. He was dizzy with rage. He had a crazy impulse to dash over to the office safe and grab the nine-millimeter they recently pulled off a drug peddler and fire off a few rounds. If Sean Duffy and Centrick Cline were not there, he'd just shoot . . . whomever. Get Rider and White first. Instead, he flung the cardboard box aside and placed Lulu's empty cage on top of his wastebasket. He raised a pebble-leather, oxblood brogue over the cage and then stepped down several times, crunching the glass.

The police officers braced for action, but then Hammermeister sagged. The only picture that came to his mind now were those of the flattened tires of his Ford. Gone was the movie, the new and better wife, the Lincoln, polo, and country clubbing. His shoulders slumped and he turned to them defeated. "I'm ready," Harold said with a melodramatic flourish, presenting his hands for cuffing. "Read me my Miranda and let's clear out of this place."

The police officers, one short, one tall, exchanged a significant look. The short one said, "No need for the handcuffs, sir. They just want you off the grounds. It's a routine eighty-six, that's all. They just want you to leave."

Hammermeister seemed disappointed that he was not under arrest. He felt cheated but let the police officers lead him through the party of "concerned" but not entirely unsympathetic office secretaries. They led him out into the throng of students who had heard the sound of smashed glass and had gathered to witness what they intuitively knew was a very strange and very bad scene. Several of the students wondered out loud as to what was going on. One of these, a student who had once been mesmerized by Hammermeister's power of positive thinking spiel, and who had a certain affection for the former junior vice-principal asked, "Wha'chew got, man?"

Hammermeister looked over his shoulder and cried, "Murder one."

And with that he was led out to the parking lot to a squad car, driven to the bus stop, and dumped off. He had never taken a bus in America, didn't know how, didn't know when one was coming, and when he could no longer stand the cold, he gulped down a couple more codeine tablets with a slug of vodka and surveyed the landscape before him. Hammermeister realized he was the only Caucasian in the neighborhood, and he began to feel conspicuous. A couple of thugs, also brown bagging, joined him at the bus shelter. One carried a ghetto blaster. Clarence "Frogman" Henry was singing, "I'm a lonely frog, I ain't got no home."* Hammermeister watched as the man inserted a rock in a crack pipe and took a hit off of it before passing it to his companion.

---

* "Ain't Got No Home" by Clarence Henry. ©1956 (Renewed) Arc Music Corporation. All Rights Reserved. Used by Permission.

Moving from the shelter of the plexiglass bus stop, Hammermeister dropped his head down against yet another *Nanook of the North* sleet storm. A mere pedestrian in the heart of the Motor City, new citizen John Harold Hammermeister caught the shoe-leather express back to his apartment.

Suketu Mehta

Gare du Nord

From *Harper's Magazine*

EIBRAHIM rented the back room in the Café du Nord, where he had set up four tables and to which he brought, through a small window in the cramped kitchen, masala dosas, idlis, meat curry, vegetable curry, and parathas.

Outside the café, on the sidewalk, was a blackboard that said, "Masala dosa is ready."

Eibrahim was a Tamil from Vietnam. He spoke, in order of fluency, Vietnamese, French, Tamil, Hindi, and English. As we left, he would always give us a paratha wrapped in aluminum foil—"from the heart," he would explain, pressing the package to his heart before presenting it to us.

A mixed lot ate at Eibrahim's. Mostly they were Tamils from Pondicherry or Sri Lanka, with the occasional French tourist of ethnic food who would try to eat her dosa clumsily with her fingers, all the while reading Nâzim Hikmet in translation. Then Eibrahim would bring her a fork. He was always very solicitous of his female French customers, though in a kind rather than an obeisant way. We once went to the restaurant with Françoise, and all four tables were full of Tamil men. Upon seeing Françoise, Eibrahim motioned to three men at a table, and they quietly took up their plates and marched to the café in the other room.

The boundary between the restaurant and the café was invisible—there was no wall between the two; nonetheless, the division was as palpable as if it were of concrete. In the café were Algerians, Moroccans, travelers from the station, and working-class Frenchmen. There was a fight, often involving knives, almost every night. But none of the tough guys came to the back, although we had to pass through the café to get to the restaurant, and if we wanted a beer Eibrahim had to get it from the woman who ran the café. So, eating our dosas, we could watch the fracas in the café in comfort and safety. Nobody fought in the restaurant. Ever. Although we suspected that many of the Tamils eating with their heads close together over their curry were discussing ways to finance the Tigers in their homeland.

Eibrahim's was always a good place to take visiting relatives and friends; it showed a side of Paris not represented in the better arrondissements. No statuary or multicolored fountains, no aged ornate structures, no harmonious marriage of stone and river. The tables and chairs were the cheapest available; the room was filled with the noise of the video game and the jukebox from the café. Physically, the restaurant could have been in any large metropolis where exiles gathered. And it was cheap. For thirty francs, one could get a masala dosa with chutney and sambar and a beer. The sambar would be hot on alternate days; the other times it would be reheated without patience. But, we reasoned, it was the one and only place in Paris we could get dosas. And our guests liked to see Eibrahim recognize us, talk to us; it reassured them that we had found our bearings in the large city, that someone would notice if we were absent for long.

Those were very good times that year in Paris. We had plenty of money, plenty of friends, and the weather was fine. In the mornings we drank coffee and in the evenings we drank wine. Yes, in the mornings we drank coffee and in the evenings, wine. The tourists came in busloads around Notre Dame and the world was on holiday. Everyone was under thirty. The sunlight fell down in sheets on the white walls of the buildings outside our window. Sometimes we could see people in the windows facing us. Two girls in the spring afternoon came and sat by the window and smoked cigarettes as the light fell on their white faces and legs. It became hot, but it was the heat of Paris in June, warming rather than enervating, the kind of heat in which you go out after seven, walk endlessly, and have your dinner at a sidewalk table around eleven: a glass of slightly cold Beaujolais and a large salad. The university students spent long afternoons in the small cinemas that showed American films of the Forties: Spencer Tracy and Frank Capra never died here. In the evenings we would go to the house of our friend Françoise, and she would put on scandalous songs by Serge Gainsbourg. Two rooms full of people would go about their business of eating, laughing, talking, while the loudspeaker poured forth the prolonged ecstasies of a couple making slow and intense love.

It was a very long summer. The heat began in early May and increased in intensity till by the end of July the Parisians fled the city in masses for the sea. We had the city to ourselves, except for the tourists. The cafés near the river were filled with voices from Atlanta, San Francisco, the Upper West Side of Manhattan. But the population at Eibrahim's remained stable—the Tamils could not afford to go away on holiday and besides quite welcomed the heat. It may have been our imaginations, but the food seemed to get hotter as the summer progressed. When we went with Françoise, we would have to ask Eibrahim to tone down the heat for her sake.

It was toward the end of one of those long days, when it seemed impossible that the light would ever go out of the sky, that Eibrahim sat down with us. There were about seven of us, and we had been eating and drinking for over three hours. We had run through the limited repertoire of his kitchen, and the Tamil woman in there had hung up her apron and gone home. But the beer was still flowing, and we were in an excellent mood. We offered to buy Eibrahim a beer.

"I cannot," he said, indicating the white cap on his skull. "Mussulman."

"And yet you have no problems serving the devil's drink to us unbelievers!" said Jean.

Eibrahim laughed and said, "Even in my country I ran a bar."

"What *is* your country?" Françoise asked.

Eibrahim put his hands on the table, crossed them, and finally responded, "I come from Vietnam. I am Tamil but I come from Vietnam."

"Do you still have family there?"

"Yes." He was speaking very slowly. "I have . . . my wife is there, and my three children. I have not seen them since 1973. Nineteen years. And four months."

No one was left in Eibrahim's side of the café but us; in the outside room a swarthy man stood at the counter drinking his beer in silence. All of a sudden the pinball machine in the café erupted in a staccato medley of sounds. No one was standing in front of it; the machine was singing to the void.

"It was because of the war?" asked Françoise.

"The war." Eibrahim wiped his forehead with his hand. "Yes. You know, when I first met my wife she was only a baby. She was . . . she is my uncle's daughter. We used to play in the street, in Saigon. You know I grew up with my wife. Almost every day for twenty-five years I spent with her. So then, since 1973 I have not seen her. Do you know what it means? It means that one day I see her, and then the soldiers come, and the next day I am in Paris and my life is completely different. Three children she gave me, two sons and a little daughter. But she is alive. She will come to me, of that I am sure."

"Why did you leave?" asked Jean with his usual tactlessness. "Why did you abandon your wife and children?"

Eibrahim's face jerked up. "It is none of your business," he said, and stood up. He looked down at us, and we knew we would have to leave.

After we left the restaurant, we walked around outside the Gare du Nord. It was a Tuesday night, and we were the only people out, but we were in such good spirits that we were a crowd all by ourselves; we made the street feel inhabited. The buildings around the Gare du Nord are filled with immigrants; it is as if having come off the train from their distant homes, they were so exhausted by the journey that they put bag and baggage down in the first empty room they saw. It is not a pretty area, and the noise of trains and cars consumes the neighborhood from an early hour. But maybe what keeps the immigrants in the area is the knowledge that the first door to home is just there, in the station, two blocks away. The energy of travelers is comforting, for it makes us feel that the whole world, like us, is transient.

We were walking along the street when two Arab boys strode toward us very fast. They plunged right into the middle of our group, and Françoise gasped, whirled, and called out at their departing backs, *"Salaud!"* The boys stopped, turned, and walked slowly toward us. Françoise and the boys started arguing vehemently. We gathered that one of them had squeezed her body as he brushed past her. "I am Arabian and I can do what I want!" said the boy to Françoise.

There were only two of them, and there were four men in our group, but except for Jean we were all foreigners, and we could not follow the argument. Jean stood next to Françoise and grabbed the boy by the throat. At this, the boy's friend pulled out a knife and slashed at Jean, cutting his arm. For a moment we all stopped, astounded, because now we had no knowledge of what we were supposed to do. The boys ran. We clustered around Jean helplessly as blood leaked out from his arm. But it was not very much blood, and it stopped soon. Somebody had Band-Aids in her purse, and we put a couple on Jean's arm.

We took the Metro to Les Halles in silence. Then somebody or the other joked about the incident and everyone laughed desperately. Out beside the fountain in Les Halles there were hundreds of people enjoying the summer night, and we all felt better. There was a café open facing the fountain, and we sat on the terrace and drank and laughed. All around us were young Greeks, young Swedes, Koreans, Americans, Argentineans, Britons; from all the continents of the world they had come to Paris with their backpacks and their savings from part-time and summer jobs as store clerks, apple pickers, temporary secretaries, and messengers. Now they could enjoy the fruits of their labor. They ate little but bread and cheese, stayed four to a room in miserable no-star hotels. Their frugality with money lasted during the day, but at night these young people spent fantastic amounts on drinks in expensive nightclubs and cafés—at night they saw the person with the enchanting smile sitting in the other corner of the room. It was the night they had wept and fasted, wept and prayed for.

Then one day Eibrahim's restaurant vanished. When we went to the café, after being out of the country for some months, we were told by the Arab owner of the room in front that she now owned the whole place. No more masala dosas. But, the new owner also told us, we would find Eibrahim in his apartment, close by, and she gave us the address.

Françoise was with us; she wanted to see him. So we all went to the address and climbed the six flights to the top. We knocked. Eibrahim himself opened the door. He did not recognize us. Then we spoke to him in the few Tamil words we knew and he smiled. *"Bonjour,"* he said, opening the door.

Eibrahim's apartment was very small, very neat. We sat on the same chairs we used to sit on in his café. Françoise leaned forward. "We missed you, my friend. And your dosas."

Eibrahim rose. "I cannot give you dosas here. The woman is gone. But you will have some tea?"

We consented and he went into the kitchen. We all turned, out of habit, to the window, which looked out over a courtyard and blue-gray rooftops, studded with red chimneys standing like sentries. It was very quiet here and none of us said a word, afraid we would say something so inconsequential it would be stupid, when the situation demanded the question we could not ask, could not even think to ourselves in the silences of our own minds: "What are we doing here?"

Eibrahim returned with the tea things on a tray, beautiful inlaid teacups from Vietnam, and he poured the tea for us. We asked why he had closed his restaurant.

"I lost too much money," he said solemnly.

We all burst out laughing. It had been evident to everybody that Eibrahim was a lousy businessman: he undercharged his customers more often than not, he was always giving out free food "from the heart," and the prices he charged could barely have covered his costs. He was surprised at our mirth, but then he laughed along with us. He confessed, "I don't know about restaurants. It wiped out my savings."

He looked so comically despondent that we couldn't stop laughing.

"The Algerian madame of the café was kind. I owed her three months' rent, which she did not collect. She told me I am welcome to come back to her café, but only to play pinball."

We laughed long and hard. We wiped the tears from our eyes and sipped the tea.

"So what will you do now?" Françoise asked him.

Eibrahim treated her question with respect. He took his time, then he looked up and replied, "I must wait. My wife will come here."

He had made his choice. Of all the countries in the world he could go to, or return to, Eibrahim chose to stay here in this high room in Paris, and wait. We talked to him some more, and then we had to go. But Françoise wanted to stay. We said goodbye to her and to Eibrahim.

It was January then, and the trees by the river stood frozen and white against the very blue sky. When we walked, our footsteps echoed on the stone. It was a fine thing to get up very early and warm ourselves with a large bowl of chocolate at the corner *tabac,* and watch the tradesmen, deliverymen, and cleaning women come in and get cigarettes, papers, and coffee. Then we turned our attention to the *International Herald Tribune* and read with a pleasant sense of distance about the tumult back home. Outside the window we could see the stalls being set up for the market on the *place.*

Jean came up to the table and sat down opposite. *"Un petit noir,"* he said to the waiter. "Have you spoken to Françoise?" he asked. "She has been with Eibrahim for a month. She goes home to him." Jean did not look as if he were happy with this development.

We said nothing; we did not need to. Jean had plenty to say for all of us. "It is not right, there is something not right about this. A married man . . . with children also. And they are so completely different. I see nothing but sadness. Nothing but sadness to come out of this." He shook his head, drank his coffee, threw a coin down on the table, and left to go to work. Jean worked in the Eighth, and the Eighth was a very different district from the Fifth, where all of us lived. Poor Jean could never make sense of the difference.

We saw Françoise twice that winter, first alone and then with Eibrahim. The first time, a few of us went to listen to a Polish choir in L'Église St. Julien. Françoise closed her eyes during the music, swaying slightly with pleasure as the singers whispered, *"Pax, pax, pax,"* before breaking out into a tremendous "Amen" in time with the organ. She was smiling, and in that light her face was suffused with color; she looked beautiful and fragile, as if she were made of Dresden china.

Afterward, at dinner, she told us, "I didn't think it could happen to me. Really, I am so in love." Again she could not help smiling, but she lifted her hand with the fork still in it to cover her face. Then she looked at us trying to conceal her smile, but we could see it in her eyes. We stopped eating and broke out in laughter. Someone raised his glass and we all clinked, twice, *"Chin. Chin."*

The second time, Françoise and Eibrahim had dinner at our apartment. He was very grave, and he ate with great decorum. It felt a little strange, we told him, for *us* to be feeding *him*. Our cooking had made the apartment feel quite warm. Through the opened window we could hear the buzzer of the door to the building below, and footsteps in the courtyard. There was Debussy on the radio and a bouquet of lilies on the table. Françoise and Eibrahim avoided touching each other, but we could sense an intimate connection between them, as if they were really sitting very close. When he spoke, her body would turn toward his.

Françoise had led a proper Sixteenth-Arrondissement life until she fell into our company. She told us about how, when she was growing up, she was ill for a time, and for a month every year she would be sent to St. Honoré-les-Bains to take the waters. Her world was as exotic to us as if she had been raised on the steppes of Mongolia or the streets of Beirut, and we listened with interest. "When I am out of France," she said, "all my thoughts are clearer, I am filled with curiosity, and I can make connections between random events. Even when I am away for very long, exile is tonic for me."

"For me, it is not a matter of choice," said Eibrahim. We all turned toward him. He had finished his coffee, and rose from the table and walked over to the window. He was looking out, trying to see beyond the buildings, but the window only opened onto the courtyard and he could see just a little sky. He had his arms stretched out, holding the sides of the open window, his back to us. Françoise got up and went over to him, standing by him in silence, her eyes looking at his face.

He said something to her, very softly, so that only she could hear, and she put her arm up and touched his shoulder. Many worlds met in that gesture, vast distances were shattered. That light touch was more intimate than the most passionate embrace, and all of us, the spectators, felt our hearts breaking. Then they turned back to face us and smiled, both at the same time.

As they left, we presented Eibrahim with the rest of the cake he had so liked, wrapped up in a piece of foil, "from the heart." He looked astonished for a moment, then he got the joke and laughed, very naturally. They went out into the cold, holding hands.

One day in the spring his wife came to him. She called him from the Gare du Nord. When he met her at the station, she had all their children with her, and they looked at Eibrahim with dark, luminous eyes. They stood on the platform for a moment, Eibrahim's wife and children facing him, then he reached out and touched his eldest son on his head. His son stood still. Eibrahim withdrew his hand, and all of them walked down the platform toward the exit.

We did not hear from either Françoise or Eibrahim for a long time after that. Eventually, we became worried about Françoise and decided to drop by her apartment. When she opened the door, we didn't recognize her for a moment, she had lost so much weight. She smelled strongly of cigarettes, and the apartment was filled with a blue haze. The first thing we did upon entering was to open the windows and let in the sun and the air. Françoise sat silently on the sofa, her head down. For the next hour, we cleaned her rooms thoroughly, washed all the dishes, got the junk off the floor, and rearranged the books and CDs. When the place was more habitable, we poured some wine for Françoise and ourselves, and sat down with her on the sofa. We waited for her to speak. We had time. The afternoon sun came slanting and sneaking into the apartment, coloring our thoughts insidiously. We sipped the wine and looked out of the window at the clouds moving across the sky. The refrigerator motor stopped with a shudder, and we realized that we notice the absence of sound more than we notice sound itself. Silence is tangible; you can run it between your hands like folds of silk.

"You know, he has beautiful eyes," Françoise said. "When he takes off his glasses, he has very beautiful eyes." Then she was crying, a little.

There are people who come to Paris and never visit the Louvre or the Eiffel Tower. We were like that. The entire time we stayed in Paris, we went around these two monuments, we looked at them from a distance, we directed visitors to them, but we never went there ourselves. This was not a conscious decision. It was just that . . . these two landmarks were so much *there*. We had heard so much, read so much about them, seen them in so many films, that we felt we had experienced both without being *in* them. Maybe this is the process of understanding a love that is not yours.

When we left Paris, a little while later, both Françoise and Eibrahim, arriving separately, came to see us off. We were taking the boat train to London from the Gare du Nord. They sat with us for one last coffee at the station café. People waited with their bags at the tables around us, listening to the messages echoing through the station. Some would go on to Belgium and Köln; some had taken the night train from Moscow and were rousing themselves from the journey with a strong coffee, waiting for their relatives to come and claim them. Nobody in this café was there by design; we were all in transit. The morning newspapers were filling up the racks in front of the *tabac* with urgent messages from all over the world.

When the waiter brought our coffees, Eibrahim's head dropped.

Françoise understood immediately and gave the waiter a fifty-franc note for all of us.

"When do you come to Paris again?" she asked us. The situation seemed so normal, all of us sitting around a table talking as if nothing had changed, as if it were the previous summer. And, in fact, Eibrahim's former restaurant was not two minutes' walk from where we were sitting; we could all so easily go there, forget everything, and sit down to a meal of dosas and idlis and a couple of beers.

We let Françoise's question lie on the table between us; we could not answer it. And she knew that, for immediately after asking it, she leaned back in her chair. She had made her effort. Now she was very tired.

"I have a little present for you," said Eibrahim. He reached into his jacket and came out with a small package badly wrapped in a red-and-green paper that had *"Joyeux Noël"* written all over it.

The little present was a heart; that is, a clear plastic model of the human heart, showing, in different colors, all the multiple arteries, veins, chambers, and valves. Accompanying it was a little booklet titled "The Illustrated Heart," which explained in scientific detail the parts of the heart and their functions. As we held the heart, and all of us looked closely at it, it seemed almost to throb with life.

"It is such a complicated thing, the heart," explained Eibrahim.

"No, it is not," said Françoise. "To me it is very simple." She was not looking at anybody, but her palms were open on her lap as if they were a book and she was trying hard to read what was written on them. Or maybe she was just trying very hard not to show us her eyes.

There was a vast silence, shadows between the seconds. Everything—all questions, answers, and possibilities—was suspended. Then Eibrahim leaned forward and gently covered Françoise's palms with his.

Our train was called and we stood up to leave.

It was cloudy, threatening to rain. Ten minutes out of the station the train slowed, then stopped altogether, in the desolation. All around us were housing projects. Brown faces looked out at us from some of the windows. The faces stared at us without moving, looking at the stalled train.

Then, summoning up some last reserve of will from the depths of its being, the train lurched forward, and we were once again on our way.

Carolyn Cooke

Eating Dirt

From *New England Review*

W E TURNED at the Cheese House, which was round and painted yellow, gouged with black holes. After that, the country seemed real. Horses stood bored behind barbed wire. The skeletons of gray barns rattled beside long farmhouses painted white and green. Old cars multiplied, so did snowmobiles tilted on the green humps of yards, toy tractors, red bicycles leaning up against red maples, tire swings.

Mum drove. Grand sat wide and ladylike beside her and asked, wasn't it comical to see reindeer on the roof in June? I looked up and saw ropes of metal in the shape of a sleigh and a broken plastic Santa Claus hung down behind the sleigh instead of commanding it, his black whip broken in two. "Isn't it just like those Burnses? Haven't they always been nothing?" Grand said.

"Oh, Mumma, you old snob," Mum said, and laughed.

"Old mother Burns, Sue Burns, Gem Burns, that whole crowd—nothing," said Grand. "The old man didn't know a toilet from a washbowl."

"Oh, Mumma. I bet they're saying in there, There goes old Maggie. Remember her father, that mean old gardener?"

"My father was the son of a duke!" Grand said. The words flew up like hands in front of her face.

"That's what he said," Mum said.

Grand clutched her big square purse in her lap like a baby she kept smoothing down. A car passed around us. Mum veered the wheel. "Jesus God, maniacs!" she said.

"Did you bring a bottle?" Grand said.

"I brought a bottle of wine," Mum said.

"Coo, wine!" Grand said.

"They don't have to drink it today," Mum said. "They could put it aside."

"I brought a *bottle*," said Grand.

We rode through a jungle of birches and hackmatack and maple and pine. Aunt Annie and Uncle Owen and all their kids had just moved back from wherever they had been living, and had been camped out at the Dysharts' for two months. The Dysharts had five or six kids. It was supposed to be a picnic.

We drove up alongside the Dysharts', where they kept more cars than people. They all stayed in two toy-looking houses—one house where they ate, with the TV and the stove, and the other house where some of them slept. The first person we saw was Louise in the yard with her horse, her Palomino; her hand on the side of the horse's head reminded me of last time, of the head coming down to take the shucked clams we held out on our palms. Louise was my age, eight. She had pink cheeks and wore a dirty pink dress. She never seemed exasperated by anyone. She waved and ran on toward us, her bare feet kicking up to the backs of her knees.

The Dysharts' other four or five kids and Aunt Annie and Uncle Owen's four kids were running all over the field between the two houses. Aunt Annie and Mrs. Dyshart spilled out the kitchen door. They both had curly hair to their shoulders and pink-and-white checkered one-piece bathing suits that tied at the backs of their necks. They had red toenails and cut-off blue jeans for shorts, and glasses rattling ice in their hands. Uncle Owen and Louise's father, Mr. Dyshart, walked out behind them, two skinny men holding cigarettes cupped behind their hands, all dressed in long pants and black shoes and socks, and short-sleeved shirts. They all four stood in the driveway.

Mum drove carefully, her knuckles curved over the steering. She slammed on the brakes whenever she saw a person. "Jesus God!"

she said. "These kids are *right under* my wheels." Grand ran red lipstick over her lips and kissed a Kleenex. Mum parked the car and jumped out of her side. She had on blue jeans shorts too, but she was still dramatic—skinny in a black tee shirt, with her pixie cut and cat's-eye dark glasses.

Louise ran up and looked in the window. "Oh, hi," she said. "I like your haircut. What's your name?"

"I am *Molly,*" I said.

"I forgot. You can see my horse if you want."

My cousins and the Dyshart kids yelled in the yard. Aunt Annie opened the car door on Grand's side and she and Grand jabbed their cheeks at each other. Grand brought a bottle of Jim Beam out of her purse and snapped the clasp closed again, a rich-sounding sigh and a click. "Oh, Maggie, we were hoping for one of your pies," Uncle Owen joked. Grand flapped her arms at him, smiled and puckered her lips.

"Isn't he comical?" she said. Uncle Owen took the bottle and Grand's arm and hauled her out of the car. Grand's dress spread out when she stood up and shrunk up her leg past the knee.

Troy was the only one of the kids Grand didn't know about. He was already two, and Aunt Annie and Uncle Owen hadn't mentioned him yet because Grand would have had such a fit it would probably have sent her to bed for a year. We all said this, but Grand had gone to bed for a month every time Aunt Annie had another baby, and even if Grand *had* gone to bed for a year because of Troy, she would have been out now.

It was exciting, having Grand not know, wondering when she would add it up. Troy, who no one ever noticed or thought about, didn't usually seem real. He sat on the ground away from the kids on the field. His hair hung in white whips on his shoulders, and he didn't really play. He never looked up at any of the other kids, just kept his head bent over his stick, talking to it. It was easy to tell which one he was. He was small for his age, not real. He wore a pair of overalls that all my cousins had worn before. He was stirring dirt in a tin cup with a spoon and talking to a stick. It seemed impossible, even among my running cousins and five or six Dyshart kids on the field, that Grand did not notice Troy now, and see who he was. It made her seem stupid—there was Troy, big as life, and Grand didn't even notice. The adults made their eyes wide and rolled them at each other while Grand made her way to the kitchen house, busy looking down the two white poles of her legs to her sneakers in the rutty dirt.

The day dragged the way it always did once we got out of the car. I had forgotten my cousins the way Louise had forgotten me. Cousin Trudy stayed close to Troy, not playing with him. She had a dirty doll hanging from her hand by the hair and she didn't remember me from the last time. We all stood around the dirt yard for a long time with our arms hanging down—my cousins Ross and Lenny and Trudy and Troy and then the Dyshart kids, all names and faces, and Louise.

"What'd you get for Christmas, Molly?" Lenny asked.

"A desk," I said.

"A *desk?* I got about $300 worth of tropical fish," he said.

"Where are they now, big shot?" Ross said.

We climbed stairs in the second house, up to the room where the kids lived. It seemed to be made of girls' dresses, blue jeans and red flannel printed with cowboys and Indians, and everything smelled warm of wood and sugar and pee.

"I'm so bored," Lenny sighed.

"We're never going to eat, they're having drinks," Ross said. He lit matches and tossed them lighted out the window.

"I thought it was a picnic," I said.

"Yeah, right," Ross said. "A *picnic.*"

"What'd you have before?" Lenny said.

"I had a honey bun at home," I said.

"You're so goddamned rich," Lenny said.

Ross held a lighted match in his fingers and closed his mouth around it. When he opened his mouth again the match had gone out.

"All we ever get here is goddamn cereal," Lenny said. "Yesterday we didn't even have any milk. Goddamn Annie made us put goddamn water on it."

"Just one day," sneered Ross. "What's the matter, baby, you can't take it?"

"Eat dirt, jerk," Lenny said.

"Who sleeps here?" I said.

"We all do," said Ross. "Lenny sleeps over there with the little kids who wet their beds and I sleep with Louise."

"I don't wet."

"You do so wet."

"You don't sleep with Louise."

"I do too sleep with her. Louise lets me ball her," Ross said.

"You lie."

"Molly won't let me ball her," Ross said. He lit a match and held it until it burned down to his finger, then he jerked it out the window and watched it fall. "I can't wait to get out of this place," he said.

Uncle Owen cooked all day in the kitchen, laid spoons down on the stove that bled spaghetti sauce down the cupboard. Aunt Annie scrubbed clams with a wooden brush and dropped them live into a pot of water. The kitchen table filled up with ashtrays and glasses and rings on the table and Grand's bottle of Jim Beam and other bottles, a bottle of coffee brandy and a bottle of milk. When we kids ran in Mum said in a sensational voice, "Head for the round house, they can't corner you there!" She didn't like kids.

Mrs. Dyshart and Aunt Annie seemed to expand in the warm kitchen. They untied their bathing suit strings and tucked them into the bosoms of their bathing suits, pulled off their earrings and laid them down on the kitchen table. Pins slid from their hair. They played a game with Ross where they took turns burning holes with a lighted cigarette in a napkin that held a dime suspended over a water glass. Mrs. Dyshart had yellow and blue on the top of her brown arm, like a vaccination scar, but wider and fresher. She and Aunt Annie wore their tans like masks, and they took turns holding the cigarette in the same stiff, careful way, as if the cracked, broken-up red polish on their nails was still wet and fresh. Ross kept taking drags on the cigarette to keep it going until finally Aunt Annie said, *"Ross."* A fan of white lines unfolded around her brown mouth. She burned another hole in the napkin and the dime clunked into the glass.

"Junk man came and gave me twenty dollars for that alabaster statue I kept on the mantel," Grand said.

Mum's back shot up straight in her chair. "Not the bust of William Shakespeare," she said.

Grand nodded. "That old thing, I don't know where it came from. Junk man gave me twenty dollars, isn't that rich?" said Grand.

"Oh, Mumma, I would have given you fifty dollars," Mum said.

"Coo!" said Grand. "Where would you get cash?"

"How could you, Mumma, that bust was part of our family. I remember that bust in Grandma's kitchen at Dumbartons'. William Shakespeare," Mum said.

"Oh, Lucy, you're so dramatic," Grand said. "I think I paid twenty-five cents for it at the Episcopal church fair. Junk man wanted to look at Grampy's Civil War rifle he bought in Bangor for a dollar, but I couldn't find it."

"I'd sell the gun before the Shakespeare," Mum said.

"I could probably get you a hundred bucks for a Civil War gun," Uncle Owen said.

"Oh, coo," said Grand.

Mum told the old stories about Grand. When Grand was young she had red hair and she was a star forward on the girls' basketball team. They called her "Shimmy" Purton because of the way she danced with boys.

"Isn't that wicked?" Grand asked. "Your fat old Grand dancing the shimmy? My mother Purton used to have a fit."

"Shimmy, shimmy, coconut," Uncle Owen teased Grand, swaggering his hips. Grand waved him away, but she bunched her lips at him.

"Now I remember Grandma Purton's rice pudding," Mum said. "She would bake it for hours in that old Clarion cookstove. It would cook there all afternoon and her kitchen smelled of cinnamon and sugar and the raisins she used, the currants. And when the pudding was done she would say, 'I shouldn't,' but we always had bowls of it together with cream on top."

"I don't remember that," Aunt Annie said. She slid Mum's pack of Kents across the table and lit one for herself with Mum's lighter and blew out a smoke ring.

"How do you remember that, Lucy? If that isn't comical," Grand said.

"I think my life was more real to me when I was six than it is now," Mum said.

"Isn't she something? How does she think of it?" said my aunt.

Mum told the old story of when Grand was just a little girl and her sister Doris died. Grandma Purton screamed: *Why did this one have to be taken?* The whole house shook, and Grampy Purton had to come and quiet her so the Dumbartons wouldn't hear her. And then when they laid Doris out—they laid her on the kitchen table where they ate, dressed in a new dress that cost thirty-five dollars—Grand was sitting with her and she saw Mrs. Dumbarton coming down the walk to pay her respects and she ran and hid under the stairs so Madam wouldn't see her. Can you imagine? Mum said.

"Isn't it something how she remembers it so vivid? I don't remember it that vivid," Grand said.

Ross reached for Aunt Annie's cigarette but Aunt Annie glared at him without moving her face at all and dropped the cigarette into the glass with the dime.

The fallen cigarette smoked in the glass. Aunt Annie opened up a magazine and turned the pages with just the pads of her fingers.

"I don't think it was terrible," Grand said. "It was what we knew."

"That's Lucy, trying to make a tragedy out of everything," said Uncle Owen.

"It *is* a tragedy," Mum said.

"Boo hoo, I'm crying," Uncle Owen said.

Mum looked around for someone who would understand her.

Uncle Owen sat down beside her with his drink in a coffee mug. He leaned toward me and cigarette smoke drifted up between his teeth and floated out of him as he sang:

Your teeth are yeller
Who's your feller?
You some ugly child.

"Why don't you get married, Lucy?" Uncle Owen asked Mum.

"I can't take care of a man," Mum said. "I have a kid to take care of. I have dreams of my own, damn it," she yelled, suddenly furious.

"You want to make a home for someone, have more children," Owen said.

"Oh, for God's sake, Owen," Mum said. "I want . . . to understand my life."

But Uncle Owen wasn't listening.

"Now my kid is my life—or is a kid a life?" Mum said. She picked up her drink and sipped it.

Uncle Owen leaned close to her. "I remember first time I saw Molly. I said, 'A baby's a miracle, isn't it? Just imagine this little bundle twelve or thirteen years from now drinking jiz in the back seat of a Ford.' Hey, Lucy?" Smoke rolled out of Uncle Owen's mouth.

Mum threw her glass at Uncle Owen. It bounced off his chin and clunked on the table. "Shut up, you filthy man!" Mum yelled in the deep voice she used for drama.

Uncle Owen licked spilled Jim Beam off his chin and wiped some of it on the back of his hand.

"Pig! Troglodyte!" Mum boomed.

Uncle Owen poured spaghetti sauce over plates of noodles and bowls of clams. Suddenly Grand put down her glass of Jim Beam and looked at Troy. "Oh my Lord, you've got another one!" Grand said. You could see from the way she laid down her cigarette in the big round ashtray in the middle of the table that she had guessed about Troy, had figured it out.

A line between Grand's eyes and Troy was clear as a rope in the air, tying them together. Troy had sat down in a corner of the kitchen with his plate of spaghetti and clams and his stick and he was talking to his stick, but not in any voice you could hear. "You've got another one, haven't you?" Grand shrilled.

"Say hello to your grandson, Troy, Mumma," Aunt Annie said. She held out a plate of clams to Grand. But Grand didn't take the plate. She uncrossed her legs and spread them out and she leaned toward Troy for a minute across the table of her lap with her elbows on the table and really looked at him.

Everybody looked at Grand look at Troy.

"You got another one?" Grand asked. She heaved up on her feet. Her legs looked like two white flagpoles holding up a nation.

"We have Ross and Lenny and Trudy and Troy," Aunt Annie said.

Uncle Owen wasn't anywhere around, just a long brown spoon stuck out of the pot. Suddenly all the adults jumped on Grand and held her arms, all except Aunt Annie, who was still holding the plate out to Grand. Louise put down her plate and picked up Troy and his stick, and walked out the front door.

Grand was just breathing. "You must be crazy for it," she said to Aunt Annie.

We kids, except for Louise and Troy, sat on the floor with our backs against the kitchen wall, buttering rolls, skimming gray veils off the necks of clams, rolling forksful of spaghetti against the sides of tablespoons. "Oh, Mumma," Mum said. *"Jesus,* Mumma." She banged over to the counter and put more ice and then more Jim Beam into her glass, so it was just the Dysharts holding Grand lightly at her arms, and Grand leaning forward to Aunt Annie, hissing at her, but not trying to break away, to go beyond.

"You must be crazy for it," Grand said, spitting a little toward Aunt Annie. "I'd think you'd be ashamed!"

"I am not ashamed," Aunt Annie said. She put down the plate of food and sat down at the table and lit a cigarette. She sat there facing Grand, her wide brown chest puffed out from the top of her pink-and-white checkered bathing suit, keeping the smoke out of Grand's eyes with her hand back and her elbow lifted up to smoke the way Grand herself did it. The spaghetti tasted delicious, hard and then soft against your teeth, and the soft bellies of the clams tasted gray and grainy from the tiny pearls of sand they had eaten.

Grand, who hadn't ever noticed Troy for two years, didn't notice he was gone. "I'm not going to say hello to it," Grand said. "I don't want it!"

"Troy almost died of infant diverticulitis in the hospital when he was three months old," Aunt Annie said. White lines fanned out at the corners of her red, watering eyes.

"I wish it had died!" Grand said. "Why didn't you get yourself fixed when I gave you the money?"

"I used the money to pay for Troy's operation, Mumma," Aunt Annie said.

After the picnic we left our paper bowls on the kitchen counter and climbed back to the kids' room with our hands full of Oreos. We talked about who was wanted and who wasn't, scraping the white frost of sugar from between the cookies with our front teeth. All of Aunt Annie and Uncle Owen's kids were mistakes, especially Troy. I thought I had been planned and wanted.

"Yeah, *right*," Ross said, his gums swollen with cookie.

All of the Dyshart kids were surprises but were wanted, so Louise claimed.

Inside the house no light snapped on. Ice cracked and broke. Grand yelled, "I could shoot that man!" Mum and Aunt Annie yelled back at her, but Grand's voice soared up over them and hung in the yard. "If I had a gun, I'd shoot him!"

Louise, the thrill of violence lighting her eyes, kneeled down around Troy and told him that Grand would shoot him if she found him. She pulled him close and in a rough motherly way explained over and over that it was his fault Grand was mad and she would shoot him with a gun unless he did exactly as we said. Troy did not say he understood but he spoke syllables to his stick. He stood still while we wrapped him up with his stick in red flannel printed over with cowboys and Indians. Then we hid him in a trunk in the kids' room—closed him up with some toys and old sneakers and left him there. We built a maze around him, so if Grand were to come up with a gun she would have to crawl between chairs overhung with snow jackets and Louise's dresses.

We all went outside to keep watch for Grand.

Louise took me out to the corral where her horse stood in the wet black muck out front of his stall. He was old, or maybe he was a sick horse with cloudy eyes. His head hung over the ground.

Louise didn't have a saddle—I don't know if she could ride the horse or not, whether the horse could see well enough to be ridden or run. Crossing the piles of dung was like walking through ice-glazed snow, at any time your foot could crack it and sink down. We made the crossing, and rubbed the horse's long nose and talked to it as if it were a baby. Together we mucked out the stall with shovels, heaved the black piles over the fence and laid down new hay. Louise pulled out an extra pair of hip boots for me to put on over my blue jean shorts and sneakers. Everything was in the little stable that we needed.

The sun flattened and turned orange, the trees turned black, the crickets rubbed their wings. Ice rattled through the walls of the house where the adults sat and talked. Grand yelled something tearful and Mum yelled back in a hard voice, *"Mumma."*

Louise and I peeled off the spongy rubber hip boots and left them fallen on the ground like legs. We thumped up the stairs of the second house. All the other kids had gone out to the field to play chicken with the old pickup they drove. Louise and I crawled through the maze of sheets and chairs and opened the trunk and unwrapped Troy. At first we thought he was dead, he was so pale and a vein showed blue on his forehead. We pulled him from the trunk and laid him out on the floor. While we were laying out his arms on his chest he opened his eyes and vomited his dinner. Louise kneeled around him and wiped his mouth with dirty towels. We were still playing, but it felt serious and real.

She cleaned Troy and dressed him in footed pajamas, then picked him up. He was long and heavy, like a monkey in her arms. We walked across the yard to the kitchen where she dropped him in Aunt Annie's arms. He slid down her legs and soon fell asleep on the floor near Grand. Grand, now she had discovered Troy, did not notice him. He was just another one.

They were finishing their drinks, then suddenly Mum stood up and said it was time to go. Troy sat up and rubbed his eyes. We all got up and went outside where the mosquitoes buzzed and bit, and blue bats orbited the yard. Ross and Lenny nagged Mum with their hands, "Please, Aunt Lucy. Do Bette Davis."

Mum tapped a Kent out of her pack and lit it with her Bic. She gave her lighter and her cigarettes and her dark glasses to Ross to hold, then she puffed out a few clouds of smoke and raised her chin so the cords showed in her throat. She waved her arm toward Uncle Owen's car at the other end of the yard. Uncle Owen was sitting in the driver's seat, not going anywhere, smoking a cigarette. The little light glowed down on him from the roof.

"You want to speak to my husband? He's in there," she said, waving to Uncle Owen. "But you can't speak to him. You see, I've just killed him," Mum said. She puffed more on her cigarette and let go of Bette Davis slowly. She was Bette Davis, a smoking killer, then she was both Bette Davis and Mum, and then finally she dropped her chin and her face softened into the usual worry lines on her forehead, and she was just Mum.

Mr. Dyshart took his cigarette from the cup of his hand and stuck it in his mouth while he clapped. Aunt Annie said, "Isn't she something?" and tapped her palms together in silent, useless applause.

Uncle Owen still sat in his broken car on the other side of the yard, slumped down so all you could see was the smoke from his cigarette and the coffee mug on the dashboard and the yellow bulb glow.

Mum stuffed her cigarettes and her lighter and her cat's-eye dark glasses in the pocket of her blue jeans shorts.

"You're such a card," Ross told Mum.

"OK, Molly, you work the pedals and I'll steer," Mum said, her old fall-down drunk joke. But I climbed in back as usual and put my seat belt on. Aunt Annie and Mr. and Mrs. Dyshart turned toward the kitchen and Aunt Annie saw Troy squatting near the front door. "Oh, Jesum *Crow,* he's eating dirt again. Look at you, you little dirteater," she said, swatting the tin cup out of his hand. It rattled across the rutty yard. Troy's head hung a little sideways and he looked up at his mother with one eye and showed a row of small square teeth. It was his smile.

"Come on," Aunt Annie said, and pulled him up with one hand, and they all walked back into the kitchen. Mr. Dyshart closed the door behind them.

Grand whimpered in front. She spent half an hour opening the big purse on her lap and finding a Kleenex. Then in a slow thumping way she began to take off the jacket of her suit. Mum reached over and helped peel the jacket back from her shoulders and the car pitched from one side of the road to the other. "I'm so moist," Grand complained.

"Jesus, Mumma, you could at least have taken the jacket off. We're *family*."

"My arms are fat," Grand said.

Mum drove past the reindeer and the broken, hanging Santa Claus on the Burnses' roof. "It's just as bad as those Burnses, all those kids and *nothing!*" Grand said, and blew her nose. "We Purtons weren't much. But we were something," Grand said.

"Your legs still look nice, Mumma," Mum said. "Your calves."

"You think so?" Grand said, dabbing her Kleenex at the end of her nose.

"Your calves are very shapely for a woman your age," Mum said.

"Troy thought you were going to shoot him, Grand," I said.

Grand and Mum both spun their heads around, then Mum recovered and looked back at the road. "What?" Mum said, the *T* rattling out behind the word.

"She thought I wanted to shoot that baby," Grand said. "My Lord!"

"Grand isn't going to shoot anybody, you got that?" Mum said.

"She thought I wanted to shoot the baby!" Grand said again. She wiped her eyes with the Kleenex. "What must you think of your Granny," she said.

We drove a while without talking.

"Owen was using that old coffee mug," Mum said to Grand. "No wonder he has diverticulitis. What that man drinks. Gee, God."

"That's what I call an alcoholic, someone who drinks out of a coffee mug instead of pouring a cocktail with everyone else," Grand agreed.

Mum smiled tightly at the Cheese House as we came up to the turn.

"What on earth is that building over there?" Grand asked, pointing at it, her finger bent against the window glass. "When did they put that up? That used to be the MacFlecknie farm."

"That's the Cheese House, it's been there forever, Grand," I said.

"It's round, is it?" said Grand. She didn't trust herself. "I never saw it."

"You need to use your eyes, Mumma," Mum said.

"A house shaped like a cheese," Grand said. "Isn't that comical."

Peter Ho Davies

Relief

From *The Paris Review*

SOMETIME between the cheese and the fruit, while the port was still being passed, Lieutenant Wilby allowed a sweet, but rather too boisterous fart to slip between his buttocks. The company around the mess table was talking quietly, listening to the sound of the liquor filling the glasses, holding it up in the lamplight to relish its color against the white canvas of the tent. It was, Lieutenant Bromhead had just explained, a bottle from General Chelmsford's own stock, and not the regulation port issued to officers. A hush of appreciation had fallen over the table.

Of course, Wilby had known the fart was coming, but it was much louder and more prolonged than he had anticipated and the look of surprise on his face would have given him away even if Major Black to his left, the port already extended, had not said, "Wilby!" in a sharp, shocked bellow.

"Sorry, sir," Wilby said. His face burned as if he'd been sitting in front of the hearth at home, reading by the firelight. He risked one quick glance up and around the table. "Sorry, sirs." Chaplain Pierce was looking down into his lap, exactly as he did when saying grace, and Captain Ferguson's mustache was jumping slightly at the corners, like the whiskers of a cat that had just scented a bowl of cream. Lieutenant Chard, however, sat just as he appeared in his photographs, his huge pale face tipped back like a great slab, rising above his thick dark beard.

As for Bromhead, he looked only slightly puzzled.

"What?" he said. "What is it?"

Wilby, staring down at the crumbs of Stilton on his plate, groaned inwardly. Bromhead's famed deafness was going to be the end of him.

He looked up under his brow as Bromhead's batman, who had just placed the fruit on the table, leaned forward and whispered all too audibly in his ear, "The lieutenant farted, sir."

"Chard?" Bromhead asked. Behind his beard the old lieutenant turned the color of claret. Bromhead, himself, wore only a thin mustache and sideburns, and Wilby thought he saw a flicker of a smile cross his face.

The batman leaned in to him again.

"Wilby," he whispered.

"Ah," Bromhead said sadly. He stared at his glass. An uncomfortable silence fell over the mess table. Wilby's mortification was complete. And, perhaps because he wished himself dead, a small portion of his recent life flashed before his eyes.

The lieutenant had been suffering from terrible flatulence all the way from Helpmakaar. At first, he had thought it was something to do with his last meal (a deer shot, several times, by Major Black, which he could hardly have refused in any case) but as the column approached Rorke's Drift his bowels seemed in as great an uproar as ever. Fortunately the ride had been made at a canter, and he'd been able to clench his mount between his legs and smother the worst farts against his saddle—although the horse had tossed her head at some of the more drawn out ones—but as they came in sight of the mission station the major spurred them into a trot and then a run so that their pennant snapped overhead like a whip. Legs braced in the stirrups, knees bent, his body canted forward over his mount's neck, the lieutenant had had no choice but to release a crackling stream of utterance.

At first, there was some undeniable relief in this, but as each dip and rise and tussock jarred loose further bursts, he was obliged to cry, "Ya," and "Ho," as if encouraging his horse, to mask the worst outbreaks. He was grateful that over the drumming of hooves and the bugler who had hastily run out to welcome them to camp no one seemed to notice, but the severity of the attack made him doubt that he had not soiled his breeches and at the first opportunity he sought out the latrine to reassure himself.

Having put his mind at rest, seen to his tentage and placed his horse in the care of the groom he shared with the other junior officers, Wilby had taken himself off to the perimeter of the camp. Despite the newly built walls and the freshly dug graves—they were overgrown already, but their silhouettes were clearly visible in the long pale grass—it was all familiar to him from the articles in the *Army Gazette,* and in his mind he traced the events of the famous defense that had been fought there not three months before.

Fewer than a hundred able-bodied men, a single company plus those left behind at the mission hospital, had fought off a force of some five thousand Zulus—part of the same *impi* that had wiped out fifteen hundred men at Isandhlwana the previous day—holding out for upwards of ten hours of continuous close fighting and inflicting almost five hundred casualties on the enemy. It was a glorious tale and Wilby didn't need to look at the page from the *Gazette* that he kept in his tunic pocket to recall all the details. He had read and reread it so often on the ride out from Durban that it felt as fragile as an illuminated manuscript. "You'd think it was a love letter," the major had scoffed.

He should be rejoicing to be here, standing on the ground of the most famous battle in the world, and yet he only felt the churning of his wretched stomach. Tomorrow they would ride out, the first patrol to visit the site of Isandhlwana since the massacre.

He stared out in the direction they would take in the morning. The ferry across the drift was moored about two hundred yards away and on the far bank the track ran beside the river for a half mile or so and then cut away over a low rise and out of sight. Wilby found himself thinking of the Derbyshire countryside near his home . . . and fishing—up to his thighs in the dark cool water, feeling the pull of the current but dry inside his thick leather waders. He supposed the sight of the river must have brought it to mind.

It was Ferguson who found him out there. He saw the captain running towards him, his red tunic among the waving grass, shouting his news.

"Wills, we are invited to dine with Bromhead and Chard. You, myself, the major and Pierce."

"Truly?" Wilby caught his friend's arm, and Ferguson stooped for a moment to catch his breath. Then he shook himself free and took a step back, squared his shoulders and held up his hand as if reading from a card.

"Lieutenants Bromhead and Chard request the pleasure of Major Black and his staff's company for dinner in their mess at eight o'clock."

Of course, it was a little unusual for two lieutenants to invite a major to dinner, but by then Bromhead and Chard were expected to be made majors themselves—not to mention the Victoria Crosses everyone was predicting—and the breach of etiquette seemed altogether forgivable to Wilby. A dinner with Gonville Bromhead and Merriot Chard was simply the most sought after invitation in the whole of Natal in the spring of 1879.

"Good Lord, Fergie," he said. "Why, I must change."

He had spent the next hour in his suspenders and undershirt polishing the buttons of his tunic, slipping a small brass plate behind them to protect the fabric and then working the polish into the raised regimental crests and burnishing them to a glow. Next he worked on his boots, smearing long streaks of bootblack up and down, working them into the hide with a swift circular motion, and then bringing the leather to a shine with a stiff brush. He thought hard about the thin beard and mustache he had begun to grow three weeks before and with a sigh pulled out his razor. Ferguson, waxing his own mustache, paused and watched him in silence, but Wilby refused to meet his eye. His mustache would never be as good as the captain's anyway. Fergie's mustache was justly famous in the regiment, said to be wide enough for troopers riding behind him to see both ends. Wilby knew that wasn't quite true. The captain had made him check. He stood behind him trying to make out both waxed tips. In the end, they had had to call in the chaplain and standing shoulder to shoulder, about five feet behind Ferguson, Wilby and Pierce had each been able to see a tip of mustache on either side.

Wilby lathered the soap in his shaving mug and applied it with the badgerhair brush his father had given him before he'd come out on campaign. The razor was dull and he had to pause to strop it, but he managed to shave without drawing blood.

Finally, he extracted his second set of epaulets and his best collar from the tissue paper he kept them in and had Ferguson fix them in place. The fragrant smell of hair oil filled their tent as they each in turn vigorously applied a brush to each other's tunics. Without a decent mirror, they paused and scrutinized each other carefully, then bowed deeply—Wilby from the waist, Ferguson taking a step back and dropping his arm in a flourish.

The meal had gone well at first. The major had introduced him to first Chard and then Bromhead and he'd looked them both in the eyes (Chard's gray, Bromhead's brown) and shaken hands firmly. In between, he had made to clasp his hands behind his back and been sure to rub them on his tunic to ensure they were dry. "How do you do, sir?" he had said to each in turn.

"Very well," Chard had said in his gruff way.

"Splendid," Bromhead had told him a little too loudly. The story of his deafness, that he would almost certainly have been pensioned off if his older brother had not been on Chelmsford's staff, was well known among the junior officers. It was said that he had only been given B company of the 2nd/24th because it was composed almost entirely of Welshmen and it was thought that his deafness wouldn't be so noticeable or important to men who spoke English with such an impenetrable accent. There was even a joke that Bromhead's company had only received its posting at Rorke's Drift because the lieutenant thought the general had been offering him more pork rib at the mess table. "Rather," he was reputed to have said. "Sounds tasty."

Some of the officers still made fun of Bromhead, but Wilby put it down to simple jealousy. For his own part, he thought it more not less heroic that Bromhead had overcome his disability. He had a theory that amid all the noise of battle a deaf man might have an advantage, might come to win the respect of men hoarse from shouting and deafened by the report of their arms.

At dinner, Wilby had waited until the major and Ferguson had each made some remark or other, nodded at each response and echoed the chaplain's compliments on the food. Only then, as the batman passed the gravy boat among them did he ask a question of his own.

"How does it feel?" he said. "I mean, how does it feel to be heroes?"

Bromhead looked at him closely for a moment, but it was Chard who answered.

"Well," he began. He stroked his beard and it made an audible rasping sound. "I would have to say, principally, the sensation is one of relief. Relief to be alive after all—not like the poor devils you'll see tomorrow—but also relief to have learned some truth about myself. To have found I am possessed of—for want of a better word—courage."

"Rather," Ferguson said. He grinned at Wilby.

What a blowhard, Bromhead thought. It pained him that Chard's name and his own should be so inextricably linked. Bromhead and Chard. Chard and Bromhead. He felt like a blasted vaudevillian.

"It's an ambition fulfilled," Chard went on, ignoring the interruption. "Since I was a little chap I remember wondering—as who has not?—if I were a brave fellow. Cowardice, funk—more than any imagined beast or goblin, that was my great terror. And now, I have my answer." He paused and looked around the table slowly and this time it was harder for Wilby to hold his gaze. "If the chaplain would be so good as to forgive me, I rather fancy it is as if I have stood before St. Peter, himself, not knowing if I were a bally sinner or no, and dashed me if he hasn't found my name there among the elect."

The chaplain smiled and bobbed his head complacently. Wilby

and Ferguson glanced at each other again, their eyes bright, but not quite meeting in their excitement.

"Heavens!" said Bromhead, clearing his throat. "For my part, being a hero is nothing so like how I fancy a beautiful young debutante must feel." There was a puzzled round of laughter, but Wilby saw Chard press his lips together—a white line behind his dark beard—and kept his own features still. "You've seen them at balls, gentlemen, there are one or two each season, those girls who aren't quite sure, but then discover all of a sudden quite how delightful they are. Oh, I don't know. Perhaps their mamas had told them so, but they'd not believed them. After all, that's what mamas are for. They'd not known whether to listen to their doting fathers and all those old loyal servants, surely too ugly to know what was beautiful or not anymore. And then, suddenly, in one evening, confound it, they know. And all around them, instantly, why who but our own good selves, gentlemen—suitors all."

Wilby could see Ferguson smile and he knew he was thinking of Ethel, his betrothed. He had seen such women as Bromhead described himself, but his own smile was more rueful. (He remembered one long conversation with a certain Miss Fanshaw who had cheerfully told him that she had sent no less than five white feathers to men she knew at the time of the Crimea—"And you know," she had told him earnestly, "not one of them returned home alive.") The major he knew would be thinking of his wife, home in Bath, and the chaplain, he supposed, of God. He saw Chard, bored, study his reflection in the silverware.

"Anyway," the major said. "Put us out of our misery. Let's hear all the details of this famous defense of yours, eh? Give us the story from the horse's mouth, so to speak."

"Oh, well," Bromhead opened his hands. "It was fairly fierce, I suppose. The outcome was in doubt for some hours." He faltered and Wilby who had been leaning forward eagerly, sat back and saw the others look disappointed. This was after all what they had come for.

Chard, however, stepped in. He was an officer of engineers and he believed in telling a tale correctly.

He told them about the hours of hand-to-hand combat, of the

bayonets that the men called "lungers" and of the *assegais* of the Zulus. How the men's guns had become so hot from firing that they cooked off rounds as soon as they were loaded causing the men to miss, so hot that the soft brass shell casings melted in the breeches and had to be dug out with a knife before the whole futile process could begin again. He told them about men climbing up on the wall they'd built of biscuit boxes and mealie bags and lunging down into the darkness; of the black hands reaching up to grab the barrels and the shrieks of pain when they touched the hot glowing metal. Shrieks that were oddly louder than the soft grunts men gave as a bayonet or assegai found its mark. He told them about the sound of bullets clattering into the biscuit boxes at the base of the wall, and rustling in the mealie bags nearer the top, so that you knew the Zulus were getting their range. He described men overpowered, dragged over the walls, surrounded by warriors. How the Zulus knocked them down and ripped open their tunics, and the popping sound of buttons flying loose. "That would be the last sound a lot of our chaps heard," he said. With their tunics open the Zulus would disembowel them, opening men from balls to breastbone with one swift strike.

"I swear I'll never be able to see another button pop loose from a shirt without thinking of it," Chard said. He took a sip of wine. "Of course, you'll see a good deal of that handiwork tomorrow, I'll warrant."

That was when Wilby began to feel his flatulence return, and his discomfort grew even when Bromhead broke in and explained that the Zulus believed that opening a man's chest was the only way to set his spirit free from his dead body.

"Really, it's an act of mercy as they see it," he said. "I hope so, at least. There was one poor chap of mine, a Private Williams. Bit of a no-account, but a decent sort. I saw him get fairly dragged over the wall before I caught hold his leg. This was quite in the thick of it. There were so many Zulus trying to rush us from all sides they were like water swirling round a rock in a stream. Quite a ghastly tug of war I had for him with them. Every time they had him to their side he'd give one of those little grunts Chard was talking about, but then I'd pull like mad and when I had him more to me he'd look up and say in a cheery way, 'Much obliged, sir.' In the end, they began to swarm over the walls all about us and I had to let him go to draw my pistol. I told him I was sorry—I fancied he'd be in a bad panic, you know—but he just said, 'Not at all, sir,' and 'Thank you kindly, sir.' "

Bromhead paused.

"I was going to write to his people. Say how sorry I was I couldn't save him. But dashed if he didn't join up under a false name. A lot of the Welshmen do it seems. For a long time I thought they were all just called Evans and Williams and Jones and what-have-you, but it turns out that those are just the most obvious false names for them to choose. His blamed leg—you know I can't get it out of my mind—how remarkably warm it was."

He sat back and the batman took the opportunity to step forward with the port. Bromhead watched in silence as the glasses filled with redness.

Wilby had managed a few quiet expulsions, but then came the surprising and ruinous fart.

The silence around the table seemed to go on for hours—Wilby could hear the pickets calling out their challenge to the final patrols of the evening. Finally, Bromhead looked over and said genially, "Preserved potatoes." He shook his head. "Make you fart like a confounded horse."

He waved his man forward with the cigars and as they passed around he leaned in towards the table and looked around at them all.

"Reminds me of a story," he said, cutting the end of his cigar. "I haven't thought of it in years, mind you—about a bally Latin class, of all things." He ran the end of the cigar around his tongue and raised his chin for the batman to light him. "Hardly the story you expected to hear, but I'll beg your indulgence." He took a mighty puff and began.

"Well, we had this old tyrant of a teacher, Marlow, his name was, of the habit of making us work at our books in silence every other afternoon. Any noise and he would beat you with a steel ruler that he carried from his days in the navy. Now that was fear.

I swear it was rumored among us—a rumor spread no doubt by older boys to put a fright on us and, who knows, still attached to some teacher down to this day—that boys had lost fingers, chopped clean off at the knuckle by that ruler.

"I must have been upwards of twelve or so. I can't recall quite the circumstances, but I'd bent over from my desk to retrieve a pen I'd dropped—or more likely some blighter had thrown—on the floor. We were always trying to get some other poor bugger to make a sound and bring down the tyrant's wrath upon their heads, but anyhow, as I say, I'd bent over to pick up my pen—I was in the middle of translating 'Horatio on the Bridge' or some such rot—and, what do you know but I farted. Quite surprised myself. Quite taken aback, I was. Not that it was an especially, you know, loud one. More of a pop really. Or a squeak. Hang me if that's not it either. Let's just say somewhere between a pop and a squeak. Hardly a decent fart at all, if the truth be told, it's rather astonishing I can remember it so well. No matter. Whatever the precise sound of the expulsion, in that room with everyone trying to be still it was like a bally pistol shot, like the crack of a whip.

"Well the fellows behind me, of course, went off into absolute fits and gales. Up jumps the tyrant brandishing his ruler and I fancy I'm for the high jump now. The whole room falls silent as the grave and the old man stalks up the aisle between our desks looking hard all about him.

" 'John Beddows,' he says to one of the chaps behind me, and his voice is veritable steel. 'Would you mind telling me what is the source of this hilarity?'

" 'Nothing, sir,' says John—a decent enough sort, loafer that he was—and I begin to think I might be spared, but dash me if the old man doesn't persist.

" 'Nothing,' he says. 'You had to be laughing at something, boy. Only idiots laugh at nothing. Are you an idiot, Mister Beddows?' And he bent that ruler in his hands.

" 'No, sir,' says John pulling a long face. 'Please, sir. Gonville Bromhead farted, sir.' "

Wilby risked a glance around the faces at the table and saw that Ferguson was grinning broadly, his teeth showing around his cigar. The chaplain, too, was struggling to keep a straight face and even Major Black had a curious look in his eye. Only Chard showed no glimmer of humor. He had stubbed out his cigar and taken an apple which he was chewing steadily.

"Of course," Bromhead went on. "You can imagine the pandemonium. You'd have thought there was a murder in progress and to be honest I could have cheerfully strangled Beddows. I let out a swear or two under my breath, but the tyrant himself was at a loss for a moment. All I could do was snatch my hands up from where they'd been lying on the desk and press them into my pockets.

" 'Silence!' the tyrant finally bellowed, and then with me cringing, 'That's quite enough drollery, gentlemen. Back to work. All of you.'

"Of course, it was only a reprieve of sorts. The worst was still to come. By-and-by, we came out for our break and the other chaps started up a game of tag. I was too angry or ashamed to join them. I took myself off to a corner of the yard and watched. One person would be on, his tie would be undone, and he'd tag another who'd also pull his tie open and they'd keep tagging until everyone had their ties hanging loose. Only when some of them ran closer to me did I catch the name of the game. 'Funky Farters.' " Bromhead looked around him, his face a mask of tragedy.

"That dashed game became the craze at school for months, although I can tell you I never played it. I had dreams, nightmares really, of boys going home at the holidays and teaching it to their friends and in this way the detestable game—and my disgrace—spreading to every durned school in England. Can you imagine? I couldn't shake the notion. I thought with certitude that affair would be the only thing I'd be known for in my whole life. I thought, I'll die and my only lasting contribution to this life will be a fart in a confounded Latin class."

The table was roaring with laughter by now, the chaplain dabbing at his eyes with his napkin, Ferguson clutching his sides, and the major positively braying. Ash from the almost extinguished cigar in his hand peppered the table as he shook. Wilby found himself laughing, too, uncontrollably relieved. He caught Bromhead's eye and the older lieutenant nodded.

❑ ❑ ❑ ❑

The meal broke up shortly after—the major's patrol would have to leave camp at first light—and the men went out into the night to find their own tents. Bromhead leaned back in his chair and watched the major sidle up to Wilby and Ferguson and say, "I remember once letting loose a mighty one on parade in India," and the two young officers staggered with laughter. The chaplain was the last to leave. He smiled at Bromhead and shook his head. "An edifying tale." Then he hurried after the other three and Bromhead saw him put an arm around Wilby's shoulder.

Only Chard stalked off alone, his back straight and his chin held high. "Now that man," Bromhead said to his batman, "mark my words—has never farted in his life. It'd break his back to let rip now." He lit another cigar and smoked it thoughtfully, while the batman cleared the plates from the table.

"It's a terrible thing being afraid, Watkins, do you not think?"

The batman said he thought it was.

"Join me," he said and he poured two glasses of the celebrated port and they sat and drank in silence for a moment.

"Bloody rum thing. Zulus thinking to find a fellow's soul in his entrails, eh?"

The batman nodded. The port tasted like syrup to him and later he would need a swig of his Squareface—the army-issue gin in its square bottle—to take the taste away.

It was late and the light breeze through the tent felt cold to Bromhead. He always took more of a chill when he'd been drinking. He pulled a blanket off the cot behind him and draped it around his shoulders. "Like an old woman," he said. He wrapped his arms around himself under the blanket, clutching his shoulders, and thought again how really remarkably *warm* Private Williams's leg had felt.

"Wake me," he said to the batman, "before the major's patrol leaves in the morning. I think I should like to see them off."

Reginald McKnight

Boot

From *Story*

I

NO, THAT'S NOT what I'm saying. I'm not saying it's okay to lie. All I'm saying, Coburn, is—if you'll let me—is that there's lies you believe in, and lies you don't believe in. This is a lie I believed in, and it took me a long time to shake it off.

I think it was the punishment that made it so hard. I mean, look, they made you haul around sixteen-pound hammers everywhere you went. You had to carry these things around like they were your M16s. Spent *eight* hours a day making cement blocks into powder with those hammers, dude. I'm telling you. You were fucking chained together at the ankle with at least forty other recruits, brother. You're damn right they did. And hot? Let me tell you, Coburn, when you get to thinking that packing bags and humping groceries at our little Safeway is a burden, just think about old Bones here chained like a bald-headed slave to other slaves in ninety-by-ninety weather. Think about this poor bastard breathing hot white dust for eight hours a day while he's wrestling a sixteen-pound hammer to the sound of his keeper's whistle. One blast for up, one for down.

You're damn right it's hard, but the rest of it was hard, too. In the Corrective Custody Platoon they had this problem: they had to make it harder than regular boot camp, but not actually kill people. In regular boot camp they make you run, march, polish shit, climb obstacle courses, and so forth. You take courses in rifle maintenance, first aid, close combat, swimming. None of it's fun, but it's never boring, especially when they punish your ass. Mostly it's push-ups and squat-thrusts, which you do for the slightest infractions.

Say you fold your towel wrong, say you're talking in formation, say you look your drill instructor in the eye, say you refer to yourself as "I" instead of "the private," say you refer to your DI as "you" rather than Drill Instructor, Staff Sergeant So-and-so, say you're caught cussing under your breath while the DI is picking on some dumb little recruit you feel sorry for, or you move too slow when you're called, or you roll your eyes when your Drill Instructor barks at you, or you wipe sweat out your eyes, or swat a bug when you're supposed to be at attention. Say you're ugly and the DI just can't stand the sight of you. These are the times the DI will put you on your face. And they don't just do you till you break into a little sweat and get a touch winded. Nope, they do you till the floor is slick with your sweat, till your muscles tremble like you got the flu. I seen some guys cry. Swear to God.

I remember one time the DI was bending and thrusting us in this sand pit outside our squad bay. This one guy spits a loogie onto the sand, like a guy'll do when he's overworked. Well, the DI says, "Say, Boot, whachu doing spitting on my nice clean deck. You pick that goop up and put it back where you found it." And the guy did, sand and all.

So this is typical boot camp stuff. It won't kill you, and neither will CCP, but it does make regular boot camp look like sex with your fantasy girlfriend. It lasts for one week, CCP, if you're lucky—two or three if you really don't get it the first time. But an hour in that place will change you fast. Make you feel wronged by the man, make you feel like your lie wasn't a lie cause it was all so hard. And even though they keep you busy for sixteen hours a day, like they do in regular bootsville, it feels like you got more time to think. I guess it's the monotony, the one-track rhythm of the system. You spend one-third of the day collecting dust and pain in every pore of your body. You spend another third washing the dust out your clothes, eating, shining your white boots back into black glass. You shine your brass, reblock your cover, which before the end of the day, the DIs have knocked off your head at least a half-dozen times, and forty guys have tromped on. They put you on your face for so much as blinking without permission, but it's all so quiet-like, except for the whistle.

In regular bootsville, when they put you on your face, you hear this sound, like the air sort of crackling. Everybody's—you know—angry. There's a sound to it, like fluorescent lights in a gym. But in CCP, it's quiet—everybody's bummed, everybody's thinking about what they didn't do wrong. You feel used, and used up.

The last third of the day's supposed to be about rest, and it pretty much is, for regular boot camp, but in Corrective Custody, you don't hear the crackling sound until the lights are out and everybody's in the rack. Then, it's like everybody's in bed eating walnuts, it's so loud with anger. Punishment makes you think about shit, but it doesn't make you see the light. No sir. All night long you're knotted up in blind anger, your sheets twisted round your neck, your fists still hard enough to grip the hammer.

I know you, Coburn, you're one of them romantic dudes who think prison would be like some movie where the hero gets real mad while breaking a rock and he just starts flailing away at it. Then we're supposed to know that the hero's pretending the rock is the head of the evil guard, or the reptile-heart motherjump who turned him in, or some such nonsense.

Well, as a matter of fact, that's not true. When you're actually busting rocks, you're pretty much busting rocks. You're too tired to dabble in imagination. Your brain shuts off, your body goes robot on you. All you can see is your rock, and your boot, a sixteen-pound blur, and white dust. It's in that last third of the day when you think about how that piece of concrete you're working on is Captain Hoeg's head, or Drill Instructor Allen's head, or that weasely bucktoothed-ass Private Grice's head, but mostly what you think about is what you did to get yourself there. For me, it was what I thought was the truth. I swear to you, young blood, the more I twisted in those sheets, the more I believed I hadn't lied.

What? No thanks, man, I'm not doing meat these days.

No, it's nothing moral, nothing religious. It's just I've spent over seven thousand hours of my life cutting up meat, and I'm sick of looking at it. If it was a moral thing, I couldn't do the job. Besides, how could I give up these nifty little paper hats?

I will have a taste of that pie there, though.

Well, it's okaay. A little stale, maybe.

Well, lemme get back to my story.

When Drill Instructor Staff Sergeant Allen asked me to cheat on the firing line, I said, "Sir-yes-sir; aye-aye-sir." I'm sure you've heard military talk before. You've seen those movies. The first and last words outta your mouth are supposed to be "sir." What they don't say in the movies, though, like I said before, is you can't use personal pronouns like "you," or "me," or "I." If you say, like, "I feel sick," instead of, "The private feels sick," the DI'll put his face as close to yours as the brim of his campaign cover'll let him, and this prick'll say something to you like, "Eye? Eye? You got something in yo eye, Prive?" And so like you say, "You don't understand. I'm really sick."

"Ewe? Ewe? Do I look like a sheep to you, boy? Do you wanna fuck me, Private?" And he'll start peckin at your forehead, or your ear with the edge of his campaign cover, like his name's Woody Wood, Jr. and your name's Bob Sycamore. No man has ever got in your face like that, and stunk like that, and yelled like that, and didn't move away without a fat lip, but you are scared. For one thing, DIs wear about a quart of bad cologne every day, and some of them chew tobacco, so as to work this subliminal crap on your head. The heavy smell overwhelms you, but you believe it's the DI. For another thing, you know they can have your narrow ass arrested if you so much as raise your hand to them. And for another thing, the military scrubs brains smooth in boot camp.

But like I'm saying, this DI'll say, he'll say, "Are-you-tryin-to-piss-me-off-to-day-Maggot? Are you trying to put me on the rag today?" By this time, you're so angry and worked up, you wanna bite his nose off, but you won't move, cause you're too angry and too scared. You're afraid you'll kill everybody, and you won't stop killing till you've left a blood-red ribbon around the whole stinking globe. Naw, I don't think so, Coburn, not even a badass like you would move. And then he'll point to the ground and say, "Get down on my deck and give me fi'ty bend-and-thrust, Bitch." And it's a good thing he does, too, cause it helps you work off the rage.

Well no, Staff Sergeant Allen didn't actually say "cheat," but that's what he was asking me. I knew that right away. I mean all this bullshit about, "Ah, well, Private Hay-riss, I cain't give you a lawful order to do this, but some of our privates are injuring our platoon average on the range here." Fucking gorilla was as nice as could be, which told me everything I needed to know. Even put his hand on my shoulder, like his name was Jimmy J. Coach or something. I mean, please, the guy hated me. It killed him I was his best shooter, and it killed him there were so many assback shooters in his platoon that season.

But it's not like what we did was original. I was told a couple years later that DIs pretty much always use ringers on the firing line to raise their platoon marksmanship averages. The higher the average, the more easy the guy gets promoted. Everybody does it.

But there he was, *asking* me—hell, considering how he felt about me, and considering this was Marine Corps basic training, he was practically on his knees, kissing my smoothies. Yeah, he dropped his big old fuzzy mitt on my shoulder, scrunched up those big-assed hedgehog eyebrows all serious-like, and gets all confidential in my face. It freaked me out, him getting so close to me like that without him yelling. He had a jaw like half a watermelon, and it always looked like he needed a shave—you know, with that blue-green look to it? His eyes had these big droopy Robert Mitchum lids. And his teeth were splayed and bucked, like some kind of cartoon ogre. He had that whole fear-o'-God-in-you stuff screwed down tight partly because he was so ugly. It shoulda been a hick face, one of them faces that say, Hey, I'm the biggest slack-jawed, no-intellect-having, proto-sea urchin-brain-having, shoe-drooling, motherless lizard that ever put feet to dirt.

But, no, it wasn't quite that kind of face. No, this guy had some of the blackest, coldest eyes I'd ever seen in my life. And they were smart eyes. Eyes that kinda went, I know that you know that I know that you know.

Hey, I won't lie to you, by the time we were in the rifle range phase of boot camp—about six weeks in?—I was afraid of him. Of course you're supposed to be afraid of DIs or the whole damned thing wouldn't work. You fear the DI; you fear looking like a puss in front of the other boots; you fear shaming your family. You fear going to jail. It's that fear that keeps seventy-five recruits with loaded M16s from shooting their drill instructors to fucking rags. But like I tell you, DIs play so many mind games with you in the first phase of boot camp that you'd shoot your little sister before you'd shoot one of them puppies.

From the very first night of basic training, they make you hurry everywhere, but you stand in formations and lines, waiting for nothing for hours at a time. If you talk or move without permission in that line, they put you on your face. They cut all your hair off in less than a minute, just as soon as you get off the bus. I mean, straight from the bus, right to the barber shop. (I know that don't mean nothing to you nineties boys, with all that skinhead shit you do, but in the seventies? It shocked the pants off you.) They make you strip, shower, and shave. They make you pack all your civilian trash in boxes and address it to your parents. They bark at you constantly in this guttural language you can't understand any better'n you can understand a seal.

Hell yes it works. It's worked for over two hundred years or better in this country. In the first few days, they keep you tired, never let you get quite enough sleep, or get quite enough to eat, so you're always just a little off balance, and your mind's empty. And, man, they keep at you. I once saw three drill instructors standing around this one recruit on the third floor squad bay balcony?

What? Oh, well the Marines stopped using the old Quonset huts back in the late sixties, pretty much, and started housing recruits and others in these buildings that looked like big pastel motel complexes. Three stories high, with a small balcony for the DIs to use. Well, anyhow, this guy I'm telling you about? They had him in one of those deals where if you agree with one DI, you're calling the other one a liar. They were pros at this one. Did it every chance they got. It'd make your head do three-sixties. Well, this poor boot's mind popped and he jumped off the balcony. So, the next thing you know, one DI's calling for an ambulance and the other two tear downstairs, drop to their knees beside the recruit and keep on yelling at him. "Get up, you pussy, and answer my question: You calling me a liar? Do I look dishonest to you, you weak bitch?"

But I was afraid of Sergeant Allen like nobody else in my platoon was afraid of any DI. Now, try not to lose me here, cause this all has to do with the cheating on the range, the lie, rock busting, and the point I'm trying to make.

See, one Thursday night, during phase one of training, all us recruits were ordered to sit quietly in the squad bay while one by one, Allen called us into his office. Each guy went into the office from anywhere between thirty to sixty seconds and then left and sat back down with the others. We were all polishing our boots and brass. Pretty soon, Private Harrell walked out Allen's office and hollered, "Private Harris, report to the duty hut." I popped up all military like, hauled myself to Allen's office and said, "Sir, Private Harris reporting as ordered, sir."

Allen kept an eight-and-a-half by eleven-inch sign on the wall behind his desk. It had two crappily drawn bloodshot eyes on it, and stenciled beneath the eyes were the words KEEP YOUR EYES HERE!! So I locked onto the bloodshot eyes, but I could still see Allen's crew cut, cause it was like a shoe brush sitting on his head. Very noticeable. I could even see the sweat on his forehead, and I could feel those cold black eyes on my throat. "Private Hay-riss," the guy said, "I am required by law to ask you for your religious affiliation so you can be billeted to the appropriate religious service on Sundays. Take your pick, Protestant or Catholic."

Yeah, that's what *I* was thinking, too, cause it happened to *be* the case with me. Still is, except I'm not a Muslim or Mormon, like you're saying, but I'm a Buddhist, that is, if you can actually *be* a Buddhist.

No, I'm not joking, I've studied Tibetan Buddhism since high school, but forget about that. I'm talking about this, cause this all has to do with why Sergeant Allen ended up hating me. Now, there I was standing in front of this huge hairy DI from North Carolina, and I'm figuring he probably doesn't like blacks as it is. But put a black *Buddhist* in front of him, and you mize well make your black Buddhist a commie vampire coprophiliac child molester, too. I wasn't telling this man shit. But it was a mistake, it turns out. Looking back on it, I should have said, Sir, the private is a Catholic, sir, and been done with it. I mean, at least they burn incense, Catholics, and it doesn't really matter what church you go to if you study Buddhist thought anyway.

Okay, instead of saying, "Sir, the private is Catholic, sir," I said, "Sir, the private can't say, sir."

So the little office got real quiet for a minute and he said, "Why idn't it you cain't say, Private Hay-riss?" And I said, "Sir, it's one of the tenets of the private's religion that he can't speak his religion's name." I guess, right away, you can see the mistake I was making. That dude musta been thinking, Well, well, weee-el, what have we got us here, a fuckin black candle-burnin, cowl-wearing cannibal? A nigger Aztec astral traveler?

So he leaned back in his seat and locked his fingers behind his head. And when the chair finished creaking, he said, "Well, what are some of the other tenets of your faith, Private. I'm sort of a student of religion, though I don't believe in no god."

I said, "Sir, the private doesn't believe in killing, sir."

He dropped his arms to his desktop and leaned forward and said, "You don't believe in what?"

I said, "Sir, killing, sir."

And then, under his breath, he said, "Pfffuck," then his voice got loud. "Well, god*damn,* Private Hay-riss, why on earth did you join my Marine Corps?"

I told him I joined to serve my country, but he said, "Serve your—Oh goddamn, boy, if you wanted to serve your country, why didn't you join the fuckin army, or the air force? The Corps ain't about serving your country, boy, it's about killing people. It's about body count, son." He sat back in his chair and folded his arms. He started shaking his head. "What are you planning to do in combat, pray your enemy's bullets turn into flowers? Figger they'll bring Frisbees ruther than rifles?"

I didn't have anything to say, of course, and by then I was just thinking, Catholic, Sir, the private's a Catholic, okay?

You're damn right I should have; that's what I'm saying, but it was way too late for that by then. Staff Sergeant Allen just stared at me for a spell, then said, "Are you telling me you wouldn't kill under any circumstances?" And I said, "Sir, it's what the private believes, sir," and he said, he goes, "Private, do you have a mother, I mean is she still alive?"

"Sir, yes, sir," I said, and he said, "Do you have a sister?" I told him I had two. "Well," he said, "All right, Private, let's say the Communists invade our country and they break into your home and kill your father, if you got one, and rape your mom and sisters *before* they kill 'em, then they burn your house to the ground. All right? Would you feel like killing then, Private Hay-riss, would you feel like cutting their balls off and putting them up their asses?"

Thank you. Who *you* telling? I was standing a short *yard* from the man.

Coburn, son, I was so nervous and shook up, my hands felt cold and my heart was doing triple-time. What was I doing in his Marine Corps? Truth be told, I'd wanted to join the navy, and did go see a recruiter, but on the way out the man's office, this other dude, a little cricket-sized marine, slick as a photo and about as deep, convinced me the navy was a racist yacht club and I'd never be promoted. "But hey," the man told me, "if you're into swabbing decks and scraping barnacles for four years, fill out the guy's application. No skin off my pecker. I'm just telling the truth." No way was I going to make Allen privy to that. But I did try to tell him about how I could do anything anyone else would do, out of passion, but that wouldn't make it right. I tried to say that probably everybody feels like killing at one time or another in their lives, but feeling strong about something doesn't necessarily *make* it right, but I don't know how much of this got out of me, considering my mouth was dry, and considering how hard all that, Sir, the private this-and-that crap makes it to talk like a human being.

Anyway, before I could finish, he sighed real hard and said, "Stand at ease, boy. Stand at ease." I did but I knew I still shouldn't look him in the eye or even lower my head. Well, the sergeant said, "Frankly, Private Hay-riss—and this is just between you and me—frankly, I love killing. To me, there's no better feeling in the world than killing somebody. Plain and simple. I served three years in the bush with Third Recon Battalion before I came to the drill field. Three tours, all volunteer, and by the time I left the bush I had me a hunnerd and nineteen accredited kills." He paused a long time, till the little office filled all the way up with the smell of his Brut, or his Hai Karate, or whatever it was, and then he said, "Accredited." He leaned forward in his chair, then stood, and I could tell his hands were spread flat on his desk. Held his left cheek two inches from mine. Talked right into my ear. His voice got deep and low. I could smell his breath like it was my own. Sweet with Copenhagen.

"Accredited, Private. I was good at it. Wasn't nobody better at it in my platoon. I've used .45s, Ka-Bars, M16s, M14s, M1s, AK-47s, and explosives. I've used branches, bootstraps, and steel-toed boots. I've used my bare goddamned hands. I've used my teeth. I don't care what it is, if it'll snuff a son of a bitch, it's for me. Now, you're wasting my time, and I got at least fifty more recruits to interview before reveille. I don't give a flying fuck what you are, or whether you pray on your ass, or on your knees. But when you see that god a yours tonight when you hit the rack, you tell that asshole to send me another war before I start snuffing privates. Now. Take your pick, Protestant or Catholic."

For some reason, I said, "Sir, the first one, sir," and he put me down as Protestant instead of the other. Look I gotta get back to the shop for a couple hours and bloody up this clean white apron some more. See you next break.

What? Yeah, I'm serious, I haven't had meat for three months.

II

Coburn, what's this I hear about this old lady slapping your hand for packing her stuff too fast?

Really? Too weird. So why didn't you just walk off and let one a the other kids do the order? You don't have to take that kind a crap. What, did my story make you think you were in the Corps?

Hell, that's the kinda thing Sergeant Allen used to do to me after the religion interview. That whole thing made him feel something personal for me, which you really don't want from a DI. You wanna be just another green boot, with a name he can't pronounce, and a face he can't tell from any other. But as soon as he starts feeling something personal for you, the assistant DIs and the other boots start to pick up on it. If they see the DI pick you for the close-combat "dummy" every single time he wants to demonstrate something. If the other boots see him picking on you, they get the idea you're the platoon shitbird, and they can mess with you whenever the DIs look away. And I assure you, they do a lot of looking away in the rifle range phase of boot camp.

Don't really *know* why, but I think they figure you're disciplined enough by the end of phase one, and they probably figure it's better to let the boots fight amongst themselves rather than stay pissed at them. But even at the range, Allen barely let up on me. Like this one morning we're marching to the range, and suddenly Allen says, "Private Hay-riss, you're out of step. Quit messing up my formation," even though it was obvious to everybody I wasn't. Hell, I loved to march, if you can believe that. And I was good at it, too. I loved the chop! chop! chop! sound the boots make, and to really appreciate the sound, you got to be inside the rhythm. You had to be in step. "Sir?" I said. And he said the same thing, so I did the little skip step they teach you so you can get back in step, but naturally I was out of step now, and we marched along a few feet more. "Stop!" he yelled, "Just stop!" which is what a DI says when he's all worked up. You see, when he says that instead of "Pla-toon, halt!" you're supposed to know you've really screwed up.

So he said, "Stop. Just stop." And, "Hay-riss, boy, get outta my formation." I did get out and I was pissed enough to snatch my rifle off my shoulder and knock his watermelon jaw off his neck. I said, "Sir, the private was not out of step, sir," and he said, "Close your hole, Maggot." And I said, "Sir, the private wasn't out of step till—" but before I could finish, one of the assistant DIs, Sergeant

Plumber, zipped up to me and said, "Staff Sergeant Allen just gave you a lawful order, Screw, and you better do it."

I said, "Look, man, I was in step—"

Yeah, I just went off, called the DI *man*. I surely did lose my mind.

Then Sergeant Plumber, that little shrew-faced, dog-breath prick slapped me on the right ear with his left palm and the left ear with his other and said, "Shut up! Shut up! You want a piece a me, Screw? You want some a this?" and he punched me in the chest, right over the heart, but he was on his heels so I barely felt it. Little prick.

It is. It is illegal, but that never stopped anyone from doing it. Hell, the only thing Plumber did wrong was hit me in front of seventy-seven witnesses, but if you think I or anyone else thought about reporting it, forget it. All it did was open me up to being messed with by everyone. And let me tell you something: after I finished my bends and thrusts, Sergeant Allen told me to get my sorry ass to the end of the formation, and for the first and last time, I let our eyes meet. And the mother let me. He didn't say one word, and I let myself look as long as I wanted to. I could tell he was enjoying himself.

It never got too bad, though, because I choked the devil out this big dope named Polar Bear, this jerk from Alaska, when he came at me one morning in the head.

Yeah, there I was one morning shaving, and this big, *big* white boy—head like a bus—lumps over to me and starts this rap about how his brother died over in Nam, and how it was pussies like me got good marines killed. Please. So, this boy racks up his big red knuckles like his name is Mr. G.W. Hope, and like I'm gonna get the thrashing to end all thrashings. I mean, please. I mean, really, like the great pacifist isn't gonna throw hands if some reprobate starts pushing him around. Now that's something that blows the back of my head, Cobes. Like just because you believe in God, a mother-fucker thinks you got no will to live. Like you ain't got blood and nerves. Like you don't get annoyed. It ain't but saints who can lotus-pose and burn like a minute steak without a peep. I threw myself his way, clamped my right hand around his tube, and squeezed like I didn't care. Which I didn't.

Sure he hit me, hit me a couple times. Hurt, too, afterward, but I didn't let go till a couple squad leaders yanked me off him. I'm glad they did, too, or he probably would have killed me. The cool thing, though, was when they pulled me off him I was struggling for them to let me loose, like they do in the pictures, but man I'm glad those boys had me good. Hell, I acted so crazy, Polar Bear even apologized to me after morning chow, and no one much bothered me after that. Not enough to make any difference, anyway. Besides, when Allen learned I could shoot, he got real nice to me, and what I liked about it so much was that I knew it was like cancer of the dick to this man. That's the only good thing about looking him in the eye that time. I knew how bad it ate him, being chummy with me. I was one of only four qualified expert riflemen in the whole damned company, which is four platoons—three hundred men—and I had the high score, so if he wanted ringers, he pretty much had to come to me first.

Naw, I hate guns, and I wasn't raised around them, but that's probably why I was so good at them. I came to the whole thing like a blank slate. Learned to do everything right and didn't have to unlearn the wrong stuff. It was kind of fun being good at something I'd never much thought about or cared about, and at the time I liked the way the rifle twitched in my arms, like a woman does when she climaxes.

Well, it's true. And at the time I liked the smell of cordite and hot metal, the way the targets would rise up from behind the mounds and roll back down a second after you'd squeezed the trigger. And I was always surprised when the scorecard read anything less than a five, cause it happened so rarely. I shot a two-thirty-eight out of a possible two-fifty, and for a while, it's all I wanted to do with my life. So I said sure to the sergeant, and I fired in the prone and the standing positions for one dude, and the kneeling and the standing for this punk named Grice, who was the guy who dropped the dime on us all.

Now that boy Grice was a serious piece a work. Weasely little shitbird. He had a big nose and buckteeth and chewed on the skin around his fingernails till they bled. He constantly got us in trouble for talking when we weren't supposed to, or sleeping through classes. He couldn't keep still. Ever. Even in his sleep. He twitched, jerked, laughed out loud at every lame thought that came into his nut. He was dark skinned, like a Gypsy, a Greek, an Armenian, so I'm pretty sure a lot of the other recruits and the DIs thought he was a Jew. And lemme tell you, the only military that's comfortable with Jews, it's Israel's. I can't explain that, I just know it's pretty much true. Only thing worse, I guess, would be a Buddhist.

Anyway, about half the time a recruit messed up, they'd punish the whole lot of you, and seven times out of ten, it was pretty much Grice at the bottom of things. He'd washed out of another platoon in phase two cause he couldn't qualify as a marksman, and he still couldn't shoot after retraining with our platoon. I hate to admit it, but the pressure let up on me even more when Grice was transferred into our platoon. Well, at least I helped him qualify, but I can't say that was an even trade. But he qualified along with everybody else, and the next week we marched to another camp for phase three of our training, which was all about battle formations, infantry tactics, and whatnot.

Well, look, Coburn-bud, I gotta do my last two hours, then close up shop. If you get some free time, throw on a jacket and I can finish telling you about this junk while I'm cleaning up.

Hey, kid, watch out for those old women.

All right, now.

III

I told you to bring a jacket, man; it's always about thirty-three or -four degrees up in this igloo. Go on, get your . . . Okay, suit yourself. I got some coffee here if you want.

All right, so yeah, so we were in third phase now, and it's about the best bootsville is gonna get because when the infantry stuff's over, there're only two weeks left, and you spend those back at the recruit depot where you began phase one, back at the place where they cut all your hair and brainwashed you, the place with the squad bays that look like a big Florida motel complex. No fond memories, but still it's sort of like coming home after camp. They ease up on you here. You even get to see a movie, if you behave yourselves, and they let you have all the pogey bait you want on movie night: popcorn, Coke, candy bars. The smokers are allowed to smoke more during these last two weeks; the food gets better; you spend more time polishing shoes, buckles, doorknobs, etcetera, than you do bending and thrusting. It's still boot camp, and they still drive the nails in your butt if they feel like it, but you can see things are winding down, and the DIs' hearts ain't in it. You're getting your uniform ready for final inspection. You clean your rifle till the black metal is gray. They teach you how to tame the hair in your nostrils, your ears, the tip of your nose.

Everything's being fine tuned now. They want you to feel like that big-dick polished sword in the Marine Corps recruiting ads. You're almost a leatherneck, a devil dog, an all right, high-and-tight, hard-pecker jarhead, who can rhyme like Ali and get a hun-nerd and nineteen accredited, that's accredited kills, son.

All right, man, so I sound excited. I am excited. It was an exciting time. I was almost through it. Almost a marine. Two weeks to go, I had two weeks to go till I could drive a car again, see women, listen to music, read a dozen books if I wanted to. Drink a beer. Hey, I knew I was still enlisted for another three years and nine months, but I knew that military life after boot camp wouldn't be as bad as this had all been. And boot camp is bad, young blood. It's only three months out of your life, but they use the time well. And let's face it, it takes a lot to make a fighter out of a kid born in America in the nineteen fifties. As you young bloods say, we was born "phat." And I'm not sure if the Corps ever really succeeded with me. I just don't know. I was never put into the position of having to kill anyone with my own hands.

Hey, toss me that there scrub brush, Buckaroo. Yeah, thanks.

Okay, so Grice qualified with the rifle, but Allen and Plumber and Staff Sergeant Grafton, the only human being among our DIs, just didn't like the dude. No one did. They canned him, basically, for being the cat box of the platoon. He wasn't a likable guy. Even for a so-called nice guy like me he was hard to like. He was still hard to like even when I found out that he was the clown who'd jumped from the third-floor squad bay, and even though he'd washed out twice. I couldn't stand him, even though it was clear he was terrified, that he wanted so bad to be a marine, probably cause he'd always been picked on all his life. I mean, you looked at a guy like Grice and you knew he'd wet the bed till he was eleven years old, and you knew his mom's legs and face were all bruised up, that guys in his high school gym classes put Ben-Gay in his jock strap, that people invited him to parties only to serve him piss-filled beer bottles, and he and his family lived in a home that—

Forget the "clean up" on aisle ten. Jack can get it. Let me tell this now, Coburn, before I go home, cause I'm not talking about this stuff on Wednesday or any other day of the week. Ask me about it Wednesday and I'll tell it another way. I'll add new stuff, or leave stuff out, and end up God knows where. Hell, I might even disprove my point about lies, and then where would we be? Okay then.

Grice had no place else to go. His home was a cabbage-smelling dump, and he never had a girlfriend. He looked like a Gypsy, and they figured he was Jewish so they treated him like a nigger. He wasn't good at anything. His constant flinching and rippling and nail biting got under everyone's skin. No, he wasn't good at anything, but he was gonna to be a marine. In the Marines they like to say that you never go any faster than the slowest man, which means that boot camp isn't so hard you can't make it. All you have to do is keep on trying, and you'll make it. I could see that Grice was bound and determined to make it. See, if I could have talked to Allen and Plumber and Grafton man-to-men, without all the sirs and privates and by-your-leaves, I'd have slipped up to them after chow and said, "Hey, fellas, uh, lookee here. I hope you guys aren't thinking of canning Grice, cause, hey, it looks like to me, my brothers, that my boy Grice don't got no place else to go. I mean, think about it. He jumped out a window, but he's still here. Convinced his doctor he wasn't crazy, wasn't stressed, just tripped, just fell, Doc, an accident. No, really.

"Never said an unkind word about his DIs either. He's your thinking man's shitbird, see. Laid up in a GI hospital for forty-seven days, foresaw and forgave, and came right back. Washed out in phase two, and he's still here. Nobody likes him; they kick his ass—nightly, daily—or call him names every time you guys look away, but he's *still here*. And, uh, Coach Allen, buddy—you ever look at that motherless lizard's eyes? Black, hard, cold as October. Better watch your back, your highness."

I woulda said, "Look guys, this punk's been here fifteen—eighteen weeks already, three times longer than a regular phase-two recruit. You cut him loose and he'll fight back. He'll find some way to still be here, guys, till you make him a bona fide jarhead." But I couldn't say stuff like that. They bum-rushed Grice, most likely without giving it five-minutes' thought. And besides, at the time when they were bagging him, I never thought about those things. This is the kind of stuff a guy works out at nights in a place like Corrective Custody Platoon.

It ended up like this.

Roll me that cart, man.

Well, it's just before the last week of boot camp, and it's night. Everybody except the guys on fire watch are in the rack. It feels like the holidays, the week before Christmas. Guys aren't really asleep. They're half-asleep, or half-awake. Some are whispering to their bunkies about their girlfriends and wives; some are whacking off; some of them are getting high on mouthwash or by huffing shoe polish. They're looking at the planes taking off from the San Diego airport, which was only about a five-minute walk from the squad bays. You're almost at the end, and even if you couldn't care less about either serving your country *or* killing people, you feel good that you're not guys like Grice who were put back, or guys like this phase-one boy from Platoon 2015 who froze to death in the wheel well of a passenger jet bound for Albuquerque.

So, that night, just before I slipped into full sleep, Private Johnson shook me awake and said, "Harris. Hey buddy, Staff Sergeant Allen wants you up and dressed." And I was up and dressed. Then the sergeant called me and three other men into a small formation outside the squad bay. Allen told us that after Grice had washed it, he ratted to the company commander about the ringers. The C.O., this Captain Hoeg, was fairly new to the company. He hadn't come on till we were halfway through phase three, and I didn't know a thing about him. He had a funny look, though, that bugged me. The thing I most remember about him was his huge calves. Big as rutabagas, these things were. He was built solid and low to the ground and had pink-pink skin. He had gold hair and gold-rimmed glasses that made him look more like a banker than a jarhead. He didn't look like a regular guy, and I could tell Sergeant Allen thought so, too, cause he kept saying things like, "If we stonewall this guy," and "If we deny everything to this guy," and "If we stick together like Marines do . . ." Allen marched us toward company headquarters.

We halted in front of the captain's duty hut, this Quonset hut I'm sure he'd chose in order to get the feel of the old Corps and that guts-and-glory, Pokechop Hill nonsense. Allen parked us about fifteen feet from the door, like we were a little Marine hatchback. The first guy walked in scared white and walked out whiter about five minutes later. The next guy went in and came out the same way. Then came my turn.

The dude's office was cramped and small, and the light was copper. His pink skin and gold glasses were copperish, too, and I noticed he had a cleft in his chin, which made him look even more prep than I'd remembered him. His office was lit with just this one little lamp, one of those things with the green rectangle shade and the brass stem. The whole scene felt like something out of the past, you know, a camp scene from World War I, or one of those Haitian campaigns a hundred years ago, which I'm sure was the effect my boy was shooting for. There was no air in the hut, and even less when the captain slipped one of those skinny brown More smokes from the pack on his desk and fired it up. "Stand at ease, Private," he said after a couple drags, and he tapped some ash into the big glass tray behind his name plate. Then he said, he goes, "Private, I would like to congratulate you on winning company series high shooter." He cleared his throat and said, "I suppose you know that series high shooter graduates with a meritorious promotion to private first class.

"I've seen your service record, young man, and I can see you're pretty much starting off on the right foot: high marks on all your tests, extremely high IQ scores, excellent proficiency and conduct marks. It all looks good for you, provided we can clear up a little matter concerning an accusation made by Private David T. Grice that Staff Sergeant Allen led you and several other recruits to fire in the place of certain recruits on the rifle range last month. Can you tell me anything about that? Does any of this sound the least bit familiar to you?"

And then, Coburn, man, it started feeling like I was in some kind of movie about some guys in a POW camp who were being interrogated by the camp commandant. All this dude needed was a monocle instead of glasses, suede gloves, and a foot-long holder for his smoke. Did it sound familiar, he asked me. I was just about to tell him, Suh, hell no, suh—beggin de cappin's pardon—but de private don' know nuttin bout dat dar rifle rain stuff, suh—but he said, "Before you answer me, recruit, I want to caution you about the consequences of perjuring yourself in a lawful military investigation of an Article Fifteen offense." He talked about me losing my stripe before I even got it, which meant less money. He talked about the lowering of my pro and con marks, which, believe it or not, I cared about. He told me I had never been under any obligation to honor Sergeant Allen's order cause it hadn't been lawful.

He said, "I can appreciate your being loyal to your DI. I respect it. I encourage it. By now, you're family. We're not investigating you or charging you with anything, but we have to heed the very serious charges leveled against Staff Sergeant Allen, even though they were made by a worthless little shitbird like Private Grice. But you see, even worthless little shitbirds can be right about the wrongs good men do."

Then he started talking about CCP, about what it's like to be there when you've got twelve weeks of basic under your belt. "In some ways it's easier, Private, because you're in great shape, and your mind is more disciplined than it's ever been. I've no doubt you can hack CCP. But there's another side to Corrective Custody for phase-three recruits that I've seen time and again. You're cockier than the newer recruits, and so you're more likely to mouth off at the wrong time or lose your temper and do something stupid. It could get worse for you if you screw up there, too. A fall from

CCP means a fall into the brig, and after that, Leavenworth Federal Prison, maybe.

"And besides, you could be home in a week," the guy told me. "One week from tomorrow. A ten-day leave, to see home, friends. I know what it's like, Private; boot camp is challenging in the extreme. And those ten days are close as your hands. But if you lie to me or try to willfully mislead me . . . and I find out about it, I'll have no choice but to sign you into CCP." Then he told me what he'd seen when he observed CCP. He told me everything about the week from hour to hour, so I could feel it in my mind and practically see it shining off his little gold-rimmed glasses. I didn't know what to do. I didn't know what to do.

Okay, so he carefully rolled his cigarette cherry on the bottom of his ashtray till it went out in stages, like, with the smoke getting thinner and thinner until he was all gone. And I just focused on the smoke till my brain cooled a little. He cleared his throat again and folded his hands on his desk. I noticed how long I'd been in his office and wondered what it was about me made military types blow sermons and speeches. Other guys went in and out, and I was there philosophizing like my name's Bob Confucious. The captain said, "Tell me what you can about Private Grice's accusations, Private Harris."

I didn't know what to do, so I lied, lied my ass off. Lied like a poet. Lied so long and sweet, I'm sure he believed me. It was the sweetest song you ever heard, like Ripple, and Smokey Robinson on AM radio. *No, sir, the private can't remember the slightest thing. No, your majesty, the private never fired for Privates Grice or Durant. No, sire, I don't know nuttin bout birfing no bullets. No, my liege, nothing about rifles at all, but can I rub your back for you? You look tired, good King.* What could the guy do? I'd backed up everything the first two guys had said, and evidently the last guy backed me up, cause when the captain sent the last guy out, Sergeant Allen looked happy. He marched us back and told us to get some sleep. "Well done, gentlemen," he told us.

I'm getting to that, just relax.

Well, along about 3:30 A.M. they came back for us, which I wasn't expecting. Allen marched us over and sent us into the office in the same order as before. The captain sat up straighter in his seat than he had before. He never asked me to stand at ease this time, and the overhead light was on, so the room looked pink and bright as the captain's skin. "Private Harris," he said, "let's do this quickly. One of the shooters has confessed to the whole thing and named himself and you as two of the ringers. This is it, Private Harris: deny it, and you end up in Corrective Custody for at least a week. Choose your words carefully."

Now I want you to listen to me, Coburn, cause here's the lie I believed. I know all what I told you about the two kinds of lies, and I still stand behind what I said to you, but when I was there under that dirty pink light with my body locked at attention, and the captain looking pissed off, and his thick pink fingers shuffling papers around on his desk, and the papers making this snapping noise that's making it hard to think—Hell, man I just said, "Sir, yes, sir, the private knew about everything, sir. The private would like to apologize, sir. The private shot for a couple guys, sir. That's all the private knows, sir." And he dismissed me.

I don't remember being marched back, and I don't remember sleeping that night. Only one guy stood by Allen the whole way, a guy whose name I can't remember. He was the only one of us who went to CCP. I found out later he graduated just one week after we did, and they made him platoon guide, you know, the guy who graduates with the highest pro and con marks and carries the platoon colors and gets a meritorious promotion to private first class. None of us guys in platoon 2013 graduated as PFCs. Not even our guide. Staff Sergeant Allen was busted to corporal and removed from the drill field for about a year. He did come to our graduation, though, in order to shake the hands of the guys he still liked. I acted like I didn't see him, and he did me the same favor. That's the way it should have been. Staff Sergeant Grafton told me that Allen would have his stripes back in a year and would train new DIs till he could go back to the field. "He'll be okay, Harris. Don't worry about him."

I know you're disappointed, Coburn, I can see it in your face, bud, but it wasn't a lie till now. Not to you. Or even me, really. I'm sorry, man. I was going to tell you the story the way I've always told it. Told it that way to everybody I knew, but this time I just couldn't lift the hammer. It's always been the truth I said, but it was a lie. You see, I can describe CCP so well because I *was* there, in some way. Every year I've added details, made it fuller and realer, and it was mine, Coburn, it was mine. But I'm telling the story this way now, kid, because it proves my point better than the old way, those other ways. You're that important to me, man.

No, no, it's not that simple. Understand this. I could taste the cement on my tongue. I could feel sixteen pounds tear up my biceps, my shoulders. I could see my clothes go white with all that dust. The cuff on my ankle cut me one hot afternoon—I told Munoz and them in dairy it was a Friday—and it makes me limp to this very day. I've dressed and shaved and fed myself with hands that were calloused by that steel handle. I've showered and walked and chewed to the sound of the two-blast whistle for better'n twenty years. I know how the dust gets between your teeth, how hard it is to brush it away. Can't get it out of my head. It's a lie I've always believed because I lived it.

Goddamn you, Coburn, man, don't look at me like I'm bullshitting; this ain't simple bullshit. Don't go dim on me. This proves my point. I was there. It's taken me years to shake it off, and my back still gets tight when I think about it—about that hammer, about all those nights I couldn't sleep and twisted up my sheets. Even to this day, this second, I still feel ashamed that at the last minute I sided with Grice the shitbird instead of the Drill Instructor Staff Sergeant Allen, who would have killed for me, I'm sure.

See you Wednesday, kid.

Josip Novakovich

Crimson

From *Mānoa*

THE SULFUREOUS RED TIP of Milan's match tore trails in the wet matchbox and fell into a puddle that filled a large boot imprint. The match tip shushed, and a little frog leaped out, young, brown, and merry. Milan threw away his wet cigarette, spat into the puddle, thumbed his aquiline nose, and pressed his knuckles into the eyes beneath the high-arching brows, but he couldn't get a sensation of alertness.

This tedium was not what he had expected. The war was supposed to be over in two weeks, and the Pannonian Plains of Eastern Croatia would become part of Serbia, but this was the army's fourth month of lingering in the woods and cornfields.

Most nights the Serb soldiers, who had crossed the Danube into Croatian territory and now encircled the town of Vukovar, fired from mortars, tanks, and cannons into the town. They aimed wherever the Croat soldiers could hide, and they also fired randomly at the houses. "Don't pay any attention to what you hit," said the captain. "They are just Croats, *ustasha* children, *ustasha* parents, *ustasha* grandparents. If you don't wipe them out, they'll wipe you out." As he talked, the captain's disheveled silvery hair shook, and beneath thick black eyebrows, his eyes blinked quickly.

Half of the cannons did not work because they were rusty and soldiers often forgot to oil them. When the weapons would not fire, the soldiers played cards and watched American porn movies on VCRS hooked up to tank batteries. And they sang: *Oh my first love, are you a bushy Slav?/Whoever you rub and mate, don't forget your first hate./Oh my first hate, who should I tolerate?* He wondered why so many songs dealt with first love, lost love—why all this nostalgia? His first love was only a childhood thing; on the other hand, childhood was perhaps the only genuine time of his life, the time to which all other experience was grafted, like red apples on to a blue plum tree, where apples grow stunted.

At the age of fifteen he'd had a crush on a girl, Svyetlana. For a New Year's dance party, he had put his shoes on the stove to warm them and gone to the bathroom to shave, though he had no need of shaving yet. The rubber soles of his shoes melted, but he didn't have another pair, so he went to the dance in them. Waiting to meet Svyetlana atop a stairway, Milan dug the nails of his forefingers into the flesh on the edge of his thumbnails so deep that several drops of blood dripped onto the ochre tiles of the floor.

He had then followed Svyetlana to the gym, where the dance had begun. To avoid stepping on her feet, he stood away from her. Her friends whispered and giggled—probably about his melted soles. Like Svyetlana, they were Croats and the daughters of engineers and doctors; to them he was just a Serb peasant. He slipped out of the room, his cheeks brimming.

Several days later he and Svyetlana talked in front of her house. He walked around her, desiring to touch her and kiss her, though he knew deep down that he could not. His tongue probed several cavities from which the fillings had fallen. He feared that his breath was bad, and he cursed the dentists at the people's clinic.

Thinking back on it now, he felt ashamed again. He drank more *rakia*. At the beginning of the campaign, they had had fine *slivovitz*, gold colored and throat scorching, but now only this rotten, pale *rakia*, made from doubly brewed grapes. There was no coffee. The captain had thrown a sack of it into the river, saying, "No more stinky Muslim customs and Turkish coffee dung here— is that clear?"

"But coffee originally comes from Ethiopia," Milan said as he watched brown fish surface and open their yellow mouths to swallow the black beads, which looked as if they'd spilled from rosaries used to pray for wakefulness.

"That's Muslim," the captain said.

"Didn't use to be, and it's Coptic too—that's very similar to Orthodox."

"That doesn't matter. We don't have any filters, and if you don't filter the coffee, it's Turkish."

"You could filter it through newspapers," Milan said.

"Yeah? You'll get lead poisoning."

"You will anyway," Milan mumbled, thinking of bullets.

"What did you say?"

Milan didn't respond. The captain was edgy, and Milan thought he should be quiet.

To recover from drink, Milan and many other soldiers drank more. The soldiers were festive, although the festivity seemed forced. Milan did not want to be there. But going back to Osijek, his home town in Croatia, would not do. Once, he might have lived there unmolested; now, after being a Serb soldier, he certainly could not. Officially, he was in the Yugoslav—mostly Serbian—reservist army, but, the Croats would not make that distinction. To them he would be just a *chetnik,* a Serb loyalist striving to create Greater Serbia by subjugating Croatia and Bosnia—just as to the Serbs all Croat soldiers were *ustashas,* striving to purify Croatia ethnically. He had heard that Croats had burned his home, and now he hated them. He ground his teeth, but carefully, because one of them hurt. He resented the Serbs around him as well.

One night, three Serb cops had come to his home and asked him to join the army. When he hesitated, they threatened him with knives. The Serbs would soon conquer the town, he was sure. Still, he could have stayed back. His brother, older and stronger than Milan, had not joined. Neither had a friend of his, who'd spent his young days in fights. Most of the violent and brave guys had stayed behind, and nothing had happened to them. Croats respected them for remaining in Croatia and not joining the Serb armies. The strong guys had the courage to say no. Those who had no courage, the yes men, would be the military heroes.

Many soldiers had deserted, and several companies from Serbia had left. Still, with twenty thousand well-armed soldiers surrounding a city with two thousand poorly armed and untrained Croatian soldiers, the Serb army ought to be able to take the city in a day. He did not understand what they were waiting for, launching thousands of bombs every night. What would be the point of taking a devastated city, a mound of shattered bricks? But when the tanks had gone forward, heat-seeking missiles had blown up many of them. The Croats had smuggled in some arms.

By the middle of November, the Serb ring around Vukovar seemed impenetrable: Vukovar hadn't received any supplies from Zagreb, the Croatian capital, in weeks; and the Serb guards would not allow the U.N. ambulances through for fear they concealed weapons. The Croats had run out of food and bombs. The tanks and the infantry made steady progress, taking a suburb of Vukovar. Milan's company moved from house to house, block to block, smoking people out of their cellars with tear gas. No water flowed through the pipes and most of the sewage system was empty, so the people had lived like rats, together with rats, and the rats waited for them to die, so they could eat them.

Serb soldiers killed men, even boys. Milan's captain said, "Just shoot them. If you don't, someone else will, so what's the difference—as long as there are no journalists around, and if you see a journalist alone, shoot him too." In a dark cellar, Milan stumbled as he leaned against a dank, sandy wall and slid forward. The captain shouted from above, "What are you waiting for? Keep going. There's nobody down there." Milan saw a man's silhouette against the light of a window in the cellar. The light fell in shifting streaks, hurting his eyes. The man was quietly crawling out the window. "Stop or I'll shoot," Milan said. The man slid from the window, the sand shushing. Facing a tall, bony stranger, Milan felt neither hatred nor love, but he did not want to shoot him. Could he save the man if he wanted to? He could not escape from the army himself. Still, he said, "Do you have any German marks? Give them all to me and I'll get you out of here."

"I have nothing."

"That's too bad."

"If you know God, don't shoot," the man said in a tremulous voice. "You have kids?"

"You'd better come up with better reasons for me not to pull the trigger."

"I can't harm you, why should you want to harm me?"

"Let's get out of here, with your arms up." They walked up the stairs, into the light. Milan's captain said, "What's taking you so long? Shoot him." Milan raised his rifle unsteadily and stared at the Croat's widow's peak and the deep creases separating his cheeks from his thin mouth.

"You haven't shot anything in your life," said the captain, "have you?"

"A bunch of rabbits and birds, that's all."

"You must start somewhere. What kind of soldier are you if you're squeamish?"

Milan said nothing. You can't be in a war and not kill. Although Milan was scared and embarrassed, he suddenly became curious, not so much about how men died but how they killed, about whether he could kill. Who knows, from a distance some of the bombs he had handed to the cannon man might have killed, probably had. But he had not seen it. Maybe killing an unarmed man was wrong—of course it was wrong, what else could it be—but he thought that to be a soldier he needed to pass the test: to be able to kill.

Milan still could not shoot. He imagined this man's grandchildren, and how much misery his death could mean to the people close to him. If they exchanged places, would anybody miss Milan? Probably not, he thought, and that thought irritated him, and he pitied the man a little less.

"Do you want a cigarette?" Milan asked.

"What, are you doing the last-wish bullshit?" the captain said. "If you don't shoot the bum, I'm going to shoot both of you." He lifted his pistol. "You got to be able to pull the trigger."

Several other soldiers gathered to watch this initiation rite. "Come on, Milan, you can do it!" a voice shouted. "This guy probably killed your grandfather in the world war!"

"He's only about fifty-five," Milan said.

"Then his *ustasha* father did," the voice said.

"My father was a partisan," the tall man responded.

"Yeah, right—now you are all partisans," the captain said.

Milan abhorred this public performance. His hand trembled and he tried to hide it. He used to have stage fright when he addressed audiences; holding a glass of water, his right hand would tremble, simply because once, during his high-school oral exams, it had. He was scared of groups. In that way, he and the man had more in common than he did with the other soldiers: they both were outside the group. The man could do nothing about it; for him, this was fate. Milan, on the other hand, could pull the trigger or not pull. Not pulling would be the right choice, obviously. But in front of the deranged group, it would be the wrong choice. Whatever he did or did not do would work against him. He should not have the illusion that he had a choice. He breathed hard, as though he was about to have an asthma attack.

"I know you're a good man," the man said hopefully, in a shaky voice. "You can't kill the defenseless, right?"

Milan thought that the man saw through him, through his anxiety, through his thin guts, straight to his shit. Milan saw that the man's knees shook; the man spoke out of desperation. The man's green pants sagged. There was a streak of urine on the pants, growing bigger and bigger. When Milan had been in the second grade, the teacher had called him up to the green blackboard to subtract numbers. Out of Milan's fear that he could not do it, crap, solid and dark like cattails, slid down onto the floor and smoked while the class laughed, and for a whole semester, he could not look anybody in the eye.

Milan pulled the trigger, three times, quickly.

The man fell. His hazel eyes stayed open while blood gushed from his neck onto the brick-laid yard, the narrow yard between two three-story buildings—the dank, dusty smell blowing from out of the cellars, as though the Danube water had softened the clay beneath the cracked cellar cement, and the river mud exhaled its old air of rotting caviar yolks. Uneven over the melted soil, the rain-drenched bricks darkened slightly in the new blood.

Milan breathed in the gun smoke and coughed. So that was it. It did not feel like anything as long as you concentrated on the details. He watched the crushed snail houses on the bricks, and red earthworms sliding straight, unable to coil, in the cracks between the bricks.

The captain poked his finger into Milan's buttocks. "Good job. I was worried for you, that you were a sensitive Croat-loving homosexual. You passed the test."

Milan cringed and thought he wouldn't mind shooting the captain.

"See, you passed the test." The captain's laughter smelled of onions and cigars.

Accordion music, a bass, and shrill voices came from around the corner, from a tavern with a burned-out, red-tile roof. Milan waited for a long while, then walked in. Water leaked through the ceiling, and beads of precipitated steam slid down the walls, like sweat on a harvester's back. In their muddy boots, disheveled bearded soldiers danced the *kolo,* the Serb *rondo,* more slowly than the accordion rhythm called for. They yodeled derisively and fired their guns into the ceiling. Mortar was falling off the reeds and thudding onto the wooden floor. They tilted gasoline-colored bottles of *slivovitz* and emptied half-liter bottles of beer into their mouths, pouring some of the liquid down their chins, beards, shirts.

Milan gulped down half a liter of beer and then heard a scream in the pantry. He kicked the door in with his boot and saw the hairy buttocks of a man above the pale flesh of a woman. Milan's lips went dry with a strange excitement: was he appalled, yes he was; was he lustfully curious, yes he was. He grabbed a bottle of pale brandy from the shelf and gulped, tasting nothing, but feeling a burning on his cracked lips. The woman's face was contorted in pain, but even so, he was sure he recognized the stark, pale skin, the black eyebrows under streaks of wet brown hair falling across high cheekbones: Svyetlana. And the man was his odious captain, who turned to look at him and said, "After I'm done, you go ahead too, dip your little dick, and enjoy. *Hahaha.* You'll have a complete education today. You know, Stalin recommended rape as a way of keeping up the aggressive impulses. You'll make a soldier yet."

"Don't worry about my aggressive impulses," Milan said. He lifted the rifle and with its wooden butt struck the captain's head. The captain's head collided with the woman's, driving hers onto the brick floor. Milan kicked his head away from hers, and when his rifle struck the captain's skull again, the bones cracked. The man bled from his mouth onto the woman's belly. She had swooned. Milan dragged him away from her and covered his head with an empty coffee bag. What to do with her? How to protect her from the bar? His heart beat at a frantic pace, and his windpipe wheezed.

This was she, his childhood memory, Milan thought, as though all that singing about first loves and hates had summoned her. He gazed at her parted scarlet lips, thin vertical lines ruffling the shiny skin. The swollen lips were shapely, twin peaks of a long wave, a wave of blood, whipped by internal winds from the heart and netted in the thin lip-skin, which prevented it from splashing out, onto the shore, onto Milan. Only the thin membrane, the lips, separated his rusty plasma from hers.

He remembered how Svyetlana's lips had looked when he had leaned forward to kiss her. Her lips had parted like now, but when it was clear that he would not lean closer, she chewed her bubble gum loudly and, it seemed, challengingly, disrespectfully—her saliva gluing and ungluing foamily beneath the blue belly of her tongue. Coldly she stared at his lips through her deep brown eyes with their black stripes. And then she vanished without a whisper through a large wooden gate, into a dark garden with vines of ivy and grapes. As he gazed after her, his heart bounced in his chest like a wild dog on a chain. After that, they were strangers to each other, but he continued to yearn for her.

Milan suspected that his longing had been unrequited because of his cowardice. He had not had the courage to declare his love to her. In a dangerous world, wouldn't a woman be attracted to courage? She went to Zagreb, graduated from the school of architecture, married a doctor, and stayed a class above Milan. Perhaps out of despair, he was loud and unruly and flunked out of the engineering school at the University of Belgrade. Once, when it was his last chance to pass an exam in thermodynamics, he'd stayed in the chess-club room because he thought he'd figured out a mate in five. He stayed for the romance of it, for the sake of freedom, saying in his way, *Fuck you!* to school, ambition, and class—instead of going to the exam, which he thought he'd flunk anyhow. After that, he became a subdued engine man, driving cargo trains all over the damned federation: a blue-collar worker, the most despised in the socialist worker's state.

All his failures had to do, Milan was sure, with Svyetlana's aloofness. She could have seen what he was up to and could have helped him approach her. And now he had killed a man, two men, for her, for himself.

He stared with a sorrowful glee at the woman lying at his feet, her skirt and bra ripped open and her supple breasts tilting downward and trembling with her uncertain breath. He felt a thrill and a shudder. Below her blood-smeared ribs, her thighs, ample, curvaceous, defenseless, loosely stretched before him.

Milan carried the woman outside and gave her aspirin and water to drink. She looked at him disdainfully and asked, "You saved me or something?"

"I don't know whether anybody saved anybody, but you could thank me. Maybe I saved you."

"Will everybody be free to rape me now?"

"No, you can go. Nobody will rape you."

"I have a horrible headache." She blinked.

"The captain's head knocked against yours pretty hard. Just a concussion would be my guess."

As he escorted her to a bus crowded with Croat women and children, she stumbled alongside him, but refused his support. He wondered if the rusty bus with bullet holes would make it or if at some drunken sadist's whim a sulfureous bomb would strike the bus on the road and burn up all the passengers, including her, and if—the way things were going—he would be the one throwing the bomb. He felt sorry for the woman and asked, "What's your name?"

"What difference should it make?"

"Come on, aren't you Svyetlana?"

"No. Olga."

"Are you sure?" Milan gripped the woman by the shoulders so he could look into her face and compare it with his memory of Svyetlana's—and so he could lean on her, because he was stunned.

She pushed his arms away. "Sure I'm sure, at least about my name. Probably about nothing else."

"Olga in the Volga. And I'm Mile in the Nile," he muttered drunkenly as she stepped onto the bus. How was the confusion possible, he wondered. But the woman was not lying: her voice was higher and her eyes darker than Svyetlana's.

In a ditch, Milan took the uniform from a dead Croat soldier. He walked into the tavern, where his comrades still danced. In the pantry he dressed his captain in the uniform, and then he carried his body out and dumped it on a horse-drawn carriage, onto a pile of a dozen corpses. Milan shifted uncomfortably because the blood had soaked through his cotton uniform and shirt, gluing the fabric to his skin. A dark-orange horse with strong round buttocks stood, his head bent to the road, which was covered with empty gun shells. His hoof screeched over shards of glass. The shrill sound shook the horse's ears, reddened and pierced by the sun's rays so that a thick vine of veins stood out. A round fly sat on an ear, filling up its green belly on a vein. Milan was jittery, as though he'd had delirium tremens. Who knew what diseases lurked in this city, where cats had been eaten and rats frolicked in the walls; where cat and rat skeletons lay entwined together; where maggots formed shifting gray mounds over loose flesh detached from bones. He did not dare take a deep breath, for fear of inhaling a plague. Piles of bodies lay on almost every street corner, yellow eyes looming out of purple faces. Soldiers—some with their teeth chattering as though they suffered from hypothermia—poured gasoline over the piles and burned them.

After taking Vukovar, Milan's army progressed north to surround Osijek. One night while on guard duty in a far-flung trench beneath oak trees with long branches and water-darkened trunks, Milan sat on a sack of sand. Loud rain was knocking the last brown leaves off the branches. Drops hit the mud, splashing it.

The wetness carried the smells of poisonous mushrooms and old leaves, not only the leaves that had just zigzagged to the ground but also the leaves from the last year, and from hundreds of years ago, with mossy, musty whiffs of old lives in the soil, and new lives that slid out of the cloudy water and soiled eggs: snails, frogs, earthworms. When the rain let up, the leaves sagged and a cold wind swayed them, and water continued sliding down in large drops, which hung glittering in the moonlight before falling onto Milan, into his shirt and down his hairy neck.

The other guard on duty snored. Irritated, Milan stood up and then realized there was nobody else in sight. The series of events in Vukovar had changed him: he no longer feared what would happen if he were caught deserting the Serb army or if he were apprehended by the Croat police. Milan crawled out into a cornfield, threw away his gun, tore off the army insignia, and by dawn walked into a village near Osijek. He went to his brother's place, where his brother let him sleep on the sofa.

When Milan walked in the streets, those who recognized him merely looked at him suspiciously, as they did everybody, more or less. Milan joined the citizens who placed sandbags in front of all the shops and windows, and while doing so he wondered whether he was sandbagging his conscience more than the buildings. One afternoon three months after the fall of Vukovar, Milan had just finished piling sandbags. Dusty and sweaty, he walked past the scaffolded red-brick cathedral, where masons plastered up grenade holes in the bricks. Wet cement kept falling and thudding like hail. Listening to the thudding and to the ringing of a tram, he noticed a graceful and pale woman with black hair and a full figure walking toward the Drava River, frowning, her eyes glassy and luminous. Milan recognized Olga, and at first was surprised that he could have confused her for Svyetlana, then scared that she might jump off the bridge. But she had survived Vukovar, so ending her life now, when it was no longer threatened, would be absurd.

"Hello," he addressed her, "what a fine day, isn't it?" She shrank back as she recognized him. He was thinner than before, and white streaked his oiled brown hair. Still, his face had to be unmistakable: the eyes set deep and wide apart under the brows;

large ears that stuck out the same way they did when he was a boy. He thought that he still looked like a boy, had the same expectant, big-eyed look, of desire, hunger, envy, even love, perhaps: he had been dreaming of Olga many nights.

"What are you doing in Osijek, of all places?" she asked.

"I'm looking for a job." He was so nervous he could hardly breathe.

"That's brave of you, after what you've done."

"What have I done?"

"You know best . . ."

"Where do you want me to go? To hell? Where isn't it hell these days?"

"Go to Canada or Britain, and give them a story of how oppressed you are here. They love those stories."

"Why shouldn't I be here? I killed a Serb officer. Anyhow, the Croatian government wants to prove to foreigners that Serbs can live in Croatia, and I'll test them. I can't live in Serbia. In Belgrade, from what I've heard, if you are a Serb from Croatia, the police look for you where you live, in cafés, bars, and even churches, to draft you for the war in Bosnia. And the Belgraders, you think they'd be grateful to someone like me? They'd say, 'What are you doing here? You brought the sanctions and poverty upon us, and now you want to sit on your butt, sipping espresso? Go back to the war, get the hell out of here!' "

"That's not a particularly touching story."

"I know it."

"So now you want to live here as though nothing had happened."

"What else?"

"It might be easy for you."

"I saved you from—"

"I guess. But I'm pregnant—since then."

"I thought I killed him before he could do it."

"Sorry, but I have to rush. It's almost two o'clock—the abortion clinic will close."

"Don't do it."

"Why not? Who'd take care of the baby?"

"I will. I don't mean that we should get married. But then, why shouldn't we?"

"Why would you do that? We don't know each other."

"We do."

They stood in front of a café, and in silence they looked at each other. With blue lines under her eyes, she looked tired, but she was also curious, scrutinizing him.

She motioned toward the café and they walked in. They sat by the window. "I replaced the windows here." Milan proudly knocked on the glass. He didn't like his part-time job fixing windows, but he could bear it full time, he thought, if he lived with Olga. He enjoyed looking at her mouth as she answered his questions about where she worked (taught high-school science), whether she had other kids (didn't), parents (mother died a while back, father was killed in Vukovar), a house (no, but apartment, yes). He had kissed those crimson lips while she was still unconscious in Vukovar. He thought he should tell her about it, but he was certain that if he did she'd leave right away, and he wanted her to stay. Still, he thought that he should tell her, but instead he said, "What kind of music do you like?" and decided to tell her later.

"You want to make small talk? Years ago, that's how people talked—wasn't it nice? I don't like to listen to music anymore, but I play it on the piano, mostly Bach."

He clasped his hands, which seemed to want to touch hers of their own will.

"How many people have you killed?" she asked, staring into his eyes.

"Yes, I've killed. I don't know what counts. Feeding bombs into cannons that I didn't fire myself—how do you count that?"

"There'll be an accounting formula in hell, I'm sure." She grinned at him.

"Come on, that's not funny. You're right: I'll pay for it somehow. I wish I'd run away sooner. But then I wouldn't have met you."

A waiter with a round tray and a black apron came by, and Milan ordered a bottle of red wine. He looked through the crimson wine at his thin fingers. Her glass beads below her long neck glittered through the wine like rubies.

They gulped the wine.

"Don't go that abortion clinic," said Milan. "I got divorced because my wife and I couldn't have kids—we were married for a year. Since my twenties I've always wanted to have a baby. Wouldn't you love a little wet infant to crawl between us, and look up at us, with hazy, filmy eyes, to see the world for the first time— a world that would be new, innocent, big, admirable, imitable, and that we would be a part of? Wouldn't you like those astonishing little fingers to grasp your finger, barely closing around it, and to tug at it?"

Olga smiled and did not say anything.

Milan imagined the power of a new life sleeping with his dreams inside her, and the dreams caressing her. He had not dared to think so concretely about a baby. Now he liked imagining a biological happiness with her, more with her than with any other woman, more than with his lost childhood loves or pretty young women.

She pursed her lips. "But the kid's not yours."

"We wouldn't tell him. Or her."

"Mixed marriages aren't exactly in fashion." She stood up as though she'd had enough nonsense.

Leaving behind a crumpled blue bank note on the tablecloth, he followed her into the windy and darkening streets. "Eventually Serbs and Croats marrying each other will be all the rage," Milan said. "You'll see. People will want to prove they're not nationalists."

They walked to the river bank, then looked into each other's eyes, calmly, and listened to the ice in the Drava River cracking. They watched floating ice pieces piling on top of each other, breaking, sinking, rising, colliding, exploding—sharp, white, jagged, glaring in the sun like gigantic glassy swords clashing with slabs of marble. He imagined that the ground they stood on floated north like an iceberg while the river stayed in place.

"You think the ice comes from Austria?" Milan asked.

"And Hungary."

"And it's flowing down to Serbia. See how we are connected."

"Who is? The rivers?"

"Our waters, we."

The wind that blew chilled them, and they walked past an aluminum kiosk with postcards, cigars, and a saleswoman who yawned with her gleaming silver teeth. From behind them, the wind pushed Olga and Milan, and they walked effortlessly, with their chilled ears red and translucent against the sunshine, which shone in thick rays though black branches of leafless acacias. They pulled up their collars, and stepped into the tobacco cloud of a tavern, listened to the Hungarian *chardash,* and drank more red wine. They walked out into the sleety winds, with lips purple from the dried wine, and they huddled against the weather, against each other, making one standing mound, a man and a woman against each other.

Milan now worked full time as a glass cutter. Because of occasional shelling and frequent low MIG jet flights, which penetrated the sound barrier above the town with loud explosions, there was no shortage of broken windows. He and Olga enjoyed each other's company, and he moved in with her. When the baby was born, he held her hand in the hospital, and cut the cord with a pair of scissors. They got married, and lived happily—almost. Milan had rat and war nightmares and ground his teeth in his sleep, and during the day, if he wasn't playing with Zvone or working, he'd sit in the armchair and brood. He couldn't talk about all that had happened in the war. Not saying wasn't good; saying might be worse. In a way, it was the same kind of bind he was in when he shot the poor man in Vukovar. And, to a large extent, it was the poor man who troubled him, until one evening at home, two years later, when Olga showed Milan her family pictures while their boy slept with a light snore that made them both laugh.

"This is my dad, see," she said, pointing to an old, brown photo. "Here he's teaching me how to walk. Today would be his birthday, is his birthday." Tearfully, she looked at Milan, who winced and bit his lips.

"So still no word on him? Do you think you'll ever know what happened to him?" His voice was barely coming out of his throat.

"He was in Vukovar when you were there—maybe you saw him?" she asked.

"Such a tragedy—it really saddens me to think about the loss you've suffered." He paused. "Is there any brandy?"

"You drink too much."

"Or too little." She ignored his request and showed him more pictures of her father.

"This is awful. I don't know how to say this. But I must—I killed him in Vukovar."

She dropped the family album on the floor.

As soon as he'd spoken, he regretted what he'd done. After all that had happened, why did he feel the need to be honest? Why not keep secrets to himself, live lovingly, and cling to the bit of life that he had left?

"I didn't want to kill anybody, least of all my future father-in-law. I didn't know it was your father, at the time I didn't know you either, but the man I shot looked exactly like the one in that picture."

"Oh, my God."

"The captain had me at gunpoint, and if I hadn't done it, he and the soldiers around us would've killed us both. So it's just a technicality who pulled the trigger. I would've been forced to pull the trigger on my own father."

She moaned.

"I can't say I'm sorry—it wouldn't make sense to be sorry for something I had no control of."

She moaned and lowered her chin to her collarbones.

"That's amazing bad luck. How many people lived in Vukovar? Thirty thousand? Two thousand men in their fifties? And to chance upon your father . . . But not to chance upon anybody would have been even more unlikely."

"Why didn't you tell me sooner?"

"I only saw a small, hazy picture of him before, and while I could tell there was a similarity, I couldn't be sure—there's often a similarity. I'd even mistaken you for someone else. I'm no good at recognizing faces. Even if I had been sure before, how could I have simply come out with it: 'Listen, I killed your father.' Why wreck a family—for we have been reasonably happy, haven't we?"

After this, Olga would not allow him to stay in the bed with her and Zvone anymore.

One evening while Milan brooded, Olga said, "All right, we can't live like this—you can join us."

But he continued sitting and sulking.

"What's wrong?" she said.

"There's always something," he said.

She stood above him and said, "Why are you talking in riddles? I know what else there is. That captain of yours who, you said, raped me? Strange that we never talked about it."

"It's not strange. I didn't think women liked to talk about such things. Yes, he was doing it when I bludgeoned him."

Lately she had remarked several times that Zvone looked like Milan: he had the same kind of drop-off between his forehead and the rest of his face, and his broadly separated, large hazel eyes peered hungrily from beneath his brows.

It angered Milan that, no matter how hard he tried, just one hour out of whack made it impossible to live the rest of his life honestly and peacefully.

She paced the room, kicking her way through plastic cars, trucks, and animals donated by UNICEF, Caritas, and German Protestant churches. "Zvone looks like you. How come?"

"Isn't it obvious."

"I can't believe it."

"Listen, throughout the war, I was shoved around. Once I killed your rapist and my rapist, I felt free for the first time ever, and I was in a frenzy, beside myself, and I couldn't control either the drink or the lust. I couldn't handle anything consciously anymore. And I didn't know that I could have children—I was told my sperm count was too low. So later, I didn't think it made any sense to tell you; I thought it was either the captain's seed or, who knows, there could have been people before him. But when I noticed the similarity, I thought that in a way we should be happy: we are the biological parents."

"So you killed the rapist, to rape me, and you never told me!"

"What could I tell you? At that time I was unconscious, drunk, and there you were. I just lay with you. I did not force anything. I did it in some kind of dizzy grace period, when I was free from everything, even from the past and the future—lucky to be alive, and unlucky, doomed."

"But I was unconscious!"

"So?"

"That's rape."

"No, rape is done against a person's will, not without the will."

"That's a sophism. You raped me."

"Come on. If we were both unconscious, how could it be rape?"

"But you weren't."

"I wouldn't be so sure. Anyway, I put you on the bus. If I hadn't, the whole bar would've raped you and they would have shot you after it."

"So you're saying I should thank you?"

He didn't respond, but threw up his arms in despair. What could he do about it—about going off the edge for an hour of his life? Suffer for the rest of eternity? Kill himself?

She was wearing a gold necklace with a cross. She grabbed it, tore it from her neck, and twisted the cross in her fingers. "If it weren't for the child, I'd kill you."

She wept. He came close to her and put his arm on her shoulder. She shuddered and pushed his arm away.

They paced the room. Lightning filled the room with flashes of blue light, and he saw her as if she were in a series of blue snapshots. In silence they stumbled over chairs and walked on toys, crushing them.

Milan thought how strange it was that he should be held responsible for the past, three years ago, when he was conscripted and enslaved—when he wasn't even himself. "We all have multiple personalities," he said. "One of us is the past, and another the future, and there's no present me. We are vacant right now—spaces through which the past and the future disagree." He sounded academic, but he was trying to articulate his alienation—and while alienation and displacement usually troubled him, now he wanted them to help him. Yes, it would be good to be as alienated from Vukovar as possible.

"What nonsense. Don't philosophize. Philosophy is an excuse. You have no excuse," Olga said. There hadn't been a lightning flash in a while, but thunder grumbled and rattled the loose windows. Zvone cried in the bedroom, and Olga went to him. Milan watched from the door. Zvone sucked eagerly, kneading a breast with his little fists, sinking his untrimmed nails into the opulent flesh. Milan could see that she did not mind the scratchy nails, the little loving kitten's claws, nor the raspy tongue. Letting one of his hands roam, Zvone caught the other venous breast and smiled when he got it to squirt.

Milan undressed and went to the sofa. The baby, as though sensing the tension in the room, kept sucking for an hour, and Milan heard Olga say, "It's empty, they are both empty—can't you stop? Do you want some bread?"

"No. Milk, I want my milk," he said.

"Time to go to sleep," she said and turned off the light.

"Light. I want light!"

She switched the light on and read him a book about happy bears and happy eagles eating happy fish.

The lightning storm resumed, and the thunder rumbled the silverware on the table. "Lions are fighting," Zvone said.

Loud raindrops hit the windowpanes. "They are crying too," Olga said. "They are knocking for us to let them in."

After a while Milan's mouth was sticky, tasting of plum brandy and onions. He didn't want to walk to the bathroom to brush his teeth, in case Olga slept, and he wondered how much she must hate him at that moment. She probably wanted him to die in his sleep. He dozed off, then awakened to a stabbing pain. Olga was lifting a hand that held a large kitchen knife, and before he had time to realize that he was not dreaming, she drove the knife down into his abdomen. She leaned hard on the knife until the stainless steel ground against his rib.

The pain scorched him. He pushed her and then kicked her

against the wall. He stood up and staggered, bleeding, then collapsed, but stayed half-conscious in the burning pain. The boy woke up and screamed, "Mama, I'm afraid! Lions are biting! Where's Dada?"

Now she panicked too: the cold blue lightning revealed the spooky aspect of her deed—a man in a black puddle. She called an ambulance and went to the hospital alongside Milan, with Zvone at her breast. She did not know her husband's blood type, so finding out took time. The hospital was out of supplies of his blood group. As she belong to group O and was thus a universal donor, she gave as much as she could: three pints of blood, enough to keep him alive until new blood came, and enough to exhaust her. Now her blood would stream through him. Zvone wanted to suck, but she was empty.

As Milan came to, Zvone cried, "Milk! I want more milk!" Zvone sucked hard.

Milan's body hurt and his ears buzzed, but he listened in elation to Zvone's voice, which he'd thought he'd never hear again, and the voice cried, "Milk!"

"No, no more milk," Olga said. "Maybe blood, if you like. Keep sucking, it will come. There's some left."

Peter Weltner

Movietone: Detour

From *Fourteen Hills*

1.

GULLS STRUT on the dock. His fresh blue shirt spangling in sunlight, Sayler sweats as he coils hawser around bollard. If his crotch itches, he stops to scratch it. While he works, a tug nudges a sludge barge up river. Train-flats, two freighters, and a fireboat glide past. Chain pulleys carrying supplies clatter shipside as swarming men on deck funnel down planks to the pier and race toward shore. Back on board, his crew the last done, almost alone, Sayler tries to rest in his bunk. His mind sinks into a sleep like the sea.

Dead eyes are as lusterless as scratched marbles. On oil-slicked water, burning hair and skin crackle. As you hook them out of the drink, their stiff bodies squeak like wet rubber. Blood seeps from their noses and ears. When in her small garden Sayler's mother, clipping roses, pricked her thumb on a thorn, her blood did not gush, but trickled. Just before the crash, his father threw his body across Sayler to keep his son's head from smashing into the windshield. Afterwards, all Sayler heard were tires whirling, the wind, and his father's voice rasping, "May God work more miracles through this boy." When he looked at the gash across his thigh, his blood was barely oozing out of the wound. He wakes in his bunk sweating.

An old guy sitting on the crapper to his right whistles "Jingle, Jangle, Jingle" to himself. In the shower, a fog-like steam veils the men's bodies and clears only once they've all left the room. Alone Sayler stands in the corner prodigious and alert, like a boy hidden by a wall of bushes and woods, scrubbing himself in a clearing under heavy rains. No undertaker has laved a body more carefully, no sea washed one more clean.

He spit shines his shoes to a bootblack's pride. His fresh whites stick to his skin. With a small steel mirror, Sayler checks the tilt of his hat on his head. He flips open his wallet and counts the bills. If he is careful, they will last until the end of his leave.

He smartly salutes four times before he steps back on land. His watch says it's already half past nine. When he stares beyond the reach of the city's lights into the sea-dark sky, he finds neither moon nor stars. Their absence twitches a nerve in his groin.

Times Square lures him like a pulp book cover. His lips shape the names spelled out on a dimmed marquee. A barker wearing a weather-worn, snap-brim fedora pulled down to his ears tugs on the sleeves of the two marines who peek into the crack between the doors to a peep show. At the end of the block, another calls to the crowd and points to where the jazz band's playing some Dixieland. Globes hanging in a triad draw Sayler's eyes to the front of a honky-tonk bar where soldiers huddle singing "Who Wouldn't Love You," slurring the words. At each mistake they make, they laugh harder. Sayler claims a surveyor's patch of vacant pavement and tries to count the pinpoints of the skyscrapers. He needs to find a place to sleep. Across the street, GIs fire rifles at metal targets in a shooting gallery. Two whores wearing short yellow skirts stroll past him, their arms linked, their heels clicking on the sidewalk.

The hot night sky sweats. Heading uptown, Sayler reaches a street as black as the sea, the air sharp with the smell of brine, and turns away from the piers. Close to Third Avenue, he stops where the sidewalk and part of the street are slashed by slats of light from a window in which a sign reads, Cheap Rates. By Day, By Week. On the El, a train screaks past.

The desk clerk is as thin as light at dusk. When he speaks, his voice bat-squeaks. He studies the blocks pencilled in on a large torn paper sheet, deliberates, and slips Sayler a key to six fifteen, saying, "You tell 'em yours is the cot." Sayler looks at the clock that ticks above the rows of empty pigeonholes and slides the key toward him under the grate.

The elevator doesn't work. From the sixth floor stairwell landing, he hears some shouts, a few curses, laughter. When he reaches his room, the door is wide open but, though he knocks loudly, no one bothers to answer. Two sailors are playing cards. Smoke fogs the room. Sayler drops his sack in a spare corner and leans against the wall near an unmade bed where a guy, wearing only his skivvies, lies smoking a cigar, a round glass ashtray nestled in the black mat of his chest hair. He glares at Sayler and blows three perfect smoke rings. "You gotta be kidding. Where you supposed to sack?"

Sayler scratches the back of his neck. "Desk clerk said that cot."

"Tough luck." A fourth ring drifts toward the ceiling. "It's taken."

The card dealer twists around to take a look at the newcomer. "Aw, let him have it, Doc."

"Yeah," a red-haired kid winks. "Better him than that stinking spic. Where'd he go to, anyhow?"

The dealer throws down another card. "Ben spooked him. Scared him shitless with that knife of his."

"Hell, Atkins," the red-haired kid complains, "another humping deuce. Next time, let me cut those fucking cards."

"Your first night back on shore?" Atkins asks Sayler without taking his eyes off the deck.

"Yeah."

"Which ship?"

When Sayler tells them the name, the guy on the bed snickers. Sayler sees he likes to show his body off, his sinews pulled tight, his thews taut. "Where's the head?" Sayler asks, "I got to pee."

The guy in his skivvies crushes out his cigar and sets the ashtray down on the bare floor. "Down the hall." He studies Sayler like a cop a suspect. "What do you think, Chuck?"

"He looks okay to me," Atkins says, reshuffling the deck. "What do you think, T.K.?"

The red-haired kid shrugs. "Sure. Hit me, Chuck."

"Ben'll have to talk to you too," the guy on the bed explains.

"What is this?" Sayler says. "The third degree?"

Doc's tongue probes the inside of his cheek. He spits. "We're going crawling later. Before the bars close. Maybe find us some girls. We're particular about who we get drunk with, that's all. Ain't that right, Chuck?"

"Damn." T.K. snorts. "A lousy trey."

"Want to come along?" Chuck invites Sayler.

"Not tonight, guys. Too tired. Maybe tomorrow," Sayler says. Outside in the corridor, Sayler passes two soldiers, both drunk, each barely supporting the other. In the john, as his piss floods the urinal, he reads the numbers and names etched or scrawled on the crumbling wall and studies the crude pencil sketches. But he wants mostly to sleep.

He waits downstairs in a corner of the crowded lobby for the others to leave. After they've gone, back up in the room, he opens the window, strips, and stretches out on the cot. Hours later, when Sayler wakes as if startled from another bad dream, the red-haired kid is spewing vomit out the window as Atkins clutches the boy's waist to keep him from falling. The wall across the alley is a black backdrop to the struggle of a four-legged man.

"Jesus, T.K.," Atkins pleads, "take it easy, buddy. Keep still."

A big guy Sayler hasn't seen before leans back against the closed door and wolf whistles. "Ain't they cute?" he says to Doc.

"Shut up," Atkins hollers, "and give me a hand, damn you, Ben."

"Not a chance," Ben says. "I'd like to see him fall."

"Get a hold of yourself, T.K.," Atkins orders, "I mean it now."

"Fuck him. The fruit can't hold his liquor," Ben says, sneering at Doc who upends a nearly empty bottle and drinks it dry. "Who's the new girl in the cot?" he asks Doc, grabbing the bottle from him and tossing it across the room toward the window where it shatters only a few feet from Atkins and T.K.

"Damn it, Ben," Atkins yelps.

"Okay. He's okay," Doc says, his speech slurred.

Ben's nostrils widen. "Sure he is."

"No, really."

"What's your name, sailor?" Ben commands, officer-like. His voice sounds as if it means to stalk him.

When Sayler tells him, the big guy whoops and slaps his hands together. "My mother's maiden name," Sayler explains fast and spells it twice.

"Oh, Christ," T.K. moans and staggers toward his bed.

"Let's go," Ben nudges Doc. "We got better things to do than play nursemaid to these old ladies. The night's still young and there's money to be had and whores to lay, right, Doc?"

"You better believe it, Ben," Doc says, racing him out.

When Sayler finds sleep again, he hears his mother crying and he wants to tell her there's no need. He'll be all right. But she continues to rock in her chair like someone beyond comforting. A torpedo hits below the waterline. After the last blast, the ship slowly sinks. Then the sea is calm and empty again. Sayler sees a distant shoal and feels less frightened as he swims toward it. But no one is there. Nothing is ever there.

When he wakes at dawn, the shade blows in from the open window, and a single bar of light crosses Atkins's and T.K.'s heads where they lie sleeping side by side in a narrow bed. The big guy sprawls on an uncovered mattress laid out on the floor and snores like a horse snorting. Doc has bunched his sheets into a corner of his bed and lies on his back, his stub cock flopping through the fly of his shorts. The room smells like a drying pond.

2.

Before the others wake, Sayler showers in a rusted stall, dresses, and escapes, though it is already nearly noon. Under the shadows of the tracks of the elevated railway, he slowly eats an orange he's just bought at a stand and cut open with a penknife he carries in his pocket, picking out the seeds with the blade. An ancient Chinese woman in slip-slop slippers passes. A young girl wearing a blue cotton frock and Minnie Mouse white high heel shoes strolls by, then turns around to stare and wink. In the air, he sniffs grease, smoke, malt. Already the bars are as packed as troop trains. He walks west, then north toward the park he remembers from his last leave. Down narrow streets, delivery trucks rumble and reverberate. Fleshy women sit on the stoops of smoky brownstones, sipping the sun, their lips thick and wet. All around him, tall buildings shine bottle-bright.

Sayler reaches the park at the circle. Paradise, his father had preached, was the park which the Lord had built for Adam in Persia or Mesopotamia. No other will ever be like it. On the plains where Sayler grew up there were only dust and wind. Every day he had to sweep the dirt out of the white clapboard church and the small frame house where they lived across the road. When the winds stilled, his father would point to the clouds, "White as a good man's graveclothes," and to the sun which he said coursed through the sky like a burning and a shining light to all the gentiles. As they mopped the church one April close to Easter, his father, seized by the spirit, laid both hands on Sayler's head and, re-baptizing him Jonah, delivered him to the Lord.

Sayler stops at the streetlight and watches the driver in the wing-fendered Checker cab curse the stooped driver of an old hansom. The sky sparkles, quiet as the sky over the sea. In the park, children are flying kites. A solitary man dressed all in green sets up croquet hoops near the boating pool. On the other side of the path, four fat and grizzled men toss horseshoes. Sayler squats on a hump of basalt rock. A heart-shaped leaf spirals down onto his lap, its broad blade tough and shiny. Sayler jumps up, brushes off the seat of his bell-bottoms, and exits from the park onto the street where everyone he sees looks wrinkled and rich.

He starts up the steps to the museum where he senses he doesn't belong. Once inside, he imagines himself in a mansion or palace, himself its lord or prince. He passes quickly through the chambers filled with gloomy religious pictures or portraits until he finds the room he remembers liking best during his first visit here, where the paintings' colors are billboard-bright and the surfaces thick with juicy gobs of paint as tempting as the candy buttons he used to scratch off paper to eat. He approaches one in which lilies flicker where they float on turquoise water, checks both doors for guards, and leans into the painting to squeeze a bubble of pale yellow to see if it will ooze like a popped pimple onto his thumb and fingers.

He escapes fast, almost running down both flights of stairs, laughing so hard he can barely breathe. At the park wall, he slows down and leans against it, rubbing his thumb against his forefinger, darkening the yellow pigment with his skin's own oils.

"Hey you. Sailor," he hears.

Sayler stuffs his hands between his armpits and glances over his shoulder. The man is dressed in a white suit like those men wear in hot places in movies, his face angular and ax-head thin like an actor whose name Sayler can't remember. "You talking to me?"

His sharp chin juts out as he jangles change in his pocket. "Don't you realize that Monet is a masterpiece? Irreplaceable?"

Sayler eyes him nervously. "So what?"

"So what?" the man burbles. "So what? I should have you arrested is what."

Sayler arches his back and yawns. "Anyone ever tell you you look like that actor? You know, the one in all those shoot-'em-ups."

"What?" The man smiles like a child still half asleep. "Oh, I see. You're flattering me. For a price, I imagine. Well, then. How much?"

Sayler grins back boyishly. "Not much."

"Why is it I doubt that? Boys like you are all expensive." The man steps closer. "Let me take you to the Hotel Lexington first. We can go to the Hawaiian Room and drink out of coconut shells and talk. Would you like that?"

"I don't drink," Sayler says.

"What a pity." The man's right eyebrow crooks suspiciously. "But I won't insist."

Two boys dash past them on their bikes. A young woman leads a band of children up the museum's steps, each child holding the hand of another, all of them chattering. A taxi stops at the curb and lets out a man whose gold watch flashes in the sun. The man in white stands next to Sayler and whispers, "I can't resist blonds.

Do you understand me? They'll be my downfall, no doubt. But who would mind sinking in eyes so blue?"

Sayler shrugs and rubs a little of the yellow paint onto the man's sleeve. "I got to meet a buddy down at the Midtown Bus Terminal in a couple of hours."

"I don't live far from here. There's time."

The building is only five blocks away. Its façade shines like gilt in the noon sun. Sayler pauses to notice the bowed iron window grates and the iron scrolled glass door. As they pass through it, the doorman pretends not to see Sayler and acknowledges only the man in white linen with a salute to the brim of his cap. As they enter the apartment, Sayler observes the pictures as dark as those in the museum's darkest rooms, the closed curtains, and the gloomy wood panels and walls. When they reach the bedroom, the man is trembling and nuzzles Sayler's offered neck. Like blind men's their fingers read each other's bodies. They undress slowly, but move swiftly once naked, rushing into each other like water into a ruptured hull.

"Would you mind telling me your name?" the man asks Sayler as he dresses. "I like knowing names. Mine is Bill. Bill Blake, in fact." He finds his wallet in his suit pants and hands Sayler a fifty. "You were very sweet. Really."

"Thanks," Sayler says and stuffs it in his pocket.

"Bill Blake," the man repeats. "Please, sailor," he pleads.

" 'Sayler.' Just call me 'Sayler,' " Sayler says, laughs, and leaves.

When he steps back outside into the light, the blaring sun burns his eyes. His brain feels shackled. He breathes deep but the world under his feet buckles like the earth after he's been months at sea. He fixes his bucket hat on his head and tugs on his neckerchief. The air feels wet and salty. He checks his watch. There's plenty of time. And that fifty makes him rich. Yet as he approaches Times Square, his heart pounds and his lungs struggle for air. Like a swimmer who's gone out too far, he finds himself caught in currents which sweep him further and further from shore. Which should he try next, the Pink Elephant or the Astor Bar?

3.

The night is stubborn, the stars like pins. Sayler squats by the shore-end of the pier and watches his day's second lover disappear behind the stacks of crates and boxes that had hid them from the streetlight on the other side. A police boat churns the dark river. Water slaps at the piles. Flecks of black clouds smudge the sky lit by the new moon's thin crescent. He refastens the buttons on his bell-bottoms and wipes his lips with a corner of his neckerchief. Near the ocean, a ship's siren sounds. He brushes himself off and heads back toward the cheap hotel where he's bunking.

Its lobby is jammed with men in uniform gathered in groups. Shoving his way through, he drops the gum he's been chewing into the encrusted maw of a brass spittoon. He climbs the stairs with exhausted legs, enters the room, tosses his hat onto a dresser, and flops down on his cot. The red-haired kid is opening a beer with a church key.

Doc regards Sayler with a toothy leer. "Look who's back. Hey Sayler. You know what the definition of dancing is?"

"An old one, Doc," Atkins complains from across the room where he's pouring whiskey into the big guy's paper cup. The bed springs sag under their weight.

"A navel engagement without the loss of seamen," Doc says and guffaws. "Where you been, kid? Out getting your morale boosted?" He whiffs the air. "Only I don't smell no pussy. Do you smell any pussy, Ben?"

The big guy scratches his head with a sweaty, paw-like hand. "It all depends upon what you mean by 'pussy.' "

Doc opens another beer and chug-a-lugs. "Let's make him drop his flap and see if there's shit on his stick."

"Why, he's blushing, Doc," Ben hoots. "Blondie's blushing. I think you may be right, lookee there."

Atkins leans over and pulls a bottle out from under the bed. "You want a beer?" he offers Sayler.

Sayler shakes his head. Ben crushes his empty cup and tosses it out the window. "I bet the pussy don't even drink."

"Leave him alone, Ben," Atkins says. "He's okay. He's one of us."

"Yeah, he's okay," T.K. agrees. "Listen, we're going drinking and looking for girls," he tells Sayler. "Ben knows this place where we can drink just about for free, he says. Get us some pocket money too, didn't you say so, Ben?"

"Shut up, jerk," Ben warns.

"I need my rest, guys," Sayler says.

"Fucker thinks he's too good to drink with us," Doc says, reddening.

"Preacher's son," Sayler says to explain and yawns.

Ben lumbers off the bed and grabs Sayler by his sleeve. "We're all in the same navy, bub. Understand?"

"Okay, okay," Sayler says, relenting. "I'll go."

"Nice ass," Doc says, following him out the door.

Ben grabs his crotch and wolf whistles. "Ain't it though?"

The strip joint Ben leads them to is back closer to Broadway. As he walks down the steps first, Sayler feels almost safe in the press of men at the door. A blue light beams on the dancer doing her bump and grind to the accompaniment of a three-piece band on a narrow stage across from the bar. The fringe on her halter and g-string shimmers like tinsel. The five sailors wedge their way through the crowd to the end of the bar. Ben steps up to the brass rail and orders them all beers. When he's handed his, Sayler says a silent prayer and drinks it down.

"Sayler's okay," Atkins says.

"Sure he is," Ben says. "Did I ever say different?"

"Our kind have got to stick together," Atkins drawls.

"Damn straight," Doc says.

"Wrong kind's taking over," Atkins says. "Sayler's all right."

"Besides," Ben grins, "Blondie here's our best bait."

The beer tastes bitter and stings his throat. "What?" Sayler says.

Ben sucks on the space between two teeth as on a chunk of hard candy. "You know what I mean. Look," he calls over to Doc, "he's blushing again, just like a fucking virgin. Ain't that sweet?"

"This place sucks," Doc complains after their third round.

"Screw you," Ben says. "Fuck-face."

"Where'd that stripper go?" T.K. asks as he settles onto a just-vacated bar stool. "Where are all the dames, Ben? You said there'd be plenty of good-looking dames."

"I said later, asshole," Ben says. "First we got to get some dough."

"I like that tune," Sayler says woozily. "Nice tune. 'Who Wouldn't Love You.'" Sayler reaches in his pocket for a nickel. "Gonna play it again." He hops off the stool and zig-zags toward the juke. He watches the record spin and the colored lights flash as a man's firm hand grips his right shoulder.

"My God, it is you. After this afternoon, I never thought in my fondest dreams I'd ever see you again. But see? Fate is sometimes kind. Here you are."

Sayler does not budge. "Go away, Bill," he says, his eyes still intent on the turning record.

"You can't be worried about your friends over there. Surely they know what kind of bar this really is. Why ever else would you have brought them here?"

"I didn't," Sayler says between clenched teeth.

"Well there you are then. I was watching him from across the room. That big one certainly does look menacing. Not my type at all, I'm afraid. Too rough. Too dangerous."

"He is dangerous, Bill. Leave me alone. Please."

"Oh no, baby. I think I fell in love today. Oh my," he says, twisting around. "Who do we have here? How's every little thing?" He holds his hand to be shaken but jabs it back into the pocket of his linen jacket when he sees his gesture is to be ignored.

"Are you a friend of my friend here?" Ben inquires in a voice lacking his usual growl.

"Why, yes. I am. In a way."

"He's not. I swear he's not," Sayler says. "Get him away from me, Ben."

"I think he is. I think he is a friend of yours. A good friend. A rich friend. And so he's a friend of mine. Why don't you come join us for a drink. You'll be buying, of course?"

"Of course," Bill Blake agrees amiably.

When the bar closes, Ben talks Bill Blake into buying them a couple of bottles to take back with them to the room. "I told him to leave me alone," Sayler drunkenly whines as he follows Atkins and T.K. up the steps.

Blake glances back at Sayler uncertainly. "I think perhaps I should say goodnight here," he says as he starts to walk away.

Ben crushes his cigar on the top of the stairs and grabs Blake by the collar of his jacket. "What was that, faggot? You're coming with us."

"Watch it, Ben," Doc warns. "S.P.'s at three o'clock." Ben claps a hand over Bill Blake's mouth.

Back in the room, Sayler collapses on his cot and props his head on his pillow, trying to see what is happening in the midst of the whirl. He labors to focus his eyes on a rust-colored water stain or on the lightbulb dangling from a cord that won't stop quivering. His old pocketknife is digging into his skin. He pulls it out and drops it on the floor. Ben forces him to drink some more, pouring in straight whiskey as Doc holds his nose. Sayler fights for breath to keep from drowning. The first blows sound far away, like distant gunfire. He tries to get out of bed, he wants at least to raise his hand to stop it or to cry out, but he can't. Not even Blake screams. All Sayler hears is a steady pounding and something being slowly torn, like grass or weeds being uprooted.

4.

Bile and phlegm clog his throat. His stomach feels clotted with rot from harbor stews. Save for the distant roar of waves fading in his ears, the room is as quiet as if he were waking there alone. He holds his breath and hears no other breath, but on his tongue he tastes brass and acidic, slightly rotten tomatoes. When he breathes again, he smells blood. His cock swells from fear. In the hall, a body falls against the door and starts to puke. Sayler's stomach churns. Blood rains in his closed eyes.

When Sayler opens them, the light on the ceiling from the window is gun barrel gray. He needs to piss and rolls onto his side, but his vomit erupts and splatters on the floor before he is certain what he has seen. He steps out of his cot and wipes his mouth on a towel that reeks of sweat and mold.

Blake's body lies on the floor between the beds. Drool has trickled down the chin and dried like snail slick. Rust-colored stains streak the sheet which binds his naked body. His ears have been sliced off, his fingers and toes have been severed, his penis has been sliced down the shaft by a blade as broad as a bayonet's. But from Blake's heart rises the handle of Sayler's penknife, its mother-of-pearl almost lustrous against the pool of blood.

Sayler recoils to the darkest corner of the room where his clothes have been tossed over his bag. He fumbles for his wallet and finds all his money still there, but it won't be enough. His eyes blur as if the room were suddenly filled with death-mist or fog. With the corner of a pillow case, he tries to wipe away the lick spittle from Blake's face and to close the bulging eyes. His stomach heaves again. He hurriedly cleans himself off, dresses, grabs his bag, and darts panting out of the room like prey from a lie of weasels.

Trying not to run, he heads for Times Square, too frightened to think for long of Blake. He sees the doorman point his finger at him at the lineup. Blood throbs in his brain. The sky is lambent, though bleached and sunless. Footsteps on the sidewalk behind him scare him, and he hears someone closing doors down a narrow hall. He needs more money. Two tricks, maybe three, should be enough, a day's work. Then an early evening visit to that locker room club to check his uniform and rent himself some civies. By nightfall, he is standing on line at the bus depot, his wallet full.

Two days later, at dawn, he sits near the back of the bus and watches the country slide past him, the summer dry grass acrid in the hot breeze. At night, the stars swarm as at sea. The fourth morning, he wakes to a train's whistle filling the sky like the sun at daybreak while the bus waits at a rest stop somewhere in the plains for the last passengers to return from breakfast. He stretches and turns his head to look at the little copse of spindly, silvery trees. Beside them, a four-door Nash with sidewall tires and wheel-shields idles empty, puffs of smoke spiralling up from the muffler. Sayler feels the hand of providence grasp his shoulder and reaches for his pack from the rack above. He rushes up the aisle and jumps down onto the hard packed dirt. "We'll be leaving in a jiffy," the driver warns, stifling a yawn.

Sayler dashes around the gas pumps and past an ochre hut and hides in the trees' shadows, waiting. Slowly, he walks up to the Nash. The driver's door is open. He checks around him, sees no one, hops in, and tosses his few belongings onto the back seat. Even as he drives off, nobody rushes out from the restaurant to chase him. In the rearview mirror, he watches the motionless bus fade into the distance. The seat beside him is covered with maps. God, his father would declare, is marvelous to his saints. Sayler breathes more easily. The wind dries the sweat off his face.

When he can, he keeps to back roads and sleeps as he slept at sea in the breaks between boredom and fear. His memory tests the latches on all the rooms he's left behind him now that he's AWOL and finds them all locked. He buys food at a village general store which feels to him as safe as the shoreline seen from deck. Near the desert, the first rains begin, the lightning like sheets of foil unrolling in the sky.

He pulls off at a diner. He sits in a booth beneath a row of buzzing lights, his drained coffee cup shoved aside, and rests his elbows on a red tabletop too shiny for his eyes. Rain splatters the plate glass window to his right. When he glances out into the dark, he does not recognize himself in the reflection but sees instead a grainy snapshot of another boy, yellowed and faded, eyes bleached to white slits by the steady wear of too much light.

The guy with a broom picks a nickel off the floor and slips it into a slot of the jukebox as the cook presses the flat of the turner onto the hissing meat and stirs the mess of frying onions. Winds slap the roadside sign and streak through the roof. When the cops stomp in, dripping wet, they hook their hats and jackets onto the rack beneath which tiny pools of water slowly form like splashes of light that he watches sparkle in a corner. He reaches for his change and places a quarter under the saucer. As he drives off, no one notices him leaving. All the way through the desert, the windshield wipers go click clack, click clack.

He crosses a mountain pass barely able to see through the rain to the edge of the road. At one sharp curve, with his brights on, he sees the guard rail's red reflectors flare, brakes and skidding quickly turns. On the other side, close to the border, barricades have been set up, but he does not really believe that they are searching for him. It is only a detour, directing him a different way. Because it is so late when he gets to the town, the streets feel deserted, though the sky is now clear and the moon shines bright.

At the plain hotel, he must pay in advance before a room is made available to him. Having locked the door, he rests on a bed too soft for his body but blessed with a view of the river from where his head lies, the shade pulled up so that he can almost see the water rushing over rocks and the dark woods where owl, wildcat, shrew, mouse, and bat perform their nightly rites. In the morning, he sits on the porch, eating eggs and ham, and watches a groggy lizard slither across stones.

5.

Before he leaves, he reads another map. In less than a day he could be at the ocean. As he whistles the tune to "Who Wouldn't Love You," his muscles relax. He steers the Nash like a sailboat driven by strong winds. Green fields flow past. At a roadside stand, he stops to buy oranges. When he reaches in his pocket for his knife, panic scratches at his heart. He tears at the orange's skin and sucks it dry.

He would drive faster but the car balks and through the sleepy towns he must slow to a crawl though the billboards prod him on. In a valley of flowers, a boy stands by a eucalyptus, a straw hat tipped on his head, his dungarees too big for him, his thumb held out. Sayler brakes for him. As the boy runs toward the car, Sayler mutters to himself, That could be me almost, a few years ago. His father's sweaty palm presses down on his forehead as he leans across the passenger seat to open the door.

The boy says, "Hey," and tosses his canvas bag into the back. "I'm headed for L.A. Where you going?" His neck cords are pulled tight and the smile in his eyes is desperate.

"Same place."

The boy offers his hand. "Terry. Terry Pruett. I've been drafted."

"Sayler. Sayler Watkins," Sayler says without meaning to.

The boy slumps in his seat as Sayler cuts back onto the road. "I ran away."

"Oh," Sayler says, frowning. "So did I." The sun pounds on the dash.

"You look like me," the boy observes and laughs.

"Yeah. I noticed."

They ride in silence through orchards. The smell of the citrus etches like acid in the air. Sayler wipes his tired eyes and stares where a flock of blackbirds swoops down into a field of trees. Globes of ripe fruit are shining like lanterns. Terry rests the back of his head on the seat and gazes up at the car's ceiling. "I'm going to die. I know I'm going to die." He swallows the saliva in his mouth. Dogs on the porch of a bungalow bark at them as they pass. "I'm going to get shot. Right here," he says, pointing at his guts. "I know I am."

Sayler looks away. "Yeah. I know what you mean."

Once in the city, Sayler gets directions from an attendant at a parking lot and drives three blocks from Terry's destination to an old hotel the guy had told him was cheap. "You don't have to report until tomorrow you said. How about it, soldier?" Sayler says. "A night on the town?"

Terry shakes his head "No."

Their room stinks of fish. Sayler quickly opens the window. Outside, pigeons coo, their coral claws fixed as if snagged on the fire escape. Spider webs weave together in dusty cornices. Cockroaches scurry up the warped wallpaper.

"Stand here, next to me," Sayler directs and together they stare into the yellowed mirror. "You see, I really could pass for you."

"Maybe." The boy tosses his hat onto the bed and looks again. "Maybe you could."

"It's settled then. Tomorrow I'll go instead of you."

"Why?"

"Why not? It seems a way out is all. For us both. Listen, Terry.

That car out there is stolen. I'm running from something terrible that happened. I need to disappear."

The boy chews his cheek. "What'll I do? Where'll I go?"

Sayler steps back from the mirror and sits on the edge of the bed. "You'll have to figure that one out for yourself, kid."

In the morning, Sayler wakes first and slips on Terry's briefs, socks, shirt, and dungarees. Even the boy's shoes fit him. He shakes Terry awake. The boy's muscles ripple as he stretches and yawns. Sayler smiles grimly. "How do I look?"

Terry rubs his eyes. "You wouldn't fool my mom."

"I don't need to fool her. Just some dumb sergeant who's seen you only once or twice before. It might work. It just might work."

"You're going to die."

"Yeah," Sayler says. "I know."

"You want to die?" the boy says, puzzled.

Sayler fixes the boy's straw hat on his head, getting the angle exactly right. "No." He chucks the boy's chin. "Will I see you again?"

The boy stares back at him, uncomprehending. "I don't know."

6.

Angaur. Peleliu, honey-combed with natural caves that face each other across sheer gorges, their entrances sealed by concrete blast walls or oil drums filled with coral. Mangled corpses spew out across shallows. Leyte. Ormoc Valley where storms turn day into night. He slithers and slips from one steep muddy slope to another, from ridge to ridge where mountain meets sea. Men are bled white. Like bread or bits of cracker scattered for birds, they lie on the ground, soggy and bloated from rain. A bridge explodes. Howling men, their bodies already blackened by fire, scramble out of bunkers along a front no wider than an end zone and tumble, silenced, into a pit-like ravine. Flames billow from pillboxes as from a funeral pyre. Luzon. Each bend of the trail they cut through exposes more jungle. They march higher into the mountains. Here the thunder is manmade. At times, afraid, they hide in empty caves. His stools are bleached as bones. Though dizzy from disease, he sees the trigger wire concealed in an overgrown path to an old stone bridge and safely guides his men around it to the bank where they rest by a stream. Overhead, flocks of birds flap their wings and squawk like sullen gulls.

Akhil Sharma

Cosmopolitan

From *The Atlantic Monthly*

A LITTLE AFTER TEN in the morning Mrs. Shaw walked across Gopal Maurya's lawn to his house. It was Saturday, and Gopal was asleep on the couch. The house was dark. When he first heard the doorbell, the ringing became part of a dream. Only he had been in the house during the four months since his wife had followed his daughter out of his life, and the sound of the bell joined somehow with his dream to make him feel ridiculous. Mrs. Shaw rang the bell again. Gopal woke confused and anxious, the state he was in most mornings. He was wearing only underwear and socks, but his blanket was cold from sweat.

He stood up and hurried to the door. He looked through the peephole. The sky was bright and clear. Mrs. Shaw was standing sideways about a foot from the door, and appeared to be staring out over his lawn at her house. She was short and red-haired and wore a pink sweatshirt and gray jogging pants.

"Hold on! Hold on, Mrs. Shaw!" he shouted, and ran back into the living room to search for a pair of pants and a shirt. The light was dim, and he had difficulty finding them. As he groped under and behind the couch and looked among the clothes crumpled on the floor, he worried that Mrs. Shaw would not wait and was already walking down the steps. He wondered if he had time to turn on the light to make his search easier. This was typical of the details that could baffle him in the morning.

Mrs. Shaw and Gopal had been neighbors for about two years, but Gopal had met her only three or four times in passing. From his wife he had learned that Mrs. Shaw was a guidance counselor at the high school his daughter had attended. He also learned that she had been divorced for a decade. Her husband, a successful orthodontist, had left her. Since then Mrs. Shaw had moved five or six times, though rarely more than a few miles from where she had last lived. She had bought the small mustard-colored house next to Gopal's as part of this restlessness. Although he did not dislike Mrs. Shaw, Gopal was irritated by the peeling paint on her house and the weeds sprouting out of her broken asphalt driveway, as if by association his house were becoming shabbier. The various cars that left her house late at night made him see her as dissolute. But all this Gopal was willing to forget that morning, in exchange for even a minor friendship.

Gopal found the pants and shirt and tugged them on as he returned to open the door. The light and cold air swept in, reminding him of what he must look like. Gopal was a small man, with delicate high cheekbones and long eyelashes. He had always been proud of his looks and had dressed well. Now he feared that the gray stubble and long hair made him appear bereft.

"Hello, Mr. Maurya," Mrs. Shaw said, looking at him and through him into the darkened house and then again at him. The sun shone behind her. The sky was blue dissolving into white. "How are you?" she asked gently.

"Oh, Mrs. Shaw," Gopal said, his voice pitted and rough, "some bad things have happened to me." He had not meant to speak so directly. He stepped out of the doorway.

The front door opened into a vestibule, and one had a clear view from there of the living room and the couch where Gopal slept. He switched on the lights. To the right was the kitchen. The round Formica table and the counters were dusty. Mrs. Shaw appeared startled by this detail. After a moment she said, "I heard." She paused and then quickly added, "I am sorry, Mr. Maurya. It must be hard. You must not feel ashamed; it's no fault of yours."

"Please, sit," Gopal said, motioning to a chair next to the kitchen table. He wanted to tangle her in conversation and keep her there for hours. He wanted to tell her how the loneliness had made him fantasize about calling an ambulance so that he could be touched and prodded, or how for a while he had begun loitering at the Indian grocery store like the old men who have not learned English. What a pretty, good woman, he thought.

Mrs. Shaw stood in the center of the room and looked around her. She was slightly overweight, and her nostrils appeared to be perfect circles, but her small white Reebok sneakers made Gopal see her as fleet with youth and innocence. "I've been thinking of coming over. I'm sorry I didn't."

"That's fine, Mrs. Shaw," Gopal said, standing near the phone on the kitchen wall. "What could anyone do? I am glad, though, that you are visiting." He searched for something else to say. To extend their time together, Gopal walked to the refrigerator and asked her if she wanted anything to drink.

"No, thank you," she said.

"Orange juice, apple juice, or grape, pineapple, guava. I also have some tropical punch," he continued, opening the refrigerator door wide, as if to show he was not lying.

"That's all right," Mrs. Shaw said, and they both became quiet. The sunlight pressed through windows that were laminated with dirt. "You must remember, everybody plays a part in these things, not just the one who is left," she said, and then they were silent again. "Do you need anything?"

"No. Thank you." They stared at each other. "Did you come for something?" Gopal asked, although he did not want to imply that he was trying to end the conversation.

"I wanted to borrow your lawn mower."

"Already?" April was just starting, and the dew did not evaporate until midday.

"Spring fever," she said.

Gopal's mind refused to provide a response to this. "Let me get you the mower."

They went to the garage. The warm sun on the back of his neck made Gopal hopeful. He believed that something would soon be said or done to delay Mrs. Shaw's departure, for certainly God could not leave him alone again. The garage smelled of must and gasoline. The lawn mower was in a shadowy corner with an aluminum ladder resting on it. "I haven't used it in a while," Gopal said, placing the ladder on the ground and smiling at Mrs. Shaw beside him. "But it should be fine." As he stood up, he suddenly felt aroused by Mrs. Shaw's large breasts, boy's haircut, and little-girl sneakers. Even her nostrils suggested a frank sexuality. Gopal wanted to put his hands on her waist and pull her toward him. And then he realized that he had.

"No. No," Mrs. Shaw said, laughing and putting her palms flat against his chest. "Not now." She pushed him away gently.

Gopal did not try kissing her again, but he was excited. *Not now,* he thought. He carefully poured gasoline into the lawn mower, wanting to appear calm, as if the two of them had already made some commitment and there was no need for nervousness. He pushed the lawn mower out onto the gravel driveway and jerked the cord to test the engine. *Not now, not now,* he thought, each time he tugged. He let the engine run for a minute. Mrs. Shaw stood silent beside him. Gopal felt like smiling, but wanted to make everything appear casual. "You can have it for as long as you need," he said.

"Thank you," Mrs. Shaw replied, and smiled. They looked at each other for a moment without saying anything. Then she rolled the lawn mower down the driveway and onto the road. She stopped, turned to look at him, and said, "I'll call."

"Good," Gopal answered, and watched her push the lawn mower down the road and up her driveway into the tin shack that huddled at its end. The driveway was separated from her ranch-style house by ten or fifteen feet of grass, and they were connected by a trampled path. Before she entered her house, Mrs. Shaw turned and looked at him as he stood at the top of his driveway. She smiled and waved.

When he went back into his house, Gopal was too excited to sleep. Before Mrs. Shaw, the only woman he had ever embraced was his wife, and a part of him assumed that it was now only a matter of time before he and Mrs. Shaw fell in love and his life resumed its normalcy. Oh, to live again as he had for nearly thirty years! Gopal thought, with such force that he shocked himself. Unable to sit, unable even to think coherently, he walked around his house.

His daughter's departure had made Gopal sick at his heart for two or three weeks, but then she sank so completely from his thoughts that he questioned whether his pain had been hurt pride rather than grief. Gitu had been a graduate student and spent only a few weeks with them each year, so it was understandable that he would not miss her for long. But the swiftness with which the dense absence on the other side of his bed unknotted and evaporated made him wonder whether he had ever loved his wife. It made him think that his wife's abrupt decision never to return from her visit to India was as much his fault as God's. Anita, he thought, must have decided upon seeing Gitu leave that there was no more reason to stay, and that perhaps, after all, it was not too late to start again. Anita had gone to India at the end of November—a month after Gitu got on a Lufthansa flight to go live with her boyfriend in Germany—and a week later, over an echoing phone line, she told him of the guru and her enlightenment.

Perhaps if Gopal had not retired early from AT&T, he could have worked long hours and his wife's and daughter's slipping from his thoughts might have been mistaken for healing. But he had nothing to do. Most of his acquaintances had come by way of his wife, and when she left, Gopal did not call them, both because they had always been more Anita's friends than his and because he felt ashamed, as if his wife's departure revealed his inability to love her. At one point, around Christmas, he went to a dinner party, but he did not enjoy it. He found that he was not curious about other people's lives and did not want to talk about his own.

A month after Anita's departure a letter from her arrived—a blue aerogram, telling of the ashram, and of sweeping the court-yard, and of the daily prayers. Gopal responded immediately, but she never wrote again. His pride prevented him from trying to continue the correspondence, though he read her one letter so many times that he inadvertently memorized the Pune address.

His brothers sent a flurry of long missives from India, on paper so thin that it was almost translucent, but his contact with them over the decades had been minimal, and the tragedy pushed them apart instead of pulling them closer.

Gitu sent a picture of herself wearing a yellow-and-blue ski jacket in the Swiss Alps. Gopal wrote her back in a stiff, formal way, and she responded with a breezy postcard to which he replied only after a long wait.

Other than this, Gopal had had little personal contact with the world. He was accustomed to getting up early and going to bed late, but now, since he had no work and no friends, after he spent the morning reading *The New York Times* and *The Home News & Tribune* front to back, Gopal felt adrift through the afternoon and evening. For a few weeks he tried to fill his days by showering and shaving twice daily, brushing his teeth after every snack and meal. But the purposelessness of this made him despair, and he stopped bathing altogether and instead began sleeping more and more, sometimes sixteen hours a day. He slept in the living room, long and narrow with high rectangular windows blocked by trees. At some point, in a burst of self-hate, Gopal moved his clothes from the bedroom closet to a corner of the living room, wanting to avoid comforting himself with any illusions that his life was normal.

But he yearned for his old life, the life of a clean kitchen, of a bedroom, of going out into the sun, and on a half-conscious level that morning Gopal decided to use the excitement of clasping Mrs. Shaw to change himself back to the man he had been. She might be spending time at his house, he thought, so he mopped the kitchen floor, moved back into his bedroom, vacuumed and dusted all the rooms. He spent most of the afternoon doing this, aware always of his humming lawn mower in the background. He had only to focus on it to make his heart race. Every now and then he would stop working and go to his bedroom window, where, from behind the curtains, he would stare at Mrs. Shaw. She had a red bandanna tied around her forehead, and he somehow found this appealing. That night he made himself an elaborate dinner with three dishes and a mango shake. For the first time in months Gopal watched the eleven o'clock news. He had the lights off and his feet up on a low table. Lebanon was being bombed again, and Gopal kept bursting into giggles for no reason. He tried to think of what he would do tomorrow. Gopal knew that he was happy and that to avoid depression he must keep himself busy until Mrs. Shaw called. He suddenly realized that he did not know Mrs. Shaw's first name. He padded into the darkened kitchen and looked at the phone diary. "Helen Shaw" was written in the big, loopy handwriting of his wife. Having his wife help him in this way did not bother him at all, and then he felt ashamed that it didn't.

The next day was Sunday, and Gopal anticipated it cheerfully, for the Sunday *Times* was frequently so thick that he could spend the whole day reading it. But this time he did not read it all the way through. He left the book review and the other features sections to fill time over the next few days. After eating a large breakfast—the idea of preparing elaborate meals had begun to appeal to him—he went for a haircut. Gopal had not left his house in several days. He rolled down the window of his blue Honda Civic and took the long way, past the lake, to the mall. Instead of going to his usual barber, he went to a hair stylist, where a woman with long nails and large, contented breasts shampooed his hair before cutting it. Then Gopal wandered around the mall, savoring its buttered-pop-corn smell and enjoying the sight of the girls with their sometimes odd-colored hair. He went into some of the small shops and looked at clothes, and considered buying a half pound of cocoa amaretto coffee beans, although he had never cared much for coffee. After walking for nearly two hours, Gopal sat on a bench and ate an ice cream cone while reading an article in *Cosmopolitan* about what makes a good lover. He had seen the magazine in CVS and, noting the article mentioned on the cover, had been reminded how easily one can learn anything in America. Because Mrs. Shaw was an American, Gopal thought, he needed to do research into what might be expected of him. Although the article was about what makes a woman a good lover, it offered clues for men as well. Gopal felt confident that given time, Mrs. Shaw would love him.

The article made attachment appear effortless. All you had to do was listen closely and speak honestly.

He returned home around five, and Mrs. Shaw called soon after. "If you want, you can come over now."

"All right," Gopal answered. He was calm. He showered and put on a blue cotton shirt and khaki slacks. When he stepped outside, the sky was turning pink and the air smelled of wet earth. He felt young, as if he had just arrived in America and the huge scale of things had made him a giant as well.

But when he rang Mrs. Shaw's doorbell, Gopal became nervous. He turned around and looked at the white clouds against the enormous sky. He heard footsteps and then the door swishing open and Mrs. Shaw's voice. "You look handsome," she said. Gopal faced her, smiling and uncomfortable. She wore a different sweatshirt, but still had on yesterday's jogging pants. She was barefoot. A yellow light shone behind her.

"Thank you," Gopal said, and then nervously added "Helen," to confirm their new relationship. "You look nice too." She did look pretty to him. Mrs. Shaw stepped aside to let him in. They were in a large room. In the center were two pale couches forming an L, with a television in front of them. Off to the side was a kitchenette—a stove, a refrigerator, and some cabinets over a sink and counter.

Seeing Gopal looking around, Mrs. Shaw said, "There are two bedrooms in the back, and a bathroom. Would you like anything to drink? I have juice, if you want." She walked to the kitchen.

"What are you going to have?" Gopal asked, following her. "If you have something, I'll have something." Then he felt embarrassed. Mrs. Shaw had not dressed up; obviously, "Not now" had been a polite rebuff.

"I was going to have a gin and tonic," she said, opening the refrigerator and standing before it with one hand on her hip.

"I would like that too." Gopal came close to her and with a dart kissed her on the lips. She did not resist, but neither did she respond. Her lips were chapped. Gopal pulled away and let her make the drinks. He had hoped the kiss would tell him something of what to expect.

They sat side by side on a couch and sipped their drinks. A table lamp cast a diffused light over them.

"Thank you for letting me borrow the lawn mower."

"It's nothing." There was a long pause. Gopal could not think of anything to say. *Cosmopolitan* had suggested trying to learn as much as possible about your lover, so he asked, "What's your favorite color?"

"Why?"

"I want to know everything about you."

"That's sweet," Mrs. Shaw said, and patted his hand. Gopal felt embarrassed and looked down. He did not know whether he should have spoken so frankly, but part of his intention had been to flatter her with his interest. "I don't have one," she said. She kept her hand on his.

Gopal suddenly thought that they might make love tonight, and he felt his heart kick. "Tell me all about yourself," he said with a voice full of feeling. "Where were you born?"

"I was born in Jersey City on May fifth, but I won't tell you the year." Gopal tried to grin gamely and memorize the date. A part of him was disturbed that she did not feel comfortable enough with him to reveal her age.

"Did you grow up there?" he asked, taking a sip of the gin and tonic. Gopal drank slowly, because he knew that he could not hold his alcohol. He saw that Mrs. Shaw's toes were painted bright red. Anita had never used nail polish, and Gopal wondered what a woman who would paint her toenails might do.

"I moved to Newark when I was three. My parents ran a newspaper-and-candy shop. We sold greeting cards, stamps." Mrs. Shaw had nearly finished her drink. "They opened at eight in the morning and closed at seven-thirty at night. Six days a week." When she paused between swallows, she rested the glass on her knee.

Gopal had never known anyone who worked in such a shop, and he became genuinely interested in what she was saying. He remembered his lack of interest at the Christmas party and wondered whether it was the possibility of sex that made him fascinated with Mrs. Shaw's story. "Were you a happy child?" he asked, grinning broadly and then bringing the grin to a quick end, because he did not want to appear ironic. The half glass that Gopal had drunk had already begun to make him feel light-headed and gay.

"Oh, pretty happy," she said, "although I liked to think of myself as serious. I would look at the evening sky and think that no one else had felt what I was feeling." Mrs. Shaw's understanding of her own feelings disconcerted Gopal and made him momentarily think that he wasn't learning anything important, or that she was in some way independent of her past and thus incapable of the sentimental attachments through which he expected her love for him to grow.

Cosmopolitan had recommended that both partners reveal themselves, so Gopal decided to tell a story about himself. He did not believe that being honest about himself would actually change him. Rather, he thought the deliberateness of telling the story would rob it of the power to make him vulnerable. He started to say something, but the words twisted in his mouth, and he said, "You know, I don't really drink much." Gopal felt embarrassed by the non sequitur. He thought he sounded foolish, though he had hoped that the story he would tell would make him appear sensitive.

"I kind of guessed that from the juices," she said, smiling. Gopal laughed.

He tried to say what he had wanted to confess earlier. "I associate drinking with being American, and I haven't been able to truly Americanize. On my daughter's nineteenth birthday we took her to dinner and a movie, but we didn't talk much, and the dinner finished earlier than we had expected it would. The restaurant was in a mall, and we had nothing to do until the movie started, so we wandered around Foodtown." Gopal thought he sounded pathetic, so he tried to shift the story. "After all my years in America, I am still astonished by those huge grocery stores and enjoy walking in them. But my daughter is an American, so our wandering around in Foodtown must have been very strange for her. She doesn't know Hindi, and her parents must seem very strange." Gopal noticed that his heart was racing. He wondered if he was sadder than he knew.

"That's sweet," Mrs. Shaw said. The brevity of her response made Gopal nervous.

Mrs. Shaw kissed his cheek. Her lips were dry, Gopal noticed. He turned slightly so that their lips could touch. They kissed again. Mrs. Shaw opened her lips and closed her eyes. They kissed for a long time. When they pulled apart, they continued their conversation calmly, as if they were accustomed to each other. "I didn't go into a big grocery store until I was in college," she said. "We always went to the small shops around us. When I first saw those long aisles, I wondered what happens to the food if no one buys it. I was living then with a man who was seven or eight years older than I, and when I told him, he laughed at me, and I felt so young." She stopped and then added, "I ended up leaving him because he always made me feel young." Her face was only an inch or two from Gopal's. "Now I'd marry someone who could make me feel that way." Gopal felt his romantic feelings drain away at the idea of how many men she had slept with. But the fact that Mrs. Shaw and he had experienced something removed some of the loneliness he was feeling, and Mrs. Shaw had large breasts. They began kissing again. Soon they were tussling and groping on the floor.

Her bed was large and low to the ground. Behind it was a window, and although the shade was drawn, the lights of passing cars cast patterns on the opposing wall. Gopal lay next to Mrs. Shaw and watched the shadows change. He felt his head and found that his hair was standing up on either side like horns. The shock of seeing a new naked body, so different in its amplitude from his wife's, had been exciting. A part of him was giddy with this, as if he had checked his bank balance and discovered that he had thousands more than he expected. "You are very beautiful," he said, for *Cosmopolitan* had advised saying this after making love. Mrs. Shaw rolled over and kissed his shoulder.

"No, I'm not. I'm kind of fat, and my nose is strange. But thank you," she said. Gopal looked at her and saw that even when her mouth was slack, the lines around it were deep. "You look like you've been rolled around in a dryer," she said, and laughed. Her laughter was sudden and confident. He had noticed it before, and it made him laugh as well.

They became silent and lay quietly for several minutes, and when Gopal began feeling self-conscious, he said, "Describe the first house you lived in."

Mrs. Shaw sat up. Her stomach bulged, and her breasts drooped. She saw him looking and pulled her knees to her chest. "You're very thoughtful," she said.

Gopal felt flattered. "Oh, it's not thoughtfulness."

"I guess if it weren't for your accent, the questions would sound artificial," she said. Gopal felt his stomach clench. "I lived in a block of small houses that the Army built for returning GIs. They were all drab, and the lawns ran into each other. They were near Newark airport. I liked to sit at my window and watch the planes land. That was when Newark was a local airport."

"Your house was two stories?"

"Yes. And my room was on the second floor. Tell me about yourself."

"I am the third of five brothers. We grew up in a small, poor village. I got my first pair of shoes when I left high school." As Gopal was telling her the story, he remembered how he used to make Gitu feel lazy with stories of his childhood, and his voice fell. "Everybody was like us, so I never thought of myself as poor."

They talked this way for half an hour, with Gopal asking most of the questions and trying to discover where Mrs. Shaw was vulnerable and how this vulnerability made him attractive to her. Although she answered his questions candidly, Gopal could not find the unhappy childhood or the trauma of an abandoned wife that might explain the urgency of this moment in bed. "I was planning to leave my husband," she explained casually. "He was crazy. Almost literally. He thought he was going to be a captain of industry or a senator. He wasn't registered to vote. He knew nothing about business. Once, he invested almost everything we had in a hydroponic farm in Southampton. With him I was always scared of being poor. He used to spend two hundred dollars a week on lottery tickets, and he would save the old tickets in shoe boxes in the garage." Gopal did not personally know any Indian who was divorced, and he had never been intimate enough with an American to learn what a divorce was like, but he had expected something more painful—tears and recriminations. The details she gave made the story sound practiced, and he began to think that he would never have a hold over Mrs. Shaw.

Around eight Mrs. Shaw said, "I am going to do my bills tonight." Gopal had been wondering whether she wanted him to have dinner with her and spend the night. He would have liked to, but he did not protest.

As she closed the door behind him, Mrs. Shaw said, "The lawn mower's in the back. If you want it." Night had come, and the stars were out. As Gopal pushed the lawn mower down the road, he wished that he loved Mrs. Shaw and that she loved him.

He had left the kitchen light on by mistake, and its glow was comforting. "Come, come, cheer up," he said aloud, pacing in the kitchen. "You have a lover." He tried to smile and grimaced instead. "You can make love as often as you want. Be happy." He started preparing dinner. He fried okra and steam-cooked lentils. He made both rice and bread.

As he ate, Gopal watched a television movie about a woman who had been in a coma for twenty years and suddenly woke up one day; adding to her confusion, she was pregnant. After washing the dishes he finished the article in *Cosmopolitan* that he had begun reading in the mall. The article was the second of two parts, and it mentioned that when leaving after making love for the first time, one should always arrange the next meeting. Gopal had not done this, and he phoned Mrs. Shaw.

He used the phone in the kitchen, and as he waited for her to pick up, he wondered whether he should introduce himself or assume that she would recognize his voice. "Hi, Helen," he blurted out as soon as she said "Hello." "I was just thinking of you and thought I'd call." He felt more nervous now than he had while he was with her.

"That's sweet," she said, with what Gopal thought was tenderness. "How are you?"

"I just had dinner. Did you eat?" He imagined her sitting on the floor between the couches with a pile of receipts before her. She would have a small pencil in her hand.

"I'm not hungry. I normally make myself an omelet for dinner, but I didn't want to tonight. I'm having another drink." Then, self-conscious, she added, "Otherwise I grind my teeth. I started after my divorce and I didn't have health insurance or enough money to go to a dentist." Gopal wanted to ask if she still ground her teeth, but he did not want to imply anything.

"Would you like to have dinner tomorrow? I'll cook." They agreed to meet at six. The conversation continued for a few minutes longer, and when Gopal hung up, he was pleased at how well he had handled things.

While lying in bed, waiting for sleep, Gopal read another article in *Cosmopolitan,* about job pressure's effects on one's sex life. He had enjoyed both articles and was happy with himself for his efforts at understanding Mrs. Shaw. He fell asleep smiling.

The next day, after reading the papers, Gopal went to the library to read the first part of the *Cosmopolitan* article. He ended up reading articles from *Elle, Redbook, Glamour, Mademoiselle,* and *Family Circle,* and one from *Reader's Digest*—"How to Tell If Your Marriage Is on the Rocks." He tried to memorize jokes from the "Laughter Is the Best Medicine" section, so that he would never be at a loss for conversation.

Gopal arrived at home by four and began cooking. Dinner was pleasant, though they ate in the kitchen, which was lit with buzzing fluorescent tubes. Gopal worried that yesterday's lovemaking might have been a fluke. Soon after they finished the meal, however, they were on the couch, struggling with each other's clothing.

Gopal wanted Mrs. Shaw to spend the night, but she refused, saying that she had not slept a full night with anyone since her divorce. At first Gopal was touched by this. They lay on his bed in the dark. The alarm clock on the lampstand said 9:12 in big red figures. "Why?" Gopal asked, rolling over and resting his cheek on her cool shoulder. He wanted to reassure her that he was eager to listen.

"I think I'm a serial monogamist and I don't want to make

things too complicated." She twisted a lock of his hair around her middle finger. "It isn't because of you, sweetie. It's with every man."

"Oh," Gopal said, hurt by the idea of other men and disillusioned about her motives. He continued believing, however, that now that they were lovers, the power of his concern would make her love him back. One of the articles he had read that day had suggested that people become dependent in spite of themselves when they are constantly cared for. So he made himself relax and act understanding.

Gopal went to bed an hour after Mrs. Shaw left. Before going to sleep he called her and wished her good night. He began calling her frequently after that, two or three times a day. Over the next few weeks Gopal found himself becoming coy and playful with her. When Mrs. Shaw picked up the phone, he made panting noises, and she laughed at him. She liked his being childlike with her. Sometimes she would point to a spot on his chest, and he would look down, even though he knew nothing was there, so that she could tap his nose. When they made love, she was thoughtful about asking what pleased him, and Gopal learned from this and began asking her the same. They saw each other nearly every day, though sometimes only briefly, for a few minutes in the evening or at night. But Gopal continued to feel nervous around her, as if he were somehow imposing. If she phoned him and invited him over, he was always flattered. As Gopal learned more about Mrs. Shaw, he began thinking she was very smart. She read constantly, primarily history and economics. He was always surprised, therefore, when she became moody and sentimental and talked about how loneliness is incurable. Gopal liked Mrs. Shaw in this mood, because it made him feel needed, but he felt ashamed that he was so insecure. When she did not laugh at a joke, Gopal doubted that she would ever love him. When they were in bed together and he thought she might be looking at him, he kept his stomach sucked in.

This sense of precariousness made Gopal try developing other supports for himself. One morning early in his involvement with Mrs.

Shaw he phoned an Indian engineer with whom he had worked on
a project about corrosion of copper wires and who had also taken
early retirement from AT&T. They had met briefly several times
since then and had agreed each time to get together again, but
neither had made the effort. Gopal waited until eleven before calling, because he felt that any earlier would make him sound needy.
A woman picked up the phone. She told him to wait a minute as
she called for Rishi. Gopal felt vaguely deceitful, as if he were
trying to pass himself off as just like everyone else, although his
wife and child had left him.

"I haven't been doing much," he confessed immediately to Rishi.
"I read a lot." When Rishi asked what, Gopal answered "Magazines," with embarrassment. They were silent then. Gopal did not
want to ask Rishi immediately if he would like to meet for dinner,
so he hunted desperately for a conversational opening. He was
sitting in the kitchen. He looked at the sunlight on the newspaper
before him and remembered that he could ask Rishi questions.
"How are *you* doing?"

"It isn't like India," Rishi responded, complaining. "In India the
older you are, the closer you are to the center of attention. Here
you have to keep going. Your children are away and you have
nothing to do. I would go back, but Ratha doesn't want to. America is much better for women."

Gopal felt a rush of relief that Rishi had spoken so much. "Are
you just at home or are you doing something part time?"

"I am the president of the Indian Cultural Association," Rishi
said boastfully.

"That's wonderful," Gopal said, and with a leap added, "I want
to get involved in that more, now that I have time."

"We always need help. We are going to have a fair," Rishi said.
"It's on the twenty-fourth, next month. We need help coordinating
things, arranging food, putting up flyers."

"I can help," Gopal said. They decided that he should come to
Rishi's house on Wednesday, two days later.

Gopal was about to hang up when Rishi added, "I heard about
your family." Gopal felt as if he had been caught in a lie. "I am
sorry," Rishi said.

Gopal was quiet for a moment and then said, "Thank you." He did not know whether he should pretned to be sad. "It takes some getting used to," he said, "but you can go on from nearly anything."

Gopal went to see Rishi that Wednesday, and on Sunday he attended a board meeting to plan for the fair. He told jokes about a nearsighted snake and a water hose, and about a golf instructor and God. One of the men he met there invited him to dinner.

Mrs. Shaw, however, continued to dominate his thoughts. The more they made love, the more absorbed Gopal became in the texture of her nipples in his mouth and the heft of her hips in his hands. He thought of this in the shower, while driving, while stirring his cereal. Two or three times over the next month Gopal picked her up during her lunch hour and they hurried home to make love. They would make love and then talk. Mrs. Shaw had once worked at a dry cleaner, and Gopal found this fascinating. He had met only one person in his life before Mrs. Shaw who had worked in a dry-cleaning business, and that was different, because it was in India, where dry cleaning still had the glamour of advancing technology. Being the lover of someone who had worked in a dry-cleaning business made Gopal feel strange. It made him think that the world was huge beyond comprehension, and to spend his time trying to control his own small world was inefficient. Gopal began thinking that he loved Mrs. Shaw. He started listening to the golden-oldies station in the car, so that he could hear what she had heard in her youth.

Mrs. Shaw would ask about his life, and Gopal tried to tell her everything she wanted to know in as much detail as possible. Once, he told her of how he had begun worrying when his daughter was finishing high school that she was going to slip from his life. To show that he loved her, he had arbitrarily forbidden her to ski, claiming that skiing was dangerous. He had hoped that she would find this quaintly immigrant, but she was just angry. At first the words twisted in his mouth, and he spoke to Mrs. Shaw about skiing in general. Only with an effort could he tell her about his fight with Gitu. Mrs. Shaw did not say anything at first. Then she said, "It's all right if you were that way once, as long as you aren't that way now." Listening to her, Gopal suddenly felt angry.

"Why do you talk like this?" he asked.

"What?"

"When you talk about how your breasts fall or how your behind is too wide, I always say that's not true. I always see you with eyes that make you beautiful."

"Because I want the truth," she said, also angry.

Gopal became quiet. Her desire for honesty appeared to refute all his delicate and constant manipulations. Was he actually in love with her, he wondered, or was this love just a way to avoid loneliness? And did it matter that so much of what he did was conscious?

He questioned his love more and more as the day of the Indian festival approached and Gopal realized that he was delaying asking Mrs. Shaw to come with him. She knew about the fair but had not mentioned her feelings. Gopal told himself that she would feel uncomfortable among so many Indians, but he knew that he hadn't asked her because bringing her would make him feel awkward. For some reason he was nervous that word of Mrs. Shaw might get to his wife and daughter. He was also anxious about what the Indians with whom he had recently become friendly would think. He had met mixed couples at Indian parties before, and they were always treated with the deference usually reserved for cripples. If Mrs. Shaw had been of any sort of marginalized ethnic group—a first-generation immigrant, for instance—then things might have been easier.

The festival was held in the Edison First Aid Squad's square blue-and-white building. A children's dance troupe performed in red dresses so stiff with gold thread that the girls appeared to hobble as they moved about the center of the concrete floor. A balding comedian in oxblood shoes and a white suit performed. Light folding tables along one wall were precariously laden with large pots, pans, and trays of food. Gopal stood in a corner with several men who had retired from AT&T and, slightly drunk, improvised on jokes he had read in *1,001 Polish Jokes*. The Poles became Sikhs, but he kept most of the rest. He was laughing and feeling proud that he could so easily become the center of attention, but he felt lonely at the thought that when the food was served, the men at his side would drift away to join their families and he would stand alone in line. After listening to talk of someone's marriage, he began thinking about Mrs. Shaw. The men were clustered together, and the women conversed separately. They will go home and make love and not talk, Gopal thought. Then he felt sad and frightened. To make amends for his guilt at not bringing Mrs. Shaw along, he told a bearded man with yellow teeth, "These Sikhs aren't so bad. They are the smartest ones in India, and no one can match a Sikh for courage." Then Gopal felt dazed and ready to leave.

When Gopal pulled into his driveway, it was late afternoon. His head felt oddly still, as it always did when alcohol started wearing off, but Gopal knew that he was drunk enough to do something foolish. He parked and walked down the road to Mrs. Shaw's. He wondered if she would be in. Pale tulips bloomed in a thin, uneven row in front of her house. The sight of them made him hopeful.

Mrs. Shaw opened the door before he could knock. For a moment Gopal did not say anything. She was wearing a denim skirt and a sleeveless white shirt. She smiled at him. Gopal spoke solemnly and from far off. "I love you," he said to her for the first time. "I am sorry I didn't invite you to the fair." He waited a moment for his statement to sink in and for her to respond with a similar endearment. When she did not, he repeated, "I love you."

Then she said, "Thank you," and told him not to worry about the fair. She invited him in. Gopal was confused and flustered by her reticence. He began feeling awkward about his confession. They kissed briefly, and then Gopal went home.

The next night, as they sat together watching TV in his living room, Mrs. Shaw suddenly turned to Gopal and said, "You really do love me, don't you?" Although Gopal had expected the question, he was momentarily disconcerted by it, because it made him wonder what love was and whether he was capable of it. But he did not think that this was the time to quibble over semantics. After being silent long enough to suggest that he was struggling with his vulnerability, Gopal said yes and waited for Mrs. Shaw's response. Again she did not confess her love. She kissed his forehead tenderly. This show of sentiment made Gopal angry, but he said nothing. He was glad though, when Mrs. Shaw left that night.

The next day Gopal waited for Mrs. Shaw to return home from work. He had decided that the time had come for the next step in their relationship. As soon as he saw her struggle through her doorway, hugging sacks of groceries, Gopal phoned. He stood on the steps to his house, with the extension cord trailing over one shoulder, and looked at her house and at her rusted and exhausted-looking station wagon, which he had begun to associate strongly and warmly with the broad sweep of Mrs. Shaw's life. Gopal nearly said, "I missed you" when she picked up the phone, but he became embarrassed and asked, "How was your day?"

"Fine," she said, and Gopal imagined her moving about the kitchen, putting away whatever she had bought, placing the tea kettle on the stove, and sorting her mail on the kitchen table. This image of domesticity and independence moved him deeply. "There's a guidance counselor who is dying of cancer," she said, "and his friends are having a party for him, and they put up a sign saying 'RSVP with your money now! Henry can't wait for the party!'" Gopal and Mrs. Shaw laughed.

"Let's do something," he said.

"What?"

Gopal had not thought this part out. He wanted to do something romantic that would last until bedtime, so that he could pressure her to spend the night. "Would you like to have dinner?"

"Sure," she said. Gopal was pleased. He had gone to a liquor store a few days earlier and bought wine, just in case he had an opportunity to get Mrs. Shaw drunk and get her to fall asleep beside him.

Gopal plied Mrs. Shaw with wine as they ate the linguine he had cooked. They sat in the kitchen, but he had turned off the fluorescent lights and lit a candle. By the third glass Gopal was feeling very brave; he placed his hand on her inner thigh.

"My mother and father," Mrs. Shaw said halfway through the meal, pointing at him with her fork and speaking with the deliberateness of the drunk, "convinced me that people are not meant to live together for long periods of time." She was speaking in response to Gopal's hint earlier that only over time and through living together could people get to know each other properly. "If you know someone that well, you are bound to be disappointed."

"Maybe that's because you haven't met the right person," Gopal answered, feeling awkward for saying something that could be considered arrogant when he was trying to appear vulnerable.

"I don't think there is a right person. Not for me. To fall in love I think you need a certain suspension of disbelief, which I don't think I am capable of."

Gopal wondered whether Mrs. Shaw believed what she was saying or was trying not to hurt his feelings by revealing that she couldn't love him. He stopped eating.

Mrs. Shaw stared at him. She put her fork down and said, "I love you. I love how you care for me and how gentle you are."

Gopal smiled. Perhaps, he thought, the first part of her statement had been a preface to a confession that he mattered so much that she was willing to make an exception for him. "I love you too," Gopal said. "I love how funny and smart and honest you are. You are very beautiful." He leaned over slightly to suggest that he wanted to kiss her, but Mrs. Shaw did not respond.

Her face was stiff. "I love you," she said again, and Gopal became nervous. "But I am not *in* love with you." She stopped and stared at Gopal.

Gopal felt confused. "What's the difference?"

"When you are *in* love, you never think about yourself, because you love the other person so completely. I've lived too long to think anyone is that perfect." Gopal still didn't understand the distinction, but he was too embarrassed to ask more. It was only fair, a part of him thought, that God would punish him this way for driving away his wife and child. How could anyone love him?

Mrs. Shaw took his hands in hers. "I think we should take a little break from each other, so we don't get confused. Being with you, I'm getting confused too. We should see other people."

"Oh." Gopal's chest hurt despite his understanding of the justice of what was happening.

"I don't want to hide anything. I love you. I truly love you. You are the kindest lover I've ever had."

"Oh."

For a week after this Gopal observed that Mrs. Shaw did not bring another man to her house. He went to the Sunday board meeting of the cultural association, where he regaled the members with jokes from *Reader's Digest*. He taught his first Hindi class to children at the temple. He took his car to be serviced. Gopal did all these things. He ate. He slept. He even made love to Mrs. Shaw once, and until she asked him to leave, he thought everything was all right again.

Then, one night, Gopal was awakened at a little after three by a car pulling out of Mrs. Shaw's driveway. It is just a friend, he thought, standing by his bedroom window and watching the Toyota move down the road. Gopal tried falling asleep again, but he could not, though he was not thinking of anything in particular. His mind was blank, but sleep did not come.

I will not call her, Gopal thought in the morning. And as he was dialing her, he thought he would hang up before all the numbers had been pressed. He heard the receiver being lifted on the other side and Mrs. Shaw saying "Hello." He did not say anything. "Don't do this, Gopal," she said softly. "Don't hurt me."

"Hi," Gopal whispered, wanting very much to hurt her. He leaned his head against the kitchen wall. His face twitched as he whispered, "I'm sorry."

"Don't be that way. I love you. I didn't want to hurt you. That's why I told you."

"I know."

"All right?"

"Yes." They were silent for a long time. Then Gopal hung up. He wondered if she would call back. He waited, and when she didn't, he began jumping up and down in place.

For the next few weeks Gopal tried to spend as little time as possible in his house. He read the morning papers in the library, and then had lunch at a diner, and then went back to the library. On Sundays he spent all day at the mall. His anger at Mrs. Shaw soon disappeared, because he thought that the blame for her leaving lay with him. Gopal continued, however, to avoid home, because he did not want to experience the jealousy that would keep him awake all night. Only if he arrived late enough and tired enough could he fall asleep. In the evening Gopal either went to the temple and helped at the seven o'clock service or visited one of his new acquaintances. But over the weeks he exhausted the kindheartedness of his acquaintances and had a disagreement with one man's wife, and he was forced to return home.

The first few evenings he spent at home Gopal thought he would have to flee his house in despair. He slept awkwardly, waking at the barest rustle outside his window, thinking that a car was pulling out of Mrs. Shaw's driveway. The days were easier than the nights, especially when Mrs. Shaw was away at work. Gopal would sleep a few hours at night and then nap during the day, but this left him exhausted and dizzy. In the afternoon he liked to sit on the steps and read the paper, pausing occasionally to look at her house. He liked the sun sliding up its walls. Sometimes he was sitting outside when she drove home from work. Mrs. Shaw waved to him once or twice, but he did not respond, not because he was angry but because he felt himself become so still at the sight of her that he could neither wave nor smile.

A month and a half after they separated, Gopal still could not sleep at night if he thought there were two cars in Mrs. Shaw's driveway. Once, after a series of sleepless nights, he was up until three watching a dark shape behind Mrs. Shaw's station wagon. He waited by his bedroom window, paralyzed with fear and hope, for a car to pass in front of her house and strike the shape with its headlights. After a long time in which no car went by, Gopal decided to check for himself.

He started across his lawn crouched over and running. The air was warm and smelled of jasmine, and Gopal was so tired that he thought he might spill to the ground. After a few steps he stopped and straightened up. The sky was clear, and there were so many stars that Gopal felt as if he were in his village in India. The houses along the street were dark and drawn in on themselves. Even in India, he thought, late at night the houses look like sleeping faces.

He remembered how surprised he had been by the pitched roofs of American houses when he had first come here, and how this had made him yearn to return to India, where he could sleep on the roof. He started across the lawn again. Gopal walked slowly, and he felt as if he were crossing a great distance.

The station wagon stood battered and alone, smelling faintly of gasoline and the day's heat. Gopal leaned against its hood. The station wagon was so old that the odometer had gone all the way around. Like me, he thought, and like Helen, too. This is who we are, he thought—dusty, corroded, and dented from our voyages, with our unflagging hearts rattling on inside. We are made who we are by the dust and corrosion and dents and unflagging hearts. Why should we need anything else to fall in love? he wondered. We learn and change and get better. He leaned against the car for a minute or two. Fireflies swung flickering in the breeze. Then he walked home.

Gopal woke early and showered and shaved and made breakfast. He brushed his teeth after eating and felt his cheeks to see whether he should shave again, this time against the grain. At nine he crossed his lawn and rang Mrs. Shaw's doorbell. He had to ring it several times before he heard her footsteps. When she opened the door and saw him, Mrs. Shaw drew back as if she were afraid. Gopal felt sad that she could think he might hurt her. "May I come in?" he asked. She stared at him. He saw mascara stains beneath her eyes and silver strands mingled with her red hair. He thought he had never seen a woman as beautiful or as gallant.

D. R. MacDonald

Ashes

From *Epoch*

RODERICK FELT the faint line crease his middle as he emerged from the brook path, not strong like wire but enough, even in its give, to vex him. He thought it no more than a strand of vine and he twisted it in his fist, but it bit and didn't break: tough white twine and it stretching almost invisibly down the wooded hill behind him, toward that hidden turn of the brook where light swayed the thick crowns of trees. A soft wave of alarm rose in his chest. This was marker line, strung by someone he did not know, or for what purpose. He drew the string back slowly until it snapped and leaped like flyline into the leaves. But this did not comfort him long and his breathing was louder as he climbed further up into the high and shady birches he had encouraged all the years he owned, and did not own, this land. Along the contours of the hill, grasses and ferns and wildflowers grew, not scrub, not thickets of spruce and alder. Up where he could see through the red maples to the road, there was some yellow thing on the meadow and he stumbled toward it. He didn't know any yellow truck or car, but Jesus yes, sure, it was a dozer, a great hunk of yellow iron down off the road, careened there.

Parked. Who'd been at the levers, a drunk? Christ, it was a serious machine. Blade higher than his head. Roderick placed his foot ankle-deep into a rut its treads had channeled, the clay laid slick and bare. In some way it seemed worse sitting than running, its silence immense, more disturbing than sound. He had worked in the roar of machinery years ago, in the steel plant, immersed in the hot ringing din of the rod mill. But here on the old land, the noise of his life was done with. He'd never been in war but surely somewhere between battles a tank had sat just as this dozer was, under summer leaves, waiting. He put his hand on the cool steel tread, polished and scarred. Lord, what this metal could do to the bits of flowers down in his clay soil shade, its thin kind of grasses good for nothing but their soft greenness, no, he wouldn't have it. No iron down there. He did not love that place exactly, that was not what he would say if he were to tell someone about it. Love was too careful a word. Something akin, but no matter: that particular spot he did need, and he had claimed it a long time ago.

Maybe the bulldozer was here to dig a foundation, here near the road. Maybe the owner of the property was building a summer house at last? Unless there was a new owner. Bad enough, but surely he wouldn't have this big rig marauding down the hill, for God's sake, with sixty acres to play with? Then again, would he have even seen it? People these days bought country land from a book, from a picture, from nothing at all but a sales pitch and a good price.

The brook place you had to seek out since no path would take you near it. Who could it matter to but himself, Roderick John MacRae?

His dinner was on the table but Roderick stood at the kitchen window and ran his eye again and again from the road, from that yellow streak in the shadows, down through the wooded hill to the shore woods, to the water behind them. All that land had once been his family's, his. Father's, grandfather's. Although his dad had moved them into Sydney when he went to work for the steel mill, they had held on to the place, kept the house up as best they could, summers and time off, until his dad died, and Roderick came into it. Twenty-four years ago, Roderick, himself ill and out of work, sold all but the house and a few acres to a Toronto man because he wanted it only for summers. Just that, the man said, the shore and the pastures to roam in, the cove where he could keep a boat. New woods had taken over much pasture and field but there was still a path to the beach. I might put a cottage somewhere, Roderick, he said, nothing bigger, look, I wouldn't spoil this for a second. And he hadn't, hadn't put so much as a cabin there, a lean-to. A big silver trailer had sat awhile, and there were a few summers of expensive tents, beach fires, hollering and firecrackers around Dominion Day, the speedboat humming off up the strait on calm, fine afternoons, and some odd noises in the woods at night, the shrieks and laughter of drinking and drunken pursuits, from what Roderick could tell. He was never part of that. Then no one came, no one showed up any time of year and he had it alone, all seasons, all summer. And he'd kept it the way he wished, thinning the softwood out so hardwoods could thrive, an open woods, curving along the hills and gullies to the shore. And of course, the brook spot. Even beech had come back, if not the grand trees of his youth, but there anyway, tall and yellow in autumn. The man who bought the land always sent a Christmas card, nothing religious, just a humorous one of holiday pratfalls and excess. Roderick remembered the broad handwriting: it had seemed reliable, frank, good-natured, nothing sly or deceptive there. But no card had arrived in three years. You're the caretaker, the man had told him, keep it looking fine, I've been a bit sick.

Roderick sat down to his salt cod, good cod. Lord it wasn't easy to get it anymore, the fish he'd fed on as a kid, fresh, salted, the fish every poor soul had fed on, that and herring, no matter what else failed you had salt fish. Once you could jig them from your boat on bare hooks, dozens, haul them in clear to the gunnels. What cod would you find in the waters here now, when offshore the catch was so poor there was talk of shutting it down, the whole show? Fatories had their place, but not out there on the ocean. The fishery was wrecked.

Roderick didn't eat. The plate cooled.

Maddocks. That was the owner's name. He wondered, were the man dead and buried, what sort of stone they'd have put over him.

Where would he have wanted his name set down, what words under it. Something comical maybe, like his cards at Christmas.

"So," Archie Bugle said, resting his chin on his cane handle. "You've got yellow iron on your old land eh?"

Archie's porch faced nicely toward the water, grayer now than the afternoon sky, whiteflecked. Archie's sister Peg, with whom he lived, did not join them but stood just inside the hallway, looking out like a cook at a galley door.

"It is mine and it isn't mine, as you know," Roderick said. He had given Archie Bugle the bare bones of his situation and was regretting it already. "Somebody new owns it, I'm thinking. I fear their plans."

"Well, they're in the tank of that bulldozer, you can be damn sure of that."

"He made me a promise, that man I sold it to. A long time ago we shook hands." Roderick extended his own large hand and closed it. "Yes, you can be buried there, he told me. Pick your site and it won't be touched."

"Buried down there? In the woods?" Archie raised his shaggy white eyebrows. "What for, Roderick John, when there's a cemetery not two miles down the road?"

Roderick wished he had not mentioned the gravesite. It was like releasing something he had captured in his hands and watching it fly away. He did not want to be thought peculiar, but was it morbid and foolish, choosing a grave on family land that went back 170 years? Was it simply normal to let somebody tuck you away in the back corner of Man O'War Point, under another piece of polished red granite chiseled with scant particulars? How was that preferable, if any man stopped to think about it, to a lovely secluded hollow of your own, the water a stone's throw from your feet, the mountain beyond and sun setting over it? Whether the bones of your family were ten feet away or two miles could hardly matter. Death, so they said, was not just a reckoning but a gathering together.

"It's a personal thing," Roderick said.

"It's a queer thing, if you ask me. You've got people on Man

O' War Point and you want to plant yourself where there's nobody at all?"

"There *was* people there."

"Not *in* the ground, Roderick John. Anyway, a verbal agreement is what you got, boy. A new owner, all he says is I never heard tell of it. Worthless. Got to be on paper."

"Maybe it isn't a new owner," Roderick said, without conviction. A man's word worthless? Not around here. But it seemed that today wherever he stepped, there was the bulldozer. Whatever was on his mind, there it sat, latent with destruction. He found he was listening, even this far away, for the sound of a diesel.

Archie Bugle said, "That's not a local dozer, is it."

"Not hardly."

"Well now, here's Corry, here comes our man." Archie drummed his cane. He loved Corry's salacious conversation, a certain kind of talk that was all but gone among them. Peg was always in earshot of Archie's life, but Corry said what he pleased, Peg or no. "He'll know something."

"He always knows *something*." Roderick found the man good company, there being damn little of that this part of his life. But he could get on your nerves sometimes, and here was Roderick seeing bulldozers left and right.

Corry's vast brown Cougar eased up the driveway like a ship toward a dock, waxed finish gleaming. He had moved to St. Aubin Island after retiring from the steel plant, bought himself a little house near the shore. People knew the car even if they didn't know him.

"Don't tell Corry anything about this," Roderick said.

"Why? He worked at the coke ovens over twenty years." Archie Bugle, in the country all his life, had always been awed by the smoky clangor of the mill, the corrosive fumes of the coke plant.

"Yes, he should be dead."

"There you are. He's held up to everything."

Corry roamed the island in that huge old car, a California vehicle some summer widow had brought here not long before she died, coated with expensive paint, wide enough to sleep in, a hood like a foredeck, sidewalls whiter than a piper's spats. Corry emerged from it slowly, appraising it as he closed the door. He stood for a few moments brushing the vinyl roof, then locked it and approached the porch in his stiff, careful gait that could be taken for a drunk's if you didn't know him.

"Will you look at him lock her up?" Archie Bugle said loudly.

Corry placed his polished shoe on the first step of the porch. He winked. "It's not what I'm locking out, Archie B., but in."

"For instance what?"

"Things drifting around in there, California things." He noticed Peg behind the screen and gave her a sarcastic little bow. "Pleasures of the flesh. It's not a hearse, you know."

"Make a good one," Roderick said.

"Roderick John's got a dozer problem, you see, on the old place," Archie Bugle said. "Don't know the why of it."

Corry, slashing at a deer fly, took his chair between the two men. He shook the crease in his trousers. Their coppery sheen resembled his Cougar's and he was looking at it now, his squint tight but favorable. He had a fierce red face, thin and alert. Age and the coke plant: they burned you down. But he believed in keeping up the fires of sex, as he liked to say, and wherever he found any smoke at all, he blew on it. "Didn't I see it. I thought, construction. Digging a septic. Foundation for somebody, and not for Roderick John."

"Of course it wouldn't be for myself. I got nothing to build. The point is, over what ground is it going?"

"No ground, this day." Corry lit a long thin cigarette. He was dressed up smartly in a dark tartan sport coat and clashing tie. When he had a date, he often stopped here, especially if Peg was at the door. "Whoever owns it got better things to do. Three days just sitting. Makes you wonder, yes."

"Roderick John's afraid . . ."

"Never mind about that, Archie Bugle," Roderick said. "I'll figure it out."

"Well, God, man, you never should've sold the place," Archie said, "if you wanted to be laid out in a piece of it."

"He seemed like a good fella. I thought it wouldn't be bad."

"What wouldn't be bad?" Corry said. "Everything gets bad if you live long enough."

"The land, the arrangement, me looking after things."

Corry smacked a blackfly off the back of his hand. "But the land is his, you see. Don't matter how many years he don't show up there."

"Roderick John's got a plot down there," Archie Bugle said.

"Plot of what? A book?"

Roderick closed his eyes. "Burial," he said. "Mine."

"Jesus, Roderick John, I didn't know you were so shy," Corry said, turning to him. "But you, you won't need much of a spot in any case. They won't let you lay your big body in the ground, boy. Ashes it's got to be."

"Ashes?"

"Dust to dust. Cremation, if it's burial on private land. That's the law now."

Roderick had never considered cremation, not for himself, not ever what it might be like. That he should be forced into it angered him: he'd had that part thought out. Now he had to imagine fire, and himself a handful of ashes. Cremation. High class, something educated and clean, and they could stow you afterward in a nice container, out of the way, shelved. And wasn't the fire gas, blue flame, neat and cold? Hot, God yes, but burning down did not appeal to him, putting his remains in the hands of stokers in white coats, sliding you into a furnace. He knew furnaces. He had seen a man tumble into molten iron, as bright and dancing as a pool of lava, and he was quickly no more than another plume of smoke. No. Too fast, bone and powder, no chance to let death know what you look like, what life has made of you: the man lying there had to be the same man who stood. Ashes were stuff you shook out of the kitchen stove, clinkers and grit. Nothing to find, if ever they dug, those people who studied graves. Could sift till doomsday for him. He wanted to be face up, hands folded, everything at rest, in one piece, down there by the brook, like the way they found people in the *National Geographic* magazine. There would be no mistaking that shape was him, not a handful of fertilizer or something you scattered across an icy sidewalk to keep from falling.

"It's not cheap, you know, Roderick John," Corry said. "You can't have it done out back, with a few pals and kerosene. Regulations is what we live by now."

"If that's the law, then . . ." Roderick said. He felt a little hot, embarrassed. How could he not have known about this? When was it law?

"Little pot of your ash," Corry said. "Put it in a nice dish with a cover on it. Good for the soil. Won't harm the water. Who could say no to that? New owner, old owner, he might not care. Just don't set one of those goddamn monuments on it, those big granite pricks. Tourist attraction he might not like."

"Then again he might go for it," Archie Bugle said, urging Corry on. "You know, the idea of it like."

"*Idea* of what? Of Roderick John MacRae? Or his prick? I like the man but you'd have to do better than that. Peg? Come out here, girl. Give us your opinion."

"Corry, hush." A long time ago Archie Bugle had brought a young wife here to live, and in less than a year she had left him. Corry referred to Peg as Miss Primpot, the Holy Old Maid. I could certainly buckle her knees, he claimed once, if ever I could get near her.

"You only talk dirt," Peg said firmly. She had stepped back from the doorway.

"Archie B., was it Peg your sister that scared your young wife away? Did she listen in?"

"God, no, Peg had nothing to do with it."

"Damned foolish thing, Archie B., bringing a young wife here with a spinster sister in the house. You upstairs in that old creaky bed of yours, bumpety-bump."

"But this was my *house*," Archie Bugle said, flaring up, not amused about his wife. "So I took her *to* it."

"Peg's always been here," Roderick said, as if she were a rock or a tree.

From somewhere behind the screen door, in the dusk of the

hallway, Peg stirred. She didn't move near the door but she said, "I wouldn't listen to you if I could hear, Corry Matheson."

Corry did not look around but he smiled. "It's not just talk, Peggy Mary. Mysterious things do happen. Look at Roderick John here. Perplexed by a big machine."

"All that's going to happen to you has happened." She had moved further back in the hallway and her voice was dimmer. "As for Roderick John, he might try praying."

"Like I pray for you, Peggy Mary John Archie MacLean," Corry said. "Someday I'm coming in there to see you. I'm coming in, all done up like chocolates."

"You're an awful man."

"That's what they tell me, dear. I'm going to see a lady this very afternoon, and awful I'm going to be. Awful's what they want. Enough talk about ashes and graves."

Somewhere in the house a door closed.

A breeze trembled through the field grass where the Cougar rested in the laziness of the afternoon. "Good as new," Corry said. "Seats still *smell* new, for Lord's sake. The leather of money."

"Maybe you could tow that dozer out," Archie Bugle said. "A lot of wasted horsepower there. The lady can wait."

But Corry didn't seem to hear. "What do you suppose makes a woman talk like that?"

"Like what?" Archie Bugle said.

"Harrying a man, raising questions about his character."

"You had a wife a long time, Corry," Roderick said. "You should know, if anybody."

"We didn't talk much, my friend. She wouldn't shed any light on it."

They watched the weather coming east, long easy clouds, rolling shades of gray in an unencumbered sky. Down in the woods, the flies would be light in a breeze like this. Roderick had things to do. More than ever his foot was tapping but he stayed in the chair, in the company of these men, listening for a sound, not sure what he would do when he heard it. When dark came he'd have to sleep and what if he didn't wake early enough to plant himself in front of that dozer in the morning and demand what it intended, where it was to go. He was not afraid of any man driving, he'd wrestle him down off that seat if he had to. He'd always been strong, a catcher in the rod mill had to be strong. It still came back to him easily, all its heat and exertion, he loved remembering it. Fifteen minutes on, fifteen off, that's how hot and hard the work was. Sometimes you could stay at it a half hour if the rod was thin. Walk out in the factory yard, get the air. This breeze carried for a moment that pleasure, that possibility of relief. Then back into the loud heat, poised in your thick leather apron, gripping tongs, waiting to spot the reflection of the rod, glowing and sparking in the gloom, cast ahead of it, coming steady and fast, and when it bloomed on the wall, you counted: *one, two,* and then *catch,* and you clamped your tongs to the nose of that rushing, looping rod and whipped it around and thrust it into the next mill that would reduce it yet further. An athlete's timing, you had to have that. If you missed, you were catching nothing, and the mill had to be stopped and tangled coils of rod balled up for the scrap machine, and they did not allow you many misses. But if you were quick and strong, you caught every rod, you didn't miss. You were young then, they all were, the catchers, sometimes they'd scream above the noise, Get 'em out Get 'em out, they were so keyed up, the pressure right there end to end, one molten rod after another wheeling toward you to be snatched and turned like a living thing. Dust, smoke, 120 Fahrenheit, white hot steel, there was nothing else that made any difference when you were really moving, in the hot center of it, blazing through, proof that, because you had brawn, you needed to know only this much about the world, and the noise of your life was loud.

"Intercourse," Corry said precisely. He lowered the long cigarette he was smoking and tapped its tip between the decking. "Was made for it, that car."

The whetstone rasped into the scythe's curve, a calming singsong of metal and stone. Roderick wanted it sharp, sharp. His grandpa at eighty had swung into a hayfield on a hot afternoon, sleeves of his white shirt rolled, his torso swaying as he cut and stepped, his wind good even then, a slow but still-useful machine. Two months before he died, he was loading hay bales all afternoon. "If I can still grab it, I can lift it." Roderick had the same build, thick through the middle, nothing could dent his belly or back, and what made his grandpa a good reaper had made Roderick a good catcher, big shoulders, handy down the ages, if you swung a sword or a pick or a catcher's tongs. All he needed to live and to keep himself in trim were tools like this one with the stamp of family on them, a good double-bitted axe, a crosscut saw. When the blade drew a little blood from his thumb, Roderick sliced the air, wishing the scythe still mattered, that it was a needed thing. He set out through the old pasture running west toward the woods. It was not harvest he was after or the cosmetics of mown grass, but motion and sweat. He cut a slow circle into the hay, widening it neatly, sucking wind and perspiring as he had years ago, in a rhythm not unlike this, not in a hayfield but a mill. Yes, he'd been sick but he'd beaten the TB, he'd come back from that. He still had power in the stroke, he had the long good arms and the strong back and he could swing that scythe flat and full, and the hay, run through with bull thistle and goldenrod and wild plants he didn't even know, fell, every stalk of it. He cleared out a space until his shoulders ached and his muscles burned, leaving this swathe to dry in the sun. There. Whatever wanted to fill this circle could, spirit or motor or some whim of weather. He had turned it out, its juices were sweet in the air. Catching his breath, he blinked at the afternoon sky, a dizzying calm blue in which a contrail was dissolving, the high faint cloud of a plane's passage. They crossed this piece of country at such an altitude he rarely noticed them. So far were they separated from their sound, the airplanes, small and silver and silent, they seemed to be leaving it for good, casting it off.

What folly to have believed the land was his again, and that he could be planted in it, like a tree, a rock.

He crisscrossed restlessly the trails he'd cut and cleaned over the years and where he often walked in good weather or bad, turning eventually to the place near the brook. He whacked at weeds of scrub spruce, or the tenacious alder, one deft swipe of the scythe. But he could not destroy the hints of yellow everywhere. Light on leaves, on water. A ragged birch stump emblazoned with yellow fungus. A dozer that big could go anywhere, anywhere on this land, up hill or down dale, clear to the beach and back, there was not a goddamn tree big enough or deep enough to halt it. A hundred years worth of root wouldn't do it. He did not want to think what that machine could do, or the way it just sat up there, left behind, more dangerous than dynamite. Men he knew, he'd laughed at their love of yellow iron. The young fella up the road who bought the MacNeil place thought he'd rout the alders once and for all because some fool from town cleared a great patch of them with a dozer, its big toothed blade ripping them out by the roots, and all so easily, shoving them into huge mounds to burn. Sure, it cleared the land like he'd wanted it, he'd beaten the alders and won back a field. But it won't work, Roderick told him, that's just a big iron version of what we do with a pick and a shovel, dig them out one summer and curse them again the next until their roots are tough as cable. No, no, the man said, it gets the roots and everything, you see, the dozer does. Yes, Roderick said, and the topsoil along with it. And he'd sat in his kitchen and listened to the bulldozer grinding back and forth over the young man's land, scooping out, with its ferocious efficiency, bladesful of alders, their brittle branches crunching and snapping like gunshots. And by nightfall the trees were rubbish and during the cold weeks of January the man burned the alder piles one by one, their hot cores glowing in the early dusks, ash coiling up gray into the windy snow, and in his bed, near sleep, Roderick sometimes sniffed the smoke and it surprised him, the wild smell of it coming in the crack of his window. Alder good wood to burn, hot, hot. Melt iron, ruin grates. But by summer that bare waste ground, oh Jesus, he knew the alders would love it, they couldn't wait, they were ready with suitcases, and move in they did. By fall that field was so thick with them, you'd think they'd been sown, and the next summer too dense to walk through, roots knotted like fists. How Roderick had laughed to see them crowding there. But ashes, the ashes.

Roderick held the receiver like a hammer.

"I didn't hear from Mr. Maddocks for a couple years," he said to the unresponsive voice. "It's just that I was wondering about him."

"You're the what, the caretaker?"

"I looked after his property here. For him. Many years."

"Where's 'here'?"

"St. Aubin. Cape Breton. Nova Scotia."

"Oh yes. Yes. Well, I forgot your name. He told me to drop you a line. I thought you were a bill collector or somebody for Jesus. He's dead and gone. Awful sick. Went quickly."

"A blessing, I guess."

"What? He didn't owe you money, did he?"

"No, no. Listen, on the property, there's a bulldozer there. Parked since a couple days, maybe three." Roderick's mouth was dry. "What's up with it?"

"Up? It's not us, not ours. Tell them to beat it. We'll be out there sometime, but this summer, well. Sometime."

Roderick could detect nothing of Maddocks in his son's voice. It seemed to promise, in its vagueness, nothing good. But the dozer was not part of that, not now. He could order it away, climb into that damn seat and drive it off if he had to, the Mounties couldn't touch him. Still, he was more uneasy than before. The man he'd just talked to knew not stick nor stone of this place.

That night through the dark fields, through the woods he knew so well, every root and hazard, Roderick needed no flashlight. The spaces lit with moon cast deep shadows, a groping darkness Roderick moved through as if it were day, skirting the spot where he, in one form or other, would someday lie. He just glanced down there at the shrouded trees, moon-washed, then headed up until he saw the rectangular hulk of the bulldozer, its yellow bleached by moon. Like a thief he clambered over its metal, cool with dew, and sat himself in the steel seat. Jesus, you were high up here: it made you think you could take any land you liked. Trees might slow you up but never stop you, and what rocks were there you couldn't lift or shove? What a beast. No wonder the drivers looked dazed sometimes, like they couldn't hear anything but the diesel and the dangerous clangor of treads, just them and the machine and the levers, nothing outside all that. Destruction, and that was what all clearing and leveling was, wasn't it, gouging out, scraping clean, like you'd dig out a sod hump. He felt the instruments for a key but there was none. God, how he would love to roar it into life, direct it, clanking and grinding, into some ditch down the road and whoever owned it could get it out, their problem. He tugged at the levers, worked the pedals. There was no way he would rouse this thing on his own. The driver would come, and then they'd have it out. Roderick would set him straight: the owner doesn't want your services, doesn't need them, you've got the wrong place, shove off. Yet he could imagine a kind of satisfaction, having this machine under you, blasting trees out of your path, scooping up rocks like pebbles, mashing a landscape into whatever. *You catch it at the seventh roller coming off, grab it and swing it around into the rollers of number eight. Nearly end to end, they were, coming at you, a white molten snake, looping and narrowing from mill to mill, and you could see it brighten the dark mill wall and you knew it was arriving steady as a train and would appear with a smooth, contained, fiery light, sudden but expected, and you whirled in a splash of sparks and you captured the rod and you passed it on into the rollers eagerly spinning, always spinning.*

Roderick slumped in the seat. A foot pedal squeaked as he pumped it in and out, in and out. When the moon eased behind the hill, there was only one dark shape in the field, big and silent.

It did not occur to Roderick that he might resort to prayer even after another day and another went by with the dozer unclaimed and unmoving, as if it had been left there deliberately to absorb momentum. Peg could pray for him, churchgoer that she was. Late in the afternoon he stood where his grave was to be. Columbines were just now giving up petals for seed, dropping one by one their purple blossoms. The brook nearby purled faintly with the low, narrow water of summer. Beech trees and maples gentled the light. He had to think about this part of death all over again and he hadn't the heart for it. He had thought that taken care of, since the burial was the only portion of it he had any say in: he believed that if you were laid out in just the right place, your spirit, the only thing that lived, had something your own going for it. A site consecrated by four generations, not by their interment, for most of them lay on Man O' War Point, but by their passing over this land for a long time in the comings and goings of their lives. But here, no visitors. Just the blue-eyed grass, the wild iris. Just Roderick. And a girl once, right here. He had brought her, or had they brought each other, her hand in his, warm as light. Why did he keep thinking now that the bulldozer would come down here for sure? Rooted up, scooped and scattered. The ground, damp from a night shower, gave slightly underfoot as he paced it, back and forth, printing the sod with his boots.

He had thought that he would sit up, if there was a sitting up when the time came, toward the mountain across the water along whose ridge he'd seen many suns disappear, many kinds. In the Catholic cemetery over on the south side of the island the graves were directed eastward toward the rising of Judgment Day. So it had to matter, did it not? And that was a day he'd heard about plenty, growing up, and the necessity, or impossibility, of being saved from damnation. Roderick had chafed at all that but the questions still troubled him. Are the fires of hell hotter than the rod mill? he'd asked his dad finally, old enough to distance himself from The Gospel Hall, and the man had said, hotter than any agony you can imagine, you young pup. A hard man in a rigid denomination: it made Knox Presbyterians sound like libertines. The Gospel Hall wouldn't let you pee if they thought it would make you feel good. Roderick couldn't go to a dance or a party, and when movies came along he was forbidden them as well. When his dad relented eventually and brought a phonograph home, the only records he allowed were Gaelic hymns and devotionals, not the sort of thing that would get you up for a Saturday night. There were endless Sundays in hard chairs in rooms bare of church trappings, hours of preaching, one lay brother after another it seemed, until he was dazed with the heat and the gravity of voices whose weight seemed to grow until he was bowed down with fatigue. When Roderick got old enough to think through some of the things he heard, the notion of being saved seemed to have worrisome holes in it, and what shone through them was not sunshine. After they took him on at the steel mill, Roderick left The Gospel Hall and his dad feared for his soul, loudly at first but finally just shaking his head when Roderick did not get up for

Sunday but lay deliciously in bed. In later years his dad would sit bent over a radio, his arthritic hands deformed at the shapes they'd worked in, listening to broadcasts of The Gospel Hall in the weak kitchen sun because he couldn't travel to meetings anymore, convinced though he was of his own salvation. Roderick did not want to, could not, determine whether he was among the elect, those whom God had already, somehow, selected to be saved, or among the damned, do what he might to correct it. What occurred after dying was—spin out what you would—baffling. But he did want his own burial, here. It was all in his will, the careful instructions written out in ink, a little map. All he had known, after all, was how to be ready, how to present himself.

He knew there would come a point when nothing would be far away, going or coming. Last night he listened to another high, solitary airplane, already over the sea when he heard that long fading whisper, like letting out breath. What would shape him out of ashes? What would care to?

When you see it on the wall, you count **one, two,** *and then catch. You never say* **three** *because she's gone, you're catching nothing.*

Was that a whiff of exhaust somewhere? The beat of an idling engine? Suddenly Roderick seized a young birch tree by its trunk and struggled to bring its crown to the ground but it was too strong and sprang away in a slash of leaves, quivering upright. The air was warm and dizzy and clouds lumbered in from the ocean, solemn with rain. He had liked the moistness here, the moss a slick green on rock, and further up thick enough to lie on, dry, if there hadn't been rain. He hastened up an old back trail, winding through a dense, gloomy stand of slender spruce, so crowded their trunks were grayed with lichen, their branches, bare and brittle as sticks where the sun hardly reached. He breathed with a tense, quickening panic: the dark, good God, he was afraid of the dark. He laughed and moaned at himself—what, you fool, could any dark be compared to the big dark you know nothing about? This was nothing, night was nothing. Branches prodded his face and arms as he pushed ahead, snapping them off brutally, hurrying, but there where the path ended like a tall door someone was waiting in the field, looking his way, back-lit. "Whoa!" Roderick yelled, angry to be surprised here, scratched and perspiring as if he were lost. "Who's up there?"

"Easy, boy. I was only up looking at your dozer."

"Corry, you bastard. You know, I never run into anybody here." Roderick felt oddly glad to see him, relieved somehow. "Where's your hat? I'd have known the hat."

"With the feather? In my car. I was needing a little walk." Corry looked hot himself, his white shirt wilted, his necktie yanked loose.

"Let's walk toward whiskey."

"A mind reading man."

In the kitchen Roderick set down a bottle of rye he'd barely touched in months and two small glasses, wiped clean. He was getting untidy but he didn't much care, him who was so neat all these years. Neither spoke while Roderick, amazed at his own eagerness to be drunk, poured generously. He wanted to hear, for once, just what Corry and that woman had done this afternoon. He would listen to every nasty detail, and if Corry wanted to dress it all up a little, that was all right with Roderick too. He had forgotten what drink was capable of if you didn't sip it but simply squared up to it.

"My great-uncle Malcolm prospered in California," he said, looking down the front hall to the Cougar parked beyond the front porch. "Rushing for gold like a lot of fools out there in the 1850s, in bigger mountains than these, snow to your rooftops in wintertime. But Malcolm, he opened an inn there in the Sierra foothills, and his son years later got on me to come out, lots of work, he said. My dad said, you'd better take it, nothing going here but Depression. But the next day I got a joyful call: the steel plant had a place for me. That night I drank rum glass after glass and they put me to bed insensible. You know, the thought of packing my things and really leaving for California made me light in the gut, like coming over a wave in a small boat. I was more pleased I didn't have to go than being there could ever make me."

"Slainte!" Corry toasted and they drank, clean and quick. When Corry got tight, there was no ranting and roaring, no Sundays stupid with Saturday night. Roderick liked that about him.

"Funny how the dozer looks like she's there for good," Corry said.

"I'll get a man to fire her up pretty soon. Run her clean to the shore and watch her sink. Good-bye dozer."

"Wouldn't be legal."

"Legal got nothing to do with it."

"Yes. I know."

"You're going to be buried in that automobile," Roderick said. The quick glass of rye settled a strange calm into him, though his heart seemed to beat quietly fast.

Corry laughed. "I'd need the dozer for that. But why not? I don't want that car junked in somebody's woods, spruce shoving up the floorboards. Look at that paint. No rust, not a pinhole."

"No salt out there in California."

"Not a lot here either."

"What, the winter roads?"

"No, this man's summer. The salt's gone out of it." Corry tamped a long cigarette on the tabletop, lit it. "You ever think of the first woman you laid down with, Roderick John?"

"Wouldn't do me a bit of good."

"Lord, I can taste her sometimes. I can feel the hem of her dress, her slip. That little noise the satin makes. They always wore dresses, remember? The perfume was nothing special, dime-store stuff, but Jesus. I could tell you every inch of her."

"Don't."

"Might. Just for the hell of it." Corry sighed deeply. "For God's sake, Roderick John, I used to drive all around the island and half the time there'd be a woman in the seat beside me."

"Which half was better?"

"Do you know what I'm talking about at all, man? When were you with a woman last?"

"It's pretty dim, I admit. But there's another time, much earlier time. I'd been working in the mill a while and I brought a woman home, just into the driveway, late, driving my dad's old Ford, and we went at it in the front seat, pretty well juiced and ready for each other, the both of us, and later I stumbled out of the car for a piss but I wander upstairs when I'm done, to bed somehow, passed out.

In the morning my dad, up at daybreak wouldn't you know, discovers the poor girl asleep where I left her, her skirt to her waist and her underpants snagged on the gear shift. It was a sight you and me would've gladly exaggerated, but he told it straight, my dad. He'd woke her up as gently as he could and turned his back while she dressed, and then he sat her in the kitchen and cooked her eggs and baloney and poured coffee until she felt better. Long before I woke up he drove her home, or as close to it as she wanted to be left. But he did not preach to me about it, not a word of that. He just told me it was time I got myself a room somewhere, and that it was a mean thing to leave a girl out there in the cold. I loved my dad for things like that. He could surprise me sometimes. But I didn't love his religion. It's no good to me now."

"All I remember of church is, no, you can't do that. All out of whack to the comfort it gave anyway. Still, that Presbyterian love, it can fool you. That same fire they scare you with can heat up your blood."

"Works that well, does it?"

"Not anymore. You have to do what's required," Corry said, looking away out the back window. "That's what it comes down to and they only have so much patience, b'y. Used to be *we* couldn't wait, our foot to the floor, a few squirts and a cigarette, eh? And now there I am in the drugstore with my arm in the blood pressure machine, grinning like a fish because my heart's still beating, toting up my score. If those things gave nickels, I'd be rich. Christ."

"You've had a disappointment, Corry, boy. I'll fill your glass."

"That doesn't half describe it, my friend." Corry's voice dropped to a note Roderick hadn't heard before, sad and smoky. "No ailments, I said. I told her, let's talk about what still works, even if it doesn't work so good as it used to. But she was fixed on the broken, the pains, the aches, the threats and dangers and what's to be done about them. It's a medical world, b'y. So. I'm pulling up my trousers, and her, she's vacuuming the room. She's shaking out the curtains."

"I'm glad to be free of that," Roderick said. He let the rye heat on his tongue, then swallowed.

"You're never free of that till you're dead. My God, there's nothing sadder than a soft dick."

The back field was flowing with early goldenrod on which brown butterflies trembled, then blew about like tiny leaves. This-tle seeds scattered past the window, bits of feather. Through the screen they could hear the aspens hiss. Roderick squinted at the shades of leaves, their different rhythms of green. Truth was, he did remember that girl. He was not immune. They'd known each other as summer neighbors, knew the woods and paths to the beach, the brook: all seemed to lead to water, and they both had a thirst. As keen as he was, she was, church or no church, and they'd both spent many a Sunday in those hard pews. They knew the language of sin, they'd heard it, the rules and the risks of it. But he led her down to that spot by the brook, to that leafy privacy where their nakedness seemed so easy they laughed. But ashes?

He had never wanted marriage, to her or any that came after. They had their ways and he had his. Any fit man could cook his meals, mend his clothes, clean up after his own body. And of course a point comes when you know you're alone, that it's too late for that kind of company day by day. And there was Corry to consider, living in silence with a woman who refused to talk to him because he had taken church money she was in charge of and gone on a binge.

"How long was it, Corry, that Willena wouldn't speak?"

"Seven years," he said quickly, as if they'd been discussing her all along. "Some might say that was a blessing, but of course that's an easy thing to say. I could have left. But you know I didn't want to, and she knew it, and she punished the shit out of me. No talk but just the necessary yes or no. But it's the bits of conversation that you like in a woman and they knit you together in a way, after awhile, because it's not quite like the talk you have with anybody else. The silence, well, it was queer. I never knew what to do about it. I was proud too, you know. After a while it was just wills, mine and hers. I never stopped thinking about her. Without her voice, I was always wondering about her, harder than before. She died suddenly, as they say, too quick to tell me anything at all—yes, no, or maybe."

"Without talk, I don't see it."

"I loved the woman anyway. Hard to explain, and since she's gone, there's no point in that either."

Against the mountain an eagle, a brilliant white bit, was drifting, high over the water, its black lost in the dark green shadows of trees.

"Sunday tomorrow," Roderick said. "I haven't been to church for fifty years."

"No black suit for me, b'y."

"Was my dad's idea of heaven—one Sunday after another."

"No room for women, I suppose?"

"Not the way you're thinking, Corry, my man. That's all over with up there, so they tell us."

"I suppose. And ashes, they're so damned unreliable."

"You too?"

"They don't so much burn you as bake you. 2500 degrees. Three hours. There's bits left, but not the bits we care about."

Corry topped his glass and Roderick's. Above the mountain, sun burned a few moments deep in cloud.

"Be blazes in the mill today, eh?" Corry said.

"Lord. Basic rate plus tonnage. Always on edge. Rolled a thousand billets a day without a rejection. Rolled all sizes, right down to wire, just a weaving glowing filament."

"Chase that wire to hell and back, eh? Whiskey makes me want to dance, Roderick John. You got music here, Scotch music anywhere?"

"None on the radio, not this day and hour. Plenty of other racket, that stuff that sounds like a scrap yard."

"I'll jig my own tune then." Corry rapped out a beat with a spoon, humming, and then he stood up slowly and picked it up with the heel and toe of his shiny black shoes, his back straight, arms at his side. Roderick was surprised at the supple swiftness of his footwork, neat and close to the floor, a good stepdancer in the old style.

"I knew men could dance that all night," he said.

"They cleared the floor for me more than once, boy." Corry stepped off a few more bars and then stopped. He breathed deeply like a runner and sat down. "Short night. I'm an old dog, all the tricks are new."

"That was good, boy. I'm weary just watching."

"I never liked watching, I wanted to be in there."

"Yes, yes." In the early years after he sold the land, Roderick had gotten up from bed for no reason but restlessness, a summer night dark and bright at the same time, the moon as brilliant as snow. His illness had passed and he was strong again but in the old house living alone, and that night there seemed to be nothing ahead of him, no one close to him: everyone had gone away for good. The burden of the old house was his, every room, and the land. Then out in an old pasture, succumbing already to woods, he saw three people stepping tenderly across the chilly, dewy grass, things dangling from their arms. Two men and a woman, he could hear their laughter, their murmured remarks. In the middle of the field they flung away the clothes they were carrying and joined hands, moving slowly in a circle, cooing at the moon. They were naked, moonwhite, and as soon as Roderick apprehended that, he felt leaden with yearning. Never before or since had he so much wanted to be taken in, and he did not even know into what. When the circle of revelers parted and were soon gone toward the shore, he listened to their calls in the woods, their howls as they waded into the midnight water, keeping him awake.

"Listen," Corry said. "We'll go up there and get that damn dozer started, get it out of your life."

"No. I don't think so."

"Something else on your mind?"

"Yes. I'm going to die."

"Most certainly."

"No, I mean soon."

"Ah. At least you know. Some of us wait, some of us run. Me, I have a car with a big engine."

"I'm not afraid of it. I just thought if they could put me under a piece of my own ground, I'd get over the tough part, the surprises."

"But we don't know what the surprises are, Roderick John. Are you sick, do you have something terminal?"

"I haven't. It's got nothing to do with being sick. Now it's ashes I have to think about, and worse."

"Have another drink then, seeing as you're going to die."

"I didn't mean this afternoon. I'll wait till you leave anyway."

"That's decent of you, Roderick John. I've had enough dying for one day." Corry's gaunt face was flushed with whiskey and he blew out smoke with a long exhaling that seemed to merge with wind flowing through the back field, through the kitchen. Then rain brought down a sudden dusk.

"The peepers have stopped, have you noticed?" Roderick said, but Corry did not answer. Yes, the small frogs that in the night woods cheeped like birds. They'd quit, suddenly. But of course it was July and they should be finished mating anyway. Nothing odd about their silence except that Roderick was aware of it and missed them. He did not remember just when Corry left, did not recall even the engine of his car, only the kitchen growing darker, and on the water a brief light like ice, silvery. The room grew cooler with the evening breeze but Roderick made no move toward a supper. He watched a moon appear, large, low and richly yellow, but turning white as porcelain as it rose. He took the last of the whiskey in sips because it seemed to hone his attention in some necessary way. The deep darkness of country night. Someone's wharf at the foot of the mountain, one solitary light in a wide high blackness. Well, he would lie some way under leaf or snow. Rabbits would cross, fast if they sensed a fox in the cold air, a dust of flakes following their tracks, or they might pause, listening. The fox would move dainty, swift at the right moments, clearheaded with hunger, not panic, unless the snow were deep and the lynx, on its big soft feet, were running him calmly down. Deer hooves to the brook, marking the sod deep. He'd shot his share when he was young, skinned out their steaming insides. Meat he'd wanted, needed. Birds would brush the ground for bugs, for seeds. A grouse would scoot through the summer grass, diverting danger from her young. But that danger would not be human. He did not remember either when he slept, when his head lay on the table, and his dreams were rapid and confused, as if his sleeping consciousness dismissed everything parading across it, all enticements, fantasies, regrets, and when sun lit the back field in a sudden flicker of russet, the grasses still cool, faintly smoking, he was already hearing an engine, the clattering of tread, dirt gorging against steel, the stones tumbling, screeching, and as he got to his feet he was already counting, *one, two*.

Rick Bass

The Myths of Bears

From *The Southern Review*

I

TRAPPER IS SO OLD and tired that every August he just sits in the sun in front of his cabin with his head bowed, trying to gather up the last of it. A week of heat left, and then each day after will be cooler. He sits with his arms spread and tries to gather it all in, absorbing the vitamin D. Everything is draining from him. He used to love winter the most; now he tries only to stagger from August to August, each year, crossing the months like stepping-stones across a dangerous river.

Maybe the breadth of time he's spent in the woods turned Trapper's mind: his need to be versatile, to change with the seasons. Or maybe it's the absence of cities, towns, or villages. It wasn't something, though, that human contact could stave off in him, or else his wife would have kept it at bay. He wants her back worse than he ever wanted a pelt. Judith has been gone now almost a year.

She broke through the cabin's small window on a January night during the wolf moon when Trapper was having one of his fits. At such times something wild enters him. Trapper is as pale as a snow lion. Judith came from Tucson, and was still brown ten years after she left. It was as though in Arizona she'd stored a lifetime of sun.

Judith has curved feet, like flippers. She's six feet tall (Trapper is five nine), and her shoe size is thirteen. Judith gets around in the snow real well; the inward curve of her feet makes it so she doesn't need snowshoes.

In Trapper's nighttime fits, he imagines that he is a wolf, and the others in his pack have suddenly turned against him and set upon him with their teeth; he's roused in bed to snarl and snap at everything in sight.

And then there are the daytime fits, when he imagines he has become someone else, in the manner of a snowshoe hare or ptarmigan, whose coat changes color with the seasons; or of the deer and caribou, whose habits change; or the bear, who goes to sleep, falling down into that deep, silent place—beneath a dozen feet of snow by January—where his brave heart beats once a minute—where everything's very, very slow. . . .

When Trapper would get that way—*changed*—he'd turn to Judith and begin speaking in the third person, as if neither he nor she were there. His eyes wouldn't blink as he turned slowly to Judith to say: "Trapper says there is a storm coming"; or, "Trapper says there are too many wolves in the woods"; or—increasingly—"Trapper says he doesn't feel good."

Judith hated to leave him like that. When Trapper held his hands out in front of him they shook like leaves, and he was only thirty-five years old. Maybe his body would live forever, but his mind was going, and Judith was too smart to ride it to the end.

He had also begun to shake as he set his traps, fumbling with and bumping the hair triggers. Increasingly, he'd arrive home with crushed and broken fingers.

"Trapper says he doesn't know what's happening," he'd say, and Judith's heart would flood away from her like loose water. She'd feel wicked about it, but she was changing, too—she could hear the distance calling her some nights, could see the northern lights whooshing and crackling so close as to seem just over the next ridge. She'd want to leave right then, right there. The northern lights, or something, were calling her name. Judith stayed as watchful in bed as a cat, never sleeping now as the lights sprayed green and red beams across the dark sky: she was waiting, waiting for one more wolf fit. When it finally came, she would be up and through that small glass window.

Judith cut herself, breaking through it—Trapper had barred the door to keep trouble out, she knew, though as he grew sicker she had begun to imagine it was to keep her in—and he'd been able to track her a ways, following her blood. Howling as he went, he sounded like a wolf in his sadness. But Trapper had had to stop to pull on the snowshoes he'd managed to grab from their place by the door, and in this span Judith drew away from him. She had the advantage of speed, and she knew where she was going—up and over that northern ridge—while Trapper had to pause, going from track to track, bloodspot to bloodspot. A heavy snow was beginning to fall through the trees as if trying to wash away the moon, and Judith ran for the ridge with her 50-yard head start, and then it was 100 yards; she was crying, and tears were freezing on her cheeks, but she knew she was now about 250 yards away from him. She could barely hear his howls.

She crossed a creek, soaking her boots over the ankles; she gasped, clambered to the other side, and started up the ridge. He was the only one who had ever really loved her—*her*—with her big, crooked feet. Faintly, she could still hear him.

Her feet were numb from the creek, but still she moved on, the quick-falling snow covering her tracks.

When Judith got to the top of the ridge, his howls were gone. She considered howling once, to let him know she was . . . what?—all right? not angry? sad?—but instead she turned and went down the other side, catching herself on the trunks of trees when she tripped over her large feet. Judith ran all night to stay warm, floundering, going north. She knew he'd figure she was headed to a town.

It was true she'd be safe in a town, because Trapper would never enter one to look for her—but he might go so far as to hang around on the outskirts, like an old lobo skulking near a campfire.

Judith didn't miss the desert. Sometimes she did—in the spring usually—but right now she was thrilled to be half-running, half-swimming through rich, deep snow. The sadness of leaving him being transformed into the joy of freedom, and the joy of flight, too.

She imagined the sleeping bears beneath her. Her Uncle Harm had raised her in the desert outside Tucson, and then she took up with Trapper when they were both eighteen. Uncle Harm had been an old trapper and hunter and had tried to teach Trapper some things, but had not been entirely successful. Another year and Judith and Trapper would've spent half their lives together.

It was delicious to swim through the snow. The blizzard was a sign that she was meant to escape. A fool could have followed her tracks under normal conditions, but these weren't normal conditions. This was the first night of her life.

It wasn't about babies, or towns, or quilting bees. Domesticity. It wasn't about flowers, or about the desert in spring. It might not even have been about his snarling fits, or his lonely, flat-eyed "Trapper says" fits.

It was about those red and green rods streaking through the sky, just to the north: just a little north of where she had been living.

He was gone, Judith knew. It would be a luxury to feel sad about it. He'd been gone for years. If he'd been a deer or moose, elk or caribou—if he'd been prey instead of predator—something would have noticed his odd demeanor, his slowing step—that *trembling*—and would have singled him out and brought him down.

Judith slept at the base of a giant, fire-hollowed cedar for a short time before dawn. She took off her leather boots, her socks and leggings, and tucked them between her body and clothes to dry. She half-dozed with her hands around her naked feet, trying to warm and dry them. The cedar jungle where she had stopped offered shelter against much of the snow and wind; the deer had taken refuge there, too. They'd been living in the tangle of cedars for several weeks, ever since the storms started, shedding their antlers and milling together for warmth. Great curved antlers lay scattered all around her; the antlers were being covered quickly with skiffs of snow—the drifts weren't as deep back in the cedars—and Judith could feel the deer watching her. She dreamed that she could feel the warmth of their breath as they moved slowly over to investigate. Her coat and pants were made of deer hide, deer Trapper had shot for her to skin and sew into garments.

Judith slept as the deer circled and sniffed her and looked at one another in the deep night and waited out the storm.

The wolves would notice his odd gait, Judith dreamed. If Trapper tried to follow her too far in his condition—his *sleepwalking*—the wolves would get him.

Spring, even the hint of it, was still three months away.

She dreamed of Tucson, holding her cold toes in her hands: rubbing them in her sleep.

It was still snowing outside the cedar jungle when her shivering woke her. Judith considered whether she would forever, after this night, associate guilt with cold. She could see the deer tracks around her where they had come in the night; she could see where they had stopped to sniff and identify her. They had touched her, she knew, with their noses: they had given her her identity.

It is not that he is a bad man, or that I am a bad woman, she thought. It's just that he is a predator, and I am prey. It is the way of nature for our lives to be associated, even intertwined, for a long while. But now, if I am to survive, I have to run. It has nothing to do with him. It *used* to; but now, suddenly that I'm free, it doesn't.

It is so *sad,* she thought; but even as she was thinking this, she was pulling on her damp socks, her damp boots and leggings, and dusting the snow from her clothes and rising stiffly, her legs as bowed from the cold as the curve of her big, sorrowful feet. She stared at the deer's delicate tracks.

He is gone, Judith told herself again. I am not running from him anymore, I am running from his death. Trapper is gone.

She looked up the next ridge, into the wind-and-north-stunted alpine fir; a little farther north, she knew, there would be tundra. She definitely did not want to leave the woods.

No, she remembered then, I am no longer running from anything. I am running *to* something.

Her feet were hurting, which was good; the blood was returning. Judith limped down a game trail. Snow was still falling. Her long yellow hair shrouded her neck and face and kept the snow out. It was too cold for it to melt. Trapper used to brush her hair every night; brush and then wash it. Already she missed his broken-fingered hands.

"Trapper is gone," she repeated out loud, like a mantra, as she trudged up the trail. Later in the day, with the snow still coming down, she would find a gaunt-ribbed deer dying in the cedar jungle, starving, and she would chase it a short distance—the deer falling and floundering, crazy-legged, unable to go on—and she would kill it by cutting its throat with her knife.

Judith drank the blood from the cut throat, but only after the deer was dead and its eyes were turning waxy blue, its soul rising into the trees.

Then the liver, still hot; steam rising from it as she cut it free. Then the blood that was sloshing inside the body cavity. Judith washed the blood from her face with handfuls of snow; skinned the deer quickly while it was still warm, before it could freeze; and cut the meat from the shoulders and hamstrings and wrapped it in the congealed hide. Tied it to her back.

Judith felt the woods wrapping her, taking care of her in her sorrow, and she thanked them every step of the way for giving her a deer. She felt *embraced*. Judith knew this was how her Uncle Harm—the one who'd taught Trapper certain things, though not everything—used to feel, because he'd talked about it often, back in Arizona.

Deer stood aside, too cold to run, and watched her pass.

Judith felt badly: not knowing why she was moving, only that she must. Grizzlies will travel thirty miles in a night, she knew, to get to a good acorn crop. Deer and elk will leave a mountain, will come down off the highest peak and into the river bottoms in advance of a storm, in only a matter of hours. But Judith was not entirely sure why she was traveling—and why she was moving north, into the winter, rather than away from it.

It had been 106 degrees on the day she was born. But she'd gotten used to the cold. It wasn't that different from the heat. Both were things that got your attention.

Maybe it was as simple as the feeling that if she went south, it would be like running away; but if she went north, it would just be running.

Trapper hunted her for four days and nights, making concentric circles around his cabin, trying to pick up her sign: making the circles larger and larger; calling her name and crying and howling. Chasing the game off: ruining his season.

Betrayed; abandoned. He'd thought she was *tame*. He'd not understood she was the wildest, most fluttering thing in the woods.

He thinks, Next time, when I get her back, I will keep her tied up even tighter. I will tie her with rawhide to a stake in the front yard.

He thinks, She didn't love me enough. Maybe she even hated me. But what about all those good times in Tucson? And up here?

I will make her love me more, he thinks, wandering his woods, casting for scent—trembling like an old dog. He hunts for her harder than he ever hunted for any grizzly or wolf, fisher or marten. He abandons his traps, forgets where he's hung them: leaves them untended.

Martens dangle from the trunks of trees, a rear leg snapped, broken by the trap's jaws. At first they scramble and chatter to get free, but over time their movements become slower. They hang like small shawls against the bark, snow catching on their fur, and the traps rusting. . . .

If Judith had heard Trapper cry like a child she probably would have gone back to him and stayed until he got better, or didn't. But some instinct—and fear—told her to go all the way up to the edge of the forest, to winter away from him, in a place where she could not be lured back.

Maybe in the spring, Judith thought, she'd ease back and spy on his cabin. See if he had made it or not. See if he'd survived, or if he was bones.

Forty, fifty, fifty-five below. She can't build a fire, or he'll find her. She left in such a hurry. She builds a snow cave in the cedar jungle, makes a coat of her deer hide, but still she's cold, even with two coats. She doesn't dare build a fire. Even mind-sick, Trapper can smell smoke at a hundred miles.

Such is her fear, and the word beyond fear: *longing*.

Trapper sleeps with the window open—the one she crashed through—to punish himself for letting her escape. He knows she's not building fires—he'd smell them. If he could just find where she is, he could begin setting traps for her, but he has no idea whether she is east or west or north or south. He feels trapped by his ignorance, and thrashes around on his bed at night and moans and howls. . . . His trap-cracked fingers surge with pain; they've been frostbitten so many times that each new time they freeze, he's sure he'll lose them, that this time the blood won't return; and what good is a trapper without fingers, without hands? He'd be no better than a bear, with nothing but paws. He dreams again of August.

Trapper remembers the big grizzly he killed down in the Gila desert, back in the '90s. Its tracks were thirteen by eleven inches—the feet as long as Judith's, but so very much wider—and Trapper remembers how the bear dragged his chain and trap twelve miles up into the mountains and into a cave. Trapper had nailed the trap and chain to a twelve-foot timber, and he followed the swath the bear made as he fled. October. Buzzards shadowed the trail, knowing what was coming. It was easy for Trapper to follow at a dead run as there were the birds to look to, and the trail was like the wake of a canoe. Trapper has never owned a horse: he despises and distrusts anything stronger than he is.

As Trapper's shakes set in, Judith got that way: stronger than he was. He still had his strength, but when he was trembling it was of little use; he'd drop things. He'd have to ask for her help. The glimmer of reasoning that this might have frightened her as badly as it frightened him glows in his mind, and then fades. He's remembering this bear in the Gila.

You must tie a drag to the trap for the prey to run with, but one that will only slow the animal down. If you tie the chain too tight, the bear or wolf—with no hope of escape—will chew its damn *leg* off to get away.

This Gila River grizzly holed up in a cave. It was a smart bastard. It ambushed Trapper, trap and chain and log and all. Wrapped him up as best it could, biting at his face and neck. The only thing that saved Trapper was that the bear's teeth had been broken by the huge steel trap: he'd tried to bite it off. Still, the bear raked Trapper's back with his terrible claws. The first bear that ever got in close with him; the first one he ever wrapped up with. Trapper was nineteen. He grabbed the bear's big tongue the way he'd been told and twisted like hell; the bear released his grip, and Trapper pulled his knife free and stuck it up under the ribs, again and again, probing for the heart. Found it.

Bright red blood and froth and slobber and bits of tooth all over his face. He had to sleep on his stomach for three months. He remembers how Judith would lick the wounds; and then, when they healed, how she would lick the scars. They were living on her Uncle Harm's ranch, in an adobe by the Salt River. White-winged doves cooing all the time. The mornings were cool; everything seemed new.

Nineteen!

He didn't know if his seed was bad or if she was barren. Nothing ever happened, and he's not sure, as he trembles now, ancient at thirty-five, that that was a bad thing.

Candlelight washes across his crooked face. He can't believe he's alone.

In February it warmed to fifteen below. It had been so cold that Judith's head hurt: she got a little crazy, afraid to go to sleep for fear her head would split the way the dry fir trees had been cracking open every January night. She couldn't move around, couldn't walk through the woods with her ugly feet, unless it was snowing hard; she couldn't risk leaving tracks.

Judith figured she was about twenty-five miles north of him. She could sense by the stillness in the woods—the utter emptiness and newness and peace—that he had no idea where she was hiding.

But he would find out. He would sense that emptiness, that peace—he would feel her feeling it—and he would be drawn toward it, perhaps without ever knowing why. She would have to be ready to move again, and quickly.

She wanted to get away—but not too far away.

There were nights when she felt he was still tied to her: she knew he was out tracking her. Strangely, she felt *loved*.

But it felt fine to be alone, and to be free of his air. It wasn't bad air that he breathed in and out; it was just *his*.

When it began to snow, she would rise and go for walks in the woods, walking through the heaviest snowstorms. She'd found a winter-killed moose and made a robe of it, to add to her other coats. She wore all of them when she walked, and when she got lost and could not find her way back to her snow cave, as frequently happened, she'd build a new one. She was following a ridge above a river bottom, over into the next valley. It was a country Trapper had never worked before, and sometimes Judith would catch herself with the ludicrous thought that she would have to tell him about it when she got back.

Remember, Judith told herself, *he is gone.*

She was pretty sure he was gone.

Her hair was wild and dirty, turning darker—from white blond to dirty blond, which troubled her. But it wasn't enough to turn back for: the simple touch of his busted-up hands, brushing and washing her hair, and a warm fire.

A wolverine confronted her one day, ran scampering around her snow cave, raising his hind leg and pissing all around, a vile scent that reminded her of maggots. He stuck his snarling face into her cave, and Judith screamed and jabbed her knife at him, cutting his nose, and the wolverine ran away, lunging across the snow like a man with a broken back, squalling and leaving a trail of blood but looking over his shoulder at her as if to say, "I'll be back."

Judith cut a heavy walking stick and lashed the sharpest deer antlers she could find to the end of it. She never went anywhere without it, and had nightmares about the wolverine until she found him dead in March, where wolves had killed him.

The meat of the wolverine had been too mean and vile for the wolves; they'd eaten only his entrails. Ravens led her to the carcass. It pleased Judith to think of the wolves eating his guts. But she moved on, because he'd marked her cave as his territory with his terrible piss, and the woods were spoiled.

She kept moving north whenever it snowed, from one pocket of stillness and peace to the next.

It was exactly as if she had an injury, and had to let the muscle and bone knit and regather strength. It took time.

In February, Trapper had abandoned his cabin and gone south looking for her. By the first week he knew she could be dead and under five or six feet of snow—that he might not find her skeleton for ten or twenty years, or ever—but he pushed on, casting for scent. He knew she would cross at least one divide, possibly two. The way she had hit that window: he knew she was terrified of something.

It was the first time in eighteen years that he hadn't spent a winter trapping; it felt good. He stood by his fire each night, the trembling having spread from his hands to his shoulders and legs. He was alone, and—he acknowledged this—there was something wrong with him, something time would not fix—but he felt *good*.

He'd piss on his campfire each night to let the wolves know he was there. He heard their howls, the whole of the woods echoing with their sound. Trapper knew that in winter they were all only two days from starving.

He worked a hundred miles south in a week, then fifty miles east of that line, coming back across it, and fifty miles west.

"Sombofambitch," he said in March, when he finally felt the peace and could acknowledge its presence. He was having trouble with his speech. "She has gonb norf . . . norf . . . norf." His heart was fluttering, and his legs, when they trembled, felt like a colt's.

He was back at his cabin, padding traps with hides as he didn't want her to have an ankle broken. He would set them in the spring.

The scent, or feel, of her peace reminded him of the northern lights. No one else he knew ever claimed to hear them, but he could: the sound was faint, to be sure, but clearly there, and it was like strips of thin metal delicately chiming. Trapper believed in angels and a God, though he had never seen either, and believed without doubt that the red and green of the northern lights showed where angels had been: just a day's passage ahead of him, or two days at most.

Trapper started north with a hundred pounds of traps slung over his shoulder. He hadn't used sled dogs in five years; the wolves always killed them, and he was tired of the heartache of losing them.

Aiming north and west, he figured she'd head for the ocean—women love oceans, he thought, and men love forests.

He came near her on that trip, missing her by less than a mile. Judith was sitting on the bluff, looking out over the western river bottom, when she felt his presence in the woods and then, an hour later, saw him walking below her, all those heavy chains thrown across his shoulder: his steps with the snowshoes looking big and sloppy.

She watched him cross the frozen river with his traps. She couldn't see his face or even his beard, and certainly not his strange blue eyes, which turned almost violet in late winter, as if from the absence of something, or in anticipation, perhaps, of spring.

She could make out his wide back, the heavy robes he was wearing, and his clumsy steps. She watched as if it were her wedding day; she felt that much love for him, and that much relief that he was missing her. He stopped often to look at tracks in the river bottom, but they were not her tracks.

In Arizona, Trapper had fried everything in lion grease. Pancakes, sausage, elk steaks, or fish—it all sizzled in the sweet fat of the mountain lions he killed. Old folks said it would go to his brain and give him the trembles later in life, and maybe it did, but watching him move across the river bottom—trembling, though still somehow in possession of his strength—Judith doesn't think that's what did it.

She thinks it is the force of God blowing through the trees that makes him shake. He has chased things so long and so hard he has gotten cut off. He's gotten lost, or dead-ended, or trapped. Or something.

Anyway, he doesn't look ready to die. He looks like he's holding steady.

Judith watched Trapper cross the river: heading all the way to the coast, she suspected—salmon, boats, fishing villages—just to look for her.

It made her feel good in a way she hadn't felt in a long while.

Trapper moved slowly. Judith stayed behind a tree and watched. He was hundreds of feet below her, and half a mile off. Once he turned and looked back up the bluff, right at her. Tears began to roll down Judith's cheeks, freezing before they fell, as she felt all her precious space shattering in his gaze, his *discovery*—but he was looking right through her. Trapper turned away again.

Immediate relief became joy, but then Judith felt an echo of sadness, like a stone dropped, clacking to the bottom of a nearly dry well on a hot day.

She watched him make his way across the mile-wide frozen river. He didn't have long to get to the coast and back before the breakup of the ice left him stranded—the river would surge in a month or six weeks with jagged icebergs, cracking and booming, frothing with dead moose and bear bobbing in its torrent, young, foolish animals who'd tried to cross it. It occurred to Judith that maybe Trapper wasn't coming back.

He still had not come straight north. She believed that when he did not find her on the coast, he would come back and try the forest—the last place he would have suspected her to be. It was a miracle that he had not seen her when he'd looked up the bluff. Judith had held her breath to keep from exhaling smoke-vapor, and hadn't *blinked*—just those slow, round, crystal, frozen tears leaking from her. She had seen Trapper spot live animals hidden in the forest at greater distances. Despite the beauty of his violet eyes, he was color-blind; he saw a monochromatic world, grainy blacks and whites of tone. Winter didn't bother his eyesight because it was how he always saw the world—and animals that relied on camouflage were helpless, revealed bluntly, nakedly, before his gaze.

After Trapper was gone, Judith felt that dry-well sorrow and fear, but then the fear left and joy returned. She wished him well on his journey and worried for him, but reasoned that any time spent trembling in the woods was infinitely preferable to time spent trembling on a bed in a cabin or—worse—in a town.

Judith imagined that the space to the north, all the way to the North Pole, was hers—her *own* space.

She could not wait for spring, when color would fill that space and her world would burst with life.

They had left Arizona when the first silver and copper mines were going in and cattle were sweeping across the desert and fouling the brief rivers. In the Santa Cruz River, which steamships cruised, there had been trout a foot and a half long—but five years after the cattle showed up, the rivers had turned to silt plains, and there weren't enough wolves to turn the cattle back. Trapper regretted that he had helped see to that.

He had never poisoned wolves the way the ranchers did. He trapped them instead, then hit them in the head with a club to keep from ruining the pelts.

Judith's Uncle Harm was the one who taught him how to trap. Judith has tried to imagine Trapper being anything else in life—a miner, or a schoolteacher—but can't see it. She takes this to mean that if he had not met up with Uncle Harm and herself, Trapper would be dead. Invisible.

She takes this to mean, indirectly, that she saved his life. If he had not fallen in hot love with her, he would never have learned to trap.

Uncle Harm was seventy-seven and failing when Trapper showed up. He still hunted and trapped, but was mostly hunting with dogs by that time and no longer tried to get physically involved with his prey.

When he'd been younger—Trapper's age—Uncle Harm had hunted the way Trapper did—on foot, stalking and laying traps, shooting from ambush, and taking on the animals in his traps with only a knife or a club. Uncle Harm was the first white man to perfect the old Yaqui Indian's trick of hunting down and engaging a grizzly—getting it to charge—and then swatting its wrists with an iron bar, breaking them, thereby improving the odds considerably; dodging the crippled bear's jaws and killing it with a knife or lance after that.

The worst Uncle Harm ever got it was from a Mexican grizzly

down in Chihuahua. The grizzly was so big that it simply pulled free of the giant trap, leaving behind part of its foot and two huge claws. Whenever Uncle Harm spoke of this, he took care to mention how the flesh-end nerves of the freshly pulled claws were still red with life, glowing in the trap.

The tracks of the escaped bear were plain, and Uncle Harm, a young man of thirty-three at the time, followed them easily and quickly. At a sharp bend in the trail he found what he wanted. The hurt grizzly had backtracked to the bend to wait.

There was no time to lift his club or his knife. The bear knocked Uncle Harm down with one swat, breaking his collarbone, then bit him on the skull—Judith had heard him preach that the human skull is irresistible to grizzlies, that they like to puncture it like a ringtail cat popping eggs—and then, when the bear heard Uncle Harm's skull pop, he moved his attentions to the shoulders and began ripping them and chewing.

Uncle Harm was dying fast, and he knew his only chance was to play dead, which he was having no trouble doing. He shut his eyes while the grizzly picked him up and dragged him back and forth across the manzanita, smearing the bushes with his blood. Still Uncle Harm played dead, trying to outlast the animal's rage.

The grizzly finally dropped him and ran off, only to return to shake him again so hard that it almost broke Uncle Harm's neck. The bear bit him in the face, then stood over Uncle Harm before nosing him, as if trying to bring his victim back to life so he could kill him again. The bear leaned down and snorted in his ear, trying to make him jump, but Uncle Harm remained dead. He heard the bear limp off after that, and consciousness left him.

When he awoke it was night. He crawled back down the creek to a small spring. Another wolf hunter found him the next day. They sewed him up with veterinary supplies, "but my looks," Uncle Harm would always say, motioning to his terrible, grinning face, "were never thereafter complimentary."

Trapper loved the old man: loved him deeply. Sometimes Judith thinks Trapper should have married Uncle Harm instead of her. He loved to be with the old man. Uncle Harm fried all his food in lion grease too, though he never got the shakes. When Harm got really old and had to resort to chasing animals with dogs rather than on foot, he would circle around the desert on his mule with a gramophone horn lifted to his near-deaf ears, trying to pick up the sound and direction of his dogs' squallings as they battled a bear or a lion. He insisted on going out on his own—wouldn't share his territory, the Galliero Mountains, with anyone, not even Trapper— and when he got older still, there were days when Trapper and Judith didn't know if he'd make it back. At such times, they would search for him.

Sometimes they would find him all right—he'd have gotten tired and stopped to camp by a creek on his way in, with a grizzly hide and the quartered carcass packed across his mule, his dogs panting in the shade, all scratched and cut up from the fight— Uncle Harm looking five or ten years younger every time he killed something. But there were other times, sad times, when they'd go out and find Uncle Harm, loopy from dehydration, spinning on his back on the desert floor, staring wild-eyed up at the great white autumn clouds while his dogs stood around in a confused circle, wanting to step in and lick him but unable to move in among his flailing arms and legs. The saddled mule would be off in the shade chewing saltbush, unconcerned, with no grizzly or lion pelt across its saddle. Uncle Harm looked a hundred years old on such days, wild-eyed, too, and with his canteen stone-empty. . . .

Judith and Trapper would gather him up, lift him onto his fool mule, give him water, and put his hat back on him to shield him from the sun. They would walk home: a whole day's hunting ruined for Trapper, but he didn't care. Back then Trapper could take it or leave it. Uncle Harm's facial scars glowed pale blue whenever he had heatstroke. There was a muddy creek behind their adobe house, and they'd float him in that until he returned to himself.

By nightfall, when the coyotes were singing, Harm would be better—he'd have crawled from the creek and gone to his little house (Trapper and Judith lived in the big house), and there he would change into his white linen evening suit. He'd fix a cup of piñon-leaf tea and go sit on his porch and listen to the night. He'd tell Trapper and Judith trapping stories, and secrets, and in the morning, though there would be new scars and stretch marks upon his heart, he would be ready to go out and kill again.

He kept going. Judith thought it was half-monstrous and half-heroic—it was just the kind of thing a man would like and ad-mire—the way Uncle Harm ruined himself. He kept driving, mindless—*pursuing*. It makes her sad to realize that the times she loved Trapper most were when he was hunting the least. It makes her feel guilty, too, because when Trapper was not hunting he was paying attention to her and loving her. Does this mean she can't love Trapper for what he is, but only for what he can give her?

Nobody could be that evil, she thinks. It's simply a matter of where he puts his heart. It's very simple, Judith thinks. He puts his heart in the woods, or he puts it in the palm of her hand. His heart clinches hers as though they are two elk with their noble antlers linked, if only by accident, in combat.

Back before Harm broke off the gramophone horn to take with him, Judith would stay in bed with Trapper all through the hot part of the day, the sweet middle, falling in and out of sleep, *languishing*, rousing only to put a new record on: both of them abed in the cool shade of love, never suspecting that in a few short years the desert would be gone. Shitting cattle would scour it, and water-robbing mesquite would grow out of their manure—shit-pile muf-fins cast like steppingstones across the land—and with that the rarest and wildest creatures would leave, vanish.

The last music Judith heard, other than the howls of wolves, was in 1904. She listens for the northern lights that Trapper says he can hear, but she hears nothing: though even the sound of nothing, with enough space around her, is pleasant and sweet. Not as good as the sound of running water, which she knows will be coming— but in winter the sound of nothing is just right. The howls of wolves reassure and comfort her, as though a deal has been struck whereby they will take sadness from her heart and assume it for themselves.

Judith builds a tiny cabin out of wind-felled timbers, stretches her hide over it for a roof; packs it with snow. Trapper didn't look sick, she thinks. Maybe he has gotten better without me. This inspires in her the desire to capture him and see if it is so. Judith's not sure she *wants* him to be better off without her.

It isn't about children, Judith tells herself. She remembers the old woman they met in Yellowknife who said she'd had thirteen children by her first husband, but her new husband, "Art, his seed is bad."

Judith knows women with children who've run, and she knows women without children—such as herself—who have also run.

Uncle Harm trapped or killed almost everything in Arizona and then died in 1909 at the age of ninety-one. He'd taken to shooting cows when there was nothing else around; dropping them like buffalo, fifteen and twenty at a time, then hiding out and waiting for the coyotes and the last few lobos to come skulking in. It was easier to find him once he started shooting the cows. Buzzards would spiral above wherever he'd made his stand.

His dogs were by his side, guarding him, the day Trapper and Judith found him for the last time. Dried up, wizened, Uncle Harm had already been gone about half a day, headed toward wherever he was going beyond this life. His gramophone horn was curled tightly in his little fist, and Judith took it from him gently. After they'd buried him, she tried to hook it back up, but the gramophone wouldn't work, not even after they cleaned all the dust and grit out of it.

They had to bury him way off in the desert so he wouldn't foul the spring. Piled rocks on his grave to form a cairn, but still the few remaining coyotes and wolves gathered around it and howled every night for a month. The summer rains came, and they could see where a few grizzlies had emerged from hiding and circled the cairn as if to see for themselves that yes, it was true, they were safe now. Ravens dove and spiraled around it for weeks. Damnedest thing either of them had ever seen, with the exception of Uncle Harm himself.

They sold his dogs to a cattle rancher, opened all the doors and windows of the adobe houses to let the desert enter, and went up through the Rockies in the spring. But the grizzlies and wolves and

Indians had vanished there, too, so they kept going farther north. Trapper and Judith didn't reach the Yukon until fall.

When they started hearing wolves, they felt better. As if they had come home; as if what mattered lay south or north of their country, but not in-between.

II

It's Trapper's aim to catch wolves and martens and wolverines on his trip to the coast, and pull the hides behind him on a sled, arriving there a rich man and trading for gold, for groceries. Coffee from Africa, sugar from the tropics, to maybe keep Judith happy this time. Maybe while she's staked out in the yard he will bake her things with sugar in them. Maybe she would enjoy his new riches so much that he wouldn't have to keep her staked, at least not all the time.

She's lost her mind, Trapper muses, moving through the woods, shaking and stutter-stepping. She hit that window like a bat out of hell. It was like something old Harm might have done.

Big smoked salmon and new traps, new ammunition, too—lead and gunpowder. And jewelry: he'll trap her with gold jewelry, he thinks; he'll string it all through the woods and then set snares, or hide up in a tree so that when she reaches for the glittering-with-sun necklace he can catch her wrist in a wire noose, and he'll have her, have her again. The mistake last time was that he didn't hold her tight enough, that he gave her too much rein. . . .

He'll build smaller windows.

More leg-hold traps, more tobacco. Fuck horses! He'll pull it all home on a sled himself, the way he's always done. Fuck dogs! Whiny crybabies, always wanting to rest. Always getting eaten by wolves. His beard and eyebrows are shining dull whitish-blue with frost—it's thirty below—and he howls.

The wolves that have been following at a distance draw closer, knowing they are safe when a fit wells up from within him; at such times they know that he is not a man but one of them. They seem to believe he would be loath to kill one of his own kind—a brother, a sister.

It's so lonely without her.

What if she's not even up here anymore? What if she's back in Arizona? He's ashamed that his heart is a weak little muscle, incapable of matching the great strength of the chest in which it is housed. Can it be true that he is as weak in heart and mind and soul as Harm was in body? Can it be that he has an animal's soul trapped within him? Maybe that's why trapping never bothered him.

Delicate, ladylike weasels, their front legs bent sideways and shattered in the trap, quiver and look at him in fright as he approaches; they grasp the metal jaws with the slender fingers of their uninjured paws. Already the beautiful shawl they wear does not belong to them.

A man can be a horrible thing. Trapper sits on a log and howls and weeps, but there seems to be no escape—nor does he know where he wants to escape *to*.

He hears a movement in the brush and snow behind him. He grabs his rifle and turns and raises it and sees a pale silver wolf running away; Trapper fires and sends the wolf tumbling, but he's only wounded it, the wolf is back up and running again. There are other wolves with it, and so he will not go into the brush after them, though the blood trail tempts him.

It's not his fault that Judith got away, part of him tells himself when he's shaking—when he's trying to become whatever it is his body's trying to make him become, even if only fodder for worms—but the other part of him, the stronger part, says, "She was in your dominion, and you had control of her, and lost her."

For thirty miles slogging through snow he thinks of words like *dominion* and replays every day of their life together, putting the days together like tracks, but he's puzzled, can find no sign of error, no proof of her unhappiness with him.

He's got four wolf pelts, six foxes, a dozen weasels, a coyote, and a wolverine on his sled—his stone boat—which he drags through the forest. He tries to think like the animals, and yet at the same time to keep his wits about him and keep from plunging off the cliff of human reason and into some abyss where man, having failed at something, descends to a level equal with the animals.

Loopy with fatigue, Trapper snaps off the branches of winter-thin willows along a creek, weaves them into a crown, and continues on his way, carrying his traps with him as he goes.

On the coast Trapper asks around, speaking all three languages—Yúpik, French, and English—awkwardly: the damn woods having swallowed his tongue. But no one's seen her.

The men and women cluck their tongues. One old woman laughs at him and says in Yúpik, "If you lived here she would be easy to trap, for she would have nowhere to run to but the sea."

He stays a night, buys sex from a villager for one wolf pelt—an outrageous price—makes his trades the next day, and heads back across the tundra, back to the woods, with another storm coming in behind him from the Arctic Ocean. He'll trap on the way home, too, though he must be careful and hurry or he'll run out of snow in places and ruin his sled pulling it across the bare rocks.

And then there's the river. Trapper can't swim. He can do all manner of things, spectacular things, with his body if not his mind, but he's so freighted with muscle that whenever he gets in water he goes straight to the bottom. Like a rock.

Trapper moves through the woods herking and jerking, pulling his load, trying, with his mind alone, to trick his central nervous system into not disintegrating further; into not acknowledging that disintegration. He notices that he's trying to tie his knots backward, and it scares him.

To keep his mind off how far this nonsense can go, he concentrates on bears. He imagines how the woods are full of sleeping bears, all denned up beneath him, six feet beneath his snowshoes and curled, waiting to come to life. He thinks of bears and goes over the facts versus the myths.

Bears do *not* suck their paws in hibernation. They merely sleep with their paws pressed against their faces. The Indians in southern British Columbia maintained that a grizzly sighting a lone man in the forest would stand up and hold out one paw toward the man, even if seen or scented at a distance, to try and tell if he was *skookum*—brave.

What's it going to be like to be dead? Trapper catches himself wondering. He views the trembling as accelerated old age, or fatigue—but now he remembers Uncle Harm spinning on his back in the desert, looking up at those clouds.

The thing was, Uncle Harm always got better. They'd lay him down in that cool water, and then later in the evening they'd see him come stepping out of the Arizona darkness in his glowing white linen suit. They'd smell his piñon-leaf tea. He'd sit on their porch and tell them stories: true stories, amazing things that seemed capable of holding even death at bay.

The bear up near Prescott that kept raiding Uncle Harm's family's garden when he was a boy. Harm and his friend Dobie, fourteen years old, waiting and watching in the moonlight as the big silver-tipped grizzly came ambling into the garden and began swatting down the corn. July night thunder, monsoons walking across the far horizon, illuminated by heat lightning. A feeling, with all that thunder coming, Uncle Harm said, that you had to *kill* something.

With lanterns and rifles, Harm and Dobie would start yelling and sic their dogs on the great bear and head for the garden, running hard: half-crazy and half-brave, even then. (Dobie died young.)

The bear would gather all the corn it could carry, holding it under one arm, and run. A grizzly can hit speeds of up to forty miles an hour, and runs faster up a hill than down, due to the extraordinary piston-musculature of its hind legs. Certainly even on three legs the grizzly could outrun two boys and their pissant feist dogs. The boys tracked it more by following the spilled ears of corn than with the aid of their cowardly pets, but could never catch up with the grizzly, could never bring it to bay.

The grizzly kept coming back every night. Sometimes the boys heard him, and other times they slept through his raids. Finally one night Harm and Dobie stole a real dog—an Airedale that belonged to a friend of Dobie's father. The neighbor lived a half-mile away. They muzzled it so the owner wouldn't wake up in the night and hear his dog off on a bear trail, alone—and they tied double leashes to him so he couldn't get away. Tied the other ends around their waists.

They lay down on the dark porch in ambush and waited. August, now, and the corn beginning to dry up. They could feel something was nearing an end.

"Tonight we get him," Dobie whispered.

After midnight they heard the bear in the corn again, and they sat there and waited, letting him fill his belly so he'd be easier to chase. There was a wind in their faces, and the Airedale, with cloth wrapped around his muzzle, whined softly, but the breeze carried his soft sounds away from the bear. Lightning storms rippled across the plateaus to the south.

When the bear stood up and began knocking down roasting ears to take with him, Harm and Dobie turned the Airedale loose, and were snatched off the porch and out into the garden after him.

Uncle Harm said they each broke an arm, that the Airedale took them seven miles up into the mountains, that he would not stop, and that Dobie split his chin on a rock.

Still, the dog carried them on: across tiny creeks, farther up into the mountains. They'd spy a dropped ear of corn every now and then. Sometimes they'd see the silver bear disappearing over a ridge: running on all fours now, with the Airedale hard after him. Dobie had dropped his lantern and rifle when he split his chin, then had been whisked on, snatched along by the Airedale's mad rage. The lantern had started a small fire where he dropped it. Then, climbing farther up the mountain, the Airedale jerked Harm off his feet, and he lost his lantern as well, then was dragged along.

As they neared the summit they could see the two small fires burning in the piñon below them. At the top of the mountain, the Airedale—close to baying the bear—summoned a last charge and broke free of his harness, which probably saved the boys, allowing Harm to continue on his way to becoming an old man, and Dobie to live another two years.

The Airedale engaged the grizzly up against the mouth of a cave. The dog must have known he couldn't *bite* the bear, with his jaws still bound up in the tight-knotted muzzle, but such was his fury that he flew at the bear anyway.

Harm and Dobie crested the mountain, gasping. They saw the

bear swat the Airedale, the limp dog fly away. The bear was standing at the mouth of a penned-up cave. Four or five pigs were grunting and squealing behind him; there were corn husks everywhere as the bear had been feeding the pigs, fattening them, getting them ready to be eaten.

The bear squinted and raised his paw slowly, still standing, and held it out as if trying to feel their heat: holding his paw toward them the way a man might turn his palms to a campfire's flames to warm them.

Harm, with his rifle, was shaking so badly he couldn't begin to lift it; it was all he could do to keep from dropping it.

The bear didn't run. It kept standing there, holding its paw toward the boys and sniffing the night-storm air.

Uncle Harm said that both boys had the feeling—unspoken between them at the time but passing through the air like an electric current—that the bear wanted to catch them alive, put them in that pen with the pigs, and fatten *them* up.

They ran down the mountain stumbling and bleeding, with thunder booming all around them, and never told anyone where the Airedale had gone. Told their parents they'd gotten in a fight, is how they busted each other up.

The storm put out their fire, though for forty years, Harm said, you could see where they'd been: and the bear never came back to the garden.

"Cave's still up there," Harm had told Trapper. "Pig skeletons, too. And dog skeleton. Never did find a bear skeleton on that mountain. Could have been that bear was God. Could be too that we're all little pigs the real God's got penned up on this earth," Harm said, and then laughed.

"I want to know what happened to Dobie," Judith said.

Harm chuckled. "Drowned," he said. He looked at Trapper and laughed again, his terrible old face stretching and then falling slack, stretching and then falling slack, stretching and falling slack. "You and him resemble each other in the face," he said, reaching out to tousle Trapper's wild hair.

❑ ❑ ❑ ❑

He finds one stretch of woods that's *rampant* with game, with life. He knows he shouldn't linger—knows he should get on back to the river, and across—but he cannot help himself. He camps for a week and takes not one but two wolverines—the second being the first one's mate, who keeps coming around after the first one is taken—and he traps foxes, too.

And wolves: always, wolves.

He pushes on again, but he's running late. The snow's melting, and freezing again at night. It's rough and chopped up; roots and boulders are emerging. Trapper slips, falls often. Sometimes he can't get up and has to struggle to reach his sled, pulling a bloody wolf or fox hide from the stack to drape it across himself for warmth as night falls. The hide freezes during the night, fitting itself to Trapper's shape. He hears wolves howl and has to bite his cheeks to keep from joining in: they'd come investigate, and then his dreams might come true: the pack swarming him, casting judgment for all the pack members, the brotherhood that he's killed—all the days of life he's robbed.

Trapper knows there aren't any *proven* stories of wolves killing a white man—Uncle Harm told him that for some reason they used to eat the hell out of Frenchmen, Eskimos, and Russians—but that's no consolation as he quivers in the night, trapped in the form-fitting frozen fox hide.

Oh, for a wife or a dog!

III

The river ice changes color in the last days of March, from white to gray, and from gray to thin blue, and Judith sits on the bluff and watches this. She listens to the ice groan and creak, straining to move again. She listens to the wolves howling. It is harder for them to hunt once winter is gone. In winter they can chase hooved animals, the weak ones, onto the frozen lakes and ponds.

Poor wolves, she thinks, watching the woods for Trapper's return. The days are warm enough now that she doesn't need fires, but finally she builds them along the bluff and throws wet duff on them to make them smoke.

It's terrible without the thought of him out there chasing her, hunting her. It's horrible. There's too much space.

The river thaws first into ice floes that crash against each other, and then into fast blue water. Still he does not appear.

She remembers how Trapper gathered her urine once a month to use it with his traps; she remembers how, that one time each month, the wolves would gather around their cabin and howl for a night or two, which excited Trapper terribly, made him pace the tiny cabin all night.

He'd shout into the dark, and sometimes shoot his rifle: taking a bead on the great full grinning moon and then shouting, in the rifle's echo-roar, when the moon did not fall and the wolves did not stop howling.

Maybe her womb was barren, or maybe his seed was bad. Maybe both. Or maybe it was like the wolf and the wolverine, who were not meant to mix; like the bear and the badger.

She considers children. Remembers a man in Arizona whose son was killed by a bear, and who hunted that bear down, killed it, skinned it, and then slept on the hide every night for the rest of his life, another sixty-three years of falling asleep—or not—in the warmth of the killer's thick fur. Thinking these things, Judith grows fond of her times with Trapper, and then one day he appears. A white-haired crooked figure on the far side of the river: it's him, with about a thousand pelts on his sled.

Judith turns and runs: into the woods, leaping logs like a deer. She doesn't *want* to go back to the past, or back to the warm lovesick days in Arizona with roast suckling goat and chimichurri sauce for breakfast, margaritas, and those doves cooing while they went to bed and made love: Harm, not Trapper, off in the desert. It feels wonderful to be running again.

Trapper has been seeing the smoke from her fires for days now; it's what turned him around. He's been walking in circles, lost for the first time in his life, just a few miles from the river. He knows finally what is happening to him. He's busted open the skulls of a million animals, gathering their brains to use for tanning their hides, and he's compared the highly ridged convolutions of a bear's brain with the smoother, duller loops and folds of a marten, or the blankness of a boar-musky, raging wolverine's brain—and Trapper can feel a certain silliness, a kind of numbness, like a skullcap, settling over the top of his own mind.

The loops of his brain-folds are losing their edges.

Maybe it was the lion grease. Or maybe loneliness.

He's been walking in circles, setting traps that don't catch anything. Sometimes he steps in his own snares—by some miracle avoiding the forty-five-pound bear traps, which would cut his legs off—but even when the metal jaws clap shut on his ankle, or his hand, he doesn't really *feel* anything.

But the smoke: he still knew enough to go to the smoke. He still had the instinct, if not the knowledge, that maybe somehow she could save him.

He'd stake her out yet. His arms are wizened, slack-muscled, and he stares at them, then squints across the river. She's probably stronger than he is now, he thinks. He'll have to do it with cunning.

He feels the loops unfolding. Thinks of how wolves pull the slick entrails out first and gulp them down, sometimes while the animal is still alive.

Trapper doesn't blink. He can't feel anything. A million hardnesses are beginning to crash down upon him, and all he can think is, I want a million and one.

IV

It was thought by the savages of the North, Trapper knows, that bears are half-god and half-human; that they are linked to the spirit world because they dig below the earth each autumn and come back out each spring. A bullshit stupid myth, Trapper thinks.

Fact: a bear just rising from the so-called spirit world doesn't have any gastric juices in his stomach yet. Trapper's killed bears just coming out of hibernation and has opened their stomachs out of curiosity and found live ants crawling there, ants the bear had licked up ten, twenty, maybe thirty minutes before Trapper came sauntering through the woods.

He's building a hide boat: tanning and stretching the wolf hides on the riverbank and cutting green willow limbs. Maybe the boat will float and maybe it won't. He wonders why the Indians didn't think birds, like loons, belonged to the spirit world—diving under the water and then flying into the air. Or maybe they did. Maybe the Indians thought everything belonged to the spirit world.

When he finishes the boat, Trapper looks at the huge stack of hides he will have to leave behind. He could try and cache them, but he knows something—wolverine or bear—would find them soon enough. A damn shame. He piles branches and grass around the stack of rich furs, then chips stones until a spark catches. Soon the hides are a billowing black crackling pyre of smoke, like a small volcano on the gravel riverbank.

Trapper trembles but without feeling as he watches the smoke, as he watches the ghosts of the animals return to the sky. There *is* no spirit world, he thinks. There is just her, whom he wants to capture, on the other side of the river. If he can capture her—that blur through the forest, that movement in the corner of his mind's eye—all will be made new again.

Spirit world, my butt, he thinks, turning to look at the river. He loads his traps into the round boat, readies the paddles he's cut and carved, and pushes into the rapids. The river is wild with the loud underwater *clunks* of rocks bashing against one another. It's so frigid he won't even live long enough to drown if the boat capsizes.

He rows like crazy, his small violet eyes fixed firmly on the far shore. He feels the rocks tumbling beneath him, feels the force of this one river on this one immense earth. Rapids drench him, slicking back his thin white hair. He watches the shore without blinking. Remembers, in a glimpse, Uncle Harm's mangled face. Remembers a coyote he saw running off with one of his drag-traps. The coyote was too smart to pull the drag—a grappling hook— through the brush, where it would get hung up. Instead, he carried the hook in his mouth, running along on three legs, that fourth foot flopping whenever the trap hit the ground, but running—and he escaped: looking back at Trapper with that trapped foot raised and the drag in his mouth.

Pulling hard on the oars. The far shore closer, now: close

enough to see small blue flowers blooming on the bank. And the smell of the woods: *her* woods.

V

It's spring, and bears are coming out of the earth. For twelve days they have staggered through the woods like drunk sailors. They can't quite wake up, and their eyesight—poor to begin with—is worse than ever. The bears stretch and yawn, they walk into trees and fall over; they're exceedingly dangerous at this time. Trapper moves through the woods with caution, head down, looking for Judith's big, curved tracks. He allows himself to think of her breasts, which remind him of apples.

Bears are staggering through the woods and rolling on their backs, trying to stand up straight, and Trapper says to one, "Brother, I know how you feel," and passes right by it. He remembers that the Indians revered the grizzly so much that they wouldn't even speak its name, whether out in the woods hunting it or back in camp talking about it.

Instead, they would give the bear goofy names like "Grandfather," "Good Father," "Worthy Old Man," "Illustrious," and even "The Master."

Master, my ass, Trapper thinks, stepping around another wobbly bear just up from the earth. It is spitting up a small pile of sticky wet green leaves, having eaten too much too fast in its lust for new life.

He knows he should kill them and skin them out, but the hide's no good for trading in the spring.

For a week he sees bears rolling drunk in the woods, trying to get oriented.

"You're lucky, friend," he says to one. "You're going to get better."

Trapper's still twitching. He has it firmly in his mind now that Judith—somehow—can save him. That she will lay her hand on his forehead, and the shakes will go away.

In Arizona, after making love to her, Trapper would get a washcloth and dip it in a basin of cool water. Then he would come to the bedside and draw it slowly up the length of Judith's panting body, starting at her summer-dusty toes and drawing it slowly up her hot legs, over the mound of her sex, tickling, and like a sheet across her concave belly, and like a wet curtain across her breasts.

Up to her chin. Over her closed eyes. Patting her sweaty fore-head with the wet washcloth.

It was too long ago. He can never get back to that. But he's got to chase it. That feeling of not being weak. That feeling of being anything but weak.

Even numbness is better than being weak.

Trapper stops and rests often. He finds her tracks here and there: faint depressions in the moss. He suspects she is staying within this one forest—that it has become her new home (No! he thinks, Damn it, *I* am her home!) and that she is reluctant to leave, to be driven off. He also thinks she wants to be trapped, if only so she can try to escape again.

There's a strange *wormy* feeling in his mind, and he can hear a buzzing, like night katydids. I love my prey, he thinks, forcing himself to his feet.

Bear, lynx, and lobo all have a round, plump pad on each foot, but the older the animal, the flatter the pad wears, until the ball is finally all gone and no pad at all is left—just a flat space.

The female lynx has a shorter and smaller second toe on the hind foot than the male, and her front feet are a little rounder and neater than the male's. She carries her young farther back in the body than any other wild animal. If she is heavy with kittens, the outside toes on both hind feet spread out.

Trapper studies the ground and tries to catch Judith's scent. Near a small hot spring where he feels certain she's been bathing, he finds one of her big club tracks in the moss and gets down and puts his nose in the depression and sniffs, closes his eyes and sniffs, but she's clever, the sulfur odor of the spring confuses all scent, all instinct. Trapper has it in his mind that her beautiful shimmering yellow hair, which he so loved to brush, is a nest for static electric-ity, for glimmering ions leaving a magic, charged trail of *cleanliness* wherever she's passed. If he concentrates hard enough on it, he thinks, he can follow this trail. And he's tempted to track her that way—with *passion,* with desire: which he hasn't felt in a long time.

Trapper wants to *lunge* through the woods, hunting her hair-trail with this new, ten-years-gone passion; but he remembers how Uncle Harm taught him to hunt, and how he has always hunted—giving himself over more and more to the mindless, the barbaric, and shunning the mistakes of passion, regret, guilt.

"A hunter slipping up on a moose," Uncle Harm had preached—his face gouged and raked like the craters of the moon but invisible in the darkness of the back porch—Harm's white linen suit all they could see on his rocking chair, and his white Panama hat—"will make the animal uneasy by 'concentrating' his mind upon the animal.

"Those who would catch a woodsman of the old school asleep do well to come carelessly," Uncle Harm said. He'd been like the Indians in that respect—calling animals things like "woodsmen of the old school." Trapper had heard him refer to one grizzly as "Golden Friend of Fin and Forest" and had had to ask what the hell he was talking about.

It was when Harm started getting really old, Trapper remembered, that he began to develop all the *respect:* all that Golden Friend shit. Trapper knew it for what it really was: fear. Coyote fear.

Still, there had never been a better trapper.

"A stealthy approach," Harm had preached, "seems to establish some telepathic communication with the subconscious mind of one who lives with nature. This faculty is borrowed from the animals, and is common among Indians."

Harm was a savage, Trapper thinks. He wore a fancy-ass suit in the evenings, but all he was was a *savage.* Wouldn't fool with doctors. If he got a wound—a cut of some sort—and it became infected, he would lie in the shallows of the creek, would crawl into the reeds and let the minnows come and nibble away the afflicted flesh, and clean the wound in that way.

A savage, with a heart too hardened by killing, Trapper thinks.

Flowers, Trapper thinks, women like flowers. This time I will keep fresh flowers on the table.

From the ridge above, standing in a grove of budding-out birch trees, Judith watches as her young-old husband moves in a slow circle around the hot springs, carefully setting leg-hold traps under the rotting leaves. She watches him crouch and sniff at her new-bathed tracks, watches his smashed hands touch them, watches him lower his nose to the tracks once more and sniff. Despite herself, Judith lifts her hand to her hair and touches it, strokes it once.

At night, she hears him howling in her woods. *Her* woods! She feels the hairs on the back of her neck rising.

He's trembly, but he knows he could outrun her, if only he could catch *sight* of her. Her scent is everywhere. He'd chase her toward a ridge and catch her going up it; Trapper's legs are thick, like a bear's, so that he goes faster charging uphill than downhill.

The Eskimos hunt birds with bolas—little balls of ivory or bone at the ends of strong sinew cords a yard or more long. The hunter whirls at least half a dozen over his head and hurls them among a flock of geese or ducks so that the balls will spread out in flight. One of the bolas is sure to tangle itself around the wing or limb of a bird and send it crashing to the ground.

Trapper fashions bolas in the afternoons, resting his tired legs, lying in wait by the hot spring.

Judith watches from the ridge, furious. She slips down to the river and has to wash her hair in the cold glacier-silt water. It's not the same as her spring.

Trapper can sense Judith's fury, and knows he's being watched. He smiles.

Why won't he leave me alone? Judith wonders. All I want is my life, she thinks.

God, that Uncle Harm was a numb bastard, Trapper thinks as he whittles on the bolas. Trapper remembers a game he and Harm used to play—a game Harm taught him—called Sleep-a-Night-and-Die.

They'd whittle long, slender barbed shafts of bone and fit them into a socket at the end of juniper arrows. Then they'd sit on the porch and wait for some small animal to come out of the willows, a nose-wrinkling rabbit, a dusk-wary coyote, even a gentle doe.

They'd fire their sleep-a-night-and-die arrows at the intended victim, proud to be killing not with the machinery of guns and traps, but just *killing*.

Shot into a deer or rabbit or coyote, the barbed point would separate from the arrow socket, floating free in the flesh, and go searching for some vital part with each fleeing step of the creature; it would rankle and twist with each stride, ever enlarging and irritating the wound, until the animal died.

A myth of bears, Trapper thinks: that they'll bring food to another of their kind, caught in a trap, to ease its hunger, to give comfort. Wolves, yes—he'd seen that often—but never bears.

If she's not coming to water at the hot springs, Trapper thinks one moonless night—his wormy mind barely moving in his sleep, like the slow coils of a snake on a cold day—then she must be going to the river.

He rises in the night, crosses the ridge, and sets some new traps and snares. Builds a deadfall, too: not too big—he doesn't want to *kill* her, he says to himself, confused—but big enough, by damn, to hold her.

Then goes back to sleep: to dream of animals attacking him.

Judith wakes on the riverbank, listening to the spring sounds of geese heading back north—snow geese, Arctic geese. If Trapper approaches, she thinks, she'll simply leap up and dive into the cold river and swim away. She'll swim for a hundred years if she has to. She'll get away, or die trying. The water is so cold. She doesn't think she could make it—but she'll try, if she has to.

At dawn she rises and looks at the river and considers building her own raft: leaving her woods. She listens to the river's lovely roar, feels the great and terrible force, feels it in the gravel at her feet. Leans her head into the current, dips her head under, and washes her hair: scrubs the ions away.

All forests should have at least one man and one woman in them, Judith thinks as she washes her hair. They are on the same side of the river now, but there is still that other river that separates them—and it is no good. We spend our silly lives crossing back and forth over that river, she thinks, rather than swimming *in* it, being carried downstream in whatever manner the drifts and great force will take us.

All forests deserve one man and one woman, Judith thinks, but this man is crazy, has gone over to some other world, and this woman, she thinks—*this woman,* standing up and leaning her head back and squeezing the water out of her hair—is going back downstream. Maybe not all the way to Arizona, but somewhere: someplace.

The new birch leaves are rattling in the breeze. She will climb the ridge and look down on the poor, sick shell of her husband, the past of him, one more time.

How many others have fallen to Trapper in this manner, betrayed by curiosity and a moment's hesitation, a tempering of what was previously brute fear and headlong, terrified flight? He's caught five hundred lynx by fastening a glittering strip of metal above the bare trap. And though it is not of his planning, it works this way for Judith; while watching Trapper—that one last look— she does not pay enough attention to herself or where she is going, and walks right beneath his deadfall: bumps the branch holding it above her.

Despite herself, she cries out in pain at how it has crushed her; he hears the thump of the log landing on her, hears her cry—*What was that?* he wonders. *Lion? Wolf? Lynx? Could it be her?*—and he starts up the ridge toward the sound, eager-hearted, young again.

And caught under the deadfall, with her shoulder broken and her leg in a leather snare, waiting for him to approach, unable to twist and look back at the river below her but hearing it, hearing it, what Judith is thinking as she imagines his approach with the club is this: I know he *loves* me.

Maybe he's changed, Judith thinks.

She can't move a muscle. The river roars.

Maybe he's *well,* Judith thinks.

Then she thinks about the myths of bears versus the facts. She debates: freedom, or hope? Quitting—*flight*—or pushing on?

Does her freedom—river freedom—even exist?

She gnaws at the snare. It takes her a long time, but she's able to pull free of it. This notion—coming seemingly from nowhere—that he still loves her is confounding her efforts.

The log's so heavy. She can't lift it. With her broken shoulder she tunnels away at soft earth and then gravel, scoops out a depression barely deep enough for her to slither out from under the big log.

The river is just below. She hears Trapper coming up the other ridge, howling. Judith careens through the trees, running for the river, tripping and falling, her arm and shoulder sticking out crookedly like a bird's crippled wing. Her big, curved feet keep tripping her, but she's up and running each time she falls, the earth sending jolts of pain through her jaws and into her ears.

The diamond rushing waters of the river glitter.

There won't be time to build a raft.

She hits the water as she hit the window the night she busted out of the cabin, but this time he is right with her, on top of her, and is hauling her back out of the river.

She thrashes, broken-armed, like a bird: starts to strike at and bite him but sees, in a moment, in a glimpse—a passing shadow, passing wave of light—a thing almost like tenderness, even concern, in his face, and she does not strike or bite. She pauses, held in his grip.

She feels some part of her escape with the current—her other life, the mythical one. She feels too the other, or second, life—the real life, also just as mythical—the one he has in his grip once more.

"Listen," he says. "I'll be nice. I missed you. Listen," he says, stroking her hair as if he means to scalp her. "Oh, I love you," he says, and strokes her hair some more.

They fall back into being as they were before: as if caught in some cycle too powerful and terrible to escape: as if they might as well be trying to escape the seasons.

He sleeps with his hand tight on her wrist. He doesn't get better, but he doesn't die, either. They just settle into the soil and their lives again, like rotting trees, and the world passes over them. They keep on trapping things.

Judith dreams for a month or two of how things might have been if she'd hit the river a step or two sooner, but then those dreams fade, as if they are far downstream now, or eroded, or forgotten.

I probably would have drowned, she thinks. I probably would not have made it.

She goes back to the old life, helping him tend traps. She feels cut in half, but strangely there is no pain.

"Say it again," she tells him, nights when she thinks she must hit the window again at full stride: "Say that you love me."

"Oh, I do," he says, stroking her hair. "I do."

"Say it," she says, gripping his wrist.

Louise Erdrich

Satan: Hijacker of a Planet

From *The Atlantic Monthly*

ON THE OUTSKIRTS of a small town in the West, on an afternoon when rain was promised, we sat upon the deck of our new subdivision ranchette and watched the sky pitch over Hungry Horse. It was a drought-dry summer, and in the suspension of rain everything seemed to flex. The trees stretched to their full length, each leaf open. I could almost feel the ground shake the timbers under my feet, as if the great searching taproots of the lodgepole pines all around trembled. Lust. Lust. Still, the rain held off. I left my mother sitting in her chair and went to the old field behind the house, up a hill. There the storm seemed even likelier. The wind came off the eastern mountains, smelling like a lake, and the grass reached for it, butter-yellow, its life concentrated in its fiber mat, the stalks so dry they gave off puffs of smoke when snapped. Grasshoppers sprang from each step I took, tripped off my arms, legs, glasses. I saw a small pile of stones halfway up the hill, which someone had cleared once, when this was orchard land. I sat down and continued to watch the sky as, out of nowhere, great solid-looking clouds built hot stacks and cotton cones. The trend was upward, upward, until you couldn't feel it anymore. I was sixteen years old.

I was looking down the hill, waiting for the rain to start, when his white car pulled into our yard. The driver was a big man, built long and square just like the Oldsmobile. He was wearing a tie and a shirt that was not yet sweaty. I noticed this as I was walking back down the hill. I was starting to notice these things about men—the way their hips moved when they hauled feed or checked fence lines. The way their forearms looked so tanned and hard when they rolled up their white sleeves after church. I was looking at men not with intentions, because I didn't know yet what I would have done with one if I got him, but with a studious mind.

I was looking at them just to figure, for pure survival, the way a girl does. The way a farmer, which my dad was before he failed, gets to know the lay of the land. He loves his land, so he has to figure how to cultivate it—what it needs in each season, how much abuse it will sustain, what in the end it will yield.

And I, too, in order to increase my yield and use myself right, was taking my lessons. I never tried out my information, though, until the man arrived, pulled with a slow crackle into our lake-pebble driveway. He got out and looked at me where I stood in the shade of my mother's butterfly bush. I'm not saying that I flirted right off. I didn't know how to. I walked into the sunlight and looked him in the eye.

"What are you selling?" I smiled, and told him that my mother would probably buy it, since she had all sorts of things—a pruning saw you could use from the ground, a cherry pitter, a mechanical apple peeler that also removed the seeds and core, a sewing machine that remembered all the stitches it had sewed. He smiled back at me and walked with me to the steps of the house.

"You're a bright young lady," he said, though he was young himself. "Stand close. You'll see what I'm selling by looking into the middle of my eyes."

He pointed a finger between his eyebrows.

"I don't see a thing," I told him, as my mother came around the corner, off the deck out back, holding a glass of iced tea in her hand.

While they were talking, I didn't look at Stan Anderson. I felt challenged, as if I were supposed to make sense of what he did. At sixteen I didn't have perspective on the things men did. I'd never gotten a whiff of that odor that rolls off them like an acid. Later only a certain look was required, a tone of voice, a word, no more than a variation in the way he drew breath. A dog gets tuned that way, sensitized to an exquisite degree, but it wasn't like that in the beginning. I took orders from Stan as if I were doing him a favor—the way, since I'd hit my growth, I'd taken orders from my dad.

My dad, who was at the antiques store, gave orders only when he was tired. All other times he did the things he wanted done himself. My dad was not, in the end, the man I should have studied if I wanted to learn cold survival. He was too ineffective. All my life my parents had been splitting up. I lived in a no-man's-land between them, and the ground was pitted, scarred with ruts, useless. And yet no matter how hard they fought each other, they stuck together. He could not get away from my mother, somehow, nor she from him. So I couldn't look to my father for information on what a man was—nor could I look to my grandfather. Gramp was too nice a man. You should have seen him when he planted a tree.

"A ten-dollar hole for a two-bit seedling," he'd say. That was the way he dug, so as not to crowd the roots. He kept the little tree in water while he pried out any rocks that might be there, though our land was just as good as Creston soil, dirt that went ten feet down in that part of Montana, black as coal, rich as tar, fine as face powder. Gramp put the bare-root tree in and carefully, considerately even, sifted the soil around the roots, rubbing it to fine crumbs between his fingers. He packed the dirt in; he watered until the water pooled. Looking into my grandfather's eyes I would see the knowledge, tender and offhand, of the way roots took hold in the earth.

I saw no such knowledge in Stan's eyes. I watched him from behind my mother. I discovered what he had to sell.

"It's Bibles, isn't it?" I said.

"No fair." He put his hand across his heart and grinned at the two of us. He had seen my eyes flicker to the little gold cross in his lapel. "Something even better."

"What?" my mother asked.

"Spirit."

My mother turned and walked away. She had no time for conversion attempts. I was only intermittently religious, but I suppose I felt that I had to make up for her rudeness, and so I stayed a moment longer. I was wearing very short cutoff jeans and a little brown T-shirt, tight—old clothes for dirty work. I was supposed to help my mom clean out her hobby brooder house that afternoon, to set in new straw and wash down the galvanized feeders, to destroy the thick whorls of ground-spider cobwebs and shine the windows with vinegar and newspapers. All my stuff, rags and buckets, was scattered behind me on the steps. And, as I said, I was never all that religious.

"We'll be having a meeting tonight," he said. "I'm going to tell you where."

He always told in advance what he was going to say; that was the preaching habit in him. It made you wait and wonder in spite of yourself.

"Where?" I said finally.

As he told me the directions, how to get where the tent was pitched, as he spoke to me, looking full on with the whole intensity of his blue gaze, I was deciding that I would go, without anyone else in my family, to the fairground that evening. Just to study. Just to see.

I drove a small sledge and a tractor at the age of eleven, and a car back and forth into town, with my mother in the passenger seat, when I was fourteen. So I often went where I wanted to go. The storm had veered off. Disappointed, we watched rain drop across the valley. We got no more than a slash of moisture in the air, which dried before it fell. In town the streets were just on the edge of damp, but the air was still thin and dry. White moths fluttered in and out under the rolled flaps of the revival tent, but since the month of August was half spent, the mosquitoes were mainly gone. Too dry for them, too. Even though the tent was open-sided, the air within seemed close, compressed, and faintly salty with evaporated sweat. The space was three-quarters full of singing people, and I slipped into one of the rear rows. I sat on a gray metal folding chair, just sat there, keeping my eyes open and my mouth shut.

He was not the main speaker, I discovered, and I didn't see him until the one whom the others had come to hear finished a prayer. He called Stan to the front with a little preface. Stan was newly saved, endowed with a message from the Lord, and could play several musical instruments. We were to listen to what the Lord would reveal to us through Stan's lips. He took the stage. A white vest finished off his white suit, and a red-silk shirt with a pointed collar. He started talking. I can tell you what he said just about word for word, because after that night and long away into the next few years, sometimes four or five times in one day, I'd hear it over and over. You don't know preaching until you've heard Stan Anderson. You don't suffer with Christ, or fear loss of faith, a barbed wire ripped from your grasp, until you've heard it from Stan Anderson. You don't know subjection, the thorough happiness of letting go. You don't know how light and comforted you feel, how cherished.

I was too young to stand against it.

The stars are the eyes of God, and they have been watching us from the beginning of the world. Do you think there isn't an eye for each of us? Go on and count. Go on and look in The Book and add up all the nouns and adverbs, as if somehow you'd grasp the meaning of what you held if you did. You can't. The understanding is in you or it isn't. You can hide from the stars by daylight, but at night, under all of them, so many, you are pierced by the sight and by the vision.

Get under the bed!

Get under the sheet!

I say to you, Stand up, and if you fall, fall forward!

I'm going to go out blazing. I'm going to go out like a light. I'm going to burn in glory. I say to you, Stand up!

And so there's one among them. You have heard Luce, Light, Lucifer, the Fallen Angel. You have seen it with your own eyes, and you didn't know he came upon you. In the night, and in his own disguises, like the hijacker of a planet, he fell out of the air, he fell out of the dark leaves, he fell out of the fragrance of a woman's body, he fell out of you and entered you as though he'd reached through the earth.

Reached his hand up and pulled you down.

Fell into you with a jerk.

Like a hangman's noose.

Like nobody.

Like the slave of night.

Like you were coming home and all the lights were blazing and the ambulance sat out front in the driveway and you said, *Lord, which one?*

And the Lord said, *All of them.*

You, too, follow, follow, I'm pointing you down. In the sight of the stars and in the sight of the Son of Man. The grace is on me. Stand up, I say. *Stand.* Yes, and yes, I'm gonna scream, because I like it that way. Let yourself into the gate. Take it with you. In four years the earth will shake in its teeth.

Revelations. Face of the beast. In all fairness, in all fairness, let us quiet down and let us think.

Stan Anderson looked intently, quietly, evenly, at each person in the crowd and spoke to each one, proving things about the future that seemed complicated, like the way the Mideast had shaped up as such a trouble zone. How the Chinese armies were predicted in Tibet and that came true, and how they'll keep marching, moving, until they reach the Fertile Crescent. Stan Anderson told about the number. He slammed his forehead with his open hand and left a red mark. *There,* he yelled, gutshot, *there it will be scorched.* He was talking about the number of the beast, and said that they would take it from your Visa card, your Mastercard, your household insurance. That already, through these numbers, you are under the control of last things and you don't know it.

The Antichrist is among us.

He is the plastic in our wallets.

You want credit? Credit?

Then you'll burn for it, and you will starve. You'll eat sticks, you'll eat black bits of paper, your bills, and all the while you'll be screaming from the dark place, *Why the hell didn't I just pay cash?*

Because the number of the beast is a computerized number, and the computer is the bones, it is the guts, of the Antichrist, who is Lucifer, who is pure brain.

Pure brain got us to the moon, got us past the moon.

The voice of lonely humanity is in a space probe calling, *Anybody home? Anybody home out there?* The Antichrist will answer. The Antichrist is here, all around us in the tunnels and webs of radiance, in the microchips; the great mind of the Antichrist is fusing in a pattern, in a destiny, waking up nerve by nerve.

Serves us right. Don't it serve us right not to be saved?

It won't come easy. Not by waving a magic wand. You've got to close your eyes and hold out those little plastic cards.

Look at this!

He held a scissors high and turned it to every side so that the light gleamed off the blades.

The sword of Michael! Now I'm coming. I'm coming down the aisle. I'm coming with the sword that sets you free.

Stan Anderson started a hymn and walked down the rows of chairs, singing. Every person who held out a credit card he embraced, and then he plucked that card out of their fingers. He cut once, crosswise. Dedicated to the Lord! He cut again. He kept the song flowing, walked up and down the rows cutting, until the tough, trampled grass beneath the tent was littered with pieces of plastic. He came to me last of all, and noticed me, and smiled.

"You're too young to have established a line of credit," he said, "but I'm glad to see you here."

Then he stared at me, his eyes the blue of winter ice, cold in the warmth of his tanned blondness, so chilling I just melted.

"Stay," he said. "Stay afterward and join us in the trailer. We're going to pray over Ed's mother."

So I did stay. It didn't sound like a courting invitation, but that was the way I thought of it at the time, and I was right. Ed was the advertised preacher, and his mother was a sick, sick woman. She lay flat and still on a couch at the front of the house trailer, where she just fit end to end. The air around her was dim, close with the smell of sweat-out medicine and what the others had cooked and eaten—hamburger, burnt onions, coffee. The table was pushed to one side, and chairs were wedged around the couch. Ed's mother, poor old dying woman, was covered with a white sheet that her breathing hardly moved. Her face was caved in, sunken around the mouth and cheeks. She looked to me like a bird fallen out of its nest before it feathered, her shut eyelids bulging blue, wrinkled, beating with tiny nerves. Her head was covered with white wisps of hair. Her hands, just at her chest, curled like little pale claws. Her nose was a large and waxen bone.

I drew up a chair, the farthest to the back of the eight or so people who had gathered. One by one they opened their mouths, rolled their eyes or closed them tight, and let the words fly out until they began to garble and the sounds from their mouths resembled some ancient, dizzying speech. At first I was so uncomfortable with all the strangeness, and even a little faint from the airlessness and smells, that I breathed in with shallow gulps and shut the language out. Gradually, slowly, it worked its way in anyway, and I began to *feel* its effect—not hear, not understand, not listen.

The words are inside and outside of me, hanging in the air like small pottery triangles, broken and curved. But they are forming and crumbling so fast that I'm breathing dust, the sharp antibiotic bitterness, medicine, death, sweat. My eyes sting, and I'm starting to choke. All the blood goes out of my head and down along my arms into the ends of my fingers, and my hands feel swollen, twice as big as normal, like big puffed gloves. I get out of the chair and turn to leave, but he is there.

"Go on," he says. "Go on and touch her."

The others have their hands on Ed's mother. They are touching her with one hand and praying, the other palm held high, blind, feeling for the spirit like an antenna. Stan pushes me, not by making any contact, just by inching up behind me so I feel the forcefulness and move. Two people make room, and then I am standing over Ed's mother. She is absolutely motionless, as though she were a corpse, except that her pinched mouth has turned down at the edges so that she frowns into her own dark unconsciousness.

I put my hands out, still huge, prickling. I am curious to see what will happen when I do touch her—if she'll respond. But when I place my hands on her stomach, low and soft, she makes no motion at all. Nothing flows from me, no healing powers. Instead I am filled with the rushing dark of what she suffers. It fills me suddenly, as water from a faucet brims a jug, and spills over.

This is when it happens.

I'm not stupid; I have never been stupid. I have pictures. I can get a picture in my head at any moment, focus it so brilliant and detailed that it seems real. That's what I do, what I started when my mom and dad first went for each other. When I heard them downstairs, I always knew a moment would come. One of them would scream, tearing through the stillness. It would rise up, that howl, and fill the house, and then one would come running. One would come and get me and hold me. It would be my mother, smelling of smoked chicken, rice, and coffee grounds. It would be my father, sweat-soured, scorched with cigarette smoke from the garage, bitter with the dust of his fields. Then I would be somewhere in no-man's-land, between them, and that was the unsafest place in the world. So I would leave it. I would go limp and enter my pictures.

I have a picture. I go into it right off when I touch Ed's mother, veering off her thin pain. Here's a grainy mountain, a range of deep-blue Missions hovering off the valley in the west. Their foothills are blue, strips of dark-blue flannel, and their tops are cloudy walls. The sun strikes through once, twice, a pink radiance that dazzles patterns into their faces so that they gleam back, moon-pocked. Watch them, watch close, Ed's mother, and they start to walk. I keep talking until I know she is watching too. She is dimming her lights, she is turning as thin as tissue under my hands. She is dying until she goes into my picture with me, goes in strong, goes in willingly. And once she is in the picture, she gains peace from it, gains the rock strength, the power.

I was young. I was younger than I had a right to be. I was drawn the way a deer is drawn into the halogen lamplight, curious and calm. Heart about to explode. I wasn't helpless, though, not me. I had pictures.

"Show me what you did," Stan said that night, once Ed's mother was resting calmly.

We went into the room at the Red Lion that was Stan's, all carpet and deodorizer. All flocked paper on the walls. Black-red. Gold. Hilarious. Stan lay down on the king-size bed and patted the broad space beside him in a curious, not sexual, way. I lay down there and closed my eyes.

"Show me Milwaukee," Stan whispered. I breathed deep and let out the hems of my thoughts. After a while, then, I got the heft of it, the green medians in June, the way you felt entering your favorite restaurant with a dinner reservation, hungry, knowing that within fifteen minutes German food would start to fill you, German bread, German beer, German schnitzel. I got the neighborhood where Stan had lived, the powdery stucco, the old-board rotting infrastructure and the back yard, all shattered sun and shade, leaves; got Stan's mother lying on the ground full-length in a red suit, asleep; got the back porch, full of suppressed heat; and got the june bugs razzing indomitable against the night screens. Got the smell of Stan's river, got the first-day-of-school smell, the chalk and wax, the cleaned-and-stored, paper-towel scent of Milwaukee schools in the beginning of September. Got the milk cartons, got the straws. Got Stan's brother, thin and wiry arms holding Stan down. Got Stan a hot-dog stand, a nickel bag of peanuts, thirst.

"No." Stan said. "No more."

He could feel it coming, though I avoided it. I steered away from the burning welts, the scissors, pinched nerves, the dead eye, the strap, the belt, the spike-heeled shoe, the razor, the boiling-hot spilled tapioca, the shards of glass, the knives, the chinked armor, the small sister, the small sister, the basement, anything underground.

"Enough." Stan turned to me.

He didn't know what he wanted to see, and I don't mean to imply that he would see the whole of my picture anyway. I would walk the edge of his picture, and he'd walk the edge of mine, get the crumbs, the drops of water that flew off when a bird shook its feathers. That's how much I got across, but that was all it took. When you share like that, the rest of the earth shuts. You are locked in, twisted close, braided, born.

He smoothed his hands across my hair and closed me against him, and then we shut the door to everything and everyone but us. He stood me next to the bed, took off my clothing piece by piece, and made me climax just by brushing me, slowly, here, there, just by barely touching me until he forced apart my legs and put his mouth on me hard. Stood up. He came into me without a sound. I cried out. He pushed harder and then withdrew. It took more than an hour, by the bedside clock. It took a long time. He held my wrists behind my back and forced me down onto the carpet. Then he bent over me and gently, fast and slow, helplessly, without end or beginning, he went in and out until I grew bored, until I wanted to sleep, until I moaned, until I cried out, until I wanted nothing else, until I wanted him the way I always would from then on, since that first dry summer.

Don Zancanella

The Chimpanzees of Wyoming Territory

From *Alaska Quarterly Review*

The Frontier Index, a newspaper published from a railroad car that moved west with the colony of workers building the first transcontinental railroad, reported in their issue of June 10, 1868, that a pair of chimpanzees had recently provided an evening of theatrical entertainment at a saloon in Laramie City, Wyoming Territory.

June 9

Left Laramie City at sunrise. A rough, disorderly settlement—just what one would expect to find at the farthest edge of civilization. To our advantage, the residents had money to spend and were starved for entertainment. Our performances were well attended and when I passed the hat, it came back overflowing.

For the first few hours today, I followed the new railroad tracks. They are truly marvelous, the bright steel rails like two lines of quicksilver drawn across the undulating plains. Although I had hoped to see the encampment where the actual laying of the track is occurring, I turned north, following the trail as I had been advised. I feel compelled to continue toward South Pass City without delay, for I have been warned about foul weather and hostile

Indians so often that I expect to see bolts of lightning and flying arrows over the crest of every hill.

The apes are travelling well, if a bit subdued. Whenever I stop, I open their cage, but they seem stunned by the immense openness of the landscape and will come forth only with great coaxing. During the afternoon they slept, lulled by the rocking of the wagon. We are all three pleased with our new outfit—two sorrel mules and a small buckboard wagon. My only worry about the apes is the rough diet our journey has forced upon them. Fresh fruits and vegetables, which they prefer above all, have become increasingly unavailable since Omaha. Tonight, their dinner consisted of potatoes and an oat porridge which I spoon-fed to them like babes.

June 10
A day spent plodding over an unbroken plain. I am bone-tired. One of the mules chomped me on the shoulder as I unharnessed her for the night. They are both ill-tempered but strong.

June 11
Forded the North Platte today. Had been told that it could be easily crossed by mid-June, but it took all my courage and ingenuity to get the team and wagon across't. I released the apes from confinement so that, if the wagon overturned, they would have a fighting chance. To my surprise, the Duchess plunged in immediately and swam to the far shore. I knew the beasts could swim, but not with such ease and grace. For his part, the Duke lolled about in the back of the wagon as if it were an emperor's chaise, dipping his long hand into the current from time to time to bring up a cool draught. I saw no human nor any sign of one for the entire day. Nonetheless, I have convinced myself that Indians are lurking just out of sight. The apes were exhilarated by the river crossing. They screeched and chattered all through a sunny June afternoon.

June 12
If yesterday was lonely, today was a social whirl. A party of five men overtook us just before midday. First came the usual ques-

tions and excitement about the apes, and then speculation about prospects for gold in South Pass. They had all heard fantastic tales of riches, but the letters I received from my brother have all been much more cautious in their optimism. I never thought I would view a brace of hairy apes as my financial security, but I find myself comforted by the knowledge that if Brother Andrew's claim fails to prove out, I can continue my work as—I don't believe I've ever called myself such before—an entertainer.

Later, during the afternoon, we passed a party of three men, one of whom had gotten a sizable knot on his head from being thrown by his pony. I offered to let him ride in the wagon for a spell, but as he was climbing in, he caught a glimpse of the Duke (who bared his teeth). He recoiled in such horror that he tumbled over a thistle bush. He said he'd rather crawl than ride with monsters. Then, just at dusk, I saw a small band of Indians riding single-file along a ridge parallel to the trail. I began to tremble and wished I'd convinced the injured fellow to ride along, but presently the Indians appeared to lose interest in us and turned away to the north.

June 13

The Indians I saw yesterday reappeared this morning but not to cause any harm. There were six, all on horseback, and they paralleled my path for half a mile before veering closer. They only wanted to see the apes.

—Do they speak? one inquired, in English.

—No sir.

—What do they eat?

—About anything a man will eat—though they are partial to fruits and grains.

—Are they for sale?

I hadn't given the possibility any consideration and had to gather my thoughts.

—Eighty dollars I said.

He frowned and shook his head. Before they left I allowed each of them to stroke the Duchess's arm. From their friendly demeanor, I take them to be Shoshone.

June 14

The apes appear lethargic and low-spirited. I suspect it is because their rations are so meager and inappropriate to their nature.

June 15

Last night we camped on Russell Creek with three other parties, all gold seekers headed for S.P. An air of festivity prevailed, with everyone throwing a portion of their provisions toward a grand feast. Afterward, the Duke and Duchess performed. The evening's playbill:

    acrobatics (tumbling and balancing)

    husband and wife spat

    mother and ill-mannered child

It was a lively performance, despite their poor health. I purposely did not include "Romeo and Juliet" because all who were present may become part of my audience in S.P. and I want them to be eager for more. (I have also begun to train the Duke to ride one of the mules—I see great possibility.)

Bought 1 peck carrots and 20 turnips from a man from Dayton, Ohio. The apes ate with gusto.

June 16

Rain all day. The apes seem to enjoy it, or perhaps it is their improved diet. As for me, I am wet and miserable. My slicker is one issued me during my military service. It was the only item fit to take with me when I was discharged and now it is in damn poor shape too.

June 17

We reach South Pass City. In my anticipation I had imagined it to be a metropolis, a city of gold, but it is little more than a single muddy street flanked by log huts and hastily constructed lean-tos. Slops are emptied onto the road and skinny dogs snapped at the mules as we proceeded through town. But I am delighted to have a warm bed and a tight (or only slightly leaky) roof under which to sleep.

Andrew is astonished by the apes and laughs wildly every time he looks at them. I had explained in my last letter that they would be accompanying me, but he says he never received it and wouldn't have believed it if he had. I explained how the apes had been left in a field beside Mother's house when the owner of a one-horse circus was shot dead in a barroom. How I coaxed them into the barn with a pan of molasses and saw in their eyes a pleading that I could not ignore.

Good news about Andrew's claim. It is northeast of town and has been paying out as much as $12 a day. He says the mules are a godsend. Then he asked what salary the Duke and Duchess would take for hard rock mining. And laughed uproariously.

Five of us sleep in the one-room cabin. Brother Andrew, his partner Tim Haggarty, the apes and myself. The apes are well-mannered and nest like spoons on a cowhide rug beside the stove.

June 18

To the claim with Brother A. It is in a narrow, rocky draw, surrounded by pine and juniper. The two main seams run along one side of the draw for a stretch of more than 40 feet, and then split into several smaller veins which turn back into the hillside. The bedrock is sandstone and granite. Gold mining will be an entirely new enterprise for me so I asked many questions. Gold, I find, comes not in thumb-sized nuggets but embedded in quartz that must be pulverized in a noisy, steam-powered machine called a stamp mill. The resulting rock dust is then washed with quicksilver, to which the tiny fragments of ore adhere. But though the process was unfamiliar, the work itself is as back-breaking as I had expected—digging rock and hauling rock, the fortune hunter's lot.

Inquired of the owner of the Republican Tavern about the possibility of the apes performing there on Saturday evening and Sunday afternoon. As luck would have it, he is something of an amateur naturalist and knew as soon as he laid eyes on the Duke and Duchess that they are Chimpanzees, species *Pan troglodytes*. Not only will he sponsor our performance, but he agreed to pay us a portion of the net proceeds, sure to be quite beyond what the passing of the hat generally obtains. A welcome offer, as I have today only $5.11 in ready money, a large part of my savings having been spent on the mules and wagon in Laramie City.

During the day when I work the claim, I will tether the apes nearby, in the shade of a juniper perhaps, so they may have some freedom of movement and fresh air.

June 19

This morning, as I was loading the wagon, two hard cases (pretty drunk it seemed and this at 7 o'clock) approached and began taunting the apes. The Duke screeched at one of them—a barrel-chested fellow with a yellow beard. In retaliation he took a length of cordwood from the stack by the fence and said, "I'll break his goddamn noggin if he comes at me."

At that very instant, Andrew came out the door brandishing his shotgun.

"You be on your way," said he.

The ruffians backed off, but the taller one said, "I was at Chancellorsville. You can't scare me."

Not a one of us spoke for a long moment, but finally they did move up the street. I could have told him that I was at Chancellorsville too, but he was drunk and would not have appreciated the coincidence.

Since I have owned the apes, I have made a study of the responses they provoke from onlookers. Some laugh wildly, as if these man-shaped creatures are a joke, a caricature of human form and behavior. Others approach with child-like curiosity, asking question after question, as if the strangeness they see might be dispelled by words. Still others are terrified, thinking them furry demons, hunch-backed goblins with toothy grins.

June 21

The vein Andrew and Haggarty have been digging for nigh on thirty days turned out to be blind. That is, it disappeared into the hillside more abruptly than anticipated. They conclude that it will not be worth our trouble to mine it out further and so we start on the second major ledge tomorrow, hoping it will pay out. At this rate, our labors will not even cover our expenses. But miners are like poker players. They continue because all their hardships can be redeemed by a single run of luck.

Last night I dreamed of Chancellorsville. As usual it is raining heavily and I am lost in the woods. As I walk, I begin to notice that wounded men, dying men, are somehow entangled in the branches of the trees. I will not recount the dream in more detail because I fear writing it down will hasten its return.

June 22

There is a certain nobility about the apes. They are exceedingly kind to one another, and their eyes sometimes reveal a melancholy thoughtfulness. This is the tenth month in which they have been in my possession and I have begun to view them as more than mere beasts. Indeed, they often seem at least half human. Even those who see them as curiosities are moved by their portrayal of Romeo and Juliet—when the Duchess cradles her dying mate in her arms and then lays herself down beside him.

June 23

Tonight we played the Republican. The evening's playbill:
  acrobatics
  husband and wife spat
  dancing
  Romeo and Juliet

Although the applause was gratifying, the hat was not well-filled. Miners, I begin to see, are a penurious lot. Thus, the small share of the evenings' drink receipts given us by the owner is a welcome supplement. Our earnings for the evening: $6.23.

As I gazed out across the audience, every third soul seemed to bear some mark of warfare—a missing limb or scar or clotted eye. Hardly a man in South Pass City did not fight in some great battle—at Chancellorsville or Chickamauga or Antietam or Lookout Mt. Andrew and I started off in the same unit, two knotheaded farm boys from Missouri. Then we were separated and I did not lay eyes on him for two and a half years.

Occasionally, a fight erupts at one of the mining camps over old animosities, Blue and Gray. But mostly we seem to do our best to forget. Some of the men from the South we call "galvanized Yankees" because they have so quickly and completely shed their former allegiances. But we have all been galvanized.

June 25
The apes have been stolen.

Early this morning, I tethered them at the claim, just as planned. When I returned to visit before midday, they had vanished. Andrew insisted they must have escaped, but I know they could not have untied the ropes. If they chewed through them, fragments would have been left behind. Still, we searched up and down the surrounding hills until nightfall, but to no avail. Tonight I discovered that the two men who harassed the Duke and Duchess on the street on Tuesday have left town. I am convinced they have robbed me. I will set out to hunt them down tomorrow. Andrew cannot accompany me because he does not have complete faith in his partner Haggarty and fears losing his claim. So I will go alone.

June 26
Followed the trail south but a party heading in the opposite direction said I was the first soul they'd met all day. Turned back. I am riding a small gray mare belonging to the stable smithy, having left the larger of the two mules at the livery as collateral. I carry a

carbine rifle belonging to Andrew, which I hope I will not have to use.

Late this afternoon, went a little way north toward the Wind River Mountains following a recommendation from Andrew, based upon intelligence gathered from other miners. I should have listened to him in the beginning. It has been unseasonably cold and I am sore with rheumatism. I do not believe I am cut out for tracking desperadoes.

June 27
Early today I found the remains of a recently-used camp. I do not have evidence that it was the thieves, but see no other option than to follow this trail further.

Whenever I sit beside a fire in the darkness, I am carried back to the nights before battle when we would stay up until dawn, made sleepless by fear and excitement. Then the thunder of the cannons would commence and the horses would start to stomp and moan and I would wish for my mother and father, using the prayers I learned as a boy. I think I am somewhat like a father to the apes. I know they are not Christian and cannot pray, but I hope they are now remembering me and can take some comfort in those memories.

How does a beast think? What causes it happiness and what causes it pain?

June 28
At last today I am on the trail of the thieves. Early this morning, I encountered two trappers coming down from the high country. Yes, they said, they had indeed seen the very robbers, one on horseback and the other driving a buckboard wagon on which was lashed a large crate covered with tarpaulins. "Pigs," the trappers were told when they inquired about the nature of the cargo. They estimate I am only a few hours behind. It occurs to me that I do

not know which army the man with the yellow beard fought with at Chancellorsville.

Now, as I write by the firelight and wait for the morning when I can take up my pursuit, my heart swells with compassion for the apes. Perhaps they are being beaten, or starved, or, even if not, they must be terrified to travel all day in darkness, hearing only strange voices. They have the minds of small children and cannot understand.

June 29

Tonight I am almost too tired to write. Just after sunrise, I glimpsed the outlaws on a high plateau, perhaps a mile distant. Certain I could overtake their slow wagon I spurred the little gray onward but lost them where the trail forked into two wooded canyons. Searched them both from end to end and then explored the steep ridge between the canyons on foot. Came near to a bear but did not shoot because I did not want to disclose my position. Only with luck did I find my way back to my horse. Tonight I build no fire and make these marks by the light of the moon.

June 30

It is with great sadness that I write these lines. Today, I arose at first light and rode hard. Presently, I heard a single gunshot and, following the sound, spied the smoke from a campfire rising from a copse of willows by the south fork of the creek. I urged the gray to a gallop, holding the rifle in one hand, ready to fire. But they had escaped, leaving the Duke shot dead. The Duchess sat beside him on the ground, holding his hand to her face and softly keening. What I took for a campfire was their little wagon set ablaze. I reason that they intended to shoot them both and burn the bodies but heard me coming and only finished half the job.

What unnatural evil is it in men that one would do such a deed? What motive had they for stealing the apes and what enmity for me or for them that they would in cold blood murder a husband before his very wife. I wept to see her there and then gathered her in my arms.

July 1

Today, we buried him. All night, she slept beside his body. At first I did not know how I would bring her back. She does not ride and walking would take several days and we haven't the food to last. Then I hit upon the idea of a travois of the kind I have seen Indians use. I was able to build a rude version, the Duchess seated upon a pallet of pine boughs and two long poles lashed to the saddle. It is clumsy but faster than walking. From time to time she becomes agitated and peers back in the direction from which we have come.

July 2

Late today we reached South Pass City. Andrew is outraged at the murder of the Duke and wants to mount a posse, but I am not in favor. You have been robbed of your livelihood, says he. I do not believe the courts will provide adequate redress, I tell him. Also, violence begets violence. During our dispute, the Duchess throws herself at him, teeth bared, and it requires all my strength to wrestle her away. Her fangs closed only on the fabric of his shirt or he would have been badly injured.

I pity mankind. We have contracted a disease of the spirit. It robs us of our compassion. It is a contagious madness. It is worse than typhoid. It compels us to murder the innocent. We bleed the grace from our everlasting souls.

July 4

Independence Day here is a great cutting loose. Drunken miners shoot off their pistols on Main Street and explode whole cases of dynamite in the nearby mining camps. Windows shatter and horses bolt. I was awakened at dawn by an ungodly explosion that sounded as if it were in the next shack. The Duchess shrieked and cowered on her rug. I dressed and took her into the hills near Andrew's claim, away from the cacophony.

❏ ❏ ❏ ❏

The day was warm and I napped for a time. Then fed us both a holiday picnic—tinned apricots, barley sausages, and biscuits baked by the Swede who lives in the house behind Andrew's. When we finished, we sat in the sun, and the Duchess began to frolic on a patch of grass. Presently, she executes a pirouette that is part of a dance that she often performed with the Duke. She does it a second time, now looking expectantly at me. I respond with the Duke's step, a hop and a bow, as best I can and she follows suit. Together, we perform a little minuet on the hillside. When we are finished, we drink the juice from the apricot tin. I notice that the shooting has ceased and all that remains is the faint smell of gunpowder passing now and then on the air.

Annie Proulx

Brokeback Mountain

From *The New Yorker*

T HEY WERE RAISED on small, poor ranches in opposite corners of the state, Jack Twist in Lightning Flat, up on the Montana border, Ennis del Mar from around Sage, near the Utah line, both high-school drop-out country boys with no prospects, brought up to hard work and privation, both rough-mannered, rough-spoken, inured to the stoic life. Ennis, reared by his older brother and sister after their parents drove off the only curve on Dead Horse Road, leaving them twenty-four dollars in cash and a two-mortgage ranch, applied at age fourteen for a hardship license that let him make the hour-long trip from the ranch to the high school. The pickup was old, no heater, one windshield wiper, and bad tires; when the transmission went, there was no money to fix it. He had wanted to be a sophomore, felt the word carried a kind of distinction, but the truck broke down short of it, pitching him directly into ranch work.

In 1963, when he met Jack Twist, Ennis was engaged to Alma Beers. Both Jack and Ennis claimed to be saving money for a small spread; in Ennis's case that meant a tobacco can with two five-dollar bills inside. That spring, hungry for any job, each had signed up with Farm and Ranch Employment—they came together on paper as herder and camp tender for the same sheep operation north of Signal. The summer range lay above the tree line on

Forest Service land on Brokeback Mountain. It would be Jack Twist's second summer on the mountain, Ennis's first. Neither of them was twenty.

They shook hands in the choky little trailer office in front of a table littered with scribbled papers, a Bakelite ashtray brimming with stubs. The venetian blinds hung askew and admitted a triangle of white light, the shadow of the foreman's hand moving into it. Joe Aguirre, wavy hair the color of cigarette ash and parted down the middle, gave them his point of view.

"Forest Service got designated campsites on the allotments. Them camps can be a couple a miles from where we pasture the sheep. Bad predator loss, nobody near lookin after em at night. What I want—camp tender in the main camp where the Forest Service says, but the *herder*"—pointing at Jack with a chop of his hand—"pitch a pup tent on the Q.T. with the sheep, out a sight, and he's goin a *sleep* there. Eat supper, breakfast in camp, but *sleep with the sheep,* hundred percent, *no fire,* don't leave *no sign.* Roll up that tent every mornin case Forest Service snoops around. Got the dogs, your .30–.30, sleep there. Last summer had goddam near twenty-five-percent loss. I don't want that again. *You,*" he said to Ennis, taking in the ragged hair, the big nicked hands, the jeans torn, button-gaping shirt, "Fridays twelve noon be down at the bridge with your next-week list and mules. Somebody with supplies'll be there in a pickup." He didn't ask if Ennis had a watch but took a cheap round ticker on a braided cord from a box on a high shelf, wound and set it, tossed it to him as if he weren't worth the reach. *"Tomorrow mornin* we'll truck you up the jump-off." Pair of deuces going nowhere.

They found a bar and drank beer through the afternoon, Jack telling Ennis about a lightning storm on the mountain the year before that killed forty-two sheep, the peculiar stink of them and the way they bloated, the need for plenty of whiskey up there. At first glance Jack seemed fair enough, with his curly hair and quick laugh, but for a small man he carried some weight in the haunch and his smile disclosed buckteeth, not pronounced enough to let him eat popcorn out of the neck of a jug, but noticeable. He was infatuated with the rodeo life and fastened his belt with a minor bull-riding buckle, but his boots were worn to the quick, holed beyond repair, and he was crazy to be somewhere, anywhere, else than Lightning Flat.

Ennis, high-arched nose and narrow face, was scruffy and a little cave-chested, balanced a small torso on long, caliper legs, and possessed a muscular and supple body made for the horse and for fighting. His reflexes were uncommonly quick, and he was far-sighted enough to dislike reading anything except Hamley's saddle catalogue.

The sheep trucks and horse trailers unloaded at the trailhead, and a bandy-legged Basque showed Ennis how to pack the mules—two packs and a riding load on each animal, ring-lashed with double diamonds and secured with half hitches—telling him, "Don't never order soup. Them boxes a soup are real bad to pack." Three puppies belonging to one of the blue heelers went in a pack basket, the runt inside Jack's coat, for he loved a little dog. Ennis picked out a big chestnut called Cigar Butt to ride, Jack a bay mare that turned out to have a low startle point. The string of spare horses included a mouse-colored grullo whose looks Ennis liked. Ennis and Jack, the dogs, the horses and mules, a thousand ewes and their lambs flowed up the trail like dirty water through the timber and out above the tree line into the great flowery meadows and the coursing, endless wind.

They got the big tent up on the Forest Service's platform, the kitchen and grub boxes secured. Both slept in camp that first night, Jack already bitching about Joe Aguirre's sleep-with-the-sheep-and-no-fire order, though he saddled the bay mare in the dark morning without saying much. Dawn came glassy-orange, stained from below by a gelatinous band of pale green. The sooty bulk of the mountain paled slowly until it was the same color as the smoke from Ennis's breakfast fire. The cold air sweetened, banded pebbles and crumbs of soil cast sudden pencil-long shadows, and the rearing lodgepole pines below them massed in slabs of somber malachite.

During the day Ennis looked across a great gulf and sometimes saw Jack, a small dot moving across a high meadow, as an insect moves across a tablecloth; Jack, in his dark camp, saw Ennis as night fire, a red spark on the huge black mass of mountain.

Jack came lagging in late one afternoon, drank his two bottles of beer cooled in a wet sack on the shady side of the tent, ate two bowls of stew, four of Ennis's stone biscuits, a can of peaches, rolled a smoke, watched the sun drop.

"I'm commutin four hours a day," he said morosely. "Come in for breakfast, go back to the sheep, evenin get em bedded down, come in for supper, go back to the sheep, spend half the night jumpin up and checkin for coyotes. By rights I should be spendin the night here. Aguirre got no right a make me do this."

"You want a switch?" said Ennis. "I wouldn't mind herdin. I wouldn't mind sleeping out there."

"That ain't the point. Point is, we both should be in this camp. And that goddam pup tent smells like cat piss or worse."

"Wouldn't mind bein out there."

"Tell you what, you got a get up a dozen times in the night out there over them coyotes. Happy to switch but give you warnin I can't cook worth a shit. Pretty good with a can opener."

"Can't be no worse than me, then. Sure, I wouldn't mind a do it."

They fended off the night for an hour with the yellow kerosene lamp, and around ten Ennis rode Cigar Butt, a good night horse, through the glimmering frost back to the sheep, carrying leftover biscuits, a jar of jam, and a jar of coffee with him for the next day, saying he'd save a trip, stay out until supper.

"Shot a coyote just first light," he told Jack the next evening, sloshing his face with hot water, lathering up soap, and hoping his razor had some cut left in it, while Jack peeled potatoes. "Big son of a bitch. Balls on him size a apples. I bet he'd took a few lambs. Looked like he could a eat a camel. You want some a this hot water? There's plenty."

"It's all yours."

"Well, I'm goin a warsh everthing I can reach," he said, pulling off his boots and jeans (no drawers, no socks, Jack noticed), slopping the green washcloth around until the fire spat.

They had a high-time supper by the fire, a can of beans each, fried potatoes, and a quart of whiskey on shares, sat with their backs against a log, boot soles and copper jeans rivets hot, swapping the bottle while the lavender sky emptied of color and the chill air drained down, drinking, smoking cigarettes, getting up every now and then to piss, firelight throwing a sparkle in the arched stream, tossing sticks on the fire to keep the talk going, talking horses and rodeo, rough-stock events, wrecks and injuries sustained, the submarine Thresher lost two months earlier with all hands and how it must have been in the last doomed minutes, dogs each had owned and known, the military service, Jack's home ranch, where his father and mother held on, Ennis's family place, folded years ago after his folks died, the older brother in Signal and a married sister in Casper. Jack said his father had been a pretty well-known bull rider years back but kept his secrets to himself, never gave Jack a word of advice, never came once to see Jack ride, though he had put him on the woollies when he was a little kid. Ennis said the kind of riding that interested him lasted longer than eight seconds and had some point to it. Money's a good point, said Jack, and Ennis had to agree. They were respectful of each other's opinions, each glad to have a companion where none had been expected. Ennis, riding against the wind back to the sheep in the treacherous, drunken light, thought he'd never had such a good time, felt he could paw the white out of the moon.

The summer went on and they moved the herd to new pasture, shifted the camp; the distance between the sheep and the new camp was greater and the night ride longer. Ennis rode easy, sleeping with his eyes open, but the hours he was away from the sheep stretched out and out. Jack pulled a squalling burr out of the harmonica, flattened a little from a fall off the skittish bay mare, and Ennis had a good raspy voice; a few nights they mangled their way through some songs. Ennis knew the salty words to "Strawberry Roan." Jack tried a Carl Perkins song, bawling "What I say-ay-ay," but he favored a sad hymn, "Water-Walking Jesus," learned from his mother, who believed in the Pentecost, and that he sang at dirge slowness, setting off distant coyote yips.

"Too late to go out to them damn sheep," said Ennis, dizzy

drunk on all fours one cold hour when the moon had notched past two. The meadow stones glowed white-green and a flinty wind worked over the meadow, scraped the fire low, then ruffled it into yellow silk sashes. "Got you a extra blanket I'll roll up out here and grab forty winks, ride out at first light."

"Freeze your ass off when that fire dies down. Better off sleepin in the tent."

"Doubt I'll feel nothin." But he staggered under canvas, pulled his boots off, snored on the ground cloth for a while, woke Jack with the clacking of his jaw.

"Jesus Christ, quit hammerin and get over here. Bedroll's big enough," said Jack in an irritable sleep-clogged voice. It was big enough, warm enough, and in a little while they deepened their intimacy considerably. Ennis ran full throttle on all roads whether fence mending or money spending, and he wanted none of it when Jack seized his left hand and brought it to his erect cock. Ennis jerked his hand away as though he'd touched fire, got to his knees, unbuckled his belt, shoved his pants down, hauled Jack onto all fours, and, with the help of the clear slick and a little spit, entered him, nothing he'd done before but no instruction manual needed. They went at it in silence except for a few sharp intakes of breath and Jack's choked "Gun's goin *off*," then out, down, and asleep.

Ennis woke in red dawn with his pants around his knees, a top-grade headache, and Jack butted against him; without saying anything about it, both knew how it would go for the rest of the summer, sheep be damned.

As it did go. They never talked about the sex, let it happen, at first only in the tent at night, then in the full daylight with the hot sun striking down, and at evening in the fire glow, quick, rough, laughing and snorting, no lack of noises, but saying not a goddam word except once Ennis said, "I'm not no queer," and Jack jumped in with "Me neither. A one-shot thing. Nobody's business but ours." There were only the two of them on the mountain, flying in the euphoric, bitter air, looking down on the hawk's back and the crawling lights of vehicles on the plain below, suspended above ordinary affairs and distant from tame ranch dogs barking in the dark hours. They believed themselves invisible, not knowing Joe

Aguirre had watched them through his 10x42 binoculars for ten minutes one day, waiting until they'd buttoned up their jeans, waiting until Ennis rode back to the sheep, before bringing up the message that Jack's people had sent word that his uncle Harold was in the hospital with pneumonia and expected not to make it. Though he did, and Aguirre came up again to say so, fixing Jack with his bold stare, not bothering to dismount.

In August Ennis spent the whole night with Jack in the main camp, and in a blowy hailstorm the sheep took off west and got among a herd in another allotment. There was a damn miserable time for five days, Ennis and a Chilean herder with no English trying to sort them out, the task almost impossible as the paint brands were worn and faint at this late season. Even when the numbers were right Ennis knew the sheep were mixed. In a disquieting way everything seemed mixed.

The first snow came early, on August 13th, piling up a foot, but was followed by a quick melt. The next week Joe Aguirre sent word to bring them down, another, bigger storm was moving in from the Pacific, and they packed in the game and moved off the mountain with the sheep, stones rolling at their heels, purple cloud crowding in from the west and the metal smell of coming snow pressing them on. The mountain boiled with demonic energy, glazed with flickering broken-cloud light; the wind combed the grass and drew from the damaged krummholz and slit rock a bestial drone. As they descended the slope Ennis felt he was in a slow-motion, but headlong, irreversible fall.

Joe Aguirre paid them, said little. He had looked at the milling sheep with a sour expression, said, "Some a these never went up there with you." The count was not what he'd hoped for, either. Ranch stiffs never did much of a job.

"You goin a do this next summer?" said Jack to Ennis in the street, one leg already up in his green pickup. The wind was gusting hard and cold.

"Maybe not." A dust plume rose and hazed the air with fine grit and he squinted against it. "Like I said, Alma and me's gettin married in December. Try to get somethin on a ranch. You?" He looked away from Jack's jaw, bruised blue from the hard punch Ennis had thrown him on the last day.

"If nothin better comes along. Thought some about going back up to my daddy's place, give him a hand over the winter, then maybe head out for Texas in the spring. If the draft don't get me."

"Well, see you around, I guess." The wind tumbled an empty feed bag down the street until it fetched up under the truck.

"Right," said Jack, and they shook hands, hit each other on the shoulder; then there was forty feet of distance between them and nothing to do but drive away in opposite directions. Within a mile Ennis felt like someone was pulling his guts out hand over hand a yard at a time. He stopped at the side of the road and, in the whirling new snow, tried to puke but nothing came up. He felt about as bad as he ever had and it took a long time for the feeling to wear off.

In December Ennis married Alma Beers and had her pregnant by mid-January. He picked up a few short-lived ranch jobs, then settled in as a wrangler on the old Elwood Hi-Top place, north of Lost Cabin, in Washakie County. He was still working there in September when Alma, Jr., as he called his daughter, was born and their bedroom was full of the smell of old blood and milk and baby shit, and the sounds were of squalling and sucking and Alma's sleepy groans, all reassuring of fecundity and life's continuance to one who worked with livestock.

When the Hi-Top folded they moved to a small apartment in Riverton, up over a laundry. Ennis got on the highway crew, tolerating it but working weekends at the Rafter B in exchange for keeping his horses out there. A second girl was born and Alma wanted to stay in town near the clinic because the child had an asthmatic wheeze.

"Ennis, please, no more damn lonesome ranches for us," she said, sitting on his lap, wrapping her thin, freckled arms around him. "Let's get a place here in town."

"I guess," said Ennis, slipping his hand up her blouse sleeve and stirring the silky armpit hair, fingers moving down her ribs to the jelly breast, the round belly and knee and up into the wet gap all the way to the north pole or the equator depending which way you thought you were sailing, working at it until she shuddered and bucked against his hand and he rolled her over, did quickly what she hated. They stayed in the little apartment, which he favored because it could be left at any time.

The fourth summer since Brokeback Mountain came on and in June Ennis had a general-delivery letter from Jack Twist, the first sign of life in all that time.

> Friend this letter is a long time over due. Hope you get it. Heard you was in Riverton. I'm coming thru on the 24th, thought I'd stop and buy you a beer. Drop me a line if you can, say if your there.

The return address was Childress, Texas. Ennis wrote back, "You bet," gave the Riverton address.

The day was hot and clear in the morning, but by noon the clouds had pushed up out of the west rolling a little sultry air before them. Ennis, wearing his best shirt, white with wide black stripes, didn't know what time Jack would get there and so had taken the day off, paced back and forth, looking down into a street pale with dust. Alma was saying something about taking his friend to the Knife & Fork for supper instead of cooking it was so hot, if they could get a babysitter, but Ennis said more likely he'd just go out with Jack and get drunk. Jack was not a restaurant type, he said, thinking of the dirty spoons sticking out of the cans of cold beans balanced on the log.

Late in the afternoon, thunder growling, that same old green pickup rolled in and he saw Jack get out of the truck, beat-up Resistol tilted back. A hot jolt scalded Ennis and he was out on the landing pulling the door closed behind him. Jack took the stairs two and two. They seized each other by the shoulders, hugged mightily, squeezing the breath out of each other, saying son of a bitch, son of a bitch; then, and as easily as the right key turns the lock tumblers, their mouths came together, and hard, Jack's big teeth bringing blood, his hat falling to the floor, stubble rasping, wet saliva welling, and the door opening and Alma looking out for a few seconds at Ennis's straining shoulders and shutting the door again and still they clinched, pressing chest and groin and thigh and leg together, treading on each other's toes until they pulled apart to breathe and Ennis, not big on endearments, said what he said to his horses and daughters, "Little darlin."

The door opened again a few inches and Alma stood in the narrow light.

What could he say? "Alma, this is Jack Twist. Jack, my wife, Alma." His chest was heaving. He could smell Jack—the intensely familiar odor of cigarettes, musky sweat, and a faint sweetness like grass, and with it the rushing cold of the mountain. "Alma," he said, "Jack and me ain't seen each other in four years." As if it were a reason. He was glad the light was dim on the landing but did not turn away from her.

"Sure enough," said Alma in a low voice. She had seen what she had seen. Behind her in the room, lightning lit the window like a white sheet waving and the baby cried.

"You got a kid?" said Jack. His shaking hand grazed Ennis's hand, electrical current snapped between them.

"Two little girls," Ennis said. "Alma, Jr., and Francine. Love them to pieces." Alma's mouth twitched.

"I got a boy," said Jack. "Eight months old. Tell you what, I married a cute little old Texas girl down in Childress—Lureen." From the vibration of the floorboard on which they both stood Ennis could feel how hard Jack was shaking.

"Alma," he said. "Jack and me is goin out and get a drink. Might not get back tonight, we get drinkin and talkin."

"Sure enough," Alma said, taking a dollar bill from her pocket. Ennis guessed she was going to ask him to get her a pack of cigarettes, bring him back sooner.

"Please to meet you," said Jack, trembling like a run-out horse.

"Ennis—" said Alma in her misery voice, but that didn't slow him down on the stairs and he called back, "Alma, you want smokes there's some in the pocket a my blue shirt in the bedroom."

They went off in Jack's truck, bought a bottle of whiskey, and within twenty minutes were in the Motel Siesta jouncing a bed. A few handfuls of hail rattled against the window, followed by rain and a slippery wind banging the unsecured door of the next room then and through the night.

The room stank of semen and smoke and sweat and whiskey, of old carpet and sour hay, saddle leather, shit and cheap soap. Ennis lay spread-eagled, spent and wet, breathing deep, still half tumescent; Jack blew forceful cigarette clouds like whale spouts, and said, "Christ, it got to be all that time a yours a-horseback makes it so goddam good. We got to talk about this. Swear to God I didn't know we was goin a get into this again—yeah, I did. Why I'm here. I fuckin knew it. Red-lined all the way, couldn't get here fast enough."

"I didn't know where in the *hell* you was," said Ennis. "Four years. I about give up on you. I figured you was sore about that punch."

"Friend," said Jack, "I was in Texas rodeoin. How I met Lureen. Look over on that chair."

On the back of a soiled orange chair he saw the shine of a buckle. "Bull ridin?"

"Yeah. I made three fuckin thousand dollars that year. Fuckin starved. Had to borrow everthing but a toothbrush from other guys. Drove grooves across Texas. Half the time under that cunt truck fixin it. Anyway, I didn't never think about losin. Lureen? There's some serious money there. Her old man's got it. Got this farm-machinery business. Course he don't let her have none a the money, and he hates my fuckin guts, so it's a hard go now but one a these days—"

"Well, you're goin a go where you look. Army didn't get you?" The thunder sounded far to the east, moving from them in its red wreaths of light.

"They can't get no use out a me. Got some crushed vertebrates. And a stress fracture, the arm bone here, you know how bull ridin you're always leverin it off your thigh?—she gives a little ever time you do it. Even if you tape it good you break it a little goddam bit at a time. Tell you what, hurts like a bitch afterward. Had a busted leg. Busted in three places. Come off the bull and it was a big bull with a lot a drop, he got rid a me in about three flat and he come after me and he was sure faster. Lucky enough. Friend a mine got his oil checked with a horn dipstick and that was all she wrote. Bunch a other things, fuckin busted ribs, sprains and pains, torn ligaments. See, it ain't like it was in my daddy's time. It's guys with money go to college, trained athaletes. You got to have some money to rodeo now. Lureen's old man wouldn't give me a dime if I dropped it, except one way. And I know enough about the game now so I see that I ain't never goin a be on the bubble. Other reasons. I'm gettin out while I still can walk."

Ennis pulled Jack's hand to his mouth, took a hit from the cigarette, exhaled. "Sure as hell seem in one piece to me. You know, I was sittin up here all that time tryin to figure out if I was—? I know I ain't. I mean, here we both got wives and kids, right? I like doin it with women, yeah, but Jesus H., ain't nothin like this. I never had no thoughts a doin it with another guy except I sure wrang it out a hunderd times thinkin about you. You do it with other guys, Jack?"

"Shit no," said Jack, who had been riding more than bulls, not rolling his own. "You know that. Old Brokeback got us good and it sure ain't over. We got to work out what the fuck we're goin a do now."

"That summer," said Ennis. "When we split up after we got paid out I had gut cramps so bad I pulled over and tried to puke, thought I ate somethin bad at that place in Dubois. Took me about a year to figure out it was that I shouldn't a let you out a my sights. Too late then by a long, long while."

"Friend," said Jack. "We got us a fuckin situation here. Got a figure out what to do."

"I doubt there's nothin now we can do," said Ennis. "What I'm sayin, Jack, I built a life up in them years. Love my little girls. Alma? It ain't her fault. You got your baby and wife, that place in Texas. You and me can't hardly be decent together if what hap- pened back there"—he jerked his head in the direction of the apartment—"grabs on us like that. We do that in the wrong place we'll be dead. There's no reins on this one. It scares the piss out a me."

"Got to tell you, friend, maybe somebody seen us that summer. I was back there the next June, thinkin about goin back—I didn't, lit out for Texas instead—and Joe Aguirre's in the office and he says to me, he says, 'You boys found a way to make the time pass up there, didn't you,' and I gave him a look but when I went out I seen he had a big-ass pair a binoculars hangin off his rearview." He neglected to add that the foreman had leaned back in his squeaky wooden tilt chair and said, "Twist, you guys wasn't gettin paid to leave the dogs baby-sit the sheep while you stemmed the rose," and declined to rehire him. Jack went on, "Yeah, that little punch a yours surprised me. I never figured you to throw a dirty punch."

"I come up under my brother K.E., three years older'n me, slugged me silly ever day. Dad got tired a me come bawlin in the house and when I was about six he set me down and says, Ennis, you got a problem and you got a fix it or it's goin a be with you until you're ninety and K.E.'s ninety-three. Well, I says, he's big-ger'n me. Dad says, You got a take him unawares, don't say nothin to him, make him feel some pain, get out fast and keep doin it until he takes the message. Nothin like hurtin somebody to make him hear good. So I did. I got him in the outhouse, jumped him on the stairs, come over to his pillow in the night while he was sleepin and pasted him damn good. Took about two days. Never had trouble with K.E. since. The lesson was, Don't say nothin and get it over with quick." A telephone rang in the next room, rang on and on, stopped abruptly in mid-peal.

"You won't catch me again," said Jack. "Listen. I'm thinkin, tell you what, if you and me had a little ranch together, little cow-and-calf operation, your horses, it'd be some sweet life. Like I said, I'm gettin out a rodeo. I ain't no broke dick rider but I don't got the bucks a ride out this slump I'm in and I don't got the bones a keep gettin wrecked. I got it figured, got this plan Ennis, how we can do it, you and me. Lureen's old man, you bet he'd give me a bunch if I'd get lost. Already more or less said it—"

"Whoa, whoa, whoa. It ain't goin a be that way. We can't. I'm stuck with what I got, caught in my own loop. Can't get out of it. Jack, I don't want a be like them guys you see around sometimes. And I don't want a be dead. There was these two old guys ranched together down home, Earl and Rich—Dad would pass a remark when he seen them. They was a joke even though they was pretty tough old birds. I was what, nine years old, and they found Earl dead in a irrigation ditch. They'd took a tire iron to him, spurred him up, drug him around by his dick until it pulled off, just bloody pulp. What the tire iron done looked like pieces a burned tomatoes all over him, nose tore down from skiddin on gravel."

"You seen that?"

"Dad made sure I seen it. Took me to see it. Me and K.E. Dad laughed about it. Hell, for all I know he done the job. If he was alive and was to put his head in that door right now you bet he'd go get his tire iron. Two guys livin together? No. All I can see is we get together once in a while way the hell out in the back a nowhere—"

"How much is once in a while?" said Jack. "Once in a while ever four fuckin years?"

"No," said Ennis, forbearing to ask whose fault that was. "I goddam hate it that you're goin a drive away in the mornin and I'm goin back to work. But if you can't fix it you got a stand it," he said. "Shit. I been lookin at people on the street. This happen a other people? What the hell do they do?"

"It don't happen in Wyomin and if it does I don't know what they do, maybe go to Denver," said Jack, sitting up, turning away from him, "and I don't give a flyin fuck. Son of a bitch, Ennis, take a couple days off. Right now. Get us out a here. Throw your stuff in the back a my truck and let's get up in the mountains. Couple a days. Call Alma up and tell her you're goin. Come on, Ennis, you just shot my airplane out a the sky—give me somethin a go on. This ain't no little thing that's happenin here."

The hollow ringing began again in the next room, and as if he were answering it Ennis picked up the phone on the bedside table, dialled his own number.

A slow corrosion worked between Ennis and Alma, no real trouble, just widening water. She was working at a grocery-store clerk job, saw she'd always have to work to keep ahead of the bills on what Ennis made. Alma asked Ennis to use rubbers because she dreaded another pregnancy. He said no to that, said he would be happy to leave her alone if she didn't want any more of his kids. Under her breath she said, "I'd have em if you'd support em." And under that thought, Anyway, what you like to do don't make too many babies.

Her resentment opened out a little every year: the embrace she had glimpsed, Ennis's fishing trips once or twice a year with Jack Twist and never a vacation with her and the girls, his disinclination to step out and have any fun, his yearning for low-paid, long-houred ranch work, his propensity to roll to the wall and sleep as soon as he hit the bed, his failure to look for a decent permanent job with the county or the power company put her in a long, slow dive, and when Alma, Jr., was nine and Francine seven she said, What am I doin, hangin around with him, divorced Ennis, and married the Riverton grocer.

Ennis went back to ranch work, hired on here and there, not getting much ahead but glad enough to be around stock again, free to drop things, quit if he had to, and go into the mountains at short notice. He had no serious hard feelings, just a vague sense of getting short-changed, and showed it was all right by taking Thanksgiving dinner with Alma and her grocer and the kids, sitting between his girls and talking horses to them, telling jokes, trying not to be a sad daddy. After the pie Alma got him off in the kitchen, scraped the plates and said she worried about him and he ought to get married again. He saw she was pregnant, about four, five months, he guessed.

"Once burned," he said, leaning against the counter, feeling too big for the room.

"You still go fishin with that Jack Twist?"

"Some." He thought she'd take the pattern off the plate with the scraping.

"You know," she said, and from her tone he knew something was coming, "I used to wonder how come you never brought any trouts home. Always said you caught plenty. So one time I got your creel case open the night before you went on one a your little trips—price tag still on it after five years—and I tied a note on the end of the line. It said, 'Hello, Ennis, bring some fish home, love, Alma.' And then you come back and said you'd caught a bunch a browns and ate them up. Remember? I looked in the case when I got a chance and there was my note still tied there and that line hadn't touched water in its life." As though the word "water" had called out its domestic cousin, she twisted the faucet, sluiced the plates.

"That don't mean nothin."

"Don't lie, don't try to fool me, Ennis. I know what it means. Jack Twist? Jack Nasty. You and him—"

She'd overstepped his line. He seized her wrist and twisted; tears sprang and rolled, a dish clattered.

"Shut up," he said. "Mind your own business. You don't know nothin about it."

"I'm goin a yell for Bill."

"You fuckin go right ahead. Go on and fuckin yell. I'll make him eat the fuckin floor and you too." He gave another wrench that left her with a burning bracelet, shoved his hat on backward and slammed out. He went to the Black and Blue Eagle bar that night, got drunk, had a short dirty fight, and left. He didn't try to see his girls for a long time, figuring they would look him up when they got the sense and years to move out from Alma.

They were no longer young men with all of it before them. Jack had filled out through the shoulders and hams; Ennis stayed as lean as a clothespole, stepped around in worn boots, jeans, and shirts summer and winter, added a canvas coat in cold weather. A benign growth appeared on his eyelid and gave it a drooping appearance; a broken nose healed crooked.

Years on years they worked their way through the high meadows and mountain drainages, horse-packing into the Big Horns, the Medicine Bows, the south end of the Gallatins, the Absarokas, the Granites, the Owl Creeks, the Bridger-Teton Range, the Freezeouts and the Shirleys, the Ferrises and the Rattlesnakes, the Salt River range, into the Wind Rivers over and again, the Sierra Madres, the Gros Ventres, the Washakies, the Laramies, but never returning to Brokeback.

Down in Texas Jack's father-in-law died and Lureen, who inherited the farm-equipment business, showed a skill for management and hard deals. Jack found himself with a vague managerial title, travelling to stock and agricultural-machinery shows. He had some money now and found ways to spend it on his buying trips. A little Texas accent flavored his sentences, "cow" twisted into "kyow" and "wife" coming out as "waf." He'd had his front teeth filed down, set with steel plugs, and capped, said he'd felt no pain, wore Texas suits and a tall white hat.

In May of 1983 they spent a few cold days at a series of little icebound, no-name high lakes, then worked across into the Hail Strew River drainage.

Going up, the day was fine, but the trail deep-drifted and slopping wet at the margins. They left it to wind through a slashy cut, leading the horses through brittle branch wood, Jack lifting his head in the heated noon to take the air scented with resinous lodgepole, the dry needle duff and hot rock, bitter juniper crushed beneath the horses' hooves. Ennis, weather-eyed, looked west for the heated cumulus that might come up on such a day, but the boneless blue was so deep, said Jack, that he might drown looking up.

Around three they swung through a narrow pass to a southeast slope where the strong spring sun had had a chance to work, dropped down to the trail again, which lay snowless below them. They could hear the river muttering and making a distant train sound a long way off. Twenty minutes on they surprised a black bear on the bank above them rolling a log over for grubs, and Jack's horse shied and reared, Jack saying "Wo! Wo!" and Ennis's bay dancing and snorting but holding. Jack reached for the .30–.06 but there was no need; the startled bear galloped into the trees with the lumpish gait that made it seem it was falling apart.

The tea-colored river ran fast with snowmelt, a scarf of bubbles at every high rock, pools and setbacks streaming. The ochre-branched willows swayed stiffly, pollened catkins like yellow thumbprints. The horses drank and Jack dismounted, scooped icy water up in his hand, crystalline drops falling from his fingers, his mouth and chin glistening with wet.

"Get beaver fever doin that," said Ennis, then, "Good enough place," looking at the level bench above the river, two or three fire rings from old hunting camps. A sloping meadow rose behind the bench, protected by a stand of lodgepole. There was plenty of dry wood. They set up camp without saying much, picketed the horses in the meadow. Jack broke the seal on a bottle of whiskey, took a long, hot swallow, exhaled forcefully, said, "That's one a the two things I need right now," capped it and tossed it to Ennis.

On the third morning there were the clouds Ennis had expected, a gray racer out of the West, a bar of darkness driving wind before it and small flakes. It faded after an hour into tender spring snow that heaped wet and heavy. By nightfall it had turned colder. Jack and Ennis passed a joint back and forth, the fire burning late, Jack restless and bitching about the cold, poking the flames with a stick, twisting the dial of the transistor radio until the batteries died.

Ennis said he'd been putting the blocks to a woman who worked part-time at the Wolf Ears bar in Signal where he was working now for Car Scrope's cow-and-calf outfit, but it wasn't going anywhere and she had some problems he didn't want. Jack said he'd had a thing going with the wife of a rancher down the road in Childress and for the last few months he'd slank around expecting to get shot by Lureen or the husband, one. Ennis laughed a little and said he probably deserved it. Jack said he was doing all right but he missed Ennis bad enough sometimes to make him whip babies.

The horses nickered in the darkness beyond the fire's circle of light. Ennis put his arm around Jack, pulled him close, said he saw his girls about once a month, Alma, Jr., a shy seventeen-year-old with his beanpole length, Francine a little live wire. Jack slid his cold hand between Ennis's legs, said he was worried about his boy who was, no doubt about it, dyslexic or something, couldn't get anything right, fifteen years old and couldn't hardly read, *he* could see it though goddam Lureen wouldn't admit to it and pretended the kid was O.K., refused to get any bitchin kind a help about it. He didn't know what the fuck the answer was. Lureen had the money and called the shots.

"I used a want a boy for a kid," said Ennis, undoing buttons, "but just got little girls."

"I didn't want none a either kind," said Jack. "But fuck-all has worked the way I wanted. Nothin never come to my hand the right way." Without getting up he threw deadwood on the fire, the sparks flying up with their truths and lies, a few hot points of fire landing on their hands and faces, not for the first time, and they rolled down into the dirt. One thing never changed: the brilliant charge of their infrequent couplings was darkened by the sense of time flying, never enough time, never enough.

A day or two later in the trailhead parking lot, horses loaded into the trailer, Ennis was ready to head back to Signal, Jack up to Lightning Flat to see the old man. Ennis leaned into Jack's window, said what he'd been putting off the whole week, that likely he couldn't get away again until November, after they'd shipped stock and before winter feeding started.

"November. What in hell happened a August? Tell you what, we said August, nine, ten days. Christ, Ennis! Whyn't you tell me this before? You had a fuckin week to say some little word about it. And why's it we're always in the friggin cold weather? We ought a do somethin. We ought a go South. We ought a go to Mexico one day."

"Mexico? Jack, you know me. All the travellin I ever done is goin around the coffeepot lookin for the handle. And I'll be runnin the baler all August, that's what's the matter with August. Lighten up, Jack. We can hunt in November, kill a nice elk. Try if I can get Don Wroe's cabin again. We had a good time that year."

"You know, friend, this is a goddam bitch of a unsatisfactory situation. You used a come away easy. It's like seein the Pope now."

"Jack, I got a work. Them earlier days I used a quit the jobs. You got a wife with money, a good job. You forget how it is bein broke all the time. You ever hear a child support? I been payin out for years and got more to go. Let me tell you, I can't quit this one. And I can't get the time off. It was tough gettin this time—some a them late heifers is still calvin. You don't leave then. You don't. Scrope is a hellraiser and he raised hell about me takin the week. I don't blame him. He probly ain't got a night's sleep since I left. The trade-off was August. You got a better idea?"

"I did once." The tone was bitter and accusatory.

Ennis said nothing, straightened up slowly, rubbed at his fore-head; a horse stamped inside the trailer. He walked to his truck, put his hand on the trailer, said something that only the horses could hear, turned and walked back at a deliberate pace.

"You been a Mexico, Jack?" Mexico was the place. He'd heard. He was cutting fence now, trespassing in the shoot-em zone.

"Hell yes, I been. Where's the fuckin problem?" Braced for it all these years and here it came, late and unexpected.

"I got a say this to you one time, Jack, and I ain't foolin. What I don't know," said Ennis, "all them things I don't know could get you killed if I should come to know them."

"Try this one," said Jack, "and *I'll* say it just one time. Tell you what, we could a had a good life together, a fuckin real good life. You wouldn't do it, Ennis, so what we got now is Brokeback Mountain. Everthing built on that. It's all we got, boy, fuckin all, so I hope you know that if you don't never know the rest. Count the damn few times we been together in twenty years. Measure the fuckin short leash you keep me on, then ask me about Mexico and then tell me you'll kill me for needin it and not hardly never gettin it. You got no fuckin idea how bad it gets. I'm not you. I can't make it on a couple a high-altitude fucks once or twice a year. You're too much for me, Ennis, you son of a whoreson bitch. I wish I knew how to quit you."

Like vast clouds of steam from thermal springs in winter the years of things unsaid and now unsayable—admissions, declarations, shames, guilts, fears—rose around them. Ennis stood as if heartshot, face gray and deep-lined, grimacing, eyes screwed shut, fists clenched, legs caving, hit the ground on his knees.

"Jesus," said Jack. "Ennis?" But before he was out of the truck, trying to guess if it was a heart attack or the overflow of an incendiary rage, Ennis was back on his feet, and somehow, as a coat hanger is straightened to open a locked car and then bent again to its original shape, they torqued things almost to where they had been, for what they'd said was no news. Nothing ended, nothing begun, nothing resolved.

□ □ □ □

What Jack remembered and craved in a way he could neither help nor understand was the time that distant summer on Brokeback when Ennis had come up behind him and pulled him close, the silent embrace satisfying some shared and sexless hunger.

They had stood that way for a long time in front of the fire, its burning tossing ruddy chunks of light, the shadow of their bodies a single column against the rock. The minutes ticked by from the round watch in Ennis's pocket, from the sticks in the fire settling into coals. Stars bit through the wavy heat layers above the fire. Ennis's breath came slow and quiet, he hummed, rocked a little in the sparklight, and Jack leaned against the steady heartbeat, the vibrations of the humming like faint electricity and, standing, he fell into sleep that was not sleep but something else drowsy and tranced until Ennis, dredging up a rusty but still usable phrase from the childhood time before his mother died, said, "Time to hit the hay, cowboy. I got a go. Come on, you're sleepin on your feet like a horse," and gave Jack a shake, a push, and went off in the darkness. Jack heard his spurs tremble as he mounted, the words "See you tomorrow," and the horse's shuddering snort, grind of hoof on stone.

Later, that dozy embrace solidified in his memory as the single moment of artless, charmed happiness in their separate and difficult lives. Nothing marred it, even the knowledge that Ennis would not then embrace him face to face because he did not want to see or feel that it was Jack he held. And maybe, he thought, they'd never got much farther than that. Let be, let be.

Ennis didn't know about the accident for months until his postcard to Jack saying that November still looked like the first chance came back stamped "DECEASED." He called Jack's number in Childress, something he had done only once before, when Alma divorced him, and Jack had misunderstood the reason for the call, had driven twelve hundred miles north for nothing. This would be all right; Jack would answer, had to answer. But he did not. It was Lureen and she said who? who is this? and when he told her again she said in a level voice yes, Jack was pumping up a flat on the truck out on a back road when the tire blew up. The bead was damaged somehow and the force of the explosion slammed the rim into his face, broke his nose and jaw and knocked him unconscious on his back. By the time someone came along he had drowned in his own blood.

No, he thought, they got him with the tire iron.

"Jack used to mention you," she said. "You're the fishing buddy or the hunting buddy, I know that. Would have let you know," she said, "but I wasn't sure about your name and address. Jack kept most a his friends' addresses in his head. It was a terrible thing. He was only thirty-nine years old."

The huge sadness of the Northern plains rolled down on him. He didn't know which way it was, the tire iron or a real accident, blood choking down Jack's throat and nobody to turn him over. Under the wind drone he heard steel slamming off bone, the hollow chatter of a settling tire rim.

"He buried down there?" He wanted to curse her for letting Jack die on the dirt road.

The little Texas voice came slip-sliding down the wire, "We put a stone up. He use to say he wanted to be cremated, ashes scattered on Brokeback Mountain. I didn't know where that was. So he was cremated, like he wanted, and, like I say, half his ashes was interred here, and the rest I sent up to his folks. I thought Brokeback Mountain was around where he grew up. But knowing Jack, it might be some pretend place where the bluebirds sing and there's a whiskey spring."

"We herded sheep on Brokeback one summer," said Ennis. He could hardly speak.

"Well, he said it was his place. I thought he meant to get drunk. Drink whiskey up there. He drank a lot."

"His folks still up in Lightnin Flat?"

"Oh yeah. They'll be there until they die. I never met them. They didn't come down for the funeral. You get in touch with them. I suppose they'd appreciate it if his wishes was carried out."

No doubt about it, she was polite but the little voice was as cold as snow.

❑ ❑ ❑ ❑

The road to Lightning Flat went through desolate country past a dozen abandoned ranches distributed over the plain at eight- and ten-mile intervals, houses sitting blank-eyed in the weeds, corral fences down. The mailbox read "John C. Twist." The ranch was a meagre little place, leafy spurge taking over. The stock was too far distant for him to see their condition, only that they were black baldies. A porch stretched across the front of the tiny brown stucco house, four rooms, two down, two up.

Ennis sat at the kitchen table with Jack's father. Jack's mother, stout and careful in her movements as though recovering from an operation, said, "Want some coffee, don't you? Piece a cherry cake?"

"Thank you, Ma'am, I'll take a cup a coffee but I can't eat no cake just now."

The old man sat silent, his hands folded on the plastic tablecloth, staring at Ennis with an angry, knowing expression. Ennis recognized in him a not uncommon type with the hard need to be the stud duck in the pond. He couldn't see much of Jack in either one of them, took a breath.

"I feel awful bad about Jack. Can't begin to say how bad I feel. I knew him a long time. I come by to tell you that if you want me to take his ashes up there on Brokeback like his wife says he wanted I'd be proud to."

There was silence. Ennis cleared his throat but said nothing more.

The old man said, "Tell you what, I know where Brokeback Mountain is. He thought he was too goddam special to be buried in the family plot."

Jack's mother ignored this, said, "He used a come home every year, even after he was married and down in Texas, and help his daddy on the ranch for a week, fix the gates and mow and all. I kept his room like it was when he was a boy and I think he appreciated that. You are welcome to go up in his room if you want."

The old man spoke angrily. "I can't get no help out here. Jack used a say, 'Ennis del Mar,' he used a say, 'I'm goin a bring him up here one a these days and we'll lick this damn ranch into shape.' He had some half-baked idea the two a you was goin a move up here, build a log cabin, and help me run this ranch and bring it up. Then this spring he's got another one's goin a come up here with him and build a place and help run the ranch, some ranch neighbor a his from down in Texas. He's goin a split up with his wife and come back here. So he says. But like most a Jack's ideas it never come to pass."

So now he knew it had been the tire iron. He stood up, said you bet he'd like to see Jack's room, recalled one of Jack's stories about this old man. Jack was dick-clipped and the old man was not; it bothered the son, who had discovered the anatomical disconformity during a hard scene. He had been about three or four, he said, always late getting to the toilet, struggling with buttons, the seat, the height of the thing, and often as not left the surroundings sprinkled down. The old man blew up about it and this one time worked into a crazy rage. "Christ, he licked the stuffin out a me, knocked me down on the bathroom floor, whipped me with his belt. I thought he was killin me. Then he says, 'You want a know what it's like with piss all over the place? I'll learn you,' and he pulls it out and lets go all over me, soaked me, then he throws a towel at me and makes me mop up the floor, take my clothes off and warsh them in the bathtub, warsh out the towel, I'm bawlin and blubberin. But while he was hosin me down I seen he had some extra material that I was missin. I seen they'd cut me different like you'd crop a ear or scorch a brand. No way to get it right with him after that."

The bedroom, at the top of a steep stair that had its own climbing rhythm, was tiny and hot, afternoon sun pounding through the west window, hitting the narrow boy's bed against the wall, an ink-stained desk and wooden chair, a B.B. gun in a hand-whittled rack over the bed. The window looked down on the gravel road stretching south and it occurred to him that for Jack's growing-up years that was the only road he knew. An ancient magazine photograph of some dark-haired movie star was taped to the wall beside the bed, the skin tone gone magenta. He could hear Jack's mother downstairs running water, filling the kettle and setting it back on the stove, asking the old man a muffled question.

The closet was a shallow cavity with a wooden rod braced across, a faded cretonne curtain on a string closing it off from the rest of the room. In the closet hung two pairs of jeans crease-ironed and folded neatly over wire hangers, on the floor a pair of worn packer boots he thought he remembered. At the north end of the closet a tiny jog in the wall made a slight hiding place and here, stiff with long suspension from a nail, hung a shirt. He lifted it off the nail. Jack's old shirt from Brokeback days. The dried blood on the sleeve was his own blood, a gushing nosebleed on the last afternoon on the mountain when Jack, in their contortionistic grappling and wrestling, had slammed Ennis's nose hard with his knee. He had stanched the blood, which was everywhere, all over both of them, with his shirtsleeve, but the stanching hadn't held, because Ennis had suddenly swung from the deck and laid the ministering angel out in the wild columbine, wings folded.

The shirt seemed heavy until he saw there was another shirt inside it, the sleeves carefully worked down inside Jack's sleeves. It was his own plaid shirt, lost, he'd thought, long ago in some damn laundry, his dirty shirt, the pocket ripped, buttons missing, stolen by Jack and hidden here inside Jack's own shirt, the pair like two skins, one inside the other, two in one. He pressed his face into the fabric and breathed in slowly through his mouth and nose, hoping for the faintest smoke and mountain sage and salty sweet stink of Jack, but there was no real scent, only the memory of it, the imagined power of Brokeback Mountain of which nothing was left but what he held in his hands.

In the end the stud duck refused to let Jack's ashes go. "Tell you what, we got a family plot and he's goin in it." Jack's mother stood at the table coring apples with a sharp, serrated instrument. "You come again," she said.

Bumping down the washboard road Ennis passed the country cemetery fenced with sagging sheep wire, a tiny fenced square on the welling prairie, a few graves bright with plastic flowers, and didn't want to know Jack was going in there, to be buried on the grieving plain.

A few weeks later, on the Saturday, he threw all the Coffeepot's dirty horse blankets into the back of his pickup and took them down to the Quik Stop Car Wash to turn the high-pressure spray on them. When the wet clean blankets were stowed in the truck bed he stepped into Higgins' gift shop and busied himself with the postcard rack.

"Ennis, what are you lookin for, rootin through them post-cards?" said Linda Higgins, throwing a sopping brown coffee filter into the garbage can.

"Scene a Brokeback Mountain."

"Over in Fremont County?"

"No, north a here."

"I didn't order none a them. Let me get the order list. They got it I can get you a hunderd. I got a order some more cards anyway."

"One's enough," said Ennis.

When it came—thirty cents—he pinned it up in his trailer, brass-headed tack in each corner. Below it he drove a nail and on the nail he hung a wire hanger and the two old shirts suspended from it. He stepped back and looked at the ensemble through a few stinging tears.

"Jack, I swear—" he said, though Jack had never asked him to swear anything and was himself not the swearing kind.

Around that time Jack began to appear in his dreams, Jack as he had first seen him, curly-headed and smiling and buck-toothed, talking about getting up off his pockets and into the control zone, but the can of beans with the spoon handle jutting out and balanced on the log was there as well, in a cartoon shape and lurid colors that gave the dreams a flavor of comic obscenity. The spoon handle was the kind that could be used as a tire iron. And he would wake sometimes in grief, sometimes with the old sense of joy and release; the pillow sometimes wet, sometimes the sheets.

There was some open space between what he knew and what he tried to believe, but nothing could be done about it, and if you can't fix it you've got to stand it.

Contributors' Notes

RICK BASS is the author of fifteen books, including *The Book of Yaak* (essays) and *Where the Sea Used to Be* (a novel), as well as *The Sky, the Stars, the Wilderness,* a fiction collection that includes "The Myths of Bears."

"A lot of this story came from research I was doing back in 1991 for a book on wolves. I remember an interview I had with a trapper in Alaska, who, as he was describing his craft to me, shifted into the third-person present, describing his work as 'Trapper does this' and 'Trapper does that.' I think somehow, in a way I can't pin down, that's when the story was born within me. I was also reading through the archives at Southwest Texas State University in San Marcos, fascinated by the oral histories that Texas folklorist J. Frank Dobie had gathered from the Southwest around the time grizzlies and wolves were being driven into extinction in that region. I knew I wanted to use some of that material as well, so I reconsidered what might be the oldest story advice in the world: A character wants something and goes after it. In this effort, the character will win, lose, or draw. The character will come, too, to some understanding or discovery.

"From that point, the story was easy: the physical expression of Trapper's idea of love, vastly different from Judith's, plays itself out across a landscape as he pursues her across that landscape, and of the way he is crippled by what was previously his strength—his ability and need to control the external environment.

"In the end, Trapper comes to some glimmering of understanding his fears, while Judith comes to understand the ambiguity of her need to sometimes be loved even if crookedly. It's a story whose characters are destined to collapse, held together as they are by myths, rather than facts or truths. To me it is not that fantastic a mythology, for instance, to believe that bears in hibernation enter a sleeping spirit world or that they have been rumored to build corrals in the woods and raise and fatten pigs for consumption at a later date. To me, more fantastic, more mythological, is the idea that such a numb-nuts as Trapper—who has given himself over far, far too fully, too recklessly, to his passion—trapping and controlling—can ever get his shit together and learn to love Judith as she wants to be loved.

"I'm very grateful to my editors—Camille Hykes, Harry Foster, and Dorothy Henderson, who helped me to edit this story, as did the editors of *The Southern Review,* where this story first appeared—as well as to a friend, Neal Durando, who offered comments, and to the late J. Frank Dobie, and to Dick Holland and the staff of the special collections library at Southwest Texas State University."

CAROLYN COOKE had fiction in *Prize Stories 1997: The O. Henry Awards* and in *Best American Short Stories 1997* and is a recipient this year of a grant from the National Endowment for the Arts. She was born on Mount Desert Island in Maine and now lives at the end of a dirt road in Northern California.

"Fine lines were always drawn between who was Something and who was Nothing and who could have been Something if she didn't drink so much and have so many goddamned kids. The Cheese House was the child of a reckless moment in the 1970s. For a short time it was Something—a joke: 'Head for the round house, they can't corner you there!' But it soon waned and fell. Boarded up and painted black (a disguise), it looked venereal but also somehow innocent: a wooden cheese in a field of weeds. For twenty-five years people hurled their ingenuity at it and tried to make it into something useful—a landmark, a rest stop, a towel outlet. But the Cheese House remained relentlessly what it was, innocence and ugliness bound together in a vivid, almost narrative shape, until last year somebody finally gave up and tore it down."

PETER HO DAVIES was born in Britain and now lives in the United States, where he teaches creative writing at the University of Oregon. His work has appeared in *The Paris Review, Story,* and *Gettys-*

burg Review and has twice been selected for *Best American Short Stories.* His first collection, *The Ugliest House in the World,* was published by Houghton Mifflin in 1997. He is the recipient of various awards, including fellowships from the Fine Arts Work Center in Provincetown and the National Endowment for the Arts.

"I'd known about Rorke's Drift since I was a kid (from movie matinees of *Zulu)* and was drawn to it after writing a couple of stories about Wales, and Welsh history, but I owe the actual writing of 'Relief' to a number of more specific sources. Conrad, of course, Babel, and Chekhov all informed its language and outlook and I'm indebted too to Donald Morris's fine history of the Zulu War, *The Washing of the Spears.* (Morris, I noticed recently, mentions in his foreword how he was prompted to write the story by Hemingway and I can't help wondering if a little flicker of him lurks here, too.) Mostly though I owe 'Relief' to the Fine Arts Work Center in Provincetown. The fellowship I enjoyed there in '95 provided the time to write the story, but more importantly it gave me the time to not write it *at once,* to reread Chekhov and Conrad, to read Morris and Babel, to find this rather bizarre way into the material. In the end it's more about that ludicrous, glorious state of Britishness than Welshness (though possibly more about farting than either).

"After finishing it, I must admit I had no idea if it would ever see the light of day, but I did circulate it around Provincetown and found to my surprise that people seemed to get it. I'm particularly grateful to one reader who told me how he thought of it every time he farted—a kind of immortality, I suppose.

"Of course, all this is also a rather long-winded (ahem) way of avoiding discussing the autobiographical roots of the story."

LOUISE ERDRICH was born in 1954 and grew up in North Dakota. She is of Turtle Mountain Ojibwa and German heritage. Her books include *Love Medicine, The Beet Queen, Tracks, The Bingo Palace, Tales of Burning Love,* and most recently, *The Antelope Wife.* Her next book is titled *The Last Report on the Miracles at Little No Horse.*

"I wrote this story on the Empire Builder, a train between Whitefish, Montana, and Havre. I was teaching at Stonechild College, half a day's commute."

BRIAN EVENSON has published three story collections (*Altmann's Tongue, Prophets and Brothers,* and *The Din of Celestial Birds*). He has published fiction in magazines such as *The Mississippi Review, The Quarterly, Conjunctions,* and *The Denver Quarterly.* In 1995, he received an NEA Fellowship. He is a Senior Editor for *Conjunctions* magazine. He teaches fiction writing and critical theory at Oklahoma State University. His most recent book, *Father of Lies* (Four Walls Eight Windows), a novel, will appear in winter of 1998.

"Several years ago, in Utah, we lived down the street from a granddaughter of a self-appointed prophet who had started his own church and published a book quoting from his daily revelations from God. One night she told us how her grandfather had fallen in the hallway, breaking his leg. Certain that angels were already being sent down from heaven to raise him up into health, he forbid his wife to call an ambulance. He remained on the floor of the hall for two days, slipping in and out of consciousness. 'Two Brothers' germinated from that event but became a piece less about a prophet/father than about two confused and religiously stricken sons."

KAREN HEULER's stories have appeared in *The Virginia Quarterly Review, Ms.* magazine, *TriQuarterly,* and many other publications. The University of Missouri published her first collection of short stories, *The Other Door,* in 1995. She lives in New York, where she earns a living by providing part-time computer support.

"Happily for me, this story can be read on two levels. It is, literally, a story about a stalker and a victim who gets fed up with sainthood. Symbolically, however, the narrator's own kindness is the catalyst for most of the sorry events that plague her. Her compassion is her downfall; her desire to help is a lure, a disability, a fatal flaw. The final struggle with her boss thus represents a repudiation of her own good intentions. So I think it's possible to say that on the literal level this story illustrates the triumph of good over evil, while on the symbolic level it cunningly confirms the victory of evil over good."

THOM JONES is the author of *The Pugilist at Rest,* a National Book Award finalist, and *Cold Snap.* His third collection of stories will be published by Little, Brown and Co. in January 1999.

"I wrote 'Tarantula' as I write most of my stories, one line at a time with no plan or notion how things would work out. I had spent enough time in the closed universe of a public school to believe you can't really fight city hall, and that if the universe has a healthy immune system, it will kill off such rogue cells as Harold Hammermeister, even if it requires the janitors to step forward and take on the task. Although 'Tarantula' is a work of fiction, let me just say this: Killing your second and subsequent tarantulas is a whole lot easier than doing the first. You have to work up your nerve to do the first one."

D. R. MacDonald is the author of *Eyestone,* a collection of stories. Although he lived most of his youth in Ohio, his work is set largely in the Cape Breton region of Nova Scotia where he was born. His recent stories have appeared in *The Threepenny Review, Southwest Review,* and *Epoch.* He teaches at Stanford University.

"My family's original land in Cape Breton, next to which we live in the summer, has been in the hands of other people since the eve of World War II when my father and uncle sold it in hard times. Nevertheless, it stayed, except for trees overtaking fields, more or less as it was. A few years ago, to suit the esthetics of new owners, its lower slopes were reconfigured all the way to the shore. This troubled me, since the old route to the water—as natural as the course of a stream—was obliterated. Five generations of us, from my great-grandfather to my own daughter, had traveled that path. I was also impressed by what a single bulldozer could do, and do stupidly. That machine suggested other forces beyond our will, and when I saw what it had buried, I wondered how that might move a man so deeply connected to this land that he hoped to remain under it after his death. From there, the imaginings out of which stories come—the mysterious, the unexpected—took shape."

Reginald McKnight, a professor of English at the University of Maryland at College Park, is the author of one novel and three collections of short fiction. "Boot" appears in his collection *White Boys,* published by Henry Holt.

"I always avoided writing about the military because there are so many great military stories already. Then I decided, 'What the hell.' "

Suketu Mehta was born in Calcutta and grew up in Bombay and New York. He is at work on *Alphabet,* a novel, and a personal history of Bombay, both forthcoming from Knopf. He has been published in *Granta, Harper's Magazine,* and *Indian Literature* and won the Whiting Writers Award in 1997.

"We lived for one good year, 1991, in Paris. It was actually less than a year, but it felt like one. People always ask me about this story: Is it true? A writer is a voyeur into invented lives. There was a dosa seller that we knew, a generous man who had a café in the Rue St. Denis, by the Gare du Nord. We knew nothing about his personal life. Then there were other things I wanted to say which could only be safely said in fiction. So I wrote this story, without going back over a single line, in places distant from Paris when I wanted to remember Paris."

STEVEN MILLHAUSER's most recent book is *The Knife Thrower,* a collection of stories. He is also the author of *Martin Dressler, Edwin Mullhouse,* and *Little Kingdoms.* His stories have appeared in *Harper's Magazine, The New Yorker,* and *Best American Short Stories 1990,* among other places.

"The story began, in my mind, as a very long piece with many intricate turns of plot. The outline was detailed and compelling. But only when I discarded this careful plan, and stripped the story down to the tale of a single evening, was I able to begin writing."

ALICE MUNRO: "I have written several books of short stories, many stories originally appearing in *The New Yorker.* Also in *Saturday Night* (Canada), *The Atlantic Monthly, Granta,* and several times in *Best American Short Stories.* I live in Ontario and British Columbia.

" 'The Children Stay' is about the way we make choices and how they're usually not about the things we think they are—how a woman saves herself, on what pretext, and at what cost."

LORRIE MOORE is the author of two novels and three collections of stories, the most recent of which is *Birds of America.* She lives in Madison, Wisconsin.

"Certain things one cannot write through/toward/from without the act of writing about them becoming part of the story. Such is the case here. But writing about the writing about the writing? It makes for an awkward note.

"Suffice it to say that this story followed from certain real-life events ('inspired by' would be too innocent a term; such events seize, blind, and devour). At the time I wrote the story, after having lived through those real-life events, it was the only thing I was remotely able to compose (would that I'd been able to write something, anything, else). The story, however, should not be viewed as an account. Every line of it is fictional, that is, recooked; very little happened exactly as described in these pages. Actual lived life is so much more ridiculous, clumsy, terrifying, impossible; here, as elsewhere, I give it the back (albeit the lingering back) of my hand."

JOSIP NOVAKOVICH grew up in Daruvar, Croatia, and immigrated to the States at the age of twenty. Graywolf Press has published three collections of his stories: *Yolk, Apricots from Chernobyl,* and in 1998, *Salvation and Other Disasters,* in which "Crimson" appears. Novakovich has received the 1997/98 Whiting Award, a National Endowment for the Arts Fellowship, a Tennessee Williams Fellowship at the University of the South, and three Pushcart Prizes. He teaches in the English Department of the University of Cincinnati.

"While the recent Balkan war was taking place, I wanted to understand it through fiction. In this story, I explored what a Serb soldier participating in the siege and slaughter of the population of Vukovar in Croatia could go through. The perspective of someone who volunteered and enthusiastically fired at the civilians didn't interest me, since the judgment and condemnation against it should be unequivocal. I wanted to follow a common and reluctant soldier who had difficult, almost impossible, moral choices. In almost every war, you practically have two camps of prisoners slaughtering each other, except that in this case, the Serb side had all the weaponry and logistical support. Despite the military advantage, thousands of Serb soldiers deserted, but many couldn't or didn't dare to. So what could you do if drafted and forced to kill? What is one of the worst scenarios? Well, this is—'Crimson'—how I answer the question in my imagination."

ANNIE PROULX lives and works in Wyoming. She is the author of three novels: *Postcards, The Shipping News, Accordion Crimes*.

" 'Brokeback Mountain' was written as part of a forthcoming collection of short stories set in contemporary Wyoming."

GEORGE SAUNDERS is the author of *CivilWarLand in Bad Decline,* a finalist for the 1997 PEN/Hemingway Award. He teaches in the Creative Writing Program at Syracuse University. His story "The Falls" was awarded Second Prize in the 1997 O. Henry Awards.

"While visiting California I met an aspiring actor who claimed to be a disciple of a certain well-known self-help knucklehead. This actor claimed that his studies under the knucklehead had given him a renewed sense of personal power and destiny and was also really helping him in his career, especially the Buddhist aspects of the teaching, which had made him realize that what was good for him was good for the universe. This in turn had helped him to do his work with improved focus and intensity. The proof of this was that, while filming a rape scene, he had gone 'so far over the top' that the appalled director had found it necessary to 'pull him off' of the sobbing actress. This idea—this coopting of big and beautiful ideas into the service of Plain Old Ego—was somehow the seed of 'Winky.' "

AKHIL SHARMA (who is writing this biographical note) hates writing in third person but is such a creature of consensus that he does it. Mr. Sharma is a recent graduate of Harvard Law School. Before that he was a screenwriter at Universal Studios, where the vast hopelessness of trying to write ridiculous things ("Devices," a wife-swapping murder mystery) and bumbling even these made him grind his teeth until they became as delicate as Murano glass.

"All that happens when I get something wonderful like this award is that my neuroses move into a bigger house.

"Part of this is because success appears random. When *Playboy* rejected 'Cosmopolitan,' they said it was too sad for them. *The New Yorker* explained that the story felt familiar (which, for all I know, is true and may mean that *The New Yorker* editor is better read than I am).

"Part of my sense of luck comes from having been helped by so many people. 'Cosmopolitan' would have been written without Russell Banks, but it would have been relatively shapeless and tedious (the first draft had some wife beating thrown in to make a point whose purpose I cannot remember). Russell Banks (as wonderful a teacher as he is a writer) many times raised his baffled eyes at me and offered gently phrased bits of common sense. ("In fiction, epiphanies that occur in dreams don't have that much power," he once said, referring to one of the climaxes that, thank God, I got rid of in my revisions.)

"There have been other very generous teachers. Paul Auster gave me lists of books to read and spent hours talking about what I read. Tony Kushner inspired me to see how many wild combustible elements can be brought into one room. John McPhee taught me the necessity of structure, of keeping the soufflé from collapsing. Toni Morrison, who speaks prose (gorgeous suspended sentences that you want to sketch as she says them), would watch me babbling and boasting and then when I was exhausted, she tried showing me the importance of candor. Joyce Carol Oates (wry, gentle, incredibly honest) appeared to work as hard on my stories as she did on her own. There is also, of course, Nancy Packer (a much neglected writer whose *In My Father's House* is so good that it makes my hair stand on end), my dear friend for many years.

"All these people are part of my good fortune."

MAXINE SWANN has been living in Paris since 1991. In 1997 she received a master's degree in literature from the Sorbonne for a thesis on Proust's style. She is currently spending eight months in Punjab, Pakistan, where she is collaborating on a screenplay with Juan Pablo Domenech and writing her first novel. "Flower Children" was her first publication.

"This is a story I'd been trying to write since I'd begun writing, but I couldn't for years find the way to say it. I remember feeling desperate one afternoon. It was in my mother's house, years ago. In the next few hours, I found the refrain, a simple list of sentences that read like a song:

> They (the children) don't understand how the treefrogs sing . . . They don't understand how dew falls or when . . . Although they kill things themselves, they don't understand why anything dies or where the dead go . . . etc.

"After that, the rest of the story came quite easily. The last part, the end, came in a rush, one night late. It was summer, I remember, and I was alone. I felt a delicious sensation of lightness and slept that night very hard."

PETER WELTNER teaches modern and contemporary American poetry and fiction at San Francisco State. His books are *Beachside Entries/Specific Ghosts* (short stories with drawings by Gerald Coble), *Identity and Difference* (a novel), *In a Time of Combat for the Angel* (three short novels), and *The Risk of His Music* (seven long stories). A new novel, *Lay Aside Fear*, will be published by Graywolf Press in the spring of 1999.

" 'Movietone: Detour' was deeply affected by a number of black-and-white wartime films I'd seen shortly before I started writing it. At first the story was only a sketch consisting of what are now the last four paragraphs of Part 4. Though the plot of the story as it slowly expanded owed nothing to Edgar Ulmer's *Detour,* a postwar movie from 1946, its images and much of its rhythm are frequently indebted to uncanny shots of a coffee cup with which that movie begins. 'Movietone' in the title refers to newsreels from the Second World War and, much less obviously, to *The Leopard Man, I Walked with a Zombie,* and especially *The Seventh Victim,* all movies from 1943 produced by Val Lewton in which, as in many of the newsreels from the same period, dread and beauty, horror and wonder are nearly indistinguishable."

DON ZANCANELLA is the author of *Western Electric* (University of Iowa Press) which won the 1996 John Simmons Award given by the Iowa Writers' Workshop. His stories have appeared in numerous literary magazines, including *Prairie Schooner, New Letters,* and *Alaska Quarterly Review.* He grew up in Wyoming and now teaches at the University of New Mexico.

"About ten years ago I was looking through a calendar published by the Wyoming Historical Society when I happened on a note that made an oblique and incomplete reference to 'the first monkeys to visit Wyoming.' A few years later, after I had lost the calendar, I tried doing some research to discover just what those monkeys had been doing in Wyoming, but I could find no mention of them in the historical record. Still, the image remained with me and so I decided to invent this bit of missing history (transforming the monkeys into chimpanzees in the process). I see the story as one small episode in the desecration of the American West."

JURORS

ANDREA BARRETT is the author of the story collection *Ship Fever,* which won the 1996 National Book Award, and of the novels *Lucid Stars, Secret Harmonies, The Middle Kingdom,* and *The Forms of Water;* her most recent book is *The Voyage of the Narwhal.* She lives in Rochester, New York.

MARY GAITSKILL is the author of the story collections *Bad Behavior* and *Because They Wanted to*—which was nominated for a PEN Faulkner Award—the novel *Two Girls, Fat and Thin,* and numerous stories and articles.

RICK MOODY is the author of the novels *Garden State, The Ice Storm,* and *Purple America.* The title piece from his story collection, *The Ring of Brightest Angels Around Heaven,* won *The Paris Review's* Aga Khan Prize. He lives in Brooklyn, New York.

50 Honorable Mention Stories

BAKER, ALISON, "Bodie's Glen," *ZYZZYVA,* Vol. XIII, No. 1
Colorful characters in a rural Northern California setting, including: a dope-growing, door-to-door cosmetics salesman who still lives next door to his ex-wife, the poet in love with the ex-wife, the detective she takes up with after finding a dead body in the woods, and a female wilderness guide.

BARRON, NANCY, "Lagtime," *Gulf Coast,* Vol. IX, No. 1
Noriko, a translator, language teacher, and tour guide in Tokyo, finds herself torn between her tradition-bound family and the Western world she has experienced through her education and her work.

BARTH, JOHN, "Click," *The Atlantic Monthly,* December 1997
Hyperlinks on a Web site posted by "CNG" (the center of narrative gravity) reveal the multilayered aspects of reality (and fiction) to the reader and to a couple making up on the day after an argument.

BILLMAN, JON, "Atomic Bar," *High Plains Literary Review,* Vol. XII, No. 3
A young man is taken from a boys' home in the 1950s by an old speculator and brought to Alkali, Wyoming—home of the Alkali Rodeo and not much else—to help start a uranium company based on spurious claims.

BOROFKA, DAVID, "A Train Heading South," *The Gettysburg Review,* Vol. 10, No. 1
A woman eight months pregnant loses her baby when protesters cause the train she is riding to derail. Or so it would seem. But, in

an alternative reality, she never took the train and the baby is born alive.

BRASHEAR, CHARLES, "Ghost-Faced Charlie," *Cimarron Review,* **No. 121**

A young Comanche educated at a mission school, leaves the reservation to make a life for himself in the white man's world but comes down with an ailment he believes is "the ghost sickness" and returns to the reservation to seek a cure.

BRIDGFORD, KIM, "The Dream-Life," *Wind,* **No. 79**

The whimsical, pathetic dreams of a man, including a circus with imaginary animal acts, keep his family poor and lead his daughter to a life of poverty, abusive relationships, and dampened dreams.

CHABON, MICHAEL, "In the Black Mill," *Playboy,* **June 1997**

An archaeologist uncovers the dark secrets of a town in western Pennsylvania, the site of a burial complex left by a group of mound builders. One oddity: Many of the men who work in the mill that dominates the town are missing fingers, ears, limbs, and other appendages.

CLARK, GEORGE, "Ropa Rimwe," *Zoetrope: All-Story,* **Vol. 1, No. 3**

A white boy growing up in Rhodesia, in the absence of attention from his own parents, attaches himself to the gardener and housekeeper, both local tribespeople. In a season of severe drought, the gardener is let go, with disastrous results.

DAVIS, LYDIA, "Glenn Gould," *DoubleTake,* **No. 8 (Vol. 3, No. 2)**

The legendary pianist is linked by synchronicity to a woman at home with a baby through a shared interest in "The Mary Tyler Moore Show."

DE MARINIS, RICK, "On the Lam," *Zoetrope: All-Story,* **Vol. 1, No. 3**

"Little Biscuit" takes a car trip with his mother and a Jewish gangster on the run from the FBI, who is heading to Havana to work for Meyer Lansky. They end up driving back north to Michigan, where Little Biscuit is left with his mother's Finnish family.

DIXON, STEPHEN, "The Poet," *TriQuarterly,* **No. 98**

Caught in a snowstorm in Washington, D.C., a young radio reporter is given a ride by the then poet laureate. Over many years, the reporter re-encounters the somewhat addled poet and recounts the story, which the poet never seems to remember.

DURBAN, PAM, "Gravity," *The Georgia Review,* **Vol. L, No. 4**

Each time a woman visits her mother in a nursing home, the old woman repeats the same story, of their onetime black retainer, Mamie, and her fear of crossing the bridge to the barrier island where their summer house was.

FERRELL, CAROLYN, "Tiger Frame Glasses," *Ploughshares*, Vol. 23, No. 1

A black girl, poor and victimized by bullies at school, escapes into a fantasy world where she is part of a dynamic group of girls called "The Helper Squad."

GAUTREAUX, TIM, "Resistance," *Ploughshares*, Vol. 23, Nos. 2 & 3

Appalled by the loutish behavior of a neighbor, an old man helps the neighbor's young daughter out with a science project about electrical resistance.

GORDON, MARY, "Bishop's House," *Harper's Magazine*, January 1997

In the aftermath of a failed ten-year romance, a woman goes to Ireland to stay with the parents of a friend and allows herself to succumb to the advances of a repugnant man with a sad story of his own.

HAMEL, RUTH, "Myra," *The Kenyon Review*, Vol. XIX, No. 2

Myra, a widow in her seventies, places an add asking if there are others who hate the name as much as she does. After two other Myras reply and attach themselves to her, Myra plans an intentionally bad picnic to scare them off.

HARRISON, WILLIAM, "Two Cars in a Cornfield," *The Missouri Review*, Vol. XX, No. 1

Eight teenagers in a small Missouri town share a secret—the free sexual encounters between the four boys and the four girls in the clique—until circumstances divide them.

HILDT, ROBERT, "Cam Ranh Bay," *Ontario Review*, No. 46

Vietnam vets in a VA hospital recuperate from bodily damage but cannot recover in spirit.

HOLLADAY, CARY, "Rapture of the Deep," *Southern Humanities Review*, Vol. 31, No. 1

Odd events in the life of a woman: A peck from a hen gives her the ability to call birds to her hand; the peach farm she is raised on becomes the bottom of a lake created by a dam; a marriage to a charismatic karate instructor is cut short by a freak event.

JIN, HA, "Alive," *Agni*, No. 45

A middle-aged man up for a higher position at a cannery in Changchun is sent to Tangshan to collect on a debt owed by a mining company. An earthquake occurs, throwing him out of his hotel room in his underwear and causing him to forget who he is. Months later, remarried and with an adopted son he adores, the man's memory returns and he goes home again, only to find that his old life has closed up around his absence.

JONES, THOM, "Sonny Liston Was a Friend of Mine," *The New Yorker,* November 17, 1997

Kid Dynamite, a determined seventeen-year-old boxer in Aurora, Illinois, in the early sixties, faces a rematch with an opponent who thrashed him one year earlier.

KLAM, MATTHEW, "Linda's Daddy's Loaded," *The New Yorker,* January 13, 1997

A famous newsman comes to visit his daughter, Linda, and her husband, the narrator, who is out of a job. Two questions raised: Can he accept the generous help of his father-in-law? Can he refuse it?

LAVENDAR, DAVID W., "Among the Azores," *The Georgia Review,* Vol. LI, No. 3

A man lingers underneath the dining room table he has just repaired while his family sits down to eat. Once he emerges, his twelve-year-old son says that his father's absence reminds him of the case of the *Karen O'Casey,* a ship found drifting in the open sea with all of her crew gone and everything else intact. Haunted by this story, the man begins to notice strange occurrences around him.

LEE, REBECCA, "The Banks of the Vistula," *The Atlantic Monthly,* September 1997

After a young woman plagiarizes a Soviet text in writing a linguistics paper, her Polish emigré professor asks her to present the paper at a conference.

MACDONALD, D. R., "Whatever's Out There," *Southwest Review,* Vol. 82, No. 3

In Nova Scotia, a woman recovering from a failed marriage finds a bale full of marijuana on a remote beach and enlists the aid of a rough-hewn local to help her decide what to do with it.

MCILROY, CHRISTOPHER, "Medicine," *Ploughshares,* Vol. 22, No. 4

An aspiring painter from the Crow tribe goes off to college, a place that bewilders him. He takes white women for lovers and has a gallery show in New York, but returns to the world of sweat lodges, Sun Dances, and visions that, though they've become commercialized, are part of his family's heritage.

MEYERS, KENT, "Light in the Crossing," *The Georgia Review,* Vol. LI, No. 1

The summer after a young man's father dies, he and an acquaintance take to playing a dangerous game of chicken in which they drive through the cornfields at night with their headlights on or off and see how close they can come to converging at the crossings.

MORGAN, ROBERT, "The Tracks of Chief De Soto," *South Dakota Review,* Vol. 35, No. 2

The Spanish under De Soto and their brutality in search of gold is recounted by a young Cherokee woman.

OATES, JOYCE CAROL, "The Penitent," *Fiction,* Vol. 14, No. 2

A poor, bookish girl suffers a breakdown at a Syracuse University sorority in 1963, dragging the stern, alcoholic, English house mother down with her.

OLMSTEAD, ROBERT, "Her Lover," *Black Warrior Review,* Vol. XXIII, No. 11

A man returns home early from a disastrous canoe trip wearing for several days the clothes of the farmer who pulled him from the river.

POWELL, PADGETT, "Aliens of Affection," *The Paris Review,* No. 143

A succession of strange episodes, as a man finds himself patrolling "all along the watchtower," encounters "sodiers" (sic), and is visited by "aliens of affection." Comical, enigmatic, and possibly allegorical.

ROCK, PETER, "Convalescence," *Fourteen Hills,* Vol. 3, No. 1

An old man looking after a friend's granddaughter, who is recovering from a freakish accident, has a heart attack while walking along the Erie Canal and is saved by a young man dressed as an Indian.

SCHULMAN, HELEN, "My Best Friend," *Ploughshares,* Vol. 23, Nos. 2 & 3

An actor steals a struggling writer's wife. Later, when the actor's career is languishing, the writer, turned producer of a very successful television show, exacts his revenge by giving his old friend a part, making him a star, then writing him into oblivion.

SCOTT, JOANNA, "Yip," *Conjunctions,* No. 28

A theater impresario tries to convince a mother to allow him to use her insane son, who babbles and makes yipping sounds, in a play.

SHARMA, AKHIL, "A Heart Is Such a Heavy Thing," *The New Yorker,* December 8, 1997

A twenty-four-year-old Indian man agrees to take as a bride a chubby round-faced girl he has never met. The surprisingly self-assured bride ends up winning over the man and his family.

SHIELDS, CAROL, "Keys," *Border Crossings*, Vol. 16, No. 3

A succession of unrelated characters linked by the keys they carry or find.

SMITH, LEE, "Live Bottomless," *The Southern Review*, Vol. 33, No. 4

In 1958, in a small Virginia town, a thirteen-year-old girl becomes fascinated with an eccentric artist who, it turns out, is having an affair with her father. News of this scandalizes the town and leads her mother to a nervous breakdown, forcing the girl into a temporary exile among Christian fundamentalist cousins.

SUKENICK, RONALD, "Dick and Eddie: A Narrative," *The Iowa Review*, Vol. 27, No. 2

An experimental hyperfiction in which Dick is lecturing his one-time lover, Eddie (a woman), on texts. They decide to go out for a bit to eat and end up on a Norwegian freighter in New York Harbor, bound for the sea.

TERRY, GENE, "Mind the Gap," *Fourteen Hills*, Vol. 3, No. 2

On the day of a trip to London, a man awakes to find a giant slug in his bed, which he believes is his soul. He packs the slug in a suitcase and brings it to London with him, but loses it on the Underground.

TREADWAY, JESSICA, "Oregon," *The Boston Book Review*, December 1997 (Vol. 4, Issue 10)

A woman dreams her friend has a three-month-old daughter. The friend, it turns out, is three months pregnant and considering an abortion. Instead, she has the baby and names the friend the girl's godmother. When the girl is nineteen, she comes to visit her godmother, pregnant herself and wanting an abortion.

VOLLMANN, WILLIAM T., "The Royal Family," *Grand Street*, No. 61

A man in search of the Queen of Whores in Sacramento. Edgy literary noire reminiscent of William Burroughs.

WALLACE, DAVID FOSTER, "Death Is Not the End," *Grand Street*, No. 60

Poolside with a celebrated American poet at 10:20 A.M. on May 15, 1995.

WAXMAN, NATASHA, "The Emperors of Ice Cream," *Zoetrope: All-Story*, Vol. 1, No. 2

A woman notices she has grown fat and embarks on a diet. After her husband joins her, they spur each other on to greater and greater deprivation.

WICKERSHAM, JOAN, "Cold Front," *Glimmer Train Stories,* **Issue 21**

An old woman living alone in a beach house is visited by her granddaughter, her precocious but spoiled five-year-old great grandson, and the granddaughter's male friend.

WILLIAMS, DIANE, "The Brilliants," *Gargoyle,* **No. 39/40**

Clouds, water, a man and a woman, and the value of it all.

WILSON, CINTRA, "Red Spiral Notebook," *Zoetrope: All-Story,* **Vol. 1, No. 3**

Via notebook entries, a young man details his descent into heroin addiction, the result of his efforts to save a friend in trouble. In the process he loses his job, his girlfriend, his identity, his sanity, and a woman he falls in love with while bingeing on the drug.

WOLFE, TOBIAS, "Nightingale," *The New Yorker,* **January 6, 1997**

A physician drops his young teenage son off at a military boarding school, then gets lost on the way home and thinks twice about his decision. Is he asking too much of the boy, punishing him for being who he really is?

WOLITZER, MEG, "Tea at the House," *Ploughshares,* **Vol. 23, Nos. 2 & 3**

A young woman growing up in a house on the grounds of a mental institution is molested by a young patient invited over for tea by her psychiatrist father.

WYSONG, BRENNEN, "The Sin-Eater's Tale," *Black Warrior Review,* **Vol. XXIII, No. 11**

A man tells a fable to his granddaughter that has obsessed him all of his life, about a man who ate the sins of the Civil War dead, and thus took them on himself. The devil eventually comes for the sin-eater. Grandfather and granddaughter embellish the unresolved tale in an effort to free the sin-eater from the devil's clutches.

1998 Magazine Award: The New Yorker

SINCE 1925, *The New Yorker* has shown a consistent devotion to publishing and promoting the short story. As the only weekly magazine currently doing so on a regular basis, it publishes more literary fiction each year than any other magazine, and its stories reach a larger audience than any other venue for short fiction. What sets *The New Yorker* apart, however, isn't just the volume of fiction it publishes, nor is it the audience it reaches or the attention a story appearing in its pages gets, but the consistent high quality of its fiction. Though known for publishing great short story writers such as John Cheever, J. D. Salinger, John Updike, Edna O'Brien, Raymond Carver, William Trevor, and Mavis Gallant, *The New Yorker* is also a magazine that seeks to promote the work of new talents—after all, some of these greats were new to many readers before appearing in the magazine.

This year *The New Yorker* has four O. Henry Award-winning stories, more than any other magazine: the First Prize-winning "People Like That Are the Only People Here" by Lorrie Moore, the Third Prize-winning "The Children Stay" by Alice Munro, "Brokeback Mountain" by Annie Proulx, and "Winky" by George Saunders. It also, in 1997, published stories by four other of this year's O. Henry Award winners: Rick Bass, Thom Jones, Steven Millhauser, and Akhil Sharma. Because of this, its four Honorable Mention stories, and the magazine's continued devotion to editorial excellence and to literary fiction, as evidenced by the two annual fiction double issues it produced in 1997, *The New Yorker* is this year's O. Henry Award winner for magazines. Congratulations to Editor-in-Chief Tina Brown, Fiction Editor Bill Buford, the rest of the fiction editors, and the writers published in *The New Yorker* during the course of the year.

Magazines Consulted

Entries entirely in boldface and with their titles in all-capital letters denote publications with prizewinning stories. Asterisks following titles denote magazines with Honorable Mention stories. The information presented is up-to-date as of the time *Prize Stories 1998: The O. Henry Awards* went to press. For more complete information, contact individual magazines or visit the O. Henry Awards Web site at:

http://www.boldtype.com/ohenry

Magazines that wish to be added to the list and to have the stories they publish considered for O. Henry Awards may send subscriptions or all issues containing fiction to the series editor at:

P.O. Box 739
Montclair, NJ 07042

Please note this address is for magazines. Send other correspondence care of Anchor Books or, via e-mail, to Ohenrypriz@aol.com.

African American Review
English Dept.
Indiana State University
Terre Haute, IN 47809
Joe Weixlmann, Editor
web.indstate.edu/artsci/AAR
*Quarterly with a focus on African
American literature and culture.
Averages one short story per
issue.*

Agni*
236 Bay Street Road
Boston University Writing Program
Boston, MA 02115
Askold Melnyczuk, Editor
webdelsol.com/AGNI

Alabama Literary Review
Smith 253
Troy State University
Tory, AL 36082
Theron Montgomery, Chief Editor
Published annually.

ALASKA QUARTERLY REVIEW
University of Alaska Anchorage
3211 Providence Drive
Anchorage, AK 99508
Ronald Spatz, Executive Editor

Alligator Juniper
Prescott College
220 Grove Avenue
Prescott, AZ 86301
Melanie Bishop, Managing Editor
Annual.

Amelia
329 "E" Street
Bakersfield, CA 93304
Frederick A. Raborg Jr., Editor
Quarterly.

**American Letters and
Commentary**
850 Park Avenue
Suite 5B
New York, NY 10021
Jeanne Beaumont, Anna
Rabinowitz, Editors

American Literary Review
University of North Texas
P.O. Box 311307
Denton, TX 76203–1307
Lee Martin, Editor
Biannual.

American Short Fiction
Parlin 108
English Dept.
University of Texas at Austin
Austin, TX 78712–1164
Joseph E. Kruppa, Editor
www.utexas.edu/utpress/journals/
jasf.html
*Quarterly. Ceasing publication at
the end of 1998.*

American Voice
332 West Broadway
Suite 1215
Louisville, KY 40202
Frederick Smock, Editor
Triannual.

American Way
P.O. Box 619640
DFW Airport
Texas 75261–9640
Chuck Thompson, Senior Editor
102521.1126@compuserve.com
*American Airlines' inflight
magazine. Twice monthly with
one story per issue.*

Another Chicago Magazine
Left Field Press
3709 North Kenmore
Chicago, IL 60613
Barry Silesky, Editor and
Publisher

Antietam Review
41 S. Potomac Street
Hagerstown, MD 21740
Susanne Kass, Executive Editor

The Antioch Review
P.O. Box 148
Yellow Springs, OH 45387
Robert S. Fogarty, Editor
Quarterly.

Apalachee Quarterly
P.O. Box 10469
Tallahassee, FL 32302
Barbara Hamby, Editor

Appalachian Heritage
Berea College
Berea, KY 40404
Sidney Saylor Farr, Editor
Sydney_Farr@Berea.edu
Quarterly of southern Appalachian life and culture.

Arkansas Review
Dept. of English and Philosophy
Box 1890
Arkansas State University
State University, AR 72467
William Clements, Editor
*Formerly The Kansas Quarterly.
Note: As of 1998, the magazine has become a regional studies journal, publishing less fiction than it has in the past.*

Ascent
English Dept.
Concordia College
901 8th Street S
Moorhead, MN 56562
W. Scott Olsen, Editor
ascent@cord.edu
Triannual.

Atlanta Review
P.O. Box 8248
Atlanta, GA 30306
Daniel Veach, Editor and Publisher
Biannual.

THE ATLANTIC MONTHLY*
77 N. Washington Street
Boston, MA 02114
C. Micheal Curtis, Senior Editor
www.theatlantic.com

Baffler
P.O. Box 378293
Chicago, IL 60637
Thomas Frank, Editor-in-Chief

Bellowing Ark
P.O. Box 45637
Seattle, WA 98145
Robert R. Ward, Editor
Bimonthly.

Beloit Fiction Journal
Box 11
Beloit College
700 College Street
Beloit, WI 53511
Fred Burwell, Editor-in-Chief
Biannual.

Big Sky Journal
P.O. Box 1069
Bozeman, MT 59771
Allen Jones, Editor
bsj@mcn.net
Glossy Montana magazine published five times a year.

Black Warrior Review*
University of Alabama
P.O. Box 862936
Tuscaloosa, AL 35486–0027
Christopher Chambers, Editor
www.sa.ua.edu/osm/bwr
Biannual.

Blood & Aphorisms
P.O. Box 702, Station P
Toronto, Ontario
M5S 2Y4, Canada
Michelle Alfano, Dennis Block, Fiction Editors
fiction@interlog.com
www.interlog.com/~fiction
Quarterly.

Bomb
594 Broadway, 9th Floor
New York, NY 10012
Betsy Sussler, Editor-in-Chief
editor@bombsite.com
www.bombsite.com
Quarterly magazine profiling artists, writers, actors, directors, musicians with a downtown New York City slant. Fiction appears in First Proof, a literary supplement.

Border Crossings*
Y300–393 Portage Avenue
Winnipeg, Manitoba
R3B 3H6 Canada
Meeka Walsh, Editor
Canadian magazine of the arts.

The Boston Book Review*
30 Brattle Street, 4th Floor
Cambridge, MA 02138
Theoharis Constantine Theoharis,
Editor
BBR Info@
BostonBookReview.com
www.BostonBookReview.com
*Also publishes fiction, poetry and
essays. Published ten times a
year—monthly with double issues
in January and July.*

Boulevard
4579 Laclede Avenue
Suite 332
St. Louis, MO 63108–2103
Richard Burgin, Editor
Triannual.

The Bridge
14050 Vernon Street
Oak Park, MI 48237
Jack Zucker, Editor
Biannual.

Buffalo Spree
3993 Harlem Road
P.O. Box 38
Buffalo, NY 14226
Johanna Hall Van de Mark, Editor
*Buffalo, New York, area quarterly
arts magazine.*

Button
Box 26
Lunenburg, MA 01462
Sally Cragin, Editor/Publisher
*"New England's tiniest magazine
of poetry, fiction, and gracious
living." Biannual.*

Callaloo
English Dept.
322 Bryan Hall
University of Virginia
Charlottesville, VA 22903
Charles H. Rowell, Editor
www.press.jhu.edu/journals/cal
*A quarterly journal of African
American and African arts and
letters.*

Calyx
P.O. Box B
Corvalis, OR 97399–0539
Editorial collective
calyx@proaxis.com
www.proaxis.com/~calyx
*Triannual journal of art and
literature by women.*

The Carolina Quarterly
CB #3520 Greenlaw Hall
The University of North Carolina
Chapel Hill, NC 27599–3520
Rotating editorship
cquarter@unc.edu
www.unc.edu/student/orgs/
cquarter
Triannual.

The Chariton Review
Truman State University
Kirksville, MO 63501
Jim Barnes, Editor
Biannual.

Chattahoochee Review
2101 Womack Road
Dunwoody, Georgia 30338–4497
Lamar York, Editor
Quarterly.

Chelsea
P.O. Box 773
Cooper Station
New York, NY 10276–0773
Richard Foerster, Editor
Biannual.

Chicago Review
5801 South Kenwood Avenue
Chicago, IL 60637–1794
Andrew Rathmann, Editor
humanities.uchicago.edu/
humanities/review
Quarterly.

Cimarron Review*
205 Morrill Hall
Oklahoma State University
Stillwater, OK 74078–0135
E. P. Walkiewicz, Editor
Quarterly.

City Primeval
P.O. Box 30064
Seattle, WA 98145
David Ross, Editor
*Quarterly featuring "Narratives of
Urban Reality."*

Clackamas Literary Review
Clackamas Community College
19600 South Molalla Avenue
Oregon City, OR
Jeff Knorr and Tim Schell, Editors
www.clackamas.cc.or.us/clr
Biannual. Started in 1997.

Colorado Review
Colorado State University
Dept. of English
Fort Collins, CO 80523
David Milofsky, Editor
Biannual.

**Columbia: A Journal of Literature
and Art**
404 Dodge Hall
Columbia University
New York, NY 10027
Rotating editorship
Biannual.

Commentary
165 East 56th Street
New York, NY 10022
Neal Kozodoy, Editor
103115.2375@compuserve.com
*Monthly, politically conservative
Jewish magazine.*

Concho River Review
English Dept.
Angelo State University
San Angelo, TX 76909
James A. Moore, General Editor
Biannual.

Confrontation
English Dept.
C. W. Post Campus of Long
Island University
Brookville, NY 11548
Martin Tuck, Editor-in-Chief

Conjunctions*
21 East 10th Street, #3-E
New York, NY 10003
Bradford Morrow, Editor
www.conjunctions.com
*Biannual. Note new editorial
address.*

Crab Orchard Review
Southern Illinois University at
Carbondale
Carbondale, IL 62901–4503
Richard Peterson, Editor
www.siu.edu/~crborchd
Biannual.

Crazyhorse
English Dept.
University of Arkansas at Little
Rock
2801 S. University
Little Rock, AR 72204
Ralph Burns, Editor
Biannual.

The Cream City Review
University of Wisconsin-Milwaukee
P.O. Box 413
Milwaukee, WI 53201
Rotating editorship
www.uwm.edu/Dept/English/ccr/
tccrhome.htm
Biannual.

Cut Bank
Dept. of English
University of Montana
Missoula, MT 59812
Rotating editorship
Biannual.

Denver Quarterly
University of Denver
Denver, CO 80208
Bin Ramke, Editor

Descant
Dept. of English, Texas Christian
University
Box 32872
Fort Worth, TX 76129
Neal Easterbrook, Editor
Biannual.

Descant
P.O. Box 314, Station P
Toronto, Ontario
M5S 2S8 Canada
Karen Mulhallen

DOMINION REVIEW
Old Dominion University
English Dept., BAL 220
Norfolk, VA 23529–0078
Rotating editorship
webdelsol.com/dreview
Annual.

DoubleTake*
1317 W. Pettigrew Street
Durham, NC 27705
Robert Coles, Alex Harris Editors
dtmag@aol.com
www.duke.edu/doubletake
*Beautifully produced quarterly
devoted to photography and
literature.*

EPOCH
251 Goldwin Smith Hall
Cornell University
Ithaca, NY 14853–3201
Michael Koch, Editor
*Triannual. 1997 O. Henry
Award-winning magazine.*

Esquire
250 West 55th Street
New York, NY 10019
Adrienne Miller, Literary Editor
Monthly men's magazine.

Event
Douglas College
Box 2503
New Westminster, British
Columbia
V3L 5B2, Canada
Calvin Wharton, Editor
Triannual.

Farmer's Market
Elgin Community College
1700 Spartan Drive
Elgin, IL 60123–7193
Rachel Tecza, Fiction Editor
*Biannual. Name to be changed to
Black Dirt: A Journal of
Contemporary Writing.*

Fiction*
Dept. of English
The City College of New York
New York, NY 10031
Mark Jay Mirsky, Editor
www.ccny.cuny.edu/Fiction/
fiction.htm
All-fiction format.

The Fiddlehead
University of New Brunswick
P.O. Box 4400
Fredericton, New Brunswick
Canada E3B 5A3
Bill Gaston, Editor
Quarterly.

Fish Stories
3540 N. Southport Avenue #493
Chicago, IL 60657
Amy G. Davis, Editor-in-Chief
*Annual with summer/fall issue.
Includes some previously
published work.*

Five Points
English Dept.
Georgia State University
University Plaza
Athens, GA 30303–3083
David Bottoms, Pam Durban,
Editors
Triquarterly started in 1997.

The Florida Review
English Dept.
University of Central Florida
Orlando, FL 32816
Russel Kesler, Editor
Biannual.

Flyway
203 Ross Hall
Iowa State University
Ames, IA 50011
Stephen Pett, Editor

Folio
Literature Dept.
The American University
Washington, DC 20016
Carolyn Parkhurst, Fiction Editor
Biannual.

FOURTEEN HILLS*
The Creative Writing Dept.
San Francisco State University
1600 Holloway Avenue
San Francisco, CA 94132–1722
Rotating editorship
hills@sfsu.edu
www.sfsu.edu/~cwriting/
14hills.html
Biannual.

Fugue
Brink Hall, Room 200
English Dept.
University of Idaho
Moscow, ID 83844–1102
www.uidaho.edu/LS/Eng/Fugue
Irregularly published, rotating editorship.

Gargoyle*
1508 U Street, NW
Washington, DC 20009
Richard Peabody, Lucinda
Ebersole, Editors
atticus@netrail.net
www.atticusbooks.com/
gargoyle.html
Published very irregularly.

Geist
1014 Homer Street #103
Vancouver, British Columbia
V6B 2W9 Canada
Stephen Osborne, Publisher
geist@geist.com
"The Canadian Magazine of Ideas and Culture."
Quarterly.

The Georgia Review*
The University of Georgia
Athens, GA 30602–9009
Stanley W. Lindberg, Editor
www.uga.edu/garev
Quarterly.

The Gettysburg Review*
Gettysburg College
Gettysburg, PA 17325
Peter Stitt, Editor
Quarterly.

Glimmer Train Stories*
812 SW Madison Street
Suite 504
Portland, OR 97205–2900
Linda Burmeister Davies, Susan
Burmeister-Brown, Editors
www.glimmertrain.com
Quarterly. Fiction and interviews.

Global City Review
Simon H. Rifkind Center for the
Humanities
The City College of New York
138th St. and Convent Ave.
New York, NY 10031
Linsey Abrams, Editor
webdelsol.com/GlobalCity
Nifty, pocket-size format. Annual.

Good Housekeeping
959 Eighth Avenue
New York, NY 10019
Arleen L. Quarfoot, Fiction Editor
Offers the seal of approval.

GQ
350 Madison Avenue
New York, NY 10017
gqmag@aol.com
Monthly men's magazine.

Grain
Box 1154
Regina, Saskatchewan
Canada S4P 3B4
J. Jill Robinson, Editor
grain.mag@sk.sympatico.ca
www.sasknet.com/corporate/
skywriter/
GRAIN_Homepage.html
Quarterly.

Grand Street*
131 Varick Street
Room 906
New York, NY 10013
Jean Stein, Editor
www.voyagerco.com/gs
Artsy quarterly arts magazine.

The Green Hills Literary Lantern
Box 375
Trenton, MO 64683
Jack Smith, Ken Reger, Senior
Editors
Annual.

Green Mountains Review
Box A 58
Johnson State College
Johnson, VT 05656
Tony Whedon, Fiction Editor

The Greensboro Review
English Dept.
University of North Carolina at
Greensboro
Greensboro, NC 27412
Jim Clark, Editor
www.uncg.edu/mfa/grhmpg.htm
Biannual.

Gulf Coast*
English Dept.
University of Houston
4800 Calhoun Road
Houston, TX 77204–3012
Rotating editorship
Biannual.

Gulf Stream
English Dept.
FIU-North Miami Campus
300 NE 151 Street
North Miami, FL 33181–3000
Lynne Barrett, Editor

Habersham Review
Piedmont College
Demorest, GA 30535–0010
David L. Greene, Lisa Hodgens
Lumpkin, Editors
Biannual.

Hampton Shorts
P.O. Box 1229
Water Mill, NY 11976
Barbara Stone, Editor
*"Fiction plus from the Hamptons
& The East End."*

Happy
240 East 35th Street
Suite 11A
New York, NY 10116
Bayard, Editor
Offbeat quarterly.

HARPER'S MAGAZINE*
666 Broadway
New York, NY 10012
Colin Harrison, Deputy Editor
www.harpers.org
Monthly.

Harvard Review
Poetry Room
Harvard College Library
Cambridge, MA
Stratis Haviaris, Editor
haviaris@fas.harvard.edu
Biannual.

Hawai'i Review
English Dept.
University of Hawai'i at Manoa
1733 Donagho Road
Honolulu, HI 96822
Malia E. Gellert, Chief Editor
Triannual.

Hayden's Ferry Review
Box 871502
Arizona State University
Tempe, AZ 85287–1502
Rotating editorship
HFR@asuvm.inre.asu.edu
news.vpsa.asu.edu/hfr/hfr.html
Biannual.

High Plains Literary Review
180 Adams Street
Suite 250
Denver, CO 80206
Robert O. Greer, Jr., Editor-in-Chief
Triannual.

Hudson Review
684 Park Avenue
New York, NY 10021
Paula Deitz, Frederick Morgan, Editors
Quarterly.

Image
P.O. Box 674
Kennett Square, PA 19348
Gregory Wolfe, Publisher & Editor
73424.1024@compuserve.com
www.imagejournal.org
"A Journal of the Arts and Religion."
Quarterly.

Indiana Review
Ballantine 465
Bloomington, IN 47405
Rotating editorship
Biannual.

Ink Magazine
P.O. Box 52558
264 Bloor Street West
Toronto, ON
M5S 1V0 Canada
John Degan, Editor
Quarterly.

Interim
English Dept.
University of Nevada
Las Vegas, NV 89154
James Hazen, Editor
Biannual.

The Iowa Review*
308 English/Philosophy Building
University of Iowa
Iowa City, IA 52242–1492
David Hamilton, Mary Hussmann, Editors
www.uiowa.edu/~english/iowareview
Triannual.

Iowa Woman
P.O. Box 680
Iowa City, IA 52244–0680
Rebecca Childers, Editor

The Journal
The Ohio State University
English Dept.
164 West 17th Avenue
Columbus, OH 43210
Kathy Fagan, Michelle Herman, Editors
Biannual.

Kalliope
Florida Community College at Jacksonville
3939 Roosevelt Boulevard
Jacksonville, FL 32205
Mary Sue Koeppel, Editor
Triannual journal of women's art.

Karamu
English Dept.
Eastern Illinois University
Charleston, IL 61920
Peggy Brayfield, Editor
Annual.

The Kenyon Review*
Kenyon College
Gambier, OH 43022
David H. Lynn, Editor
kenyonreview@kenyon.edu
www.kenyonreview.com
Triannual.

Kinesis
P.O. Box 4007
Whitefish, MT 59937–4007
Leif Peterson, Editor & Publisher
Kinesis@Netrix.Net
Monthly.

Kiosk
State University of New York at
Buffalo
English Dept.
306 Clemens Hall
Buffalo, NY 14260
Rotating editorship
Annual.

The Laurel Review
Dept. of English
Northwest Missouri State
University
Maryville, MO 64468
William Trowbridge, David Slater,
Beth Richards, Editors
Biannual.

Literal Latté
Suite 240
61 East 8th Street
New York, NY 10003
Jenine Gordon Bockman,
Publisher & Editor
Litlatte@aol.com
www.literal-latte.com/
Bimonthly. Newspaper format.

The Literary Review
Farleigh Dickinson University
285 Madison Avenue
Madison, NJ 07940
Walter Cummins, Editor-in-Chief
tlr@fdu.edu
www.webdelsol.com/tlr
Quarterly.

Louisiana Literature
Box 792
Southeastern Louisiana University
Hammond, LA 70402
David C. Hanson, Editor
Biannual.

The Madison Review
University of Wisconsin
English Dept.,
Helen C. White Hall
600 North Park Street
Madison, WI 53706
Rotating editorship
Biannual.

The Malahat Review
University of Victoria
Box 1700
Victoria, British Columbia
V8W 2Y2 Canada
Derk Wynand, Editor
malahat@uvic.ca
Quarterly.

MĀNOA
English Dept.
University of Hawai'i
Honolulu, HI 96822
Frank Stewart, Editor
www2.hawaii.edu/mjournal
Biannual.

The Massachusetts Review
South College
University of Massachusetts
Box 37140
Amherst, MA 01003–7140
Jules Chametzky, Mary Heath,
Paul Jenkins, Editors
Quarterly.

Michigan Quarterly Review
The University of Michigan
3032 Rackham Building
915 E. Washington Street
Ann Arbor, MI 48109–1070
Laurence Goldstein, Editor

Mid-American Review
English Dept.
Bowling Green State University
Bowling Green, OH 43403
George Looney, Editor-in-Chief
Biannual.

Midstream
110 East 59th Street, 4th Floor
New York, NY 10022
Joel Carmichael, Editor
*Monthly with focus on Jewish
issues and Zionist concerns.*

The Midwesterner
343 S. Dearborne Street
Suite 610
Chicago, IL 60604–3807
David A. Schabes, Publisher and
Editor-in-Chief
*Published ten times a year. Slick
magazine with focus on Midwest.*

The Minnesota Review
English Dept.
East Carolina University
Greenville, NC 27858–4353
Jeffrey Williams, Editor
Non-Minnesota-based biannual.

Mississippi Review
University of Southern Mississippi
Box 5144
Hattiesburg, MS 39406–5144
Frederick Barthelme, Editor
sushi.st.usm.edu/mrw/index.html
*Biannual. Web site posts full-text
stories and poems monthly, many
of which are not included in
regular issues of the magazine.*

The Missouri Review*
1507 Hillcrest Hall
University of Missouri
Columbia, Missouri 65211
Speer Morgan, Editor
www.missouri.edu/~moreview
Triannual.

Ms.
135 West 50th Street
16th Floor
New York, NY 10020
Marcia Ann Gillespie, Editor-in-
Chief
ms@echonyc.com
Focus on feminist issues.

The Nebraska Review
Writers' Workshop
Fine Arts Building 212
University of Nebraska at Omaha
Omaha, NE 68182–0324
Art Homer, Richard Duggin
Editors
unomaha.edu/~ahomer
Biannual.

New Delta Review
English Dept.
Louisiana State University
Baton Rouge, LA 70803–5001
Rotating editorship
Biannual.

NEW ENGLAND REVIEW
Middlebury College
Middlebury, VT 05753
Stephen Donadio, Editor
www.middlebury.edu/~nereview
NEREVIEW@mail.middlebury.edu
Quarterly.

New Letters
University of Missouri–
Kansas City
5101 Rockhill Road
Kansas City, MO 64110
James McKinley, Editor-in-Chief
Quarterly.

New Millennium Writings
P.O. Box 2463
Knoxville, TN 37901
Don Williams, Editor
www.mach2.com/books/williams/
index.html
Biannual.

The New Renaissance
26 Heath Road #11
Arlington, MA 02174–3614
Louise T. Reynolds, Editor-in-
Chief
wmichaud@gwi.net
Biannual.

New Orleans Review
P.O. Box 195
Loyola University
New Orleans, LA 70118
Ralph Adamo, Editor
noreview@beta.loyno.edu
Quarterly.

THE NEW YORKER*
25 West 43rd Street
New York, NY 10036
Bill Buford, Fiction Editor
www.enews.com/magazines/
new_yorker
This year's O. Henry Award-winning magazine. Esteemed weekly with special fiction issues in June and December.

Nimrod
2010 Utica Square
Suite 707
Tulsa, OK 74114–1635
Francine Ringold, Editor-in-Chief
www.utulsa.edu/Nimrod
Biannual.

96 INC.
P.O. Box 15559
Boston, MA 02215
Vera Gold, Editor
Biannual.

The North American Review
University of Northern Iowa
1222 West 27th Street
Cedar Falls, IA 50614
Robley Wilson, Editor
nar@uni.edu
webdelsol.com/NorthAmReview/
NAR
Bimonthly founded in 1815. Features short shorts.

North Carolina Literary Review
English Dept.
East Carolina University
Greenville, NC 27858–4353
Thomas E. Douglas, Margaret Bauer, Editors
BauerM@mail.ECU.edu
Nicely produced and illustrated annual.

North Dakota Quarterly
The University of North Dakota
Grand Forks, ND 58202–7209
Robert W. Lewis, Editor
ndq@sage.und.nodak.edu

Northeast Corridor
English Dept.
Beaver College
450 S. Easton Road
Glenside, PA 19038–3295
Susan Balée, Editor
Biannual.

Northwest Review
369 PLC
University of Oregon
Eugene, OR 97403
John Witte, Editor
Triannual.

Notre Dame Review
Creative Writing Program
English Dept.
University of Notre Dame
Notre Dame, IN 46556
Valerie Sayers, Editor
Biannual.

Oasis
P.O. Box 626
Largo, FL 34649–0626
Neal Storrs, Editor
Oasislit@aol.com
Quirky quarterly.

Ohio Review
Ellis Hall
Ohio University
Athens, Ohio 45701–2979
Wayne Dodd, Editor
Biannual.

Ontario Review*
9 Honey Brook Drive
Princeton, NJ 08540
Raymond J. Smith, Editor
www.ontarioreviewpress.com
Biannual.

Open City
38 White Street
New York, NY 10013
Thomas Beller, Daniel Pinchbeck, Editors
Downtown annual.

Other Voices
English Dept. (MC 162)
University of Illinois at Chicago
601 South Morgan Street
Chicago, IL 60607–7120
Lois Hauselman, Executive Editor
Biannual with all-fiction format.

Oxalis
Stone Ridge Poetry Society
P.O. Box 3993
Kingston, NY 12401
Shirley Powell, Editor

The Oxford American
115½ South Lamar
Oxford, MS 38655
Marc Smirnoff, Editor
*John Grisham-backed magazine
with Southern focus.*

Oxygen
Suite 1010
535 Geary Street
San Francisco, CA 94102
Richard Hack, Editor
No longer publishing.

Pangolin Papers
P.O. Box 241
Nordland, WA 98358
Pat Britt, Editor
All-fiction triannual.

THE PARIS REVIEW*
541 East 72nd Street
New York, NY 10021
George Plimpton, Editor
www.voyagerco.com/PR
Quarterly.

Parting Gifts
3413 Wilshire Drive
Greensboro, NC 27408
Robert Bixby, Editor
rbixby@aol.com
users.aol.com/marchst

Partisan Review
236 Bay State Road
Boston, MA 02215
William Phillips, Editor-in-Chief
Quarterly.

Passages North
English Dept.
Northern Michigan University
1401 Presque Isle Avenue
Marquette, MI 49007–5363
Anne Ohman Youngs,
Editor-in-Chief
Biannual.

Phoebe
George Mason University
4400 University Drive
Fairfax, VA 22030–4444
Rotating editorship
Biannual, student-edited.

Playboy*
Playboy Building
919 North Michigan Avenue
Chicago, IL 60611
Alice Turner, Fiction Editor
editor@playboy.com
www.playboy.com
"I only read it for the stories."

PLOUGHSHARES*
100 Beacon Street
Boston, MA 02116
Don Lee, Editor
www.emerson.edu/
ploughshares
*Well-known writers serve as
guest editors.*

Potpourri
P.O. Box 8278
Prairie Village, KS 66208–0278
Polly W. Swafford, Senior Editor
Potpourpub@aol.com
Quarterly.

Pottersfield Portfolio
P.O. Box 27094
Halifax, Nova Scotia
B3H 4M8 Canada
Ian Colford, Editor
www.chebucto.ns.ca/Culture/
WFNS/pottersfield/potters.html
Triannual.

Prairie Fire
423–100 Arthur Street
Winnipeg, Manitoba
R3B 1H3 Canada
Andris Taskins, Editor
*Quarterly. "Literary Immortality
Programme" provides for donors
to be written into novels ($500
Canadian) or stories and poems
($250). Pets half-price.*

Prairie Schooner
201 Andrews Hall
University of Nebraska
Lincoln, NE 68588–0334
Hilda Raz, Editor
Quarterly.

Press
125 West 72nd Street
Suite 3M
New York, NY 10023
Daniel Roberts, Editor
pressltd@aol.com
www.paradasia.com/press
Quarterly.

Prism International
Creative Writing Dept.
University of British Columbia
Vancouver, British Columbia
V6T 1W5 Canada
Rotating editorship
prism@unixg.ubc.ca
www.arts.ubc.ca/prism
Quarterly.

Provincetown Arts
650 Commercial Street
Provincetown, MA 02657
Christopher Busa, Editor
Annual Cape Cod arts magazine.

Puerto del Sol
P.O. Box 30001
Dept. 3E
New Mexico State University
Las Cruces, NM 88003–8001
Kevin McIlvoy, Editor-in-Chief
Biannual.

Quarry Magazine
P.O. Box 1061
Kingston, Ontario
K7L 4Y5 Canada
Editorial board
Quarterly.

Quarterly West
317 Olpin Union Hall
University of Utah
Salt Lake City, UT 84112
Lawrence Coates, Margaret
Schilpp, Editors
Biannual.

Raritan
Rutgers University
31 Mine Street
New Brunswick, NJ 08903
Richard Poirier, Editor-in-Chief
*Quarterly. Edited by former O.
Henry Awards series editor
(1961–66).*

RE:AL
College of Liberal Arts
Stephen F. Austin State University
P.O. Box 13007, SFA Station
Nacogdoches, TX 75962
W. Dale Hearell, Editor
Biannual.

Redbook
224 West 57th Street
New York, NY 10019
Dawn Raffel,
Books and Fiction Editor
Monthly women's magazine.

Rio Grande Review
Hudspeth Hall
University of Texas at El Paso
El Paso, Texas 79968
M. Elena Carillo, Editor
Biannual.

River Styx
3207 Washington
St. Louis, MO 63103
Richard Newman, Editor
Triannual.

Room of One's Own
P.O. Box 46160, Station G
Vancouver, B.C.
V6R 4G5 Canada

Rosebud
P.O. Box 459
Cambridge, WI 53523
Roderick Clark, Editor
800 786–5669
Quarterly.

Salamander
48 Ackers Avenue
Brookline, MA 02146
Jennifer Barber, Editor
Biannual.

Salmagundi
Skidmore College
Saratoga Springs, NY 12866
Robert Boyers, Editor-in-Chief
Quarterly.

Santa Monica Review
Santa Monica College
1900 Pico Boulevard
Santa Monica, CA 90405
Lee Montgomery, Editor
Biannual.

The Seattle Review
Padelford Hall
Box 354330
University of Washington
Seattle, WA 98195
Colleen J. McElroy, Editor
Biannual.

Seven Days
29 Church Street
P.O. Box 1164
Burlington, VT 05042–1164
Paula Routly, Copublisher
*Free weekly newspaper in the
Burlington, Vermont, area.
Occasional fiction.*

The Sewanee Review
University of the South
Sewanee, TN 37375
George Core, Editor
www.sewanee.edu/sreview/
home.html
Quarterly.

Shenandoah
Troubador Theater, 2nd floor
Washington and Lee University
Lexington, VA 24450
R. T. Smith, Editor
www.wlu.edu/~shenando
Quarterly.

The Slate
P.O. Box 581189
Minneapolis, MN 55458–1189
Rachel Fulkerson, Chris Dall, etc.,
Editors
*Not to be confused with
Microsoft's Michael Kinsley-edited
online 'zine. No longer publishing.*

Snake Nation Review
110 #2 West Force Street
Valdosta, GA 31601
Robert George, Editor
Triannual.

So to Speak
4400 University Drive
George Mason University
Fairfax, VA 22030–444
Rotating editorship
*"A feminist journal of language
and art."*

Sonora Review
English Dept.
University of Arizona
Tucson, AZ 85721
Rotating editorship
sonora@u.arizona.edu
Biannual.

South Dakota Review*
Box 111
University Exchange
Vermillion, SD 57069
Brian Bedard, Editor
Quarterly.

Southern Exposure
P.O. Box 531
Durham, NC 27702
Jordan Green, Fiction Editor
sunsite.unc.edu/Southern_
Exposure
southern_exposure@14south.org
*A journal of Southern politics and
culture that publishes some
fiction.*

Southern Humanities Review*
9088 Haley Center
Auburn University
Auburn, AL 36849
Dan R. Latimer, Virginia M.
Kouidis, Editors
Quarterly.

THE SOUTHERN REVIEW*
43 Allen Hall
Louisiana State University
Baton Rouge, LA 70803–5005
James Olney, Dave Smith,
Editors
Quarterly.

Southwest Review*
Southern Methodist University
307 Fondren Library West
Dallas, TX 75275
Willard Spiegelman,
Editor-in-Chief
Quarterly.

Spelunker Flophouse
P.O. Box 617742
Chicago, IL 60661
Chris Kubica, Wendy Morgan,
Editors
spelunkerf@aol.com
Quarterly. Started in 1997.

STORY
1507 Dana Avenue
Cincinnati, OH 45207
Lois Rosenthal, Editor
Quarterly. All fiction.

StoryQuarterly
P.O. Box 1416
Northbrook, IL 60065
Anne Brashler, M. M. M. Hayes,
Editors
Not quarterly, but annual.

The Sun
107 North Robertson Street
Chapel Hill, NC 27516
Sy Safransky, Editor
Eclectic monthly.

Sycamore Review
English Dept.
Heavilon Hall
Purdue University
West Lafayette, IN 47907
Rotating editorship
sycamore@expert.cc.purdue.edu
www.sla.purdue.edu/academic/
engl/sycamore
Biannual.

Talking River Review
Division of Literature and
Languages
Lewis-Clark State College
500 8th Avenue
Lewiston, ID 83501
Student-run biannual.

Tamaqua
Humanities Dept.
Parkland College
2400 West Bradley Avenue
Champaign, IL 61821–1899
Bruce Morgan, Editor-in-Chief
Biannual.

Thema
Box 74109
Metairie, LA 70053–4109
Virginia Howard, Editor
A theme for every issue.
Biannual.

Third Coast
English Dept.
Western Michigan University
Kalamazoo, MI 49008–5092
Theresa Coty O'Neil,
Managing Editor
www.wmich.edu/thirdcoast
Biannual.

13th Moon
English Dept.
SUNY
Albany, NY 12222
Judith Emlyn Johnson, Editor
A feminist literary magazine.

Threepenny Review
P.O. Box 9131
Berkeley, CA 94709
Wendy Lesser, Editor
Quarterly.

Tikkun
60 West 87th Street
New York, NY 10024
Thane Rosenbaum, Literary Editor
www.tikkun.org
*"A Bimonthly Jewish Critique of
Politics, Culture & Society."*

TriQuarterly*
Northwestern University
2020 Ridge Avenue
Evanston, IL 60208–4302
Susan Firestone Hahn, Editor
Triannual.

The Urbanite
P.O. Box 4737
Davenport, IA 52808
Mark McLaughlin, Editor and
Illustrator
"Surreal & lively & bizarre."

Urbanus
P.O. Box 192921
San Francisco, CA 94119–2921
Peter Driszhal, Editor
*Published two or three times a
year.*

Vignette
P.O. Box 109
Hollywood, CA 90078–0109
Dawn Baillie, Editor
*All-fiction quarterly, each issue
with a theme. May no longer be
publishing.*

**THE VIRGINIA QUARTERLY
REVIEW**
One West Range
Charlottesville, VA 22903
Staige D. Blackford, Editor

Wascana Review
English Dept.
University of Regina
Regina, Saskatchewan
S4S 0A2 Canada
Kathleen Wall, Editor
Biannual.

Washington Review
P.O. Box 50132
Washington, DC 20091–0132
Joe Ross, Literary Editor
*Quarterly D.C. area arts
magazine.*

Washington Square
Creative Writing Program
New York University
19 University Place, 2nd Floor
New York, NY 10003–4556
Annual with rotating editorship.

Weber Studies
Weber State College
Ogden, UT 84408–1214
Neila C. Seshachari, Editor
Triquarterly
weberstudies.weber.edu
*New editor for 1998: Sherwin W.
Howard. New focus on
"Viewpoints and Voices of the
American West." New, larger size.*

Wellspring
4080 83rd Avenue North
Suite A
Brooklyn Park, MN 55443
Meg Miller, Editor/Publisher

West Branch
Bucknell Hall
Bucknell University
Lewisburg, PA 17837
Karl Patten, Robert Love Taylor,
Editors
Biannual.

West Coast Line
2027 East Academic Annex
Simon Fraser University
Burnaby, British Columbia
V5A 1S6 Canada
Roy Miki, Editor
www.sfu.ca/west-coast-line/
WCL.html
Triannual.

Western Humanities Review
University of Utah
Salt Lake City, UT 84112
Barry Weller, Editor
Quarterly.

Whetstone
207 Park Avenue
P.O. Box 1266
Barrington, IL 60011–1266
Sandra Berris, Editor
Annual.

Whiskey Island Magazine
University Center
Cleveland State University
1860 East 22nd Street
Cleveland, OH 44114
Rotating editorship
whiskeyisland@popmail.csuhio.edu
Biannual.

The William and Mary Review
College of William and Mary
P.O. Box 8795
Williamsburg, VA 23187
Forrest Pritchard, Editor
Annual.

Willow Springs
526 5th Street, MS-1
Eastern Washington University
Cheney, Washington 99004
Christopher Howell, Editor
Biannual.

Wind*
P.O. Box 24548
Lexington, KY 40524
Charlie Hughes, Leatha Kendrick,
Editors
lit-arts.com/wind/magazine.htm
Biannual.

Windsor Review
English Dept.
University of Windsor
Windsor, Ontario
N9B 3P4 Canada
Alistair MacLeod, Fiction Editor
Biannual.

Witness
Oakland Community College
Orchard Ridge Campus
27055 Orchard Lake Road
Farmington Hills, MI 48334
Peter Stine, Editor
Biannual.

Worcester Review
6 Chatham Street
Worcester, MA 01609
Rodger Martin, Managing Editor
Annual.

Wordplay
P.O. Box 2248
South Portland, ME 04116–2248
Helen Peppe, Editor-in-Chief
Quarterly.

Writers' Forum
University of Colorado
P.O. Box 7150
Colorado Springs, CO 80933–
7150
Alexander Blackburn,
Editor-in-Chief
Annual.

Xavier Review
Xavier University
Box 110C
New Orleans, LA 70125
Thomas Bonner, Jr., Editor
Biannual.

The Yale Review
  Yale University
  P.O. Box 208243
  New Haven, CT 06250–8243
  J. D. McClatchy, Editor
  Quarterly.

Yankee
  Yankee Publishing, Inc.
  Dublin, NH 03444
  Judson D. Hale Sr., Editor
  Monthly magazine devoted to New England. Occasional fiction.

ZOETROPE: ALL-STORY*
  260 Fifth Avenue
  Suite 1200
  New York, NY 10011
  Adrienne Brodeur, Editor-in-Chief
  www.zoetrope-stories.com
  Triannual. Established 1997 by movie director Francis Ford Coppola. Short stories, essays on stories, reprints of classic stories adapted for the screen, and commissioned stories. Web site posts full-text stories and allows for online submissions, provided users first read and rate five stories.

ZYZZYVA*
  41 Sutter Street
  Suite 1400
  San Francisco, CA 94104–4903
  Howard Junker, Editor
  ZYZZYVAINC@aol.com
  www.webdelsol.com/ZYZZYVA
  Triannual. West Coast writers and artists.

Permissions